THE MERCY OF THIN AIR

THE MERCY OF THIN AIR

A NOVEL

RONLYN DOMINGUE

ATRIA BOOKS
New York London Toronto Sydney

ATRIA BOOKS
1230 Avenue of the Americas
New York, NY 10020

ISBN-13: 978-0-7394-6755-8
ISBN-10: 0-7394-6755-7

Manufactured in the United States of America

Interior design by Davina Mock

For Todd,
my other whole

And it is right that you should learn all things, both the persuasive, unshaken heart of Objective Truth, and the subjective beliefs of mortals, in which there is no true trust. But you shall learn these too: how, for the mortals, passing through them, the things-that-seem must "really exist," being, for them, all there is.

—Parmenides of Elea, "On Nature"

Since for the time being there is no possibility whatever of a causal explanation, we must assume provisionally that improbable accidents of an acausal nature—that is, meaningful coincidences—have entered the picture.

—C. G. Jung, "On Synchronicity"

Where do I begin?

I trace my outline in the photograph. From the crown of my head, blond curves sweep down and fringe at the ends. Each limb radiates from my body. The fingertips of my right hand touch the horizon. My left hand holds pure air. I follow along the periphery, where the contours turn, head to toe, side to side.

My body is not the one I was born into. In all the moments of breathing, each cell took its turn at the cycle: growth, repair, decay. But I still remain.

Nothing of me is mine to keep, other than memory.

In the snapshot, Twolly waves from her side of the seesaw. Her left hand is fog above her elbow. She wears the purple dress that made her face luminous in contrast. She smiles wide, pale lips drawn into a perfect arc.

Unseen, Andrew. He had used four rolls of film by the end of the afternoon. He juggled the cylinders in his pocket as the three of us walked out of the park. I touched the square silver cuff link engraved with his initials, APO, and leaned into him. Please, tell me your middle name. *He said nothing and teased me with a subtle smile. Without a word, I traced a path down his right arm, and he reached toward the familiar territory of my hand as if he expected a surprise.*

I hold the photograph so tight, so long, every open space within me fills with a consummate ache.

PART ONE

SIMON BEEKER had been dead four months.

I did not know this when I approached his house for a belated visit. Because I was no longer in the habit of skimming obituaries, I missed the announcement.

The last time I had seen Simon, in early 1991, he was seventy-four. He sat in his crimson study, his elbows angled on the arms of a worn leather chair. I watched him turn the pages of a new biography—the spine crepitated under his grip—and noticed his eyes taking in each paragraph, quick and hungry. That quality had never changed about him. As a boy, he had been a collector of knowledge who sneaked into Andrew's room to read books a page at a time between odd jobs.

There in the study was Andrew's bookcase. The piece was an outdated Eastlake-inspired design when Andrew's aunt willed it to him, but he loved it because the shelves held books two rows deep. Before he left to go to law school, Andrew gave his mother permission to sell or give away what didn't go with him. He left dozens of books, several fine suits, and the bookcase. When Emmaline, their housekeeper, asked for the historical texts, Andrew insisted that she take everything. Emmaline gave it all to Simon, her long-boned, far-sighted grandson.

On the day of that visit, when Simon was seventy-four, I stayed only a few moments. I had not been near the bookcase in several decades. The smell I detected in the closed spaces made me anxious, lonesome. With barely a stir, I left. His wife asked him if he felt a draft as she stepped into the room to hand him a cup of coffee. He turned his dark face and sage eyes toward her and answered he had not.

Now, twelve years later, he was dead. The urge to see him again had come far too late.

I knew Simon was gone when I neared his little bungalow and saw the hand-lettered sign: Estate Sale. Cars parked on the banquettes on both sides of the street. Books, kitchen items, blankets, knickknacks, and furniture cluttered the tiny front yard. People made claim to Simon's possessions, holding them tightly in their arms.

There was the bookcase, in perfect condition, the only antique on the lawn. A small man in pince-nez glasses approached it with arms wide. He dropped to his knees reverently and opened the two drawers to inspect them. Like a billow of smoke from a snuffed flame, a scent I had not smelled in many years escaped the cool, dark hollows. This time, I did not avoid it. The little man began to shiver.

Andrew's essence drew outward, then stalled. The particles suspended in a dense concentration of cold, still air. I held the salty tinge within me for the length of a breath, before anything more could make an escape, before I could linger on the question, *What happened to him?*

As the air warmed, I noticed a rich, mature scent, one that had more strength but less power. That was Simon, whose hands had rubbed a chestnut patina into the glass doors as long as I'd been gone. He would have wanted the bookcase protected. I stood guard with cold drafts, waiting.

By late morning, a couple wandered through the remaining odds and ends at the sale. The young woman spotted the bookcase, shadowed by a redbud tree in new leaf. She opened the doors. As she reached inside to inspect the shelves, she breathed deeply. A comforting aroma, almost a blend of pipe smoke and cinnamon, surrounded her.

"Scott. It's perfect for the room, don't you think? And it's not musty or mildewed inside. I like the scent," she said.

He pulled a tape measure from his pocket. "Good fit. We haven't seen a nicer one anywhere. Great condition."

"I see something in a crack." She stretched deep over the last shelf. As small as she was, she could have crawled inside. When she withdrew, there was a copy of *Family Limitation* in her hand, which she eagerly began to skim. She grabbed Scott's arm and made him read a passage about unsatisfied women and nervous conditions.

"I must have this," she said. "It would complement my mementos from our Condom Sense Days in college. Remember?" Her eyes flickered.

"Oh, I remember." He flipped through the fragile pages. "You're lucky those Bible thumpers didn't whip themselves into a bigger frenzy and beat the crap out of all of you." Scott read several paragraphs. "Hey, Amy—women used to douche with Lysol?"

"Lysol? Let me see that."

I liked her because she reminded me of myself. I liked him because her brazen little nature didn't scare him. They were darling together. She slipped the pamphlet back into its place and began to inspect the exterior wood.

"Interested?" One of Simon's granddaughters had his quiet look in her eyes. "Mamma," she shouted, "what are you asking for the bookcase?"

A woman poked her head around a porch column. "Five hundred."

Amy suppressed a grin and reached into her large, cluttered purse. Scott jumped to catch a small notebook as it fell. "I don't think we have enough cash. Would you take an out-of-town check?" she asked.

"Not usually. But you two look honest enough." Simon's granddaughter put a money box on the ground and pushed the sleeves of her baggy Tulane sweatshirt to her elbows. "You're going to give it a good home, right? I don't want my grandfather rolling over in his grave."

Amy looked at her. "You don't want to keep it?"

"No one in the family likes Victorian. It's time for it to belong to someone else."

Scott told the young woman that they would have to arrange a delivery to their home in Baton Rouge. She pulled a pen and paper from the money box. "Sarah Washington, that's my mom. You can make the check out to her. This is her cell phone number. Call her and set up a date. She'll make sure someone is here."

In block print, Amy wrote several phone numbers next to their names—Amy Richmond and Scott Duncan. "Here are ours, too, just in case."

The young woman took the check, and they wished each other a good day.

Scott wrapped his arm around Amy's shoulders. She briefly laid her auburn head against his chest. "What a bargain," she said.

"With a free turn-of-the-century sex manual."

"Birth control guide."

"What do we need that for?" He patted her at the navel once before she pulled away.

AMY FOUND six more marbles as she dug new flower beds in the front yard. When she came in to take a bath, she dropped them into a shallow bowl on the coffee table. I rubbed the filth from the one I liked best, a dark blue cat's-eye, and rolled it back and forth on the floor.

"Did you remember to buy a mousetrap?" Scott yelled from the room where he searched for the dictionary in the bookcase.

"Why?"

"That mouse is playing with a marble again." Scott told Amy that when he was a child, he investigated a midnight noise in his kitchen. There he trapped a mouse in his flashlight's glare. It sat up, sweet as you please, with a marble between its paws, then scampered under the stove. Scott was convinced that a mouse had found Amy's growing marble collection and had begun to scatter it across the house.

I heard him make his way from the front room into the larger of the two bathrooms. Over the rush of the water, he told her that he wanted to discuss it again. A baby. He had mentioned the topic, briefly, several times in the past few days. "It's spring," he said. "Nature's way of setting the mood."

"Rutting season is in the fall."

"For animals with two horns."

I always appreciated such a sense of humor.

The steamy hint of supper floated into the living room. He had checked on the skillet of shrimp seared with butter and garlic. A twinge of fresh lemon caught an air current as the pasta boiled.

One more moment, and—

"Aims, why did you move everything around in the drawers and cabinets?"

In the two weeks since I arrived, their sense of order had been upended. They found their belongings rearranged or relocated. Radio stations changed at whim, books lay open in strange places, and odd knocks disturbed the house's silence. Now and then, marbles fell from the air conditioner registers and rolled across the slightly sloped floor. Their bemusement entertained me.

The first week, each blamed the other for the way the TV and CD player turned off when they neared and turned on when they stepped away. Scott changed the batteries in the remote controls three times. When it continued to happen, after I removed the batteries altogether, they stood in the middle of the living room and giggled. They laughed at the absurdity until they started to roar, tangled in each other's arms. Minutes later, a trail of clothing led down the hall.

That's what they would miss most, I thought, the occasional

spontaneity. That's why neither one would decide it was time to have a baby. I was tempted to pin-prick her diaphragm and leave his rubbers in sunlight, to force a decision. But that was against what I always believed. I also didn't meddle so directly.

An hour later, Scott entered the living room naked with a glass of orange juice in his hand. I had been amusing myself by spinning the marbles in elliptical orbits around the ceiling fan. They fell when he entered the room. Scott turned his face to the air register in mid-sip, and a drop of pale orange liquid pulled at the edge of his chin. My incorporeal lip went slack with the memory of once eating five satsumas in a row, the acid so subtle that the sweetness masked it until the last bite. I imagined lifting the droplet away with the outline of my tongue, but the taste would have been vague. Seeing the drip suspended in the air would have made him blooey to bits.

"We have to do something about these mice," he said.

Amy snapped him on the rear with a pair of boxer briefs.

His straight, broad shoulders reminded me of Andrew's.

❧

AMY AND SCOTT'S neighborhood was peaceful. Except for the occasional power tool or shout of a distant child, all I heard was the soft rush of morning and evening traffic and the wind. I was not accustomed to the relative silence, so different from the piercing whine of New Orleans. I remembered when my hometown had not been so busy, crowded, unbalanced. Once there were quiet strolls, long conversations, clanking streetcars, slow thin tires on gravel—a warm hum of activity. Year by year, the volume of it all increased by exponents. I regretted but depended on the chaos. I needed it to lull me, the noise like a persistent thought.

I slipped into the comfy rocking chair in the front room of my new home. It was almost midnight. The house was asleep and snoring, the way old ones do, with their creaks, groans, and cracks. To my right, the bookcase covered a narrow wall, but its presence filled more than the space. The porch light illuminated pits and waves in the glass bookcase doors. I turned away from the points of reflection.

That night, I wanted to study some of Amy and Scott's photographs.

Had they wandered into the room at that moment, they would have seen the box flat on the rocking chair's seat. I let it slip through my form. There was no need to make a lap for myself. If they approached the chair—and were extremely perceptive—they would have felt the air change, similar to the instant before static shocks through a body. They would have seen the box top move up, to the right, and to the floor. They would have watched a snapshot rise from the box and suspend itself at a height and an angle as if a person were holding it to look. They would have thought they were sleepwalking, still dreaming. They would not have guessed that they witnessed a simple trick of electromagnetic energy shared among the air, the photographs, and me.

The first picture in the box was of the two of them sitting on the edge of a pool. Water amputated each leg except for Amy's left one, which was tossed over Scott's right knee, kicking blue at the camera. Their arms were wrapped tight around each other. Amy wore a T-shirt over her suit. Behind them, a young man with a Beelzebubby beard posed with his hands open near their shoulders. I wanted to see the next moment, the two of them falling into the water, sputtering with surprise.

I wondered if they had failed to hold their breaths as they went under, whether the water felt familiar in their lungs an instant before mortal panic drew them north to the surface.

In a membrane of blackness, the absence of air, the presence of water—I never expected to end the way I began.

THE DAY I DIE, I glance at Daddy's newspaper before I leave the house. I notice the date, July 10, 1929, and realize it's been almost a month since my graduation from Tulane. No matter what I've done to make these weeks drag wide and full as clouds, they've disappeared in a gust.

I walk the tree-shaded blocks in my favorite green sleeveless dress. The heat makes me dewy. I hope my extra swimsuit is at his house because I terribly want a dip. If not, perhaps I should go bare. Andrew's parents are in the Swiss Alps, avoiding mosquitoes and tropical heat, and Emmaline will be away shopping until it's time to cook lunch.

My pace quickens. Along St. Charles Avenue, I grin at a college boy who offers a ride in his coupe. His F. Scott hair weeps into his neck from the humidity. He looks familiar, someone who's cut in on me at a dance or two.

"Thanks," I reply, "but I'm limbering up for a swim."

"Mind if I join you?" he asks.

"Not today, sport."

As he drives away, I stop in my tracks. Andrew's surprise. The items are still on my dressing table. A sliver of grapefruit curls at the tip of my tongue. Go back home, brush my teeth—forgot to do that, too—sneak it out in a little bag. No one will notice, no one will know. No. Maybe.

It can wait.

I unlock the back gate with a key hidden behind the purple bougainvillea. The back door near the pool is unlocked. I find my swimsuit in one of the bottom drawers of Andrew's bookcase, where he keeps the things I've left behind.

The water sips me into the deep where I twirl against its pull. Inside the house, the grandfather clock chimes ten times; then, after several languid laps, once more. It is ten thirty. He is late returning from his tennis match with Warren. I scissor myself to the pool's bottom and watch the ribbons of light knit me among them. When I surface, I crawl out to take a dive. With a shimmy, I wriggle the leg openings and bodice of my suit into place. I am tempted to shed the wool—

Imagine his face if he found me with more than my naked toes pointed at the sky. Wouldn't he—

The words fall with my body. A second, then two, of darkness. The light around me becomes gauzy and bright. Did I dive through my thoughts and into the water? What peace, these first moments under the surface when my swimmer lungs haven't started to burn and I have forgotten that time is moving above.

An airy-fairy rush fills my limbs and lifts me like incense. I am dissipating, consumed by the weightlessness of a dream—no, I am being pulled up, out, away—

Stop.

My eyesight blurs through a veil of faint sparks. I am above the water.

Andrew approaches the pool, stifling a quiet laugh. He's not going to let me scare him this time. He's seen this before. With each slow step, he removes the layers—shoes, socks, tennis shirt, belt. Andrew unbuttons his white pants but keeps them on. He kneels on the pool's edge, pulls me up, and stretches me at his side. His smooth face goes straight to my neck, but this time I don't respond. He shakes me.

He puts his ear to my mouth. He forces his right hand into my suit, under my left breast. He withdraws, holds his palm against my diaphragm. My head bobs as his fingers, frantic in a way they've never been, search the back of my head. He feels the lump that swelled after I clumsily slipped at the edge of the pool, slammed backward on the concrete, and fell into the water. My flesh is still warm. He draws me onto his lap. He wraps around my body as if he'll never let me go.

I have never heard a man's heart break.

Emmaline, smiling, walks through the back door, a grocery bag on her hip. She hears his keen—suffocated, delirious. Her eyes shine with panic. She drops everything, rushes to us. Her shadow covers our heads. When Emmaline touches the thick black waves on his crown, Andrew lifts his face from my neck and looks up. Her hand moves to his cheek. Her palm fills with his tears. Pewter lines streak down her dark face.

Over and over, he rocks me, the lullaby, sotto voce, *no no no no no.* He will not release me. Emmaline kneels in front of him and strokes my damp tendrils. Finally, when she touches his head again, he lays me flat, kisses my lips, and takes the silver locket from my neck. He walks into the house without looking back. She traces a cross on my forehead.

I linger for a week of dawns and dusks near the pool. Each day, the haze and disorientation weakens. My body is gone, but whatever I am—the sum of my final thoughts, my last breath—has begun to take shape, vague as it is.

I slip through the back door behind Simon, who has watered the plants his grandmother, Emmaline, has neglected for days. I wander into Andrew's room. He isn't there. In the reflection of the bookcase doors, I see a short man move into view. He has the grainy look of a silent film, and he wears a baggy shirt draped over tight pants. Around his neck is a faded scapular.

"I am Noble. I have come to welcome you," he says to me. His English undulates with the rhythm of French. His giant, heavy-lidded eyes overwhelm his otherwise large nose and long, thin mouth. I know that his hair should be blond—I can sense that—but it has an inexplicable lack of color. "What is your name?"

"Raziela Nolan. Call me Razi." I watch him glance at me, tip to toe, and I look down. I am nothing but a blur. "I'm missing. Where am I?"

"You're new. It will come soon." Noble peers around Andrew's room. This man, I think, has seen castles.

"Do you know what has happened?" Noble asks.

"I drowned."

"Do you have questions?"

"Where are we?"

"Between."

"Between what?"

"I do not know."

"What are we?"

"That, too, I do not know."

"So we go about our business as if we weren't—aren't—dead?"

"That will not be possible. You will soon come into hearing, sight, and smell beyond any experience you can imagine. Your form will change, and you will be able to move fluidly through this world. There will be tricks you can do, tricks that ones who are between can observe, some that the breathing can see. Be careful of your audience."

I remain silent. I am within the sound of his voice, not near it.

"There are rules, about which we all have an understanding," Noble says. "First, do not remain with your loved ones. You can go anywhere you please, anywhere at all, but leave them alone. Second, do not linger at your grave. One brief visit will suffice. Do that when you are able, perhaps in another seven days. And finally, do not touch. You have no need for it any longer."

"Why not?"

His small hand brushes the place where my cheek should have been. I know that he touches me, but all I feel is a strange raw vibration. No texture. Nothing familiar. The gesture is hollow. "I will come to see about you again soon. *Bonne chance.*"

Noble disappears into the wall. From the window, I see him drift over the surface of the pool and through the narrow bars of the wrought-iron fence.

❧

SCOTT WAS ON THE FRONT PORCH in a haze of April sunlight. His bare torso leaned like a plank against the white table's rounded edge. He stared at the puzzle in front of him, its corners taking shape. A breeze stirred the nearby gardenia, and Scott nodded upward, instinctively, to meet the scent. I wanted to trace the slow tension of his intercostal muscles as he inhaled.

Amy stood at the open front door and watched him. Her gaze followed the curves from his crown to his chest. Then she fixed on his eyes, which scanned the tabletop for a shape that interested him. She walked up with a package in her hand. He reached out without looking up and stroked her arm.

"Had a good run with the group this morning?" She scratched the base of his skull.

"Perfect. Ten miles felt like two in this weather." He pitched his weight back against the chair. "Although a new person joined us. She can't go the distance yet, but thinks the peer pressure, or support, will motivate her."

"My Olympian." Amy's hand moved down to his first vertebra.

"Don't go lower."

She touched the middle of his neck and rubbed her nails deeper, the friction audible. He exhaled with heated satisfaction.

"I warned you." He pulled her into his lap.

"Unhand me." She laughed and put the package on the table.

"I can't help how I'm wired. Or that you take your powers too lightly."

They sat quietly for almost a minute. "That's for you," Amy said.

Scott slipped a book from the bag with his right hand. "Thanks." He turned the cover to read the flap.

"I noticed you were on a world religion kick lately. I don't recall that you picked up anything on Hinduism." Amy pressed her hand against his pectoral muscles. "That lovely new bookcase is going to fill up in no time. You and your obsessions."

He dropped his right arm against her knees. "What obsessions?"

"Oh, aside from puzzles and running and microbrews—the dead presidents' biography marathon, which led to the strange fixation with all things Roosevelt, Teddy and Franklin, which led to the Manhattan Project history deluge, and then—"

"I'm a curious sort of guy."

"Yes, you are."

"And you can feed my obsessions anytime." His hand moved to the middle of her left thigh. She relaxed into his chest. Scott kissed her forehead. "How're you doing, Aims?"

"I'm doing fine."

"Since your grand—"

"Really, I'm okay. One day at a time."

He circled his arms around her completely. "How are you right now this minute?"

"Content."

"Good. Then can we—"

"Not now."

"You don't know what I'm about to say."

"Yes, I do." She held him back. "It's quiet, it's cool, you're warm, and that's enough right now."

❧

THE WALL CLOCK RANG eight times when Amy pounded through the back door. Sketches and a graphic design trade magazine fanned from the top of her red briefcase. Lettuce balanced precariously on top of the grocery bag squeezed against her chest. I joined a draft that carried a billow of pollen and twirled the particles into a saffron spiral bracelet. Amy sneezed when I entered the kitchen. She tossed the bags to the ground with little concern for the contents and squared her shoulders within her cropped Oriental jacket.

She was breathing so shallow, I thought her fingertips would turn blue. I pushed a book from its place on the edge of the counter. It hit the floor hard. The sudden noise made her turn quickly and breathe deep.

"Must have knocked it when I came in," she muttered as she picked it up.

"I thought I heard you." Scott walked into the kitchen. He was still wearing his lab coat from the pharmacy. There was a liquid antibiotic stain on his chest—a deformed nipple, petunia pink. He kissed her temple. "Your mom just called."

As she put away the groceries, she didn't turn to him. "How did she sound?"

"Okay, I guess. She's still in shock."

"Still?"

"Well, he hadn't been sick." Scott took a container from her hands and went to the cabinet to grab a dish. "Besides, your grandmother died—what?—three months ago? That's a lot to take in a few weeks."

"I guess."

"Your mom still thinks he died of grief."

Amy faced him, holding a can in her hand as if she were going to throw it. "No one dies of grief. That's like dying of a broken heart. It doesn't happen. The will to live is stronger than grief. The world would be a lot emptier if people dropped dead like that."

"Such a realist."

"Just like he was."

Scott popped a plate of spaghetti in the microwave. Molecules from the wheat, tomatoes, mushrooms, peppers, onions, herbs, and red wine filled the air.

"Want a salad?" Amy ducked into the refrigerator.

"Sure." He put a colander into the sink, stood with his back to the counter, and watched her. His bottom lip moved slightly, a reluctant comment on its edge. "Aims, I know it's normal to be angry when someone dies. I was angry when my grandfather died. But there's something, well, unusual about how you're reacting."

"How am I supposed to react, then?" She gouged a carrot with the scraper.

"Like you're sad about it."

"He was really old. It's not like it was a complete shock."

"Yeah, but no one expected it."

"No one expected Grandma Sunny to die, either."

"You're right. But you seem to mourn her. What about him?"

"I was close to her."

"I know that, but you must feel something for him, don't you?"

Amy spun around. "I was never close to Poppa Fin. I loved him, too, I guess. But I can't mourn him. We never connected.

My grandmother is the one I miss." She turned back to their salads.

"Your mom told me what he did with her things. Why didn't you mention it to me?"

"I was too angry. He got rid of everything—her clothes and shoes, her jewelry, her pillow, her toothbrush. Mom didn't realize what he'd done until last week, when she went to get the safety deposit box keys. She found a couple of photo albums—Grandma had just started to put them together—but all of the pictures, the loose ones, those are gone. She had a collection going back generations. There were so many of *her* when she was young—I promised her we'd scan them into the computer and give copies to everyone. But I kept putting it off."

Scott wrapped his arms around her waist. She gave him a perfunctory pat on the hand. "I'm sorry, Amy. You were a good granddaughter. No one loved her more."

The microwave beeped. "Thanks. Check the spaghetti, please."

❧

MY GRANDFATHER dies June 6, 1919, a few weeks before he turns seventy. He had wanted to see that ripe, round age and what he hoped the twenties would bring—better automobiles, better airplanes. Grams says, in some way, he won't miss a thing.

Now that Grams lives with us, Mother has stopped taking me along to visit her suffragette friends. I miss eavesdropping on their conversations, but Grams lets me do whatever I want as long as I'm quiet. I'm twelve, old enough to control my impulses.

I carry an armful of books to the back porch, kick off my shoes, and wave my stocking feet in the breeze. I pile my dress between my legs and prop books on the cushion it makes. I read everything in the house. I read Poe, Twain, and Dickens to entertain me, medical books to figure out what horrible disease could disfigure me, and Grams's books to amuse me.

Sometimes she pulls a rocker near the edge of the porch and sits without a word. I sense her eyes on me, watching as I flip the pages.

"Did I ever tell you about the year I was diagnosed with neurasthenia?"

A thousand and three times. "No, Grams."

"Well," she huffs, her cheaters dangerously close to the bulby tip of her nose, "your grandfather had a room on the second floor converted for my convalescence. Some mulattos came to take everything out of the room except for a bed and a chair. They painted the walls a lovely shade of diaper stain. Can you believe he had them hang drapes on the outside of the windows to block out the light?"

"How awful."

"Indeed. I couldn't read, write, or sew. They fed me food too bland for a baby."

I pick a scab away from my elbow and repeat the story in my head. Only the high-hatty doctor and Grandfather had keys to the room. She wasn't crazy, only bored beyond tears, but at the time, no one knew what else to do with women who found being a woman unbearably dull. She had been locked in the room more than four months when she overheard the doctor suggest "removing the source of her hysteria." That was all it took for Grams to figure out what she had to do to escape. She convinced everyone she was better when she told the doctor and my grandfather what they wanted to hear. *Oh, my listlessness is gone. I know now that I should have given myself more fully to my family. The reading and public lectures I occasionally attended, nothing but folly. Never again.*

Grams was released back to the world paler, thinner, and angrier than ever. Immediately, she tricked her husband into the room to discuss new decorating and locked him away for three days. She ate her meals on the floor with her children while fanning the delicious odors under the door's crack. Grams teased his want of freedom by jiggling the key in the lock but would never open it.

She is about to tell my favorite part. For this, I think Grams is the berries:

"And I told him if he ever listened to another head doctor again, I'd shave him bald and have him tied to the Cabildo," she spits, then does so literally, an enormous pool of old fop drool right over the porch railing.

Grams left the room, that domestic cell her husband made for her, convinced she'd been talking to her dead sister for several weeks. She had no serious religious convictions before, but she became an ardent spiritualist thereafter, who regularly sat among spirit circles. I got the heebie-jeebies every time I heard her talk about it when I was little. Then I learned to read and laughed myself sick over those stupid Fox girls, who tricked everyone into believing their clickety-clackety toe joints were the rappings of one Mr. Splitfoot.

"I don't think that was your sister. You were hallucinating."

"She came from the Summer-Land to speak to me. She knew I missed her so."

Grams doesn't know I've read all the ancient copies of her Andrew Jackson Davis books. She believes in a heavenlike Summer-Land that Davis claimed was fifty million miles away from Earth. A place where spirits reunite with their true partners and parents and float around in a state of perpetual learning. She believes they can be called to Earth to communicate with the living. That slaughters me.

"Now, Grams."

"It's true. Your grandfather himself, God rest his soul, sent me a message from beyond."

"The medium played a trick on you."

"Your grandfather apologized, Raziela."

I know better than to tell her what I saw from my hiding place under the davenport at that séance. Grams would refuse to believe me anyway. The medium wrote Grandfather's name on an envelope and attached it to the edge of the table where she sat. On another identical envelope, she wrote his name again. She gave that envelope and a blank card to Grams and told her to write a name, date, or phrase—a clue for the spirit. When Grams handed the sealed envelope containing her secret note to the medium, the woman switched it with the one she'd hidden earlier. As the fake card was burned to invoke the spirit, the medium quickly read Grams's message through the thin envelope. *Is he sorry?* it must have read.

"Your grandfather and I, we shared a love till the end, in spite of it all."

I know something about love, almost. Jimmy Reynolds had slipped me a note two weeks earlier.

Do you like me?
__Yes __No

I checked *yes* and left it tucked in his arithmetic book while the boys played baseball in an empty lot. The next day, he kissed me with an exaggerated pucker. I wondered what it would have felt like had his lips been flat and soft.

"Just you wait until it happens to you. You'll want nothing more than to devote yourself to him and the precious babies with which you'll be blessed," my grandmother says, as always.

I have something new to say. "I don't know if I want babies." My fingertips twist my braids into beardy-faced serpents. "I'm interested in other things."

"A girl should have interests. But eventually you'll have babies, too."

"Not if I don't want to."

Grams laughs. "Oh, dear, that's quite impossible."

"No, ma'am. I read it. Women in Europe have been not having babies for years."

"Women in Europe?" Grams doesn't have much tolerance for Europeans. Their squabbles took her youngest son in the Great War two years ago. Uncle Roger had wanted to kill some Huns with the pointed helmets off their own heads.

"Yes, ma'am. It says so in a pamphlet by a Mrs. Sanger."

Grams's peepers widen. "Who is she?"

"A nurse. She tells poor ladies about not having children."

"And what else have you read by this Mrs. Sanger?"

"Nothing." I am lying. At Mrs. Delacourt's house, I also skimmed two copies of a magazine I hadn't seen before. I agreed with what I read. I thought it made perfect sense to help women not have babies they didn't want and to keep them healthy for the ones they did.

"Listen to me, Raziela. It's a woman's duty to have children. It's a blessing. Think of all those little souls waiting to come into the world. Who are we to stop them?"

"Maybe not all women are supposed to be mothers."

"Nonsense."

"What if, though? What if they're not?"

"Then what are they to be?"

"How about an aviator? Or an artist? Or a doctor?"

"There is no higher aspiration than motherhood, Raziela. You'll learn soon enough."

That night, I hide *Family Limitation,* the pamphlet I'd taken from Mrs. Delacourt, in one of my favorite books. I fall asleep angry. My Grams, who never forgave my grandfather for punishing her worldly curiosity, expects me to meet the same fate.

Never. I vow to myself that I will become a doctor some day, to give any woman a choice between becoming a mother of six or a mother of invention.

I HAD BECOME RESTLESS spending the days in the rocking chair near the bookcase. One evening, I followed Amy and Scott on a weekend date. After a dinner of pizza, wine, and cheesecake, they stopped by a bookstore.

They perused the new releases with cursory interest until Scott said he wanted to look in the religion section. Amy read several book covers, glancing back at authors' names. She skimmed a volume on contemporary interior design. Two teenage girls walked past as she read, commenting on her tangerine Nehru jacket. Amy did not notice them or the blond man surreptitiously watching her from the discount racks. Amy tucked a wave of auburn hair behind her seashell ear, which made the man twitch his brown eyes. He wore a well-pressed shirt and flat-front black trousers. Without a doubt, he had shaved an hour earlier. I knocked a book to the floor to see what he would do. Amy reached to grab it.

"Here, let me get that," he said.

"Thanks." She gave him a polite but distant smile.

He ran a hand down his arm slowly, smoothing a creaseless sleeve. He didn't seem to notice, or perhaps care, that she wore a wedding ring. "Like mysteries, do you?"

"It depends."

"I like mysteries, too. Especially real ones."

Amy nodded. She was absolutely oblivious.

"Are you visiting the United States?" he asked.

"No. Why?"

"You have a European aesthetic. That's a lovely beret. It goes with your eyes." He leaned against the closest upright book rack. He pushed his shirt buttons flat from his sternum to his waist.

"I like your shoes," she said.

From my location, I saw Scott coming down the escalator, his hands empty. He spotted Amy and the harmless masher. He squinted, but not in suspicion. He seemed to want a better look at the man who was making up to his wife. When he reached the floor, Scott turned left, smiled with something that looked like amusement, and wandered into the stacks. Amy didn't see him pass by.

"I was thinking about getting some coffee. Is the coffee shop in here any good?" he asked. "This is my first visit."

A flabbergasted laugh ruptured through my form and revealed itself as a loud pop in the air. Amy looked toward the sound. "Lightbulb must have blown." She glanced at the second level of the store and then at her watch. "Oh, yes, the coffee is fine here, dark roast especially. Have a good night."

He watched her walk away, visibly stunned by his lack of success.

Amy found Scott crouched near the ground, reading titles sideways.

"Good conversation?" he asked.

"With who? Oh, that guy. Chatty fellow."

"I'm sure." Scott stood up and reached for a book that lay flat on the top shelf. "Ready?"

"What'd you get?" she asked. He handed it to her. "Tantric sex." She raised her eyebrows.

"I read about it in the Hinduism book you got me. And there was some mention in the Buddhist stuff I've read, too."

"So what is it?"

"Sex that is beyond sex." He took her hand.

Amy grinned. "At least you're never boring."

Back at home, Scott put his new book on top of his puzzle-in-progress and went to take a shower. Amy collected the mail from under the brass slot in the front door. I followed her into the kitchen. She dropped it all in a pile on the counter. With a cautious smile, she opened a package wrapped in brown paper. There was a note taped on top of a videodisc.

Dear Aims—

Look what I found during the excitement of my move. I thought you might like this little flashback. You mention your grandparents. Fond memory maybe. That's all I'll say. How's Scott? Tell Captain Jigsaw I miss him. I miss you both.

Love,
Chloe

Amy held it to her chest. Her expression shifted from fondness to nostalgia to dread. She crept into the sitting room and hid the DVD in one of the bookcase's drawers, below a layer of stationery and boxed cards.

"What'd we get in the mail?" Scott yelled from the bathroom.

"Bills, coupons."

I hovered into the rocker when she left the room. I could detect Andrew's scent even though Amy had closed the drawers evenly. It was stronger than usual, and I knew I was responsible for fueling it, even though I didn't want to. I caught myself humming to compete with the drone that became more intense every time I thought of him and that pulse that I missed.

THE LAST FRIEND I ever made between was Lionel.

Most of the ones who stayed between opted for the unknown—what was beyond—within weeks after their deaths. For them, the experience was too disconcerting, in conflict with all they had been taught or imagined about what happens after the body stopped. The ones who didn't leave so soon kept company with their former interests or discovered new ones to keep them busy. In a blur of days, months, decades, they learned not to think too much.

But Lionel thought all the time. In two years, he figured out why he had avoided physics, Italian, and cello lessons. Every task he meant to do in life, he completed. Every moment that shaped him, he understood. The accomplishments and knowledge illuminated him in a way no one could have expected.

As one of my pupils, Nel questioned every lesson he received. As my friend, he questioned me. *Why are you still here?* he asked, especially toward the end, when he knew he would go. *What are you afraid of?* I couldn't answer, even though I trusted him.

"Find out what happened to Andrew, and you'll find out what happened to you," he always said. I ignored him, until the last time. He was going beyond in seven days, exactly two years after he died. He would not celebrate the beginning of 2002 with me.

I went along for his final visits because he asked for my

company. Nel wouldn't have left without saying good-bye to the ones he had befriended during his time between. For me, every moment had been a constant reminder that he would soon be gone for good. When we arrived at his old apartment, the place he had last breathed, I did not say a word.

"Why the long face?" Nel asked. "Did somebody die?"

I smirked.

"I'll sing. It'll make you feel better." He opened his mouth, and I pitched a dirty coffee mug through the hole. "Bitchy today, aren't we?"

"Don't take it personally. I'm going to miss you."

Nel flopped back an inch above the sofa. He fixed his big hazel eyes on me. "Honey, it's time. I'm done."

"I know."

"Come with me."

"Nel."

"What if there is something next?"

"Stop."

"Come see. I have something to show you."

The man who lived in Nel's former apartment never turned off his computer. Nel grabbed the mouse, found an Internet search site, and popped my edge. I finally looked at him, but not at his hand. I couldn't watch him in the act of touching. His entire form was obscured by a bright haze that surrounded him, as if he moved through water. The glow was unnerving but beautiful.

Nel typed quickly, the name Andrew O'Connell. I realized what Nel was about to do. He wanted to find my Andrew for me.

For decades, I believed I had followed my sweetheart at a distance, bending the rule about following people one had loved. At least once a year, I would take pen to the air and scrawl a couple of notes in my antiquated script. Out to the post office they went, delivered to people who forwarded news clippings about one Andrew O'Connell. The return address for this information often changed. However, those good folks who stayed in their jobs long enough remembered me and occasionally attached messages to their mysterious penfriend, Barrett Burrat. They wished me luck on the biography that was taking years to write.

Only months before, one of those kind people sent me an obituary for the man whose life I had followed. I had never questioned whether I tracked the right person because—in name, action, and deed—the man had led the life I expected my Andrew to have, the life he had planned. But there, in that obituary, never mentioned in any other clipping I ever received, was the name of this stranger's birthplace, a small town in Illinois. My Andrew had been born in New Orleans. Of that, I was absolutely certain. So in fact, I had no idea what happened to Andrew after he left with two full suitcases and tickets to New Haven in his jacket pocket.

"Razi, dammit, don't look away," Nel said as the screen flashed a page of new words. He created a list of every Andrew O'Connell who had died in the last forty years. "I've reviewed these records. None of these men was born the year Andrew was. Not even within a year or two."

"Your point?"

"That Andrew of yours might still be alive. Look at this." In seconds, he created another list. I stared. More than four hundred and fifty instances of his name. "It would take you less than half a day to glance at these sites. What if he's here?"

I filled with heat, and the electronics in the apartment buzzed, flickered, then shut off. "Why do you insist on tormenting me?"

"You did it to yourself. Why'd you track him if you never really wanted to find him?"

"I didn't need to find him. When I sent letters, I expected nothing but reassurance that he had become the man I believed he would be. You have to understand, all the pieces made sense. And you know the rule, Nel, for goodness sake."

"Yes, the rule." He glanced at the dining room table. An envelope floated toward me and landed next to the vapor of my hand. "I have something else for you. Maybe this is a start in a new direction. When you're ready."

I saw the Yale University emblem on the top left. It was addressed to Mr. Barrett Burrat. Even in his meddling, Lionel was thoughtful, using my pen name.

As I opened the letter from Yale, I let a part of him escape. Andrew's scent infused me, a clean metallic brine that deepened with heat. How often I worked not to think of him, or anyone, for more than an instant. To linger was to tempt an inevitable hemorrhage of memory, almost impossible to control. After my last breath, every moment of my life was revealed perfectly intact, the recollection effortless, the connections among them fluid and associative. I could never predict precisely what would come back to me.

"What does it say?" Nel asked.

"It just confirms what I knew. I did follow a stranger. And it says that my Andrew didn't graduate from Yale—ever. This other man—I knew he had graduated in 1933, the year after my Andrew was supposed to. I assumed he took extra time to finish his studies, all things considered. But it appears that's not the case." I incinerated the letter in midair.

"I can't imagine what happened between you two, but it had to be pretty bad for someone as smart as you to dupe yourself for so long. You know, you could tell me finally. Talk about taking a secret to the grave. It's almost beyond that at this point." Nel smirked at his double entendre, his features soft behind the glow. "I'm sorry, honey. I'm so sorry—for whatever it was."

I suddenly remembered Andrew's face, in sunlight, the first time I stretched my naked body on top of his, the whisper of his hands down my back, the relish in his voice as he exhaled, *My little succubus.*

Release me. Let me go. Please.

—stunned—naked—

blue flame—bright light—white blur—

warm blood—still blood—broken glass
—blue light broken—

ANDREW AWAKES long after the sun rises, and dresses in a daze. Six weeks of grief has made him unsteady, but today he is debilitated, drunk with it. He stumbles as he reaches for his wristwatch and bumps his injured hand. His eyes go blank with visceral rage. As the focus returns, he moves with singular purpose toward the center of his bedroom doorway. He leaves the house for lunch without uttering a greeting to his mother or Emmaline. They glance at each other, unaccustomed to such a lapse in his manners. They have no idea what last night brought in, other than the storm. They speak of the thunder now, because they can't speak of Andrew's silence.

Confused and distraught, I wander for several miles, moving southeast toward the river. I suddenly realize that I must see Eugenia, the Confederate lady Noble considers a friend. She is always in the same place, circling the grounds of her old home in this old neighborhood with manic regularity. I fall in step beside her and tell her the elementary details, all that she needs to know.

"Whatever were you thinking?" she asks.

"How much I miss the feel of him." This is only a fraction of the truth.

"Oh, goodness. No one told you? Touch will never come back."

I am horrified. After weeks of trying, I had learned to create the semblance of a solid form. I was aware that my density was not matter, not as I had been before, but a knit of energy. Several times, I had allowed myself under Andrew's hands, briefly, to practice. I was impatient but certain that sensation would return in time. What was left of me would relearn—remember—how to feel.

I stand next to Eugenia as she repeats the last twitching

dance of her physical life. She does this every day at noon sharp. Only months after the War Between the States ended, she had been stung to death, right there in her garden.

Eugenia dispels her image into a humid August breeze and reappears seconds later in mid-stride. She adjusts the brim of her frowzy rose-colored bonnet. She clucks her light tongue. "Why did you assume that he could endure your touch from beyond the grave?"

"Why didn't someone warn me?"

"Didn't anyone tell you the last rule?"

"Noble did. All he said was that I'd have no use for it anymore." I tell her that I tried to get more information to explain why. I had asked four wanderers—the ones who did not confine themselves to the places they had died. Noble only smiled and said that experience was the best teacher. Two others acted as if my questions were digging into guarded secrets, and they refused to answer. The last had burned his hands on a stove at the age of fifteen months. Although he, like the rest of us, could remember every moment of his breathing life, he had had little practice at the nuances of touch in his thirty-six years with a body. He could not understand why it mattered now.

I want to cry.

"There, there, sugarplum." Eugenia pats the space near my hand. "You will have to stop, Raziela. Do not touch him again. If you cannot refrain, I would suggest that you move away—or move, well—" She pauses and fingers the lavender bow under her chin. "Tell me, after you stopped breathing, how far did you see? Into beyond."

"I only saw light. I saw no end. The same way I remember my birth."

"Noble says he saw gates."

"That's not the only illusion he treasures."

Eugenia blinks. She, too, knows that Noble believes that he disobeyed God moments after his body failed, that he refused to meet the being that forced him to watch his wife and children slowly die. "But do you suppose there is one, an end?"

"No. What do you think?"

"I did not want to find out what was next. I was so happy before the bees came." A bumblebee hovers above Eugenia's nose. She stands on tiptoe, takes it into her mouth, and stills the air in that round space. A moment later, the insect falls to the ground, smothered to death.

"All I ever wanted to do was walk in my garden and enjoy the colors and scents of every season," she says. "What a surprise it was that my form allows me to be filled with perfume. The breathing who can sense me call me the Rose Ghost because I am always surrounded with that scent.

"The air holds many secrets, dear. A beautiful spectrum of fragrances, infinitesimally small. And when you learn to take those parts to build a whole, you return to remembrance." She moves her full bosom as if she were inhaling. "He is with you even now. Your Andrew. He is a part of your scent because he is a part of your memory. He is a part of you, now as much as before."

Since my death, I have spent most of my time learning to tolerate the incredible range of sounds I now hear and working to create a solid form. I have hardly noticed the sensitivity to scent. I hold a breeze within me for a moment. The magnolia cones will not split open for another two weeks, but I can smell a hint of the red seeds that will emerge, a cinnamon-clove fragrance as rich as their color.

"What an interesting trick." I think of the spring evening when I pinched stamens from honeysuckle blossoms and savored the delicate nectar, released drop by drop, on my tongue. An April aroma suddenly perfumes the August air. "We must attract atoms from the air and assemble them into molecules."

"I haven't a clue," she says. Her nostrils curl. She detects a dilute miasma of blood and chlorine, I know, but pretends that the air is still sweet.

"It's basic chemistry."

"Such things simply are, and I enjoy them." Eugenia pulls at the cuffs of her long sleeves. "But back to the matter at hand, sugarplum. Leave Andrew be. What happened is an example of why we leave our loved ones alone. Besides, he is not the reason you stayed between. He is the reason you refuse to go beyond."

"That's not it at all. I told you before. I wasn't finished."

"Yes, that is true. That is true. But you stayed between for a purpose. Perhaps what you think that purpose is, is not the case at all." Eugenia suffocates another bee in the palm of her hand.

I VENTURED OUT AGAIN with Amy and Scott to a party out of town. The ride west from Baton Rouge to Lafayette was lovely. I had never seen that part of Louisiana. Early May had erupted in green. Now and then, I cracked the window to get a whiff of the sap that flooded the trunks and branches. The Atchafalaya Basin spread wide and shallow. Egrets perched on jagged remains of cypress trees. I remembered the flocks that flew overhead when Andrew and I drove along the Mississippi in search of a secluded spot for a picnic lunch, and dessert.

"Oil derricks used to line this stretch." Amy looked at the open spaces near a small town's highway exit. "An old boyfriend called them earless horses."

"Why?"

"The part that bobbed down looked like a horse's head."

Scott missed the woebegone tenor of what she told him. I clicked the back window down a notch to rush the air around me. There it was, the hint of a man whose skin she had known well.

"Okay—" Scott shoved his finger against the window control lever. "Am I giving off some weird electrical charge? Anything that plugs in or runs on a battery won't behave around me anymore."

"Your magnetic personality," Amy said.

"I always thought I was attractive."

"Ion-estly think so."

"Are you positive?"

She turned to him as he chuckled. Scott had a good laugh, an honest one.

"Why aren't you laughing?" he asked.

"T minus twenty-two minutes and counting to the family fun."

SCOTT PRESSED HIS PALM against the small of Amy's back as they walked up to the house. She balanced a pretty gift in one hand and knocked with the other. The front door opened. An elderly woman turned her smile toward the guests on the porch.

Twolly.

She wore black pumps with a low heel, a simple dress the color of amethyst, and a single strand of real pearls. There was a wedding ring on her left hand, which was raised to a cygnet-soft cheek. Matching pearl earrings dotted her adorable lobes. Her brown eyes were wide inside the gold rims of her cheaters. Once dark blond hair was now white as dogwood petals.

I lunged to hug my old friend. My reaction was visceral. I forgot I had no body. Twolly teetered in her shoes. Scott and another man grabbed her elbows to steady her as I slipped from the growing crowd.

"Aunt Twolly, your legs can't keep up with the rest of you," Amy said.

"Oh, my goodness! Do you hear that pounding? My heart is about to burst." Twolly giggled.

Loud rappings knocked against the walls. I stilled myself, my energy, to quiet the sound as people began to ogle the room for the source.

"Are you okay, Mom?" said the man who was holding her arm.

"Please. Your mother is old, but she's not made of porcelain." Twolly stepped proudly, and slowly, away from her son.

A bug flew into my gaping mouth and spun out of my ear. I had not seen Twolly in nearly seventy-five years. Not since I hopped a train to Shreveport and hovered the streets until I found her family home. I longed to hold her ancient hands in mine and stroke her manicured fingertips until they tickled.

TWOLLY NEVER LIKED being the center of attention. Instead, she circled around an event, tending to details, making people feel comfortable. She was a wonderful hostess in our younger years, and that had not changed about her. Each new guest was greeted warmly and led through a sea of handshakes and kisses as she offered a beverage or bite to eat. The grace she had years before was more smooth, more noticeable, because she could no longer move as quickly. Her hands lingered on people's arms to catch their attention—and steady herself.

Her laugh was exactly the same, a sharp sneezy rush, *ahhh ha ha ha*. She had no reserve if she were amused. There was never any doubt that her response was genuine. Her childlike bursts made a room chime. When she spoke, her words vibrated slightly, but they came out as strong as they had when she was young. Her North Louisiana drawl still flowed like buttermilk. And she still said "cain't" for *can't*.

When she disappeared into the kitchen, I wandered among the guests to observe Twolly's family. Some of her grandchildren and great-grandchildren had arrived to celebrate her ninety-sixth birthday, while others, scattered across the globe, had sent cards and flowers. Her two sons and daughter moved among cousins and spouses clustered throughout the first floor of the house. Her youngest sister Sunny's three children were there as well—a son and two daughters, one of whom was Amy's mother, Nora.

I smiled to myself as I stood among them. Twolly's life had turned out exactly as she expected. Her children clearly adored her. I had known she would make a wonderful mother, even when she was young. I imagined that she had been a good wife, too, although there was no elderly man at her side to give me such a clue.

I wandered into a cozy sitting room full of furniture that had been Twolly's mother's. On a pristine Jacobean table, there were fifteen framed photographs. One was of my dear old friend and her husband at Christmas. Several others showed her children and their families. The oldest ones were of Twolly's parents and a group shot of Twolly and her four sisters. I wondered what happened to the photos she once had of us together, especially the one taken at a playground, waving from a seesaw. Andrew had told us to keep still so we wouldn't blur the shot. He had been testing his new camera that day.

Scott entered the room behind a quick, crawling baby. "Okay, you little monster, let's get out of your great-grandma's special room." Scott reached under the little boy's arms and pitched him high in the air. The baby squalled.

"Give him to me." Amy stretched her hands toward her young cousin. Scott dangled the child in front of her. She kissed him loudly on the forehead. Amy scooped him on her hip and flattened the tiny buttoned shirt over his belly. Scott twitched his right hand to stop it from moving toward her in a gesture of affection.

"Cute family. Want to take him home?" asked Julie, Twolly's granddaughter. She smelled of expensive shampoo and the waning hormones of a mother no longer nursing.

"Tempting, but he'd miss you." Amy handed the child to her cousin.

"So when are you having yours?" A dull crust of oatmeal coated Julie's hair along the back edge.

Nora slipped into the room with a glass of cranberry juice in her hand. "I've been wondering the same thing." She brushed a wisp of steel gray hair from her fair, smooth forehead. Her movement showed natural grace.

"You've been married—what—two, three years?" Julie asked.

"Two," Amy said.

"But we've been together more than four," Scott said.

"Girl, what are you waiting on? You're just a year younger than me, aren't you? Don't you feel those eggs turning into raisins in there?"

"Actually, no," Amy said, a growl of warning in her throat.

"You don't know what you're missing. You've never loved anything so much. Isn't that right, Little Bruce?" Julie made pig noises into her son's neck. He squealed with delight. "You been trying?"

Scott found the third button of his shirt fascinating.

"I'm barren."

"Amy—" Nora blurted. "Why didn't you—"

"Really?" Julie clenched her jaw to thwart a conspiratorial smile.

"Just kidding."

Nora's cheeks matched her red drink, and she exhaled with a gust.

Julie frowned. "Don't joke like that. Lord, what if you were?" She turned her ear toward the door. "I know that's one of mine tearing into the gifts. I'll talk to y'all later."

With a light stroke, Nora touched Amy's hand. "You'd tell me if something were wrong, wouldn't you? I don't mean to pry, but I would want to know, sweetheart. I'm your mother, after all."

"Mom, I'm fine. I promise." Amy paused. "I think I heard Dad calling for you."

"Did he? I tell you, my eyesight first, now my hearing. I'm too young for this aging thing." Nora squeezed Amy's shoulder on her way out.

Scott waited until Nora was out of whisper distance. "Did you have to do that?"

"Julie started it. 'When are you having yours?' It's none of her business. And she's the third person to ask since we got here. It's barely eleven o'clock. What's with this family?"

"I don't think they mean any harm."

"They might as well ask for sperm samples."

"Amy, please."

"I came in here to get away from all the talk about what Poppa Fin did. What he threw out. What he didn't. Why he did such a thing. What's the point of wondering? It doesn't bring anyone—anything—back. Then I end up in here with the Fertility Goddess who pushed out four in six years. And my mother. The way she acts, you'd think I was the only one to carry on the Richmond blood. She doesn't harass my brother like this. Maybe we should move halfway across the country like he did." Amy flopped herself into a wingback. "You're a man. You don't know the pressure."

"Yes, I do. It might be different, but it feels the same. To me, anyway."

He walked out with his hands deep in his pockets. Amy turned to look at the photos on the table. For a long moment, I watched her, marveling that she had led me back to my old friend, that I must have sensed something about her other than her brazen pluck. Amy shifted her eyes to another picture, just to the right. She peered at her Grandma Sunny's face as if she expected a word of comfort. A faint, familiar sweetness spread throughout the room. I remembered Sunny, too—fresh and bold as zinnias—although I only met her once.

OCTOBER 1926, OUR SOPHOMORE YEAR, Twolly invites me to entertain her younger sister, Sunny. Eight years old, tiny and bright, Sunny runs up to the elephant's keep at Audubon

Zoo. She watches the animal grasp alfalfa with its trunk and bring the snack toward its mouth.

"People say elephants never forget anything," I tell her.

"Really?" She twists a curl of her new bob into her finger. "So if I visit my sissie at college again and we come back to the zoo, Itema will remember this?"

Before Twolly can stop her, Sunny stands on her hands and dances her feet in the air, showing her dainties to all who care to look.

"Is she laughing, Razi?" Sunny asks.

"Soleil!" Twolly shouts.

I bend over in hysterics.

"For goodness sake, don't encourage her." Twolly grabs her little sister at the waist and turns her right side up. "Soleil, that is no way to behave in a public place. If Mother were here, you'd spend the rest of the day in a corner."

"Aw, Etoile, no one but you and Razi saw."

"That's not the point."

"It was an awful good handstand, though, Twolls. She has great balance."

Twolly glares at me. I am tempted to mention that she, of late, has violated standards of decency, but even I have the sense to know that Sunny is too young to learn certain secrets about her sister.

"There's a big old monkey here, too, Sunny. Want to see him?" I ask.

The little girl blinks at Twolly with feigned remorse.

"Go on, you two."

When I glance back, I see Twolly stifle a chuckle.

BRIGHT AGAINST HER harvest gold hair is the Newcomb College Class of '29 green beanie. This is the third time I happen to be in the art building's ladies' room when the quiet, modestly dressed blond girl comes in to wash charcoal dust from her hands.

"What a messy class you're taking," I say. "What is it?"

"Cast drawing."

"What's that?"

"We draw from plaster models, busts mainly. I've seen you around. Are you an upperclassman?" She inspects me, looking for a hint of color: freshman green, sophomore red, junior gold, senior blue and white.

"I'm a Tulane freshman, but not in your college. I'm taking a drawing class for my science courses. We draw dissections. I'm Raziela Nolan. Call me Razi."

"Pleased to meet you, Rah-zee." She has pronounced my name correctly with a slight drawl. "Etoile Knight."

"Etoile? As in star?"

"Yes. You know French?"

"Some. Enough to know it's not right to name your child Star Knight. Now I'll crack up every time I see you."

"My middle name is Luna."

I laugh. "Mind if I call you Twolly?"

"I've never had a nickname. My family doesn't believe in them. But they're not here now."

"Maybe it'll catch on."

We see each other nearly every day after school. I learn Twolly is the third of five girls. She is unimpressed that she's a nouveau riche Shreveport debutante whose daddy is in oil. Although her parents had wanted her to stay home and find a nice, ambitious young man to marry, she decided she wanted a few years to herself. Twolly studies jewelry making at Newcomb and wants to meet boys who won't have to be introduced to her family. There is no doubt in her mind that she'll be a wife and mother someday, but not now, not yet. When I see her metalwork, so simple, so organic, so beautiful, I hope that her choice is truly her own, that the subtle catch in her voice does not imply resignation to a narrow world and a woman's narrower view.

FIRST SPRING DANCE, 1927. Twolly pulls me out of the arms of a bewildered stag and drags me toward the steps. Only moments before, she was dancing across the room, tossing her head back in laughter. A boy who was waiting to cut in on me frowns as we pass him.

"Easy, Twolls. Where's the fire?" I say.

"David Kleinert's pants."

I cackle. "What happened?"

"We were dancing, and he led me off the veranda into the dark."

"Did you want him to?"

"Well, yes, he's terribly sweet, I see him on campus almost every day, and he's been cutting in on me often lately, so I figured he was interested. We were having a very personal conversation—he said he'd wanted to ask me on a date, and I said he shouldn't be so shy, and then he stopped moving and leaned in, so I kissed him—"

"How was it?" Twolly's first real kiss was worthy of hours of interrogation. Until she met me, she had no idea that kisses could involve more than lips.

"It started out just fine. Then he sort of trapped me, which—don't you tell anyone, I swear—which was a bit of a thrill, I won't lie, but then I suppose things got a little carried away, and I realized something wasn't quite in place."

"That shouldn't have surprised you."

"We had our clothes on."

"Why do you think they come off in the first place?" I lead her to a bench under a tangle of honeysuckle. I take off her hat, smooth her hair, and replace the cloche properly. "Did he get fresh with you?"

"Like pie on a windowsill."

"I mean, did he do anything you didn't want him to do?"

"I pushed him off before he had a second chance."

"You have to find him. Boys are like puppies. Their feelings are easily hurt, but they forgive you quicker than anything if you show them a little kindness."

"What do I say?"

"Make him laugh. Tell him you thought something escaped from the reptile exhibit." Twolly shook her head. "Then be honest. Tell him you're sorry. Would you still go on a date with him?" She nods. "Okay. He needs to know that. He's not a masher, Twolls, just a man. You should be a little flattered anyway. And you do share some of the blame."

"How? I didn't do a thing."

"You kissed him first. Instigator. Boys love that."

"They do?"

"You felt the results."

"This is why girls should be married first before anything happens. It's too traumatic." Twolly fans herself with the bodice of her dress. Ligustrum blossoms snow from the back of her shoulders.

"You're secretly glad I'm here to see you through these first years of womanhood. You wouldn't even know what just happened to him if I hadn't told you about it."

"You're too weird for words."

I look across the yard. David finishes a smoke by himself, staring up at the stars. He would make a good steady for Twolls. He's a bit shy, well-mannered, clumsy with words but not bad on his feet. "Go on," I say. "There he is."

A year ago, she would have avoided him at all costs. But now, she exhales and straightens her dress. Twolly walks toward him. David darts his head as if he wants to run away. I cross my fingers. I imagine her sweet little drawl and those guileless brown eyes smoothing his ruffled fur. He doesn't face her directly, but he seems to be apologizing, his fists so far in his pockets that his jacket sleeves bunch. Her innocent hand reaches for his arm, and he doesn't pull away. There, a bashful smile and the turn of his elbow. She links with him, and they walk back toward the dance floor.

A trumpet startles me with its bleat. Above and behind, dancers scuffle along the varnished wood floor. The beams underneath them groan quietly. I pick a honeysuckle blossom and touch it to my nose. No matter how deeply I breathe, the scent doesn't fulfill my want for it. The narrow petals dally against my lip. I stare at the slender elegant well and pinch the base from which it grew. Slowly, the stamens emerge. I take the bead of nectar on my tongue. For a moment, the smooth liquid aroma satisfies me. Soon, there is a pile of spent blossoms on my lap.

"There you are," says a voice to my left.

The boy who wanted to dance. I remember him from other parties. Decent dancer, easy blusher, slow with a line, goofy about football.

"Hello, Carl. Were you looking for me?"

"Just passing by." He's also a terrible fibber.

"Lucky me, then. Warm up this lonesome spot." I pat the bench. "I've been waiting for someone special."

TONIGHT IS HALLOWEEN. My twentieth. Word has it that there will be a jazz band, lots of alcohol, and no chance of a raid if the right people have been settled up. Twolly swore we didn't have to come in costume. At least that's what she heard from Anna Whitcomb, the girl who invited her to join the crowd. This evening, I have donned my glorious regalia: the clover green dress that fits just right over my barely there bosom and slight hips, the matching cloche hat, a double length of pearls, and new silk stockings.

"This fellow's father is a banker," Twolly says as we approach the immaculate Victorian house painted in mute colors. "You'd think he would have a more modern house by now. A St. Charles address is a St. Charles address, I suppose."

Twolly knocks at the door. As we wait for it to open, I give a few bats of the green peepers and smooth the blond bob waves against the curves of my face. From my beaded purse, I whip out a tulip-colored lipstick and paint the promise of a kiss for a cute boy who can dance and tell a joke, preferably at the same time.

A poppy-faced boy opens the door. We trip over his unlaced saddle shoes as he moves to let us in. "Hooch in the backyard." He lights a cigarette. "Noodle juice in the parlor."

I trot to the back of the house where I find a well-tended garden along the perimeter of a gorgeous pool. I know almost half of the people here. Everyone is a crasher these days.

Carl asks me to dance before I have a chance to mingle. We cut loose for a while, and I ask him to get me a drink and a bite to eat. As I wander along the manicured boxwoods, I notice a young man having a serious and animated conversation with two fellows on the other side of the water. He has wavy obsidian hair parted on the side, and bold eyebrows that draw my focus directly to his eyes. I suspect they are black because the luster is so deep. He glances my way as he speaks, and he stumbles on his words when I don't look away.

"What are you looking at?" Twolly startles me.

"Who's that? He's a sheik."

"Which one?"

"The one with the dark hair facing that cake-eater in those terrible Oxford pants." I nod at the boy who tries to mask his sissiness with clownish baggy, and trendy, trousers.

Twolly nudges me. "That's the host."

"You don't say?"

"You look knocked for a row of cabbages."

"I always land on my feet, don't I, my dear Twolly? What's his name?"

"Oh, him. His best friend is Anna Whitcomb's fiancé. What's his name? Andrew something. Something Irish. O'Brien? O'Malley? No—O'Connell."

"Wonder if he's so fiery that it burned the red out of his hair."

"Pet him and find out."

I pull the hat down over her ears. "Such a mouth you have now."

My dance partner returns. "Have a quilt." He hands me a glass of punch tainted with gin.

I pick at the plate of nibbles Carl brought for me and pretend to be engrossed as he spills an earful. I chew the fruit bits thoughtfully and savor two of the three petits fours. Twolly is clairvoyant, I swear, and she deftly lures him away as Andrew sips on his full drink, waiting for their exit.

"I wanted to welcome you personally." His eyes are not black, but lapis lazuli, a flawless supernatural blue. "I'm Andrew O'Connell."

"Raziela Nolan." I offer my hand, which he accepts.

"How exotic. Are you named for someone?"

"Only my mother's amusement."

He passes my laugh test. It is within the normal pitch of his voice, which is deeper than I expected, and a definite *ha.* No *haws, huhs,* or—the worst—*hees.* He fills his pearly blushed cheeks with the best liquor his father's lawless money can buy.

"My compliments to the chef." I finish the last little cake. Slowly, I lick my fingertips clean. "Pure ambrosia."

"Emmaline, our housekeeper, is an excellent cook."

A young man wrenches Andrew at the shoulders. "Happy birthday, old boy. Hell of a party. Seen Anna anywhere?" He trips on his feet as he stumbles away.

"Thanks, Warren," Andrew says. "And no, I haven't seen her."

"Happy birthday."

"Thank you."

"Do you turn into something frightful at midnight?"

"No one has ever lived to tell."

"Take a walk with me, Andrew."

We slip out of the wrought-iron back gate and around the front of his house. We stroll several blocks to Audubon Park, stunned by a comfortable silence and the intoxicating perfume of sweet olive. The scent reminds me of the time I smoked opium, the way the fragrance seeped into my pores and bronchial tubes to leave me peaceful and somewhat lusty. When we reach the edge of the park, I run to a live oak reaching half a dozen leafy-fingered arms to me.

"I haven't climbed a tree in years. I hope he's strong." I push myself into a straddle over a gently sloping limb and scoot toward the trunk. "Don't peek now." Andrew glances up furtively and sips his drink. He is a little more than half-cut. Any less, and he might have tried to call me down. A chilly, humid breeze clams my skin and brushes the leaves with more moisture than air. "Join me?"

"Someone should be down here to catch you when you fall."

I laugh. "Where do you go to school?"

"Tulane."

"So, Andrew, what do you want to be when you grow up?" I wonder why we have never met before.

"A lawyer."

"Because you believe in justice or money?"

"Because I like to argue."

There. I start to sweat. My palms throb in time with my heartbeat, a steady *whoosh-rush, whoosh-rush,* and my mouth feels like the morning after a good plaster. I hug the tree, and it returns my adoration with the tenderness of an unshaven father.

A spot of light moves back and forth in front of his face. "Cigarette?" He holds up a metal case in my direction but does not look up.

"I don't smoke."

"And you, Raziela—"

"Razi, please."

"And you, Razi? What do you want to be?"

I sit down on a meaty limb. Running in crisscrosses among a row of trees are several children draped in white sheets, moaning and wooing loudly. They chase each other and collapse in blind tangles of linen.

"I want to be immortal," I say.

"Immortal." He says the word as if it has considerable meaning, like *God* or *Freedom* or *I love you*.

"I want to live forever."

"You want to live forever."

"Pos-a-lute-ly."

"Why?" He crushes his dincher under his heel. "Wait, don't answer yet." Andrew tosses his jacket to the ground and starts to crawl up the limb to meet me. He maneuvers with cautious balance. Sitting a shoulder to elbow's distance away, he says, "Now."

"One lifetime isn't enough to make all the trouble of which I am capable."

He doesn't kiss me. I don't kiss him. Twolly doesn't believe me when I say so.

WHEN I SAW TWOLLY AGAIN at her birthday party, I decided once and for all that I had to find Andrew, dead or alive, even though I feared what I invited in that pursuit. I could no longer cling to the lie that had sustained me, the pieces of another man's life I took for his. Before that, what had become of my Andrew was a mystery I was afraid to solve. To think of Andrew, actively, consciously, left me vulnerable to recollective chaos I did not have the experience to control. It was best to avoid that which could not be undone.

I knew that I had to steel myself, find the resolve. Certainly, Twolly would not have let someone she cared about slip too far from her grasp. I remembered the last time I saw her with Andrew. She had asked him to keep in touch with her, no matter how brief. If Twolly received a letter of inquiry, she would reply, of course—she was courteous in that way—and that would be the end of it. I would know.

For weeks, I collected stamps. I visited the nearby post office to look for the straggling squares from vending machines, paid for but not claimed. From Amy and Scott's mail, I removed the ones that had not been canceled by postmarks. This practice was common among those between who needed to send letters now and then.

Behind the cornice of the bookcase, I had piled dozens of stamps. If I were to learn what became of him, wouldn't I want to know from as many perspectives as possible? I had done what Lionel told me—and not a single Andrew O'Connell who had come up on his computer search led to the one I wanted. And so I began my list: Twolly, Tulane University, every O'Connell in Massachusetts, Warren Tripp, Simon Beeker's children.

Finally, one night, as Amy and Scott slept, I lifted a pen into the air. But when I guided the nib to the paper, I froze. The lights flickered on and off. I held it back that time, the memory of Andrew's eyes, that storm, his blood, the reason I feared the truth so much, the damage I feared I had done. Once the calm returned and the lights remained dark, I wrote each letter with solitary purpose, distracting myself with thoughts of how much I missed the feel of a sleek hard rubber fountain pen.

❧

SCOTT PUT HIS WEDDING RING and watch in the same place every evening after work. He had a little soapstone box big enough for those two items on their bedroom's vanity, a Depression-era Art Deco piece with a huge round mirror and inlaid drawers. Sometimes I watched him absently slide the gold band from his hand and place it gently in the box. He never turned on the light to see what he was doing. He knew right where it belonged.

He left his clothes in a pile where he took them off and picked them up after he took his shower. Scott strolled around the house naked as an ape. I did not watch him as he walked past; he reminded me too much of another man whose body I knew in more detail than he knew his own.

Some nights, Scott pulled out a plywood board from under the guest room bed. He sat for hours without turning on a radio or TV to work on a puzzle. The pieces he'd matched were on the board, and the rest were spread across the duvet. Although he didn't work quickly, he was accurate. I could tell that he was spinning pieces in his head. When he put them down, they locked up perfectly. He completed the frame first and worked toward the middle. Once, I couldn't resist and put some of it together myself. He accused Amy of doing the work.

"I don't know how that strip got in the middle of your puzzle." She eyed one row of several dozen yin-yang symbols. "You know those things drive me crazy."

Sometimes Amy would sit at the computer in the corner of the guest room while Scott entertained himself. She shuffled full, flat boxes of papers, graphic design magazine clippings, and art supplies away from the table surface. If she caught up on work, she first spilled the contents of a red multi-pocketed briefcase on the floor and checked her date book, a spiral-bound drawing pad filled with sticky notes, colorful doodles, and three-dimensional arrows with page numbers. As chaotic as it seemed, she knew where everything was. When she didn't work, Amy searched the Internet to read news or to amuse herself.

On weekends, they went to dinner or parties with friends. The evenings they stayed home together, they watched television or a rented movie. If there was nothing that interested them, they read in the living room and listened to the radio. Occasionally, one would ask if the other wanted to hit the springs. I'd leave the house when the answer was yes.

Every night before he went to sleep, Scott read a chapter from the book he kept on his side of the bed. He squinted his brown eyes and chewed his bottom lip as he flipped through the pages. If the book was paperback, he would hold it with his left hand and stroke Amy's hair with his right. With heavy books, he lay on his right side, propped the book against her body, and let a free hand fall on whatever part of her was uncovered. She sighed as she drifted off to sleep, rousing only a little when the lamp clicked off and he turned her chin toward him for a kiss. Throughout the night, a part of him always touched a part of her.

Because Scott worked late-evening shifts sometimes, Amy got up alone to go to work. She kissed him lightly on the forehead, looked at him wistfully, and tucked the covers around him before she left. Those mornings when they woke up together, they held hands near their pillows and muttered conversations.

I tried hard not to think of Andrew and how he looked asleep. I could not indulge myself in wondering what I had missed.

ONE NIGHT when Scott worked a late shift at the pharmacy, Amy slipped into the front room and pulled the DVD from the depths of the bookcase drawer. She had avoided Chloe's surprise for several days. I could sense her nervous shivering, surges of cold vibrations filling the air.

Amy popped the disc in the player and sat on the sofa with the remote control dangling in her hand. Tucked behind her perfect ears, her damp unbrushed hair dried in auburn waves near her shoulders. Her aquamarine eyes resembled ocean water transfused by light. She wore Scott's boxer shorts and a threadbare T-shirt that billowed against her thin freckled arms and small bosom.

We watched static for a few moments until the picture came into view. A neatly printed sign filled the screen long enough to read it—*Tales from the Philosophical Border: Womyn on the Front Lines.* Amy's straight lips bent into a little smile.

For the first few minutes, a voice described the scene on film.

"Welcome to the front lines," said a confident young woman. The camera focused on a man's screaming mouth, but her voice was stronger. "I am your host, Chloe Abner. It's the Year of Our Lord 1992. Big Brother hasn't invaded our homes yet, we aren't eating people, and the planet isn't ruled by apes. What you are about to see is real. These people are not actors. They are your neighbors, coworkers, maybe even your friends. They go to church, obey God, love their families, and believe that what they're doing somehow pleases the Almighty."

There was a pop, followed by the onslaught of pure volume from the man's throat. "God's mercy is not endless. He is a vengeful God. He will smite the wicked. No punishment too great for the sinners who offend Him. The fires of hell await you, Jezebels. Repent! Throw yourself on His tender feet and beg forgiveness. The slaughter of babes is a stench that coats your soul!"

The shot widened away from the mouth. A pug nose flared. Deep brown eyes stared ahead. His brown hair was stringy across his forehead, where a vein crossed his temple like a bridge. In his right hand was a black Bible. His khaki pants fit loose under a brown stenciled belt. At his knees, there was a microphone held by a steady arm. When he came into full view, the man was standing on the hood of a mid-1970s Ford Thunderbird, which was parked behind a low fence.

The arm holding the microphone belonged to a younger Amy. Her stance and expression were serious. She gritted her teeth. She was holding back a laugh.

Another pop, and Chloe said, "As if the way he talks to people isn't shameful enough, what would his Lord think of this?"

Sitting on the sofa watching her past life, Amy let out a scream of laughter. The lens tightened toward the man's pants until it was evident that he expressed disdain for his congregation in a unique—and rigid—manner.

Several scenes followed that featured the people Chloe called the protesters. Some of them addressed the camera directly, making a case for their beliefs. A short row of Catholics on their knees in the dirt didn't say a word. Rosaries looped through their fingers.

The final clip was a shot of a portable tape player balanced on the high fence around the women's clinic. Through the speakers, a baby wailed. The cry didn't hint that she was wet, hungry, or tired. The child sounded as if someone had left her for a long time—there was no break in the tape—forcing her to beg for attention the only way she knew how. A bullhorn projected a man's voice. "Hear this, mother! This cry is coming from your womb!"

"That's your own baby, you asshole." Amy was shaking again, but now from a fury that had worked its way out of the place she buried it.

The next few scenes were personal interviews with several women, and a couple of men. They explained why they got up at dawn to huddle in front of the clinic, breaking away in pairs throughout the morning to walk a woman—sometimes accompanied by a boyfriend or friend—from her car to the door. Their passion was no deeper than that of the people who stood on the other side of the fence calling them whores, Jezebels, and babykillers. It was an ugly business, both sides agreed, but for different reasons.

The setting changed. Amy and Chloe, in their early twenties, sat on a green tweed sofa lumpy from two decades of use.

"I wanted to make this tape to remember. I'm told that I'm going to turn into a Republican"—Chloe waved her hand with a series of dismissive flicks—"and that I'll look back on all of this like any other youthful folly. Jesus, I hope not. I hope I don't forget this shit."

"Speaking of Republicans," young Amy said, "this is worth capturing. I went home last weekend, and my Grandma Sunny said she'd seen on the news that Operation Rescue is coming to Baton Rouge. She was glad to know someone was defending all those innocent babies. I couldn't believe it. I mean, she grew up when women died from illegal abortions. I told her if these people cared so much, they could show some real charity. Then I realized my grandfather was listening at the doorway. I could hear him jingling change in his pocket. That habit was so annoying. But when I ignored him and told Grandma that it should have never become a government issue—it was too private—Poppa Fin said something about true conservatives rejecting government interference like that. I told him I wasn't conservative, but he said we agreed in principle. Of all people, I wouldn't have expected him to be pro-choice."

Chloe laughed. "You share more than the color of your eyes, then."

"Grandma Sunny insists that's from her side of the family—going way back."

For nearly an hour, the two shared memories of their activism. When the picture turned to static, she looked for the remote control to shut it off.

I thought of my suffragette mother, the curt public glances between her and those who opposed her point of view, the resolute look in her eyes. I remembered the faces of women who came to me, afraid, curious, asking questions that were illegal for me to answer. I thought of Mrs. Delacourt, the woman who treated me as an equal and later protected me as fiercely as a mother.

A blurry image appeared on the screen. "Chloe, get that damn thing away from me," said a young man with brown hair tied in a ponytail.

Amy's head snapped up toward the television. "Oh, my God."

Suddenly, the room's air was heavy with patchouli and musty books. The young man's face filled the television screen. He was as big as life.

"Amy." He looked straight ahead. "Doesn't she know she's capturing my soul on that contraption?"

"What, have you switched to some weird-ass pygmy religion?" Chloe was unseen, but her voice on the recording was clear.

His hand rose in front of his green eyes, and it blurred from focus as he pushed the lens toward a pair of Birkenstocks filled with furry man feet. "This week, I'm an Aztec. I'll make you my first sacrifice." The camera pulled back and up again. Amy stood in front, facing him. "I don't have any virgins to pick from anyway." He winked down at her and grinned mischievously.

Amy leapt from the sofa and pushed the eject button. She grabbed the DVD and darted toward the front room. Before she reached the doorway, she stopped in her tracks and glanced at the chair in which I was sitting. Amy shook her head, buried the disc in a bookcase drawer, and ran into the bathroom.

I STAND NAKED in front of the vanity's mirror. I have no shame about what I see. The truth is, I'm fearless. I curl my biceps, jut out my elbows, fill my nineteen-year-old lungs until I almost look buxom. I'm in the mood to cause a spectacle today.

As I dress, I think of my mother. Lingering Victorian prudishness didn't stunt her obligation to prepare me for womanhood. Claire Burrat Nolan taught me the correct names of body parts and explained what would happen as I became a woman. My poor father spent plenty of time ducked behind a newspaper with one finger in his left ear and the other pressed to the side of his wingback chair. He agreed with Mother that I shouldn't feel embarrassed about the way nature took its course. Old Barrett simply didn't want to hear about it.

I am the one who told the girls what was going to happen to them. I didn't care if the boys overheard. I knew about their problems, too. Sometimes mothers found out what I said to their children, so I endured several lectures from mine about keeping my mouth shut. Showing decorum, Mother called it. I couldn't help it, though. Between what she told me and what I read on my own, I became a little authority on subjects that make grown people blush.

I like to see how far I can go to expose old prune-pit standards for what they are. Most of the time, I don't make a huge scene. Instead of ordering my monthly supplies from Sears Roebuck, I go to different drugstores and ask for Kotex. I don't bother to use the pharmacist's silent partner, The Box. What I do is research. A girl has to know where she won't be ashamed.

This afternoon, when I meet Twolly outside the soda fountain several blocks from campus, she knows there is going to be special trouble. The fake wedding ring dangles on the hook of my finger. She protests—as usual—but it's halfhearted. She doesn't mind being a prop. The worst that could happen is that we're kicked out and never allowed inside again. And maybe get a reputation, which Twolly needs to develop anyway.

We order chocolate malts and roll our peepers at a drugstore cowboy who makes eyes at us. Twolly sips on her malt, waving her left hand to draw attention to the ring. He twirls away on his seat, sweeping his fashionable tie across a puddle of pineapple sauce.

"Set it up, Twolls," I whisper as I bring my lips around a straw.

"God, why do I do this with you?" She is as annoyed as she is excited.

"Because it's fun."

We pretend to be deeply involved in a conversation about her husband, an appliance and radio salesman. I make sure that the pharmacist passes at least once to hear the praises of the fictional Mr. Farthingworth.

"He's promised to add more diamonds to my ring by the end of the year. Sales are that good." Nervous as she is, Twolly is a convincing actress.

"My, my, aren't you the lucky one, Mrs. Farthingworth?"

"I'll say. My husband is such a dear. And so good to me."

The pharmacist, whose embroidered coat reads Finch, waddles by again. His rear is so pinched that he must be hiding something precious up there.

"Are you sure you can't get them yourself, dear?" I ask.

She shakes her head furiously from side to side. "I *cain't* imagine."

The pharmacist is near the register. He stretches toward a shelf as high as his dwarfish arms can reach.

Dress smooth, lipstick dabbed away, I announce my presence behind him with a demure *a-hem*. Tolerant expression from him, at best.

"Could you please bag a box of Kotex and some rubbers for me?" I feel brave. I have tried to purchase rubbers only twice before. Both times, the druggists were so mortified that I asked for such items by name that they bagged them and took my money without questioning whether Twolly or I even looked old enough to be married.

As his color goes from rose to coral to crimson, with rage I'm sure, all sound in the store hushes like the trailing flutter of birds. "Are you married, miss?"

"Sir, married or unmarried, all women bleed." I smile pleasantly. Although I have been speaking softly, several people are well within hearing distance. The bell on the door dingles to announce the departure of a few weak hearts.

Pinchy-Finchy clasps his stubby, gnawed hands on the counter. "I am referring to the prophylactics."

"Oh, I mean, I have no need for them." I dart splayed fingers to my heart in mock shock. "But my friend here"—I lean close enough to count the white hairs in his mustache and whisper—"she's too embarrassed to ask."

He glances at Twolly, whose hands are flat on the counter. She inspects them with great interest. The hot streak across her left cheek is bright as strawberry sauce.

"We have a box for that," he says.

"But The Box and the unmentionable item are both behind the counter. She'd have to ask for the right box, wouldn't she?"

"One may point."

"Oh, I see. A rather telling gesture. Is a wink required as well?"

After Twolly lets out a spatter giggle and a couple of loud guffaws chime in, Pinchy-Finchy realizes what I said. The corners of his mouth twitch up. His eyes widen. Then with force, his face gnarls like a peach pit. "Skin sheath or vulcanized?" That one little question earns old Finch a lifetime of respect from me, although he will never sell me anything but aspirin, soap, and Chiclets from that day forward.

"Vulcanized. Thank you, Mr. Finch."

❧

ONCE I LEARNED to maneuver through the world without a body, I felt that it was my duty to help others adjust to our translucent world. During my first months between, I'd had no initiation, little guidance, and even less instruction. Eugenia was the only one who had any interest in teaching me how to make the most of our unusual powers. Her skill was with smell, so anything else I had to learn on my own. I didn't want that to happen to anyone else.

I found them all over the city, and those I eventually trained brought new ones to me. Some of them were lost, unaware of what had happened. For most, proof came through glances at their obituaries or visits to places where they were missed. If they chose to go beyond, they were taken to deathbeds and told to lean forward into people's last breaths. That never failed to work. Like vapor, they were gone.

The ones who stayed for instruction expected me to be dramatic and profound. Their remaining human nature was still bound to roles, perception, expectations. They wanted me to deliver the facts in the voice of a tortured poet, but our state was nothing like the fantasies they'd been told. I refused to pretend that it was.

"May I have your attention, please?" I would tell the group. "The senses that once connected you to your physical lives have transformed. Has anyone noticed a change in his hearing?

Yes? Before, when you had ears, well, made of flesh, you could hear only within a certain range of frequencies. You were limited by that physical form. But now, the rules are different. You can discern individual sounds or conversations in noisy places with little effort. You will also notice sounds in what you once thought was pure silence, or from distances you didn't think possible. You will recognize subtleties in people's voices. In this state, it is far easier to understand the meaning or intent of what they say.

"On to sight. Darkness is no longer an obstacle for us. We don't 'see' the way we used to. We had eyes that depended on the chemical reactions between light and our cells to see. Now, there are no such limitations. You will not experience complete darkness in this state. It simply isn't possible because of your sensitivities. Bright light won't affect you either. Glare coming from surfaces or glances into the sun will not make you squint as it once did.

"Smell and taste are linked, as they were before. You can't actually 'taste' in this form, but you can make a scent linger by warming or cooling the air. Smell is much more intense now because, again, you don't have the limitations of your physical form. Scents will be much richer, sweeter, odoriferous, and pungent. The air is full of molecules, and combining them in certain configurations can reproduce particular smells. Ladies, that's how much of your perfume was made. Now, you know, sometimes not consciously, that people have their own scents. You will be more aware of this in your new form. You will also notice that people will give you clues about what they are thinking. You can smell it. Somehow, if a person remembers a nice summer day, you may smell the hint of a sweet breeze and lemonade. That is his memory of that afternoon."

"What about touch?" Someone would always ask before I could admit the worst.

"We'll get to that," I'd say. "I want you to pay close attention now. There are three rules. First, leave your loved ones alone. There is still something left to you that is familiar, and they can sense that. It confuses them. A rare brief visit may be acceptable, but never, never stay.

"Second, do not linger at your grave, marked or unmarked. You will be close to your remains, the matter that you recognized as you. The physical absence will be disconcerting, at the very least.

"Finally, do not touch. Any and all attempts will result in a desire for the tangible you cannot fulfill, and it will make you very vulnerable to your memories. Contact with the breathing—the *living*—can be disruptive, even dangerous. Some of you will be able to shape your energy into a shell of what you were, inside and out, but don't let that fool you. You simply no longer have the inherent structures needed to experience touch in a way that is either familiar or satisfying."

"But—" one of them would protest.

"See me later for more explanation. Questions?"

"Are we ghosts?"

"Call yourself whatever you want. There are plenty of other words to use." Then I would give them the speech about the common elements between our former bodies and the air. I explained the postulate that subatomic particles remain after our bodies fail and do not dissipate into the atmosphere. The energy shared among the particles allows us our heightened senses and the power to manipulate matter. To me, that reduction made sense.

"Are we made of ectoplasm?" another would ask. "That white goo. You've seen it in movies, right?"

"Foolishness." My tone did not invite further discussion.

"So how come I remember everything?" One would return us to serious issues.

"The physical structure that held your mind is gone, but what was your mind still endures," I'd reply.

Silence. Then, "That's intense," or "That's deep," or "That makes no sense."

"Other questions?"

"What happens if we break the rules?"

"You suffer the consequences."

"Like what?"

"You've never felt—or inflicted—such pain." My voice was so dark and cold that they shook into spark clusters. When I said that, I was no longer their prosaic instructor, their trusted guide through the difficult first days. I spoke a warning from experience. I knew. I remembered Donna, three years old, unclothed and alone, who wanted nothing but to be held again. I remembered Andrew—naked, stunned, bleeding, damaged.

For those who didn't immediately go beyond, there were more lessons. To start, matter manipulation.

"All it takes is concentration," I'd say. "When you first start, you'll make a mess, so be careful where you practice. Look—no hands."

I would make a flowerpot loop-the-loop over their pointillistic heads or scoot a china cabinet across the floor right through one of them.

"Oooh," they said, like mesmerized children.

A FRIGID NOVEMBER MORNING, 1926. Mrs. Delacourt and I collide in the doorway of a shoe store on Canal Street. My package falls to the ground. We have not seen each other since my high school graduation, almost a year and a half ago. Custom dictates a polite exchange of handshakes, but Mrs. Delacourt embraces me with affection. I agree to join her for luncheon at her home that very day.

I take the streetcar because it's warmer than walking. When I settle on the wooden seat, I realize that a blanket of static covers my skin, and my stomach is filled with sparks. How strange, after all this time. I am as thrilled to visit her today as I was when I was a curious little girl.

I remember being among those brave and well-spoken ladies, Mrs. Delacourt the ringleader of her group of suffragettes.

Silently skimming books in a corner, I listened to the strategies used to convince certain gentlemen of power that a woman's vote could benefit all involved, from society to the gentleman's reelection bid. They often met with little success—so many men being self-interested, narrow-minded louts, unlike your fine father, Mother would tell me. These women found encouragement in subtle victories, such as daughters-in-law realizing the rightness of this position, stacks of pennies and nickels and dimes going toward the effort.

Mrs. Delacourt, beautiful and brilliant, was the most dangerous of them all. Jet hair exposed the Spaniards in her blood, while Norman ancestors revealed themselves in almond-shaped blue eyes. Although tall for a woman, she refused to slouch; her bosom rose high and wide beneath crossbow shoulders. Hips arched from a broad waist, proof that she had comfortably borne her children. Deceptively delicate hands cabled with muscles when she moved them about, whether she clenched a fist or held a teacup. Her voice was oboe sweet, brass-section strong.

Those evenings her husband was home when she hosted meetings, Mrs. Delacourt would call, "Snitchy"—his given name was Richard—"come say hello to the ladies." Mr. Delacourt was a fruit importer, for the most part, whose travels to South America and Florida kept him bronze as an overripe pear. Obligingly, he wished the roomful a good evening, blinked his sunspot eyes, and departed with a flick of a wave.

After women won the vote, Mrs. Delacourt committed herself to a cause as controversial as her former passion. Mrs. Sanger's materials were strewn about the house, mixed with issues of *The Saturday Evening Post* and *The Times-Picayune.* Whenever I could, I stole peeks at the articles, piecing together complications of the human body, the struggles between and the mysteries behind them. Each time before Mother and I left, Mrs. Delacourt always offered a stack of booklets, urging Mother to pass them along to other women.

"Gertrude," Mother said, "all the ladies I know understand such things."

"Or so they would have you think, Claire, dear."

Because Mother wouldn't take them, I secreted a pamphlet within the book I was reading and took it home. The anatomical names I knew from medical books and my mother's instruction. I understood how babies came to be, so clinically had my mother explained the phenomenon. What the pamphlet described were simple methods to avoid creating them at all, something Mother must have thought was not yet important for me to know. Mother also had not mentioned pleasure, not precisely. *The act that can create a child is special and private, to be shared within the bonds of love,* she had said. In Mrs. Sanger's pamphlet, I read that a woman should expect and feel satisfaction, physical and emotional. I wasn't entirely sure what sensations were involved and where a woman felt them, but I knew, instinctively, that Mrs. Sanger was absolutely right.

Now, as I wait for Mrs. Delacourt to answer my knock, I think of the well-worn pamphlet and how many typed carbon copies I have hidden in Newcomb's library.

The door opens, and she hugs me. "Razi, dear, come in."

We exchange small talk for a while over beef and vegetable soup.

"Still planning to attend medical school, yes?" She dips a toast triangle into the broth.

"I plan to practice in gynecology."

"Only women understand women's needs and pains."

"Speaking of which. Do you still receive those pamphlets from New York?"

"You remember them?"

"I have a confession. I took one when I was twelve."

Mrs. Delacourt didn't flinch. "Good. Did your mother know?"

"She never mentioned it." I pause. "Are you ever afraid of being caught with them?"

Mrs. Delacourt spoons the last bite into her wide mouth. The back of her hand swirls with veins. Silver hair mingles brightly within the black still remaining. She never seemed older than my mother, although there is a seventeen-year difference between them. I realize Mrs. Delacourt is old enough to be my grandmother.

"Afraid?" she replies, dabbing a napkin at her lips. "No. I'm appalled that this information is as illegal as alcohol. But I'm also aware that I am a woman of privilege. My husband could easily keep my name out of the papers."

"What do you think would happen to me?"

"You'd have your picture on the front page. I think the world of your father, but he hasn't the power to protect you."

"Do you think I'd go to jail?"

"It depends on whether the city is in the mood for a good scandal."

"It's always ready for that."

"True." She fixes her strange eyes on mine. "Why are you asking me such questions?"

"I've been copying pages of the old pamphlet and leaving them in certain books at Newcomb's library. Whenever I overhear a girl talk about these matters, I mention that I've seen the answers she needs."

"Well, well." She disappears into the butler's pantry and comes out with a crate marked *Apples*. "Save time for your studies and distribute these instead." She places several pieces of fruit on the table, reaches into the space, and pulls out a stack of pamphlets. When I thumb through one, the paper is crisp. Mrs. Delacourt sits down again, polishing an apple on the napkin near her bowl.

"Thank you," I say. "We're officially in cahoots. You're my booklegger now."

She laughs. "When you're a doctor, use that power wisely, Razi. Don't let it corrupt your principles. Don't forget why you chose that vocation." She pauses. "I do hope you will give part of your time to help ladies unlike yourself. The ones who haven't much money, many of whom couldn't read what's in that box."

"Of course."

"Claire is so very proud of you, dear." Mrs. Delacourt clamps her large incisors into the apple and slowly grinds the pulp. "This is a new era altogether. What I wouldn't give to be your age now. To be able to decide one's future based on one's own will, not on the whims or demands of her father or husband."

"People still look hard at girls with minds of their own. A girl has to be tough as an eight-minute egg to take it, Mrs. Delacourt."

"You're making me feel old. Call me Gertrude, please, dear."

"Well, then, Gertrude," I hear myself begin, "there is something I've been thinking about. You're the only person I know who could help me. I've had an idea for something I call Boyless Parties."

❧

MY FRIEND and favorite pupil, Lionel, died four days before 1999 ended. He recalled falling back on his bed when a dull burst spread under his skull. He thought the light that appeared was a particularly bad migraine announcing itself. He dismissed his father's voice as part of a dream. I found him two weeks after the aneurysm killed him.

Word spread quickly in the Garden District about the strange occurrences in a particular apartment. Rarely did one of us lose control and do the damage I'd heard described. I assumed that I would be dealing with someone who didn't know he was between. When I went to investigate, the apartment was a wreck. Even the doorknobs were out of place. Everything that could ignite had tiny burn marks.

"Hey, there. What's your name?" I asked. His blurry figure was in front of a window with a torn blind.

"Well, twenty-three skidoo. I'm Lionel Mulberry. Who are you?"

"Razi Nolan." I moved closer to him. "Are you all right?"

"I'm fine, thank you. How are you?"

"Fine, thanks. Do you know where you are?"

"I'm in my apartment."

"Who made this mess?"

"A ghost."

I smiled. Perhaps he knew he was dead after all, but dangerous if the destruction was done on purpose. "How do you know?"

"Well, I didn't see the S.O.B. who did it, so it must have been a ghost."

"Am I a ghost?"

"You could be. I dream the craziest things after a migraine."

"How did your dream start?" This was one of my warm-up questions.

"I heard my father's voice say, 'Lionel, come with me, son.' And I told him to leave me alone. He insisted that I go with him. He used this nice tone of voice he hadn't used since I was twelve." His features hadn't settled yet, but it was obvious from what was there that his eyes were squinting with suspicion. I could see the contours of him with the help of the sunlight. He had been a tall man with sloping shoulders. Long hands and feet.

"How did you feel?"

"Peaceful. The way I do when the pain is gone. Then I felt as if I were falling up. Better than falling down. You know, if you hit the ground in a dream, you die." He smiled again.

"Why do you think you dreamed your father's voice? How do you know he wasn't calling you somewhere? Maybe you're dead."

"My father barely spoke ten words to me in my entire adult life. You'd think God would be smarter than to send him to get me."

"What happened exactly four months before your fourth birthday at four in the afternoon?"

"I had a snack at the kitchen table. Twinkies and milk. Mom read *Atlas Shrugged* again over the stove. She was making pork chops."

"Date and year?"

"May 3, 1958."

"The weather?"

"Sunny. But a rainstorm was coming. Why are you asking me these questions?"

"Don't you find it strange that you can remember that much detail?"

"The human mind's a funny library." His gauzy form agitated, started to swirl like drops of cream stirred slowly into black coffee.

The room was getting hot. I quizzed him on more dates until the air snapped.

"I want to wake up. I want to wake up now."

"You're awake, Lionel. You're between."

"Between what?"

"Life and whatever comes next. You're dead."

"No, I'm not."

"You are."

"Prove it."

"Did someone take your body earlier in this dream?"

"Yes."

"Can you tell me everything that has happened since then?"

"Yes, but you can do all kinds of things in a dream."

Lionel wasn't in denial. He simply didn't know he was dead, and because he didn't know, he had tried to go about the business of living as usual. That's why his apartment was in a shambles. He had become more powerful and dangerous without meaning to be as his new form started to reconfigure. It was time for the moment of reality. This question never failed.

"When was the last time you had a bowel movement?" I asked.

"Fifteen days ago." He looked at me. His eyes had been hazel. His mouth was a connect-the-dots oval. "Oh, shit."

PART TWO

AMY DIDN'T WATCH the rest of the DVD Chloe had sent her, but I did. There were only a few minutes left. The footage was taken at a party. People waved at the camera and talked to Chloe, the voice behind the lens. The microphone hummed with music and chatter. The shot moved through a dining room next to a narrow kitchen doorway. On the wall behind Amy was a calendar, August 1992. She hugged the dark-haired young man, and he clearly didn't want them to be interrupted. They shared a strangely intimate moment for such a celebratory atmosphere. He was talking, but his voice did not come through. I strained through the noise and read his lips—*It'll be okay,* he said. *We'll have the whole drive up. Sex in at least one strange bed.* He nudged her, and she smiled. *Thanksgiving will be here before you know it. This is only temporary.*

For several days after she hid the disc, the essence of another man billowed intermittently throughout the house. More often, she snapped her head toward doorways and furniture corners for no discernible reason. Amy was not reacting to me, I knew. There was another reason for her jitters.

Within that time, Amy stopped watching Scott as he slept before she left for work. Then one morning, and another, and each one after, she didn't kiss him good-bye. The only habit she kept was to keep him warm.

Scott didn't notice the change immediately. Amy's kiss had

been a gentle alarm that nudged him closer to consciousness. He never needed the ticking Big Ben that he set in case he didn't wake up on his own. But once the kisses stopped, Scott woke up to the old-fashioned *brriinnng* of the clock.

Each morning, he raised himself out of bed, scratched appropriately, stretched, and went into the kitchen. He had a small glass of juice and a few peanuts before he put on some clothes he had casually ironed. He ran at least four times a week, every Saturday morning with a group. When the Big Ben started to wake him up, he began to take vitamins, run a little longer, and read less at night. Within a couple of weeks, he was grumpy and frustrated.

"Something's wrong with me." Scott clicked off the lamp near the bed.

I could hear him from my favorite spot in the house, the rocking chair.

"Hmm?" Amy said.

"The alarm clock's been waking me up in the morning. It's like my body forgot how to wake up on its own."

"Take some vitamins."

"I am taking vitamins."

"You've been working late shifts again. Maybe that's it."

"It's like I'm sleeping too hard to hear your alarm. You know, like it wakes me up before I wake up?"

"Could be."

Sheets rustled, and flesh whispered against flesh.

"I'm tired, Scott."

"A quickie."

"Too much trouble."

"Then we don't have to do that." Elastic snapped, and the sound pitch dropped.

"Honey, please. Maybe tomorrow. I'm really tired."

For a couple of minutes, all was quiet.

"What are you doing?" Amy asked.

"What?"

"That breathing. Opposite mine."

"I'm just trying to relax here. You like it when I pull you into me."

"That's fine. But the other thing— Breathe on your own. Good night."

The bedsheets rustled, and a pillow poofed. "Love you." Scott's voice had projected into the front of the house. He was facing their bedroom door, not her, when he said it.

"Love you, too."

A metallic smell—hot steel, blood—startled me. The odor wafted into the room where I watched moth shadows flit across the floor. There was violence connected to whatever memory had released it. For a moment, I was distracted from Andrew's scent, then reminded again. I thought of his bloodstains on the inside of the bookcase's left drawer and wondered how the wound had healed. Clean cut, jagged scar. He could never be aired completely from the possession he loved so much, the oil of his hands rubbed deep into the patina, dead skin cells caught in dark, draftless crevices.

ANDREW'S BLOOD drips on the floor, from the straight cut in his right palm down to his elbow. He narrows his eyes when he turns on the desk lamp. With no sign of pain, he pulls the glass from his hand. Blood surges toward his wrist. He takes his fine-woven white shirt and twists it around the wound. I stare at his eyes. That missing crescent of blue through his iris, an illusion, a trick of light, isn't it? I reach to hold the place where he's hurt, then pull back. I cannot help, not now. Not after what I've done.

PART OF ME wants to find Noble. I've been between six weeks, and he's told me some of the pertinent facts. He has explained how to handle circumstances like this, but we never discussed how to release a child. There is no reason to take her home, even if this naked three-year-old near my hand could tell me where she lived. The grieving parents could not welcome their daughter home, and little Donna could not understand why they'd ignore her. Instead, I lead her to the only place I can think to go.

I keep her attention by reciting nursery rhymes she doesn't know. I am grateful that the repetition is so automatic because this calms me. It is familiar and requires no thought.

"Carry me," the child says. "No more walking. It's raining."

"Donna, you're a big girl. We don't have much farther."

For a moment, we slip into a tiny garden. Thunder rumbles several miles away. Donna no longer seems to mind the rain and begins to sniff the flowers. I ask her questions about how she was feeling the last time she saw her momma. Donna tells me that her throat hurt and she couldn't breathe.

"Come here. Open your mouth." She obliges. When I look into the space, the back of her throat is a thick black membrane. Diphtheria.

Is what I am about to do, in the next few moments, few hours, perhaps few days, the right thing? I pause and pat the air near my hip. She sits with her flower. She shifts it from one hand to the other as if the stem irritates her fingertips. "Now, this is hard to explain, so I want you to listen. That flower in your hand, we are very much like flowers. We need air and food and water. Your flower can't get these things anymore because, see here, the stem is broken. That's how it got what it needed to grow and stay pretty. And you, when you stopped breathing, your little heart stopped beating. That happened to me, too. Now we need our breath and our hearts to be alive. That's when we can eat and cry and go to the potty and—hug our daddies tight. But when those things stop, that means we're dead. Do you know what 'dead' is?"

She looks at me as if I'm stupid. "It means you go to heaven."

"Is that where you are now?"

"No. That's where Daddy is. Momma said Daddy would meet me in heaven."

"Did she tell you who else you would see?"

"Angels."

I deliberately lead us through a back entrance of St. Elizabeth's. I don't want Donna to even glimpse the two beautiful, lifeless white angels that flank the front porch. They would only confuse her. Quickly, I move Donna through the orphanage to find the infirmary. I realize we are close when a desperate antiseptic smell fills a hallway.

I search the room. In a corner, past a row of beds, I see two dolls. Donna cannot be expected to heed the last rule of being between, so I point out the toys. "Play-pretties!" She cradles a ragged doll in her arms and begins to sing a strangely melodic little tune of her own. "I can't find my dollies, dollies, dollies, with hair of gold and hair of black. I can't find Momma, Momma, Momma, with hands not soft but kiss that is."

Down the long corridor between the beds, a Daughter of Charity bends toward a table. Her starched white linen cornette hovers like great butterfly wings; the deep blue habit that drapes from her shoulders to her feet is nothing but a shadow in the dark.

I don't know whether the sick girls have any of the diseases that devastate neighborhoods and orphanages so often. I think of Donna's black throat and know it's likely that diphtheria has made its mysterious way throughout the city. What mimics nausea fills my form as I allow myself to do what Noble told me—find the one nearest to death and wait.

First I begin to listen and recognize the internal hum of ten distinct human beings. The counterpoint sounds inharmonious at the start—an overwhelming drone—but within moments, I discern the beauty of all the hearts and lungs and fluids moving together. The discovery holds my attention until I realize that one of the rhythms has rests that last far too long.

A little girl lies in the farthest corner, near a window as tall and wide as a cathedral door, quarantined as best as the nuns could manage. As I approach, she is absolutely silent. A hot breeze sweeps the length of the room and lifts the scent of urine from her bed. She gasps lightly. I turn to look for the nun, but she has vanished. I want her here for this child, to soothe her, but I know it will only complicate matters. I take back the covers and see that the little girl wears a light muslin gown. Her hands and feet are splayed and the color of twilight. I assume this cannot go on much longer because I feel the way I once did when I knew a child was building up to a scream.

"Donna, come see," I say, swallowing my dread. Donna skips toward me with the doll swinging by its arm. I settle on the narrow space near the little girl's hip and invite Donna to sit close to her chest, facing her. "We're going to play the Whisper Game. We'll have to be very patient, very still, and very quiet. Can you do that?"

"Yes." Donna stares up at me and moves closer to my side. The doll separates us. "Is she sick?"

"Yes. She might be better soon." A wafer of air slips into the little girl's pale mouth. "Now, she has a secret she wants to tell, but she speaks so softly that no one has been able to learn what it is. You could be the first to know."

When Donna smiles, a surge of grief delays my response. I will myself not to pull away as her shoulder touches my arm. She doesn't react, but that doesn't mean she can't sense the agitation of energy.

"Now, baby, put your ear close to her mouth. Stay very still." Donna bends at the waist, away from me. "Listen. Just listen." Donna puts her left hand under the girl's armpit. "You are doing so well."

"Shh, I'm listening," she says.

Moments pass, and not one of us moves. Donna places her right hand on the girl's chest—I say nothing but *Lean in, lean in now*—the little girl exhales a filament—and Donna disappears in a wisp of ozone. A fleeting thin silver horizon between the body and the air curls up and vanishes.

When the aphonic wail escapes me, desire awakens with no flesh to take hold. I need a body to defy what I've seen.

I WILL SAVOR my tenth birthday cake only once. As I eat my third piece of the day, I don't use my teeth. The lemon morsel presses into my palate. I swing my jaw from side to side and enjoy the creamy tartness against my tongue.

My daddy sits at his place at the table. He chews slowly, lingering on each bite. The small cut near his bottom lip threatens to open again. "Do you want more milk, my little bovine?" he asks. The bottle is almost empty.

"Yes, please."

He leans near me to pour the last drops into my glass. A Bay Rum fog settles between us. The smell is nice, but I'm not used to his face without whiskers. "Where on earth did you get the idea to give yourself presents with nothing in them?"

"It is April Fool's day, you know."

Daddy laughs. "Clever trick, Razi. Your mother and I were horrified. I was ready to drag someone out by the collar."

"Oh, Daddy, can't you take a joke?"

"Did you like your real presents?"

"I love my new dresses. But I don't think Grams likes that I got an Erector set."

"Didn't you want one?"

"Yes."

"Don't worry about Grams. She just doesn't want you to become too much smarter than she is."

"I can't help it if I do."

"Mother said you got A-pluses on your tests last week. I'm very proud."

"Thank you." I watch him scrape light yellow icing from his plate and lick the fork. "Why'd you shave off your mustache?"

"Don't you read the papers? A furry face is no longer fashionable."

"So? It made you look like a daddy. Now you look like a boy."

"I am a boy."

"Daddy . . ."

"Your mother likes it." He juts his chin and winks. "Don't you, Claire?"

When I turn, Mother is standing near the buffet. "Except for the shaving cream puddles, I don't mind. Now he looks as young as he behaves. Time for bed, birthday girl." Mother takes our dishes to the kitchen.

I hug Daddy. He pulls me bear-tight to his lap. The starch has worn from his shirt. His breath whispers in his chest. "Good night, my double-digit darling." He wraps around me like armor. "By next year, you'll be too big for this."

"I won't grow that much."

"Oh, yes, you will."

He releases his arms. I put my hands on his sandpaper cheeks, spotted with tiny red nicks, and look into his eyes. In this light, I see my silhouette in his pupils. The grandfather clock chimes ten o'clock. I kiss him on the forehead and notice that his mahogany pate glints with silver shards, mirror bright.

WEEKS AFTER I sent the first letters to search for Andrew, the first reply came from Boston, in June. I had mailed a query to every O'Connell in Massachusetts, hoping that one recipient was a cousin with a lead, even after all these years. When I opened the envelope, I flattened a thick, shiny piece of paper first. I recognized the dark eyes looking at me from the page. The young man was Patrick, Andrew's father. Before his comfortable years made him slightly round at the edges, Patrick had a muscular angularity that showed as he stood tall next to an even taller bicycle. His kinetic young body waited to be released from the attention of the lens. In the pose, I saw the promise of Patrick O'Connell's only son.

Mr. Burrat,

I am distantly related to Andrew O'Connell, I think. What I have probably won't help much because I don't have anything but basic genealogy to tell you. My great-great-grandfather was Daniel O'Connell, Patrick's brother. Their parents and the first two children, Timothy and Mary, were born in Ireland and moved to Boston. Patrick and Daniel were born in the United States. Daniel was the only one who stayed in Massachusetts.

Patrick moved to New Orleans in the early 1890s, a few years after he graduated from college, and he was a banker. My grandfather told me once that the family was horrified that he eventually married a Southern woman, but at least she was Catholic. No one has a record of the dates of Patrick's children's births. You said that there was one son, Andrew, but my grandfather thinks there was another child. He might be confusing Patrick with Timothy, so don't let that tangent take up your time.

For whatever reason, a lot of my O'Connell clan moved to Pennsylvania around the turn of the 20th century when steel was the business to be in. Maybe that will help?

I thought you might like copies of photos that ended up in my personal collection. They are both of Patrick. He's about twelve in one and a young man at Yale in the other. Aren't that big-wheeled bike and his mustache classic? If you want to include them in the book about Andrew, I can get you better copies.

I'm sorry I don't have more to give you. I hope someone else can help you find what you're looking for.

Sincerely,
Jenna O'Connell

I WANTED TO DISCOVER more about the young man with the ponytail Amy refused to see.

In the attic, I found large boxes taped up that were marked "High School Stuff," "College Stuff," and "Other Stuff." The words were written in Amy's block lettering. I had learned long before never to trust a label to tell me what was inside.

I ran a line of hot, moist air against the tape across the top of each box to deteriorate the glue. In the "College Stuff" box were old notepads and textbooks, along with newspaper clippings about reproductive rights. The "Other Stuff" box held a tattered knapsack, grassroots organizing binders, more old newspaper clippings, and several buttons: *Against Abortion, Don't Have One; Earth Is Your Mother; No Nukes.*

I spent a long time with her teenage souvenirs. She had every yearbook since the sixth grade. The signatures inside her yearbooks filled several pages. She had had a boyfriend—or two—every year since her freshman year of high school. She served as a student government representative in her freshman and sophomore years. Her senior class selected her as Most Artistic. During those years, her hair and her clothes changed, but never her smile.

Until 1992. In every photograph after that year, Amy's smile pulled at the edge of her mouth, turning it down so slightly that no one would notice. If someone did, she could excuse it as wistfulness or preoccupation. There was a melancholy dimness in her eyes. She had been happy in the moments when the snapshots were taken. The way she looked at Scott as she dabbed a piece of white wedding cake against the tip of his nose. The gaze she held on her father on his fiftieth birthday. The look she gave to the camera as she and her elderly Grandma Sunny waved from the hump of a camel at a zoo.

I thought the box was empty until I whipped a piece of cardboard free from the bottom. A large Whitman's Sampler box fit perfectly in the space.

His name was Jeremy Wheeler. Included among Amy's mementos was the identification card he received when he started college. His hair was short, and he looked older than eighteen at the time. There were love letters, three Valentine's Day cards, increasingly intimate and serious in tone. Ticket stubs. A receipt from a restaurant. Two anniversary cards. The second one promised his love eternally. Photos dated from 1988 to 1992. His hair grew longer in each. Three picturesque postcards from Tennessee, during the span of seven days in June 1992.

It's beautiful here. Remember our trek to Tunica Hills? That, only better. No one has guessed I'm a Yankee yet. Can't understand half of what's said even though everyone speaks so slowly. Miss you.

Love, Jem

FOUND A PLACE NEAR CAMPUS. Top story of an old house, view of trees. Imagine when the leaves change. You're still coming with me, right? God, I miss you.

Love you, Jem

I'll be home by the time you get this. So horny I could die. (Is it legal to write that on a postcard?) I have a surprise.

I love you, Jem

Under a stack of maps of Louisiana, Alabama, and Tennessee, there was a photo of them in front of a sign marking the border to Tennessee. From the angle of the shot, the camera must have been balanced on the hood of the car. Their arms are wrapped tight around each other. Then, the obituary and a ring. Jem died on August 19, 1992. He was survived by a mother, a father, two brothers, a niece, and four grandparents.

Amy was not mentioned.

I suspended the ring in the darkness. A narrow slice of light cracked through a space in the clapboards. It was an engagement ring, without a doubt, a tiny diamond in its center. Simple, heartfelt.

At the bottom of the box, she had hidden a short letter dated August 11.

Amy,

I can live with a secret engagement. I can live with knowing you're six hundred miles away. Promise me forever, because you know I cannot live without you.

Love,

Jem

As I stacked everything as I found it, a harsh urgent pulse of tears rushed forward with no release, sensation without substance. I remembered the last letter I wrote to Andrew, propped on my vanity, his name written on the sealed envelope. Nearby was the package I meant to send to Twolly. And tucked against the parcel, still in its box, the ring I left behind.

I ached with empathy for Amy. She tried to keep Jem within the umbra of her memory, guarded, deep under the surface of her life. From the DVD, he had emerged briefly to remind her that she had buried him, but he was not gone. Her reaction signaled that his memory had the power to destroy. I had watched her begin the incremental drift from Scott and, like him, had assumed the deaths of her grandparents had made her introspective and withdrawn.

Although I knew it was not my role or my right to interfere, I could not help it. They still had a chance, one I had missed.

Wednesday, July 10, 1929

Andrew, my darling,

My love for you is a force of nature.

I know, such words from a woman who holds faith in nothing but what her senses reveal. But I have proof, you see. I cannot doubt the rush under my skin when you turn those unfathomable blue eyes my way, the velocity of my blood when I am naked against your body, and the ebb and flow of my breath when you whisper my name.

You asked me a question, and I have your answer now. Just

for a moment, close those eyes I adore, Andrew, then hold out your hand for me.

Always, always,
your Razi

DINNER IS OVER with Andrew's small group of friends and their dates. I stay behind in the dining room with Anna Whitcomb and the other girls while the boys smoke in the parlor. I have little to say. They are all Newcomb girls, attend the same classes, run in the same circles. I hear Andrew laugh, a surprising burst of high spirits from him, and my body jumps to meet the vibration. When Anna begins to discuss her nuptial plans—more than a year and a half away, a June wedding, scheduled for the first Thursday after graduation—I excuse myself with a coffee cup in hand. The young women are polite with their good-byes, but they don't begin to speak again until I'm well out of earshot. Twolly will certainly hear about my departure when she sees Anna in class on Monday. I can't help it. The boys are two doors away, and the sound of their voices draws me into the smoky room.

Warren Tripp stands next to the fireplace, deftly flicking cigarette ashes backhanded into an ashtray on the mantel. The gesture is so cavalier and practiced that I almost laugh. Next to him, Alan sits on the arm of an ancient, reupholstered settee with a coffee cup between his enormous hands and his legs jutting into the middle of their circle. Tom has one foot propped on his mother's little stool. Andrew moves closer to Warren to let me step in.

"Ask Razi what she thinks," Andrew says.

"What do you think of the current race suicide?" Warren asks.

I glance at Andrew. He knows I spent years eavesdropping while my mother and her suffragette friends discussed popular politics. "Whose race is killing itself?"

"Certainly, you are aware of the incredible number of immigrants in this country"—Warren exhales a puff of smoke—"as well as the deep concern over miscegenation. States across the South have banned such mixing. And for several years, the birth rate has dropped severely among the educated."

"So this race suicide, it's among the whites."

"Exactly." Warren draws smoke from the last of the cigarette. "A matter of genetics. The intelligent and strong are having fewer children while the dim and weak are having more. What kind of world will we have if we're overrun by such masses?"

"I thought you were a Darwinist, Warren," Alan says.

"Shouldn't we assume that these 'masses' will die out on their own, if natural selection prevails?" Andrew says.

Warren smashes his dincher in the ashtray. His brown eyes scorch. "I suppose their death rate from disease is rather high, but the sheer number of them weighs in their favor. Something must be done to curb this threat to our country's stability."

I glance down at my cup to roll my eyes.

"This country is more prosperous that it's ever been," Andrew says. "What makes you think we're threatened?"

"Our city alone is overrun by Italians, not to mention the Negroes," Warren says.

"Perhaps we should be reminded that they do a good deal of the work to make our lives easier," I say. "Typically, they dig and build what we don't. They clean and scrub what we won't." An electrical storm of glances shoots among the men in front of me.

"Doesn't your family have help?" Warren asks.

"We do, on occasion. Paula does our laundry, and Mae helps with special dinners and spring cleaning. My mother doesn't believe in asking others to do what she isn't willing to do herself. She believes all work has an inherent dignity."

As if on cue, Tom's family housekeeper walks into the room with a tray of cookies and more coffee. She serves us politely. I know that she has been listening to our conversation because she looks me in the eye before she leaves. Her hands have the color and strength of carved walnut.

"Thank you, Millie." Tom is sunburn pink.

"Now then, back to the issue. From an economic standpoint, it would be unwise to curtail the birth rate of these so-called undesirables," Andrew says. A familiar glint appears in his eye. He wants to argue a position simply to see if he can, no matter how much he disagrees with it.

"Depending on who you are, that's a self-serving and insidious idea," I reply. "I prefer to imagine how different things would be if all people were healthy and well nourished."

"What's your point?" Warren asks.

"There's no race suicide. You're talking about eugenics and the assumption that there is a purer race that should breed. That's bunk. It's not an issue of race. It's about one's place in the world. You can be a Darwinist as well as a eugenicist, Warren. They all believe in natural selection. But our country is much bigger than the Galapagos Islands, and we'll be long gone before we find out if such theories are true for humans."

"So what do you propose, Darrow?" Alan asks. The boys laugh.

"Birth control," I say. "The problem is not that there are too many babies. The problem is that the women—who bear the burden—don't have the knowledge to stop."

Andrew smothers a sly grin. The other young men stare at me, frozen.

"That's against nature," Warren finally replies.

"Nature isn't fixed. It changes," Andrew says.

"No, it doesn't." Warren lights another cigarette. "Things are as they have always been, from the movement of the stars to the way babies come into this world."

"Tell that to the dodo bird." Andrew raises his palms together and wraps his last three fingers down, the index fingers straight toward Warren. "Consider that evolution changed humans into creatures that no longer have multiple births. A woman bears one child at a time, usually. This allows her—and her mate—to concentrate energy on that child, ensuring that it will have a better chance of survival.

"I also think that our evolution's progress makes us curious about the function of nature. Many people might argue, Razi," he says, pointing at me, "that birth control is unacceptable, but I say that the effort to limit one's family size is a conscious, deliberate act by a being who follows his—or her—own inquisitive nature. Therefore, it seems obvious to me that those who oppose birth control are opposing the course of nature itself—man's own wish to understand and control his world."

"What next?" Alan asks. "We'll control the weather?"

"No, but just like certain impulses, we'll know when it's coming," I say, and turn to Andrew. He reaches for a cigarette but watches me with his peripheral vision.

The rest of the night isn't quite as serious once the girls join us. Anna tells Warren to stop goading Andrew into provocative conversations and ruining a perfectly enjoyable party. Warren kisses her cheek when she calls him incorrigible. After some begging, Tom shows off the new tunes he has learned on the ukulele. Andrew doesn't sing along with the rest of us. He sits on the settee and taps his foot. Once, I catch him looking at me. He hides a grin in the empty cup he keeps raising to his mouth. I wink to let him know I know he's been watching.

As Andrew drives me home, we talk about the after-dinner conversation. He claims he has never known a girl so direct. The comment is straightforward, an observation. However, I know from the way he looks at me that he remains intrigued. I tell him that I've never met anyone who defended birth control as an evolutionary outcome. He admits that he'd read articles on the topic. The position is logically defensible, he says, and it raises the ire of those who argue from irrational, subjective religious beliefs.

"I had a wonderful time," I say as the roadster stops in front of my house. "I'm still impressed that your friends were so cordial, even through our touchy debate."

"Good breeding."

I laugh. "Well, good night. Thank you."

"You're welcome. Thank you for joining me." He doesn't

move to get out of the roadster to come around and open my door. His eyes dance from my eyes to my mouth and back again, my cue to move closer.

We kiss a bit longer than we have before. He has started to relax a little, but he is still chaste compared to what I'm accustomed to. I've moved faster with boys I've known for five hours, much less five weeks. Andrew's hands haven't even wandered yet. When the kiss ends, I wrap my arms around his shoulders and don't let go. He hugs me back but seems uncomfortable, as if he's not used to being held so close so long.

He walks me to the porch steps and doesn't leave until I wave to him once I get inside.

I CLOSE THE DOOR behind me, lean against its cool, thick leaded-glass panels, and listen to the O'Connell's automobile drive away. My grandmother sits on the davenport under the amber glow of her favorite lamp.

"When do we get to meet this young man, Raziela?" Grams does not look up from her magazine.

"Soon. If he's a keeper."

My father walks into the room. He is a beautiful man whose full head of silver-streaked dark brown hair and dark eyes bring attention to his angular features. There are days I expect to see him with his long-gone beard and mustache, the way I remember him from my childhood. He locks his gentle, long-lashed calf eyes on me as he bends into his wingback. "Had a good evening?"

"Yes, Daddy." I remove my coat.

"So—" He flips his newspaper in front of his face. "Why are you still hiding him, this Andrew?" He is dying of curiosity, I know. He lives to use that gruff paternal voice on the boys who pass through my life. He feels like he's doing an important job.

"I'm not hiding him."

"You could've invited him in, you know." Daddy doesn't look up from the newsprint. "It's not that late."

"Next time. I promise."

"Did you hear that, Lily?" he says to my grandmother. "There's a next time."

Grams pushes her cheaters along the bridge of her nose and stares at me. Hard. I stand there with my coat in my hands, biting my bottom lip.

"Oh, heavens. She's in love."

"No, I'm not."

My father puts down his paper and looks at me, too. Suddenly, I notice my mother standing at the base of the stairs. She is dressed for bed. Her long blond hair is pulled back with a stretch of crimson ribbon that drapes across her shoulder. She is barefoot, as she is every night, no matter the season. My family peers at me with sentimental grins softening their faces.

"You're giving me the jim-jams. Stop it. We've only had a few dates." I put my coat on the nearby rack.

"You know already." Grams turns back to her magazine.

"What, are you clairvoyant now, Grams?" I walk into the room, heading for the kitchen.

Daddy reaches out and grabs my hand as I pass. He holds tight so that I can't brush away from him. I look down at my father who—I swear—has a tear in his eye. He brings my hand to his lips and kisses me on the knuckles. A rush of affection floods me, and I resist the temptation to fall into his love as I am now, to hug him the way only little girls can hug their daddies. Instead, I squeeze his hand and kiss him on the cheek, knowing that he has let me go, a little further, from his protective reach.

WILL ANDREW SURVIVE his first dinner with my family?

When he arrives, I leave him alone while I pour drinks for everyone. It is for the best, really, because one true test of whether a boy is worth keeping is if he can endure my father's *hrumph-hrumph-hrumphing* and Grams's prying into his relations. Mother has much better manners; the motives behind her questions are far less transparent. On purpose, I drop several forks and an old juice glass to stall for time. *So, Andrew, what area of law interests you most? Your father's people: where in Ireland did they come from? Razi took piano when she was little; were you musically trained?*

Mother peeks her head from the butler's pantry into the kitchen. I toss the glass shards into the garbage can. *Bright, well-spoken,* she says as she removes Cornish hens from the oven. *Your father is barely torturing him. I think he's smitten.* I smother my laughter as I take the tray into the parlor. They are clustered around a framed photo of me on the wall near the stairs, next to Grandfather and Uncle Roger. Andrew turns first. His shoulders drop comfortably—most boys are in knots by now—and he smiles more with his eyes than the curl of his mouth. Grams takes his arm as they make their way to sit again. Oh, he has charmed her somehow. Daddy's voice is almost normal, the alpha growl nearly a congenial *arf.* We drink tea and discuss the huge parade the city held for Charles Lindbergh, an event my father advertised.

Mother calls us to the table. The meal is delicious, the conversation pleasant, and out of nowhere, I feel an unease that makes me want to run. The nervousness isn't the tickly-prickly anticipation of being with a new crush, or the sinking-gut dread of pending disaster, or the gastric butterfly battle to the death of a public moment. All is well. All is so very well. Andrew fits so well among them. I watch my father and Andrew lean toward each other in a verbal spar over city politics—and grin as they do it. I realize that I wanted Daddy to disapprove again, to give me a reason I've never used before to turn a boy loose. In fact, I want them all to adore Andrew as much as I do.

I ignore the squirmy feeling of my skin once Mother brings out her excellent carrot cake and dark roasted coffee. Daddy offers Andrew a shot of whiskey for his beverage, which he accepts. My respectably roguish father splashes a drop into my cup, too, without asking. After the talk and eating is over, I help Mother clear the dishes. She puts her hands on my shoulders and kisses my cheek. *I like him,* she says. *You have a good eye, sweetheart.* The dining room is empty when I return. Grams says her good-nights. She has captured Andrew's hand like a kitten and pats it softly. I kiss her before she goes upstairs. Daddy, I can tell, wants to stay up to chat, but Mother creeps behind him, takes his arm, and suppresses a yawn into his shoulder. She reminds me to turn off the back porch light before I go to bed, such an odd little tone in her voice when she says it. My parents shake hands with Andrew, perfectly ebullient about having met him. They each kiss me and disappear up the stairs. I hear Daddy half-whisper, *Quite a fellow my baby girl found herself.*

Tonight, the air smells like copper, a sweet clean coldness that makes every breath snap on the way in. Andrew stands straight with his hands flat on the porch rail looking into the backyard. I'm curled under my peacock blue coat on the swing. The light is off. I flipped the switch before we came outside.

"Nice evening," he says. "Clear. Polaris is rather bright."

I duck and peer up to the North Star. "Astronomical aspirations?"

He gives a quick laugh but keeps his back to me. "I learned the constellations when I was little. My father likes astronomy. He taught me. At one time, I believed the mythological creatures and objects were truly there, held in place by giant pins. The light points of their configurations, you see. I thought if any of those pins came loose, they would be at the mercy of thin air—and they'd fall to the ground and crush me. So for a couple of years, I'd only go outside on cloudy nights. I decided that would give them something on which to land, other than me." When he turns around, he's a silhouette. "Quite an imagination."

For a moment, I cannot speak. He has charmed me to pieces. "I'll say. I appreciate creative minds."

"Speaking of which. Your family is entertaining," Andrew says. "I like them."

"They have a collective crush on you."

"I thought this went well."

"You showed no sign of intimidation. You looked my father in the eye when you spoke. If Daddy senses fear, he's simply awful, like a spy interrogator."

"Interesting. He didn't strike me that way."

"Of course not. You foiled his strategy."

"Have you lost many dates because of him?"

I laugh. "I didn't let him meet them all." My arms work into the coat sleeves. "Your parents are next."

"If you're certain."

"Don't you want to retaliate?"

"Hardly seems fair. Your parents and grandmother were so pleasant."

"Raised by goblins?"

"They're different. Less spirited, much older. Mother used to call me their miracle. She was forty-three when I was born. She was tempted to name me Isaac."

"Were there others?"

"I suspect so. Perhaps none that were formally buried."

"What's she like?"

He slips his hands into his pockets. "A walking etiquette book. She went to finishing school when it was fashionable to do so. Had I been a girl, I'm quite certain that's where I'd be now."

"Horrors. What else?"

"She gives time to an orphanage, her charity work. It gives her something important to do. She's very devout. Catholic, of course. She goes to Adoration once a week, never misses mass on holy days of obligation, certainly not a Sunday."

"Were you an altar boy?"

"I sometimes dream in Latin—and not because I've studied it."

"You poor boy."

"Mother isn't so bad. She just never seems to have enough fun."

"And your father?"

"Smart in a shrewd way. He's a banker. You knew that. He's keen on bonds. That's his specialty. He likes to play the market, too, but doesn't trust it. He says it's like a woman—susceptible to gossip, whims, and disaster. I apologize. Father has old-fashioned notions about things. At any rate, he keeps his bank safe, his own money safer. The only stocks he's focused on these days are for telephone and radio corporations. The future, he says."

"Did he say why?"

"People like noise, especially their own."

"What a funny little rationale."

"He may be right."

"Our fathers might like each other. Daddy thinks good advertising hits at the intersection between inadequacy and vanity." I stand and stretch my arms overhead. We are only a few steps apart. "Well, if I'm to figure you out properly, I'm going to have to meet your parents at some point."

"Is that so important?"

"Do I make more sense to you now?"

"At least now I know where you got your eyes."

"That's not what I meant."

"I know."

"What a line." At first, I almost kiss him. That doesn't seem right. There's a sadness, a little emptiness that revealed itself in his voice, something I didn't catch before. Without any hesitant prelude, I hug him lightly around the waist. My head fits into his throat.

His arms fold around my shoulders. Within seconds, he tries to glance at his wristwatch. "I should be on my way."

"Are you tired?" I ask as he steps back.

"Not quite."

"Come here."

"Why?"

"Come here."

He steps toward me, and I hold him again. His arms are stiff, unyielding.

"Relax, Andrew."

"I am."

"You're not."

"It's getting late."

"I doubt it's even close to eleven."

"Honestly."

"Hush." I wrap a little tighter. Through the muffle of his lapel, I hear his heartbeat.

"Razi."

"I need a hug."

"All right."

Within a few moments, he sighs quietly and bends into me. His chin rests on the crown of my head. Our contours meet with precision. I realize that our breathing has slipped into echoes, out, in, answering each other. I am tempted to mention this but afraid that it will stop if I do. At the hip, he starts a pendulum motion, so subtle at first it cannot be deliberate. The swing works upward to our shoulders until I feel the dull give and tension past my buttery knees into my calves. Each rhythm, heart, breath, sway, is harmonic through our blood and skin. My eyes shut—the sound and feel enough—and when I open them again, I notice the moon has chosen a new place to rest.

What is this . . . this ache when I pull away?

"Now it's late," I tell him.

Through my house at a quarter past midnight—the grandfather clock tells me so—he follows me to the front door. I beg the creak to whisper, and it obliges. Now on the porch, Andrew thanks me for the evening, pauses, and bends for a kiss. It's supple, gentle. He hugs me suddenly, pecks my forehead as he lets go. I watch him walk down the steps. There, under the dark oak shade to the right, is his father's roadster. Andrew turns to face me, waves, points to Polaris, and turns east. He slips into a stride. I can't call out to say he's forgotten the automobile. In the morning, if someone asks, I'll say he couldn't get it to start.

NEW YEAR'S EVE, 1927. A steamboat jazz dance. It's so cold, the band has been moved inside. We silently stand next to each other on the deck for a long time. We cannot hear each other breathe. I feel as comfortable as if we had been talking.

"Your hands must be cold," he says when he sees my fingers close around the rail. His are protected by smooth brown leather gloves.

"Not really," I say. They aren't.

"Here, take my gloves. I insist."

"No, I'm fine. Keep them."

Without speaking, he takes my right wrist and holds it steady as he slips the glove on my hand. He does the same with the left. They are big for me and retain his heat. A sensation beyond temperature makes its way through my blood.

"Thank you," I say.

"You're welcome."

He is a true gentleman. He moves with ease that is instinct more than reflex. I like the way he opens doors wide for women and lets men pass through before him. He thanks people sincerely for their service, even if it's for making a sundae. He always looks people in the eye when he speaks with them. I know—although the circumstance has not presented itself—that he is the kind of man who would be the first to stand when a lady enters a room.

"Is that better?" he asks.

"Yes."

His hands are deep inside the pockets of his overcoat. I watch his profile, crisp against the gray sky. I have never noticed what a wonderful nose he has, perfect in its geometry. His cheeks are pink from the cold. His bottom lip pouts slightly as if he's forgotten to pull it even with the top one. "May I hold your hand?" he asks with such reticence I think he expects me to refuse.

I hold out my right hand, palm down, and he slips his left underneath. I move closer to him and reach for his right arm. He turns toward me and takes my other hand as well. I step toward him so that our hands are trapped between our chests. "You don't have to ask, Andrew. Not now."

"Not now?" His eyebrows drop to make his expression inquisitive.

"Not since I decided that I—that I—like you." For any other man, that would have been his cue to give me a hasty, fervent kiss.

"I've decided that I rather like you, too." He kisses me lightly on the forehead with a gentleness that stalls my breath and makes me close my eyes to focus on that feeling alone. A few seconds later, when I feel his lips on mine, I am caught off guard. The start of this kiss is a question, really, and I respond to him by wrapping my arms around his waist under his coat and relaxing my bottom lip between his. When he realizes that he has his answer, Andrew slips his hand to the back of my neck and kisses me long and wet and passionately until the pure intensity makes me want to cry.

We pull apart, slightly. "I think we had an audience," he says.

I turn to see an elderly couple on the other end of the deck. Their arms are linked, and they are smiling at us. They wave, and we wave back. The old man takes his wife by the arm and leads her inside, where it is warm.

❧

THE METALLIC SMELL remained in the house. When it first appeared, the odor was so acute, so copious, that I had no doubt the memory was as terrifying as the event itself. The sharp taint never left Amy's presence completely. In quiet moments, she would suddenly flinch or shut her eyes—and a complex rush of scents would billow around her. Each time, a masculine essence that was not Scott's dissipated in the air.

The memory of Jem had come back. She did not welcome its return.

She had not left a clue about what happened to him. Her sporadic photograph collection showed no signs. Her boxes in the attic only had proof that he had died, but not how. I hoped that she might talk about him, even under her voice. I watched her lips, larynx, and body for signs that she muttered unconsciously, unwillingly. My hyperesthesia, that consolation prize for the loss of touch, was useless. Amy's lips were still. She was keeping it deep.

I began to leave the radio on low all the time and turned it up only when songs from Amy's college years played. Perhaps music would trigger a memory, a clue. Scott was the one struck with nostalgia, who reminded her of the years they were friends long before they became lovers, husband and wife. She would smile, but without warmth.

"Hear that?" He scraped a razor against his left cheek. "Remember when Chloe used to play that song ad nauseam?" He rinsed the blade in the sink and looked at her in the reflection of the bathroom mirror.

Amy pushed her bathwater away in waves. "Mmm-hmm."

Scott stared at her and swallowed words he had wanted to say. "It's weird how much your skin freckles when you're in the sun."

Amy had spent the day in the yard, tending the flowers. She ran her hands down her body. Small reddish-brown freckles dotted her chest, abdomen, and hips, some darker and larger than others. Her limbs and face were mottled with diluted spots.

"That scar comes out when you get some sun," he said.

From the edge of her right temple to the base of her jaw, there was a thin, neat line. It followed the contours of her face so closely that it resembled a shadow. "A little."

"Do you still think about it?" he asked.

"I try not to."

"You don't remember much anyway."

"No." She flopped a washcloth over her privates. "After I woke up, I did. The hospital, the whole family being there. Poppa Fin sitting in there all day. Even when Mom and Dad and Grandma Sunny left for coffee. We didn't even talk. He read magazines and wouldn't leave. I just wanted to be alone. I was too doped up or in too much pain to deal with anyone."

"I think such a shock makes people do things they wouldn't otherwise. At least you know they all cared, Aims."

She released a stream of hot water to refresh her bath. "Grandma Sunny was the only one who listened to me. She knew how I— She understood. I could count on her to stand up to the rest of them. I loved her for that. She gave me peace, even if she did annoy me with the platitudes. 'You'll be back on the horse in no time.' 'Time heals all wounds.' That didn't help a bit."

"But she was right. Here you are. And you have me." He leaned into the humid borders of her bath and kissed her on the forehead.

"Yes, I have you." Her tone was grateful but resigned.

He left and didn't close the door behind him. Amy ran her hands along her torso. Her hands stopped above her pubic bone, and she jutted her belly upward. She held it in that position for a long time, more than could have possibly been comfortable. When she finally relaxed, she laced her fingers together and covered her navel protectively.

Blood. I wondered whose I had smelled the night before.

AMY BEGAN to come home later each night. Within a few weeks, by July, she rarely walked in the back door before eight thirty, three hours later than usual. She arrived home with replenishing stocks of food that only Scott ate. Before she went to bed, the house was always immaculate. Not a single glass or dish was dirty. Garbage bins were emptied before they were half full. Dust didn't have time to settle on tabletops and shelves. Clean clothes spent only enough time in baskets to get them from the laundry room to a closet or chest of drawers. Her clothes—and his—were ironed for the next day. Her checkbook was perfectly balanced. All e-mail messages were promptly answered. She even read the forwarded jokes, petitions, and pleas for prayers. She cooked large meals on Saturdays, which she promptly stored in the refrigerator. On Sunday mornings, she tended all yard work before Scott got out of bed.

Her life had become neat and organized, not Amy's life at all.

She twitched and fidgeted. If she sat long enough to watch the evening news, her toes fluttered against the air, and her fingers twirled limp dreadlocks on her head. She sat in the rocker for hours, scooting along the floor with a rapid sway while she read one ridiculous fantasy novel after another that she borrowed from the library. At times, her index fingers worked overlapping figure eights on tabletops and furniture. Her lips never moved to give me a hint at what she was hiding.

Scott worried.

I remembered entire decades when most men expected their wives to do what Amy did completely and without complaint. Scott was not accustomed to such domestic arrangements. He was suddenly useless in his own home, not even needed to open an occasional jar. He watched her, unsure when she'd become the efficient creature who now made their bed with perfect folds of the sheet and blanket.

"Aims," he said sometimes as she padded through the house, involved in a task, "come see."

She would stand in front of him with blank eyes.

"Sit down and relax. I'll take care of it later. You've had a long day." He would hold her hand in both of his or grasp her pajamas tightly. Sometimes he would get her to curl on his lap for a moment.

Like a willful cat, she'd spring from his grip. "That's okay. I'm too keyed up from work to sit still."

Amy was losing weight although she rarely exercised and her diet was atrocious. When she came home at night, she dined on cheap tacos, hamburgers, and grilled chicken sandwiches. She once packed her lunch every day, but that hadn't occurred in weeks.

Scott looked scrawnier as well. He subsisted on leftover meals and strange salads concocted from cans of chickpeas, beets, and artichokes as well as packages of spinach, carrots, and coleslaw. Occasionally, he dined on a frozen dinner and chased it with a bowl of cereal. He ate apples as if he owned an entire orchard.

After his fifth week without sex or something close, he stopped asking for it. He closed the bathroom door more often.

He hadn't become visibly angry yet. He hadn't acknowledged to himself that a growl stirred deep in his throat when he spoke to her. He hadn't stopped trying to touch her when she passed by.

❧

I HAVEN'T SLEPT in five weeks. I gaze at the jade crocheted coverlet I used as a cocoon almost every night since I was fourteen. The sheets underneath, unlaundered—I sense what my flesh left behind. Pillows stacked too neatly, not at all the way I left them. There, at the edge, an imprint, a subtle swirl of yarn. Someone has been sitting on my bed. I stir the lint. Each of them, Mother, Daddy, Grams, visited this place.

Now I am a guest in my own room. So little of me remains. The watercolor of pond lilies hangs over my bed, the one Roger, my dead doughboy uncle, finished between college and the Western Front. Above the chest of drawers, there is the portrait of a Pekingese that Twolly did for one of her classes. The closet shelf holds two of my cloche hats in boxes. Hanging from the rod are four dresses, evenly spaced, nothing in common except that I was told how lovely my eyes looked when I wore them. Below, a pair of celadon evening slippers with thin straps and shiny silver buckles and my boyish brown sporting shoes, laces tied. The walnut chest of drawers is empty. My delicates, nightgowns, stockings, slips, gone. Near the double windows, sheers closed, the vanity mirror reflects only light. The pictures of Twolly and Andrew and assorted other friends have disappeared.

Oh, this is not the same. My lipsticks on their sides, my perfumes in Grams's old atomizers in a row, my powder puff sealed in its round eggshell box. Drawers empty, except for a hairpin. The nightstand uncluttered—no soda bottles, magazines, torn-out crossword puzzles, thick stationery, or leaky fountain pens—only the lamp occupies the space, its shade level and dusty. Underneath, the shelves are vacant; all of the cigar boxes full of letters have vanished.

My family is awake. The insect whine outside the wavy-paned windows does not smother their breathing. Perhaps I should take the stairs, drift down the grunting steps, leave them now, avoid the risk that they are able to feel me near. Give them absence, peace I haven't found yet.

My grandmother whiffles a drowsy sigh across the hall. I disintegrate, particles slipping through the dry oak of the door, and knit together inside her room. The sash is thrown wide. Propped high on her pillows, she looks regal with a white braid brushing her clavicle and fine-boned fingers laced against her bosom. A glint from her diamond wedding ring shoots across the room.

Hello, Grams, I say. *You look like a queen.*

Languid blinks weigh her lashes to her cheeks.

I'm glad to see you're all right. I miss you.

From her, a deep breath, slowly delivered. I ache for that release, such an organic pleasure taken for granted millions of times over. Closer, now, I see her nose twitch with mousy curiosity, her head tilt gently in my direction. She mouths a word without parting her lips, beneath sound—if I concentrate, I can seehear—*Raziela.*

I enter the hallway again. Twenty-three girl steps, sixteen frightened ninny leaps, one brief hover away from my parents' bedroom. No voices mutter, but they are entirely awake. With a tornadic swirl, I swoop under the door.

All three windows are open. The night breeze rustles the curtain edges. In bed, my parents lie on their sides. A pale yellow sheet covers them from the hips down. Mother faces the wall, Daddy behind her with his chin tucked into her neck and his left arm around her waist. Her forearm touches his, and her hand curls under her ribs. My mother is not wearing a gown.

They are pretending to be asleep. That forced slow breathing, occasional sighs, dry swallows, quiet lip smacks. Into the pewter light, they look without seeing. Daddy blinks with every eighth tick of the alarm clock. Mother stares with a haze across her green eyes. Neither has any hope of slumber; their faces are restless. From across the room, I can discern gray, swollen patches under their sockets. But worse, their orbs don't reflect. That blankness, it frightens me. My mother and father, so confident and aware, seem mystified. *How many hours do they spend—have they spent—this way?* I wonder if they give up and go into the living room to read or sip brandy or listen to the grandfather clock near the stairs. My form begins to vibrate, spreading heat near the bed, but I force it to stop. I remember a night, one of many, as I lay between my parents, infant breath sweetly curdled, my mother's lips on the pulse of my fontanel, my hand pressed to my father's chin.

Mother's fingers move over Daddy's arm. He tucks his hand deeper, pulling her into him. She closes her eyes for a moment, and when they open, they glisten. Mother clenches her jaw, which Daddy certainly feels because he nuzzles her with his cheek. She swallows loud enough to hear in this silence.

"Oh," Mother calls with quiet surprise. "Her baby scent."

"You, too?" Daddy says.

As Mother turns on her back and meets her husband's mouth, a tear slips past her temple and into her hair. The sheet twists under him. He brings his arms to her shoulders, and his naked torso, hips, and legs stretch above hers. The moonlight illuminates a converging stream that falls from him down the curve of her face. She takes a deep breath, exhales tightly. She rips the covers aside. I fall to pieces and scatter.

LATE JANUARY 1928 on a Saturday. Cool-snap morning, balmy by noon. From the moment we leave the city, we shout over the road noise, narrow rubber tires pulverize rock, wind carelessly blows our conversation through the windows. He keeps both hands on the wheel to hold us steady, but his grip is slack. I find excuses to move near him—a flock of egrets, there, to your left; a feather in your hair, must have blown in; your collar is twisted, let me straighten it. The Mississippi River hides behind the levee; the gravel road mimics each bend. Lonely trees greet us with skeletal, limber fingers. Dry bronze grasses play with the breeze. The sun embraces its sky, topaz blue infused with platinum gold.

There, see the chimney, let's find a spot, I say. Nothing remains of the old home except for its foundation and central hearth. Andrew drives past the husk, deep on the property where several oaks and a cluster of fuchsia-tipped redbud trees shade the ground. We spread a layer of blankets and unpack the picnic basket. Chicken salad sandwiches, carrot and celery sticks, pickled okra, satsumas, mint tea, pound cake. After we eat, Andrew removes his sweater and tucks it under his head. He looks drowsy.

"Your grandmother said something unusual to me before we left," Andrew says.

"Get used to that."

"She said, 'Raziela did not anticipate you. Don't forget.' What did she mean?"

"Well, you're the first steady I've had in a long time. Maybe she's afraid that you'll distract me from my studies."

"You said she wasn't especially keen on your educational pursuits."

"Grams wants me happy until I realize my true calling as a wife and mother."

"That wasn't in her tone. She seemed to be warning me."

"Of what?"

"That's why I asked you."

There is one satsuma left. I begin to peel it, trying to keep the skin whole. "She likes to be mysterious sometimes. I wouldn't be surprised if she's testing your reaction."

"You walked in before I could reply."

"Want some?" I toss the intact peel into the grass and hold a wedge near him. Andrew takes it, skims my fingertips.

"I never knew my grandparents. They died before I was born. I always wanted a grandparent who would tell me old stories. I would enjoy learning about history as they lived it."

"That's great until you hear each story for the fiftieth time. Never changes."

"Perhaps I'll borrow yours for a while. They're all new to me."

"Next time she's on a tear, I'll put her on the telephone."

"The last time we had a date, before you came downstairs, she started telling me about her sister."

I smile, shake my head. He looks at me curiously. I scoot close to him and rest a piece of fruit on his lips. "How far did she get?" Carefully, he drops his jaw to take it in.

"The confinement."

"You missed the good part about her locking up my grandfather."

"She truly believes that her sister was there."

"Ab-so-tively."

"What do you think?"

"Hallucinations. She was going mad locked up like that. No woman, no person, should live in such deprivation. Her mind had to do something to make up for the lack."

"Could it be that she was more receptive to such an experience? I've read about these men called shamans. They deny themselves food, drink, and human contact to reach another world."

"Mumbo jumbo. That's ridiculous."

"Why?"

"You've read Freud, haven't you?" I ask. "He says dreams are manifestations of our wishes and fears. When a person is in a state without physical stimuli, like in sleep, we enter some deep part of ourselves. There's nothing to distract us. So if my grandmother, or some shaman, wants desperately to see a sister or brother or friend, that's exactly what she will get."

"Interesting. But what if there is something else?"

"For example?"

"A spirit realm. One we cannot see, one as real as the one we have now."

"I thought you were no longer Catholic."

"It has nothing to do with Catholicism. Assume there is an essence to each person. We've both studied Latin. The Romans used the word *anima*. The Church translates that to *soul*. Now, let's say, when the body goes, that part remains? It must go somewhere. Perhaps it stays around us, or perhaps it enters another realm we don't yet understand."

"Heaven?" I slowly bite a satsuma wedge near the back of my mouth. The mild acid makes the side of my tongue constrict a little.

"Semantics," he says.

"Bunk."

"Why?"

"Rule of finite energy. Once we die, all it took to keep our organs and blood moving dies with us. That's what we are. Millions of amazing little cells, working in clusters of tiny machines, the parts of the big machine. It breaks; it's over. The pieces put to use in some other way."

Andrew is quiet. He stares at me until I meet his eyes. "No one knows why the heart beats."

"Voluntary and involuntary muscles."

"What makes them move?"

"The cardiac plexus, for the most part."

"And what gives it power?"

He's so clever, that's why I—I won't concede. "Maybe I'll be the one who figures that out."

"What ambition." He stretches, lifts his chest toward the sky. He holds this position long enough to make me think of the lean, tight muscles that levee around his spine. Once he settles into the position he was in before, I reach for his right hand, cupping my fingertips into his. The subtle muscle tension draws me toward him.

Andrew takes my hand, palm up, on his chest. Without a word, he begins to trace the outline. The curves near my nails spark. Across my wrist, spiral in to the palm, toward the middle, slow, restrained, light as pollen, closing inward, electric. I stop breathing as tight circles float in the hollow. Whatever he is doing, whatever current I feel, rushes through my arm, into every limb, gathers at my core. He has been watching me watch the motion, and when I realize this, my lungs shallow, and I shut my eyes.

"Razi, look at me."

The distant January sun turns his blue to sapphire. His pupils vanish. I want to turn away, down, sideways, but he takes my cheek into his palm, thumb on the rise of my lower lip. I can't breathe. He doesn't move, only gazes at me, my eyes. I am heat: I implode without warning.

There is every reason to rush, yet neither one of us does. I loosen the buttons of his Oxford shirt and see his breath animate under layers of bone and flesh. My hands drape on the rise and fall, back and forth, take the rhythm to his shoulders, turn the collar behind him, shed sleeves. My zipper trickles down my spine with an exhale, the pit of my back arches away. The slip marks territory. We touch only what we can see. Now, a kiss on my neck, another, another, a necklace of bliss, a charm brought to his lips, caught between us. At his waist, cool silver under my fingertips, leather whisper and whip, two buttons, his back forced to the earth, row of metal teeth apart, wool over cotton. He sighs, low, fast, hands at my hips, seams inside out, silk through my hair, now his hands, down, my pulse at his wrists, his pulse at mine. Herringbone in my fists, one undulation, two kicks, aside. Cotton at his knuckles, slow shimmy, left right center left, away, fingertips at garter bands, pull, grip at both calves, ankles, toes, away. My whorl at the freckle on the front of his left hip, the first point of constellation, the second here, and then here . . . Not yet, not the urgency, every place else, first with hands and eyes—don't move—next my lips, he is seamless, and before the map is complete—he charts me the same way.

I want—I want to, I want him.

Our hands embrace the release.

Andrew observes my eyes. He smiles as if he knows a secret about me.

❧

LIONEL AND I were nearly joined at the mist from the moment I started to teach him how to live between. I'd never had a brother, and Nel would have been my choice if I'd had one. He was a wonderful conversationalist, a good listener, and a wicked practical joker.

Although he knew we weren't supposed to interfere, he couldn't help himself. People's slow powers of perception were too tempting. No one relished the fun of teleportation more than he did, and he was good at the trick. Because he couldn't use his own form to distract attention from his sleight of hand, he had to be particularly observant of his victims. He could move a set of car keys, a cocktail, or a packed suitcase so often in a short span of time that he'd bring people to tears of frustration.

His favorite trick was the lap dance. Nel had learned to create the energetic membrane of the body he once had. He could not experience human touch as he once did, but he was nearly certain that people couldn't tell the difference. Now and then, he would knit his form and slip under the descending rear of a streetcar passenger or moviegoer. The depth perception startled them first, and their hands would run over the obstacle, and then, limbs gyrating, they'd fling themselves away from the blank space. I chastised him for blatantly crossing the boundaries, but he ignored me.

"I'm so mean," he'd say with a chuckle. "It's not right. To think we were once so easily bewildered. Poor breather."

When he wasn't amusing himself, Nel worked through a list of simple accomplishments during his first months. He had kept a list of movies he wanted to see before he died, so he watched films in video stores between one and eight in the morning for several weeks. After that, we spent days and nights in libraries across the city. To start, he read all of the writings of Ralph Waldo Emerson. I told him that hardly counted because we had perfect memories of anything we read before we died. Nel had only studied two key essays in high school, though. To read Emerson's body of work only took a few days. No need for sleep. Then he studied art history. What a pleasure, he declared three months later, to be able to look at a painting, know its style, and name its creator. Because he thought he should, he forced himself through *War and Peace.* Next, he studied car repair manuals and loitered in auto shops until he understood internal combustion engines and brake systems. For fun, Nel shocked an entire crew of mechanics when they arrived at work one morning and every car worked perfectly.

"Isn't there something you want to do?" he asked me six months after his body died. We were giving ourselves a tour of the Cabildo, another Lionel to-do almost done. "Aren't you bored? You haven't gone out on your own much lately."

"Am I bothering you?"

"No, no, you're never in the way. But all you do is read or stare off into space. You've hardly trained any new ones in months."

"I've put in seventy years or so. Can't I have a break?"

"There's no retirement in this state, honey. They need you."

"Thanks, Nel." I watched him rock on the balls of his feet to his heels. An old habit unbroken, only he did this hovering an inch above ground.

"I've been thinking about what you told me when I was adjusting. About what we are. What you think we are. That we're the reduction of those atoms and whatever they hold. The whole bit about elements—oxygen, hydrogen, nitrogen—what the air and our bodies have in common."

"It's only a theory. Ready to go?"

We moved under the archway, facing Jackson Square.

"I hated physics in school," he said. "I didn't have the patience to learn. Didn't think I was smart enough to understand. But it's really interesting once you get into it." He looked at me. "A lot has changed since the days you studied the subject."

"Pos-a-lutely."

"So this idea that we're reductions, where did you get that?"

"It's simply logic. The particles needed for matter are gone. The rest stayed. Here we are."

"Undiscovered bits. From atom to electrons and protons to quarks to—what is it these days—strings?"

I didn't turn to him as we passed St. Louis Cathedral and the tables of chiromancers and card readers lined up near the church's gray steps. Nel had become unusually interested in a topic that made ordinary minds drowse and wander. Although I appreciated his curiosity—I liked Nel because he was an inquisitive sort—I was unsure what motivated him. Whether he wanted an explanation or comfort, he'd get neither.

"Razi—strings, right?"

"These days, yes, strings."

"I think it's a beautiful idea, don't you? Imagine—deep down, the pieces are all the same, and how they vibrate make them unique, like a photon or an electron, and then how they move and interact make them unique again, into atoms and such."

"Quite lovely."

Nel stopped, creating a blank density in the middle of the

banquette that tourists dodged. "You haven't read anything in years, have you?"

"I've dabbled. I know about the quantum and chaos theories."

"You don't strike me as a dabbler."

"These people question what everything's made of and what holds it together. But it's all still finite, regardless of what it is. That hasn't changed."

"But explain why we're sentient. Explain why we still remember. What holds who we are? Don't you want to know?"

"You were the kid who always asked questions, weren't you?"

"You were the kid who shouted out the answers. Where's your answer now, Razi?"

❧

AMY HAD CALLED to say she was working late again. After Scott hung up the phone, he paced along the living room floor for several minutes. He went into the kitchen, and a small book rustled open. Eleven even beeps chirped in the silent house.

"Chloe?" He leaned his hip against the sink. "Hi, it's Scott Duncan."

A little howl vibrated the phone. "What's with the last name? You're not at work, right? Oh, my God. How are you?"

"Fine, thanks. How's that new job?"

"Great. Bet you didn't figure me a techno geek, did you?"

"No. But then you changed majors so often that I'm more surprised you're not still in college."

"Old friends and ancient history. Gotta love 'em. Speaking of which—how's Amy?" She paused. "What's wrong?"

"I'm not sure."

"Is she still having a hard time over her grandparents?"

"I don't know. She doesn't talk about it."

"No shock there."

"It's not that." He peeked outside the kitchen door's window. "Remember that summer at the clinic?"

"All I care to."

"Remember when Amy had that period of keeping things really neat?"

"Oh, shit."

Scott swallowed hard. "I don't think she's dealing with her grief over her grandparents. She cried every day for two weeks after her Grandma Sunny died, and then it was sort of sporadic after that. Then when Poppa Fin died, she cried only once—after his funeral. Then nothing. She doesn't even mention them."

"She's sad they're both gone, but furious at old Fin. She sent this e-mail a while back and told me what he did. I told her that happened in my family, too, one of my older cousins who lost her husband. Got rid of everything in a matter of weeks. I thought it was weird, but I see it from their point of view—it's got to hurt to have that stuff around."

"It was so soon after, though," Scott said. "And he did it alone. Amy would have wanted to be there, to save things."

"We don't have a right to tell people how to grieve," Chloe replied. "Anyway, when did her cleaning fit start?"

Scott unlocked the back door and sat on the steps. "Three, four weeks ago. At least that's when I noticed."

"Do you know what triggered it?"

"If I knew that, I wouldn't be talking to you. I hoped she'd said something. What did you do last time to get her out of it?"

"What last time?"

"That summer, after the protests."

"Oh."

"Oh what?"

"I rarely did anything. She worked it out in her own head, mostly."

"I was there that summer, Chloe. She didn't work out of that alone."

Suddenly, faintly, Jem's scent emerged. His presence was accidental, as if Scott didn't mean to remember that Jem had been there, too.

"Look," Scott said, "I don't know how you—and Jem—got her through. It's really bad this time. Not like the times when she cleans to think something out. That lasts a day or two, not weeks."

"You have to talk it out of her."

"She won't talk."

"She will. Everyone has a breaking point."

"I don't want her to snap."

"She's not a twig. You're such a sensitive new age guy. She loves that about you, whether or not you know it. Enter the millennium with a new spin, Captain Jigsaw. Sensitivity is knowing the right tack to get what you want."

"When's your self-help book hitting the shelves?"

"True gifts like mine won't be sold."

"If you knew something, you'd tell me, right?"

"If it were my place to tell you. No doubt."

"Your place?"

"Semantics. Don't be paranoid."

"I need a favor. Come here. Come see her."

She was quiet for a moment. "I have to be honest. I can't afford it. The move—"

"I'll pay for the ticket. Can you come? She'll talk to you. I know it. You're like sodium pentothal. No one can look you in the eye and lie. I've seen it happen."

Pages fell upon each other in the background of Chloe's line. "Maybe I should have gone into the CIA. No, I bet I have an FBI file from my activist days. Okay, three weeks from now, early August. That's the best I can do, buddy."

Scott's body relaxed forward. He closed his eyes. "Thank you, Chloe."

"I just wish I weren't seeing you guys for the first time in months under these circumstances. One catch, though. You have to make me some of that damn fine chili of yours. I haven't had real food in forever. A girl can eat just so much from a salad bar."

"I'll even spring for beer," he said.

❧

TWOLLY AND I primly pose on a bench as Andrew fiddles with his new toy, a Kodak camera with adjustable speed and focus. Inspired by the photographs in *National Geographic,* he wants to learn how to take his own snapshots. For now, until he becomes a world traveler, his hometown is the subject.

"Twolly, turn your head a little to the left, wait, down slightly. There. Don't either of you move. And—done." He looks down at the camera.

I stretch my legs. "Are you going to New York during the Mardi Gras break?"

Twolly squeezes her mouth into a little prune. "Daddy doesn't want me to go. Mother got him all stirred up about the foreigners there, and he has it in his head that someone will sell me into white slavery."

I can't stop laughing.

"It's not funny," she says.

"How can you be so sensible and have such a kooky family?"

"My daddy worries about me."

"My daddy worries about me, too, but he doesn't keep me from having my own life. Didn't you tell him you'd get one of your sisters to go along?"

"Terre is due in a month, Fleur is planning her wedding, and Ciel gets violently train-sick. Little Soleil would only sweeten the trade." We laugh.

"Your talent is being squandered," I say. "Your teacher wouldn't have offered to arrange those meetings if she didn't think someone would snatch you up. Imagine, Twolls, your very own line of jewelry. In New York. Maybe then France. Your name is perfect. Etoile. You'd be famous. At least try it. Have some fun."

"I don't really want to go anyway."

"Liar. I should escort you myself. And because you're such a goody-goody, you can be my chaperone."

"Chaperone for what?" Andrew stands within earshot now. Twolly summarizes the drama. "You should go. You will always wonder what if, if you don't."

As he turns little gears this way and that, I notice his square silver initialed cuff links. *APO*. "What's your middle name, Andrew? You haven't told me."

He twitches his black eyebrows. "What if I'm using an initial alone?"

"Honestly. Come on, now. Twolly can keep a secret better than anyone, and I need only a little bribe." He laughs and shakes his head. "I would trade with mine, but I never got one. Twolls, tell him your full name."

"Etoile Luna Knight."

Andrew blinks at her and finally says, "Inventive." He wants to laugh.

"Go ahead. I did when she told me."

He smiles. He's too much of a gentleman to make fun of a lady's name.

"Now," I say, "if hers can be so silly—"

"Hey—" Twolly says.

"—you can share yours."

"I may not even tell the woman I wed." Andrew doesn't blink.

"Spoilsport. Will you let me guess?" I brush my hand down his arm.

"Three."

"If I guess, will you admit that I'm right?"

"That's only fair," Twolly says.

"Yes, that's only fair," Andrew agrees.

"A name that starts with P. Hmm. Now, you must want to keep it a secret because it's terrible. And you may think it's ghastly, but perhaps it's not. You might hate it for no reason at all. O'Connell. Irish, Catholic. Oh, it must be a saint's name. Paul." Negative. "Peter." Again, no. "Phillip?"

"That was a good college try." Andrew grins, then walks away.

"You're going to burn a hole in his trousers if you keep staring like that, Miss Off-the-Market," Twolly says. "You're so cute when you're in—"

"Andrew." I run to him. "This isn't as fun as I thought it would be."

"I need practice."

"That's fine. But it won't do for us to loll about like Maxfield Parrish models, so serious and pensive." I skip circles around him. "See, I'm a fairy. Capture me if you can."

"Aye, lassie," he answers with a brogue, "you may have your wish for the price of a kiss." He winks at me in the way that makes me want to kiss more than his cheek, which is all I do before Twolly and anyone else who happens to glance our way.

"Twolls—to the playground," I say.

I run ahead of them, drop my hat on the brown grass, finger-comb my locks, and straddle the seesaw. When I turn to see where they are, Twolly has the camera in her hands, and he is explaining how some gadget works. Her deft fingers maneuver around the contraption.

"Let her take one," I say.

"Oh, may I?" Twolly looks at him with puppy eyes.

"Remember how to focus?" he asks. She nods. "Look charming, Razi."

"Look charming with me. Come here."

He refuses, several times, but Twolly pushes him gently in my direction. I get down from the seesaw, and Andrew gives me a bashful grin as he approaches. He puts a rigid arm around my shoulders. Twolly, preoccupied with the lens, doesn't see him jump when I slip my hand into his back pocket. He almost laughs, would have if he hadn't stopped himself. I turn my face up and watch the smirk take over his cheeks. My molesting hand moves to his waist. He relaxes. His hip rests right above mine.

"Hold still. Got it," Twolly says.

Andrew tries to pull away, but I hug him suddenly, my cheek on his chest. He hugs me, too, secure and affectionate, and I incandesce.

"Got that. Very cute. Oh, I think you're out of film."

"I have more in my pocket." He does not rush when he releases me. Andrew takes the camera and begins to replace the roll.

Twolly grabs my cloche. "That was fun. I think I took some good photos."

"Your artistic eye, I'm sure." I take my hat from her.

We perch on the seesaw. Twolly kicks her legs out when she's on top. She hasn't made a noise about our unladylike behavior. We wave at Andrew and blow him kisses. When he tells us to hold still, Twolly—taller and heavier than I am—anchors the seesaw to the ground as I reach for the sky. After he takes the photographs, Andrew sits on the ground and watches us brush fingertips against the clouds.

MY SAUCY DRUGSTORE theatrics with Twolly and clandestine leafleting at school lead to a new tactic—Boyless Parties.

Twolly and Andrew have tried their best to discourage me. They imagine a scandal that will embarrass my family, ruin my reputation, and destroy my chance at medical school, not to mention result in a prison term.

Although Twolly finally sees the necessity of providing women with certain information before they need it, she doesn't think it's appropriate that I should be the messenger. Of course, I disagree. Who better than another woman to share such intimacies? Look at what doctors have done to our grandmothers and mothers—quick with knives and electrical curative devices.

What do they know? No matter what the law says, what right do they have to give advice only to those whose bodies are bound in holy matrimony? By then, isn't it too late?

When I first told Andrew what I was doing, he remained quiet for several moments. He gave me a paternal look and said that he wished I wouldn't. Andrew agreed with my intent, although he didn't approve of the methods. He claimed he would personally defend me in court, if he could do such a thing, but that the ramifications were too great no matter the principles I held so dear. I was handing out material that was illegal to even mail. I was telling women things only doctors are supposed to discuss. And above all, it was indecent in the opinion of most people. I introduced him to Mrs. Delacourt, hoping that would assuage his fears. The two most politically minded people I knew gravitated into an immediate repartee over lemonade and strawberry cake. He liked her, although he didn't want to. With a tone of admiration, Andrew called Gertrude an imposing figure.

Gertrude and I do our best to protect ourselves and the other women. Through Gertrude's special connections, word spreads about hygiene classes for women. She opens her own home to them—a tactical maneuver. No dark rooms or alleys that invite suspicion; instead, a respectable home in a respectable neighborhood, the least likely place in the world. We do, however, have the gatherings late in the evening.

The parlor where I once eavesdropped has become a den of rabblerousing once again. I didn't ask her to keep this a secret from my mother, but I know that she does. My mother has never confronted me.

I hold a Boyless Party every couple of months. Somehow, through a network of whispers, women—mostly working girls and poor mothers—discover the location. At first, only one or two women came. Now, the gatherings include five or more. Gertrude has some way of ensuring a small crowd.

The front porch light is always off. The women sneak into the yard and come through the back door. I greet them and point them through the kitchen toward the brightly lit meeting place. The parlor's unusually thick drapes block all light to the street. A passerby couldn't guess that several women settle into the room with hats pulled low near their faces. If the guests say anything at all, the girls speak in nervous, staccato sentences. That is, until Gertrude enters with a rolling cart filled with tea, coffee, and nibbles from the best French and Italian bakeries in town.

I begin my talk with a little game of catch first. The ball is a rubber inflated within an inch of its life. This makes the girls laugh, even the ones who refuse to touch it, and once the tension splinters, they are ready to listen. Anatomy first—quality medical-school posters showing the mysterious organs hidden behind our belly flesh. Some take notes on paper scraps from their handbags, others borrow the tablets and pencils Gertrude leaves in the room. Most listen intently. A rare cough breaks the silence while I continue my talk:

"You must learn where your clitoris is." (I point to a giant diagram of the external female organs.) "It's a critical key to satisfying relations. A very famous psychologist claims mature women should not only achieve but also prefer vaginal orgasms. When you find the right spot, you be the judge of how much he understands about female anatomy.

"You can buy rubbers and suppositories to kill the sperm at most drugstores. The vulcanized rubbers are stronger. Men last longer with those. Yes, I mean, during the act." (A box of these items makes its way around the room for inspection.)

"There are recipes for various douches that you could try, but they must be used right after the act." (I hold a stack of pamphlets.) "However, unless you plan to sling a douche bag over the shower curtain bar, I recommend the other methods."

"Pessaries fit over the neck of the womb. Advertisements state that they are used to correct a prolapsed uterus. That's not the only purpose. The rubber pessary blocks the male fluid from entering the uterus, especially when coated with a special jelly before insertion." (I share another box full of examples.) "Diaphragms are similar to pessaries but have a spring hinge that folds so they can be properly placed. They are not yet readily available here. You must be fitted by a doctor and taught to use them."

"If you haven't married yet, get a fake wedding ring. Most doctors won't tell you a thing if you don't have a husband. They wouldn't want to break a precious Comstock law, now would they?"

At the end, the bravest ones ask questions in front of the group. *Is it true there is a safe time each month? Why does the bosom become so sensitive? Does it hurt? Is this a venial or mortal sin?* Occasionally, a woman stays behind with an inquiry the rest don't need to hear. At these times, Gertrude sends me out with dishes to wash. There are connections in the city that it's best I can't name. My purpose, she says, is to ensure that no woman becomes so desperate in the first place.

WHATEVER THE FANATICAL cleanliness had done for Amy no longer worked. She needed a new distraction. She called several members of her family to ask if they had photographs she could borrow to scan. Amy had promised her Grandma Sunny that the family snapshots would all be archived in some way, and she was going to keep that vow.

There wasn't nearly the crowd at Twolly's that Saturday as there had been for her birthday. A few boxes and albums of snapshots had been left at the house for others to sort. After an early lunch of sandwiches and salads, the small group sat at the dining room table to go through what had been delivered. Amy's uncle Stephen and her mother Nora sat together on one side. Twolly's granddaughter Julie, without her four little monsters, sat on the other.

"Okay, everybody," Amy said from the head of the table, "I'm trying to get this into some kind of order, by decade if possible. If there's a date on a picture, great. If not, take your best guess. I didn't want to mix up everyone's pictures, so use the labeled envelopes."

The room was bright with laughter from the moment photographs started passing among their hands. They enjoyed unearthing forgotten stories, reminding each other of fun they'd had. Twolly's memory was unusually sharp, although a person's name occasionally escaped her.

"Oh, here's one of Mom and Amy," Stephen said.

Amy took the photo from her uncle. Her seven-year-old face puckered tightly in the foreground. Behind her, Sunny laughed. Her waving chopsticks brushed a fan of yellow on the still frame.

"Sweet and sour squid. I can still feel the texture in my mouth. That's the only weird food favorite of hers I never developed a taste for. Who took the picture?"

"My oldest. Here, see if there's more in the pile," Stephen said.

There were several other snapshots from that day, but the remaining ones were odd. No people, only shots of a backyard. Few mature trees dotted the landscape. They were all trimmed dramatically. There was no limb closer than fifteen feet to the ground.

"Your son captured Poppa's pruning skills." Amy frowned as she pushed the photos back to her uncle.

"Time for coffee?" Nora asked.

Wood groaned and fabric whispered as they stood up to scatter across the house. Everyone moved into the kitchen. The vacuum seal on a coffee bag gasped open. The scent of dark roasted beans drifted through the dining room.

Amy returned with a glass of milk and homemade pound cake. She began to sort through her great-aunt Twolly's two boxes, which were full of paper slips, postcards, and photos. Twolly had assured Amy that there was more to see, but it was separated and spread throughout the house. This was no surprise. In college, Twolly's dorm room had been a piggy short of a sty.

My dear old friend's snapshots were much older than the rest of her family's. The sepia tones captured shadows in a way that color photography never could match. I thought of Andrew's secret photographs of me, the curves of my body so much smoother because of the way he made light cascade on my flesh.

I looked over Amy's shoulder as she shuffled through the pile. I recognized Sunny as a little girl. She smiled wide and took the center at the front of any group shot. Twolly stood with her hands tightly clasped at her waist.

Amy peered closely at one of Sunny as a young woman with a man dressed in an army uniform from World War II. Their arms were wrapped tight around each other, and they looked into the other's eyes, not at the camera. Their pose was unusually intimate, nothing like the images I'd seen of women tucked under the awkward arms of men. Amy twisted her wrist. The date on the back was April 1942. That photograph caught a moment before a good-bye. Amy held her breath.

Back in the pile, the photo swept under a wave shifted by Amy's hands. The next one that surfaced to her attention was another of Sunny from the early 1940s. She held a child in her arms who wore a military dress hat too large for his head. The face was vaguely familiar, a baby Stephen. That one was thrown back as well.

Amy went to the other box and fished deep under the overlapping layers of paper. These were in color, ebbing through Amy's childhood and adolescence. She flicked through them frantically. She saw herself with cousins and her brother, with grown-ups who seemed to stand guard above her. The depth of her breathing showed she was anxious.

I recognized Jem the instant Amy nipped the shiny paper in her fingertips. His shaggy, clean hair hovered near his shoulders. He had a sincere smile. Amy's chin was turned toward him, but she looked as if she were slowly pivoting her head to face the hidden photographer. Her smile wasn't for the camera, though. It was for Jem, soft with adoration.

Amy breathed sharp, as if she'd caught his scent.

"Oh, sweetheart. What a precious picture." Nora stood behind her. "His hair made me nostalgic for the sixties."

"I know, Mom. Excuse me. I'll be back in a second."

She rushed upstairs. Amy dashed through Twolly's bedroom and shut herself in the bathroom. Sitting on the closed toilet, she drew her knees to her chest and ducked her forehead down. She inhaled hard, and her shoulders trembled noiselessly. The essence of Jem hovered around her like a cloud from a sudden summer storm. After a few minutes of tears, she reached for a tissue. The door swung open.

"Oh, excuse me." Twolly ducked behind the door. Then, as a second thought, she peeked in.

Amy wiped her face on her shoulders and jumped up to flush the toilet. "That's okay. I was done anyway." Her voice was a warble.

Twolly stepped inside. "What's wrong?"

"I'm fine."

"I have my glasses on. Let's go in my room. Just the two of us."

Amy followed her out. Twolly locked her bedroom door, then sat in a dainty slipper chair. "I miss her, too, honey."

"It's not that. Well, not just that." Amy pulled at the edge of her shorts. "If I ask you something, do you promise to be honest?"

Twolly's milky brow creased above her serious eyes. "Yes."

"Did Grandma truly love Poppa?"

"Of course she did. What kind of question is that?"

"I don't know. I was looking at a picture of her with her first husband," Amy began, her inflection clearly indicating that she'd known this fact all her life, "and it made me think of how I remembered her with Poppa Fin. They always seemed distant. She didn't seem, I don't know, affectionate with him."

Twolly grinned a little. "Our generation didn't paw each other like yours does."

Amy scowled at her. "No, that's not what I mean. It's as if something was missing for her. Did she settle for Poppa?"

"My baby sister settled for no one. You have to understand, honey, times were different. Those war years tore out people's hearts. That's something you won't read in history books. For every boy who died over there, someone back home missed him in a way that nothing could fix. No one could fix. Sunny grieved over—oh my goodness, what was his name?—why, I can see his face, but his name—"

"Mitchell."

"Yes, of course. My sister grieved over Mitchell for years before she was ready to marry again."

"So why did she choose Poppa?"

"Plenty of reasons. He came from a good family. Our fathers were business acquaintances. He was well educated, sincere, handsome. He was protective"—Twolly noticed Amy's expression—"although he might have taken it too far at times. Sunny felt safe with him. He was a good provider. That meant something once. They had things in common. They shared the same values."

"How did she deal with losing Mitchell?"

"She had her tough times. She lived with us when he went into the service, then afterward. My children were still very young. Stephen was a baby. When that telegram came, well, you think the shock would leave you speechless, but she fell apart on the spot. It was even worse for her because there was no body to bury. She obsessed about that, about the way he died, all in pieces. You know, she had begged him not to enlist. As an only son, he could have been deferred. But Mitchell, he had principles." Twolly wiped her lashes.

"They were wonderful together, Sunny and Mitchell. He was so respectful of her, a gentle man, and she thought he was an angel. For months after he died, she went through the motions of life. She knew when to smile, when to laugh, but there was no heart in it. Slowly, she decided to be grateful for the time they'd had together. She worked hard to remember their happiness. By the time she met Fin, she was tired of being alone. He was a good, decent man."

"Did Grandma ever talk to you about what it was like having that first baby, Mitchell's baby?"

Twolly squinted at her suspiciously. "No. She worried most about him not having a father, I know that. And Fin did his duty. He was a good father. And Stephen was a comfort for her, really. He got her through those months when her husband was at war, then through those years after he was killed. She always had a piece of Mitchell in Stephen."

Amy bit the inside of her cheek. "Did she ever regret having him?"

"Of course not. What kind of question is that?" She got up and sat next to Amy on the bed. She placed her thin hand on her great-niece's knee. "What's the problem, Amy?"

"I guess I'm trying to work out who they were. As if I just realized I barely knew them at all."

"Baby, if there's one thing I've learned, it's that people are full of surprises, no matter how long you've known them. All you have now are your memories and those of whoever is left. What's that saying? The dead tell no secrets?"

"The dead tell no lies."

TWOLLY LIVED in her parents' home in the same room she had as a girl. Her double bed, unmade of course, was topped with a stunning white quilt that was stitched together with rows of flying birds. A thicker, more homespun quilt lay in a pile on the floor. Her pillows were arranged in a horseshoe so that she had something to cling to no matter how she turned in the night. All of her furniture was only a few years old and very expensive, proof that her daddy had struck it rich enough to be almost garish. Twolly crowded her solid bird's-eye maple nightstand with a lamp and books bound in leather. The armoire stood open with dresses and coats dancing wildly from their wooden hangers. A trail of shoes and hatboxes led to her vanity, which was covered in scarves, face powders, bottles of perfume, hairpins, and stray candy wrappers.

The mirror above the vanity shimmered.

I had been dead almost five months. It was the middle of December. I had adjusted to seeing my own image again, my form a shapely haze of light, an interaction between what I was and the silver of the looking glass. Seeing a photo was entirely different, a jolting reminder of the life I didn't forget. Twolly had a snapshot of the two of us on a seesaw tucked into the frame of the mirror. The presence of the photo made me think she missed me, at least thought of me now and then. I was comforted that I had not been forgotten—or shut away from her memory.

I spent a week with Twolly. She seemed restless, although she was busy all the time. Her mornings were spent reading the local newspaper and writing long letters. She watched their housekeeper set the table for the noon meal and ate slowly as she listened to her mother's gossip. There were afternoon visits for coffee with lady friends who were her age, several years married, and in various stages of pregnancy or postpartum. Twolly absently patted the little ones who were drawn to her whimsical brown eyes. Before supper, she played checkers or worked crossword puzzles with her youngest sister, Sunny, then eleven years old. Her father was home to eat with the family on those nights. A few moments of conversation were devoted to Twolly's search for a husband. On two separate evenings, two different young men came to sit in the parlor with her. Twolly was cordial, but they bored her. Neither could have sensed it, masked as her indifference was by her manners.

After her bath and a generous slathering of skin cream, she crawled into her unmade bed and read for an hour or two. Her enormous alarm clock was silent. There was no reason for her to measure time, no reason to get up before her internal rhythms stirred her conscious.

On the second to last night I was there, Sunny burst into Twolly's room holding her hands open. "Sissie, it broke. Fix it, please."

"What broke?" Twolly didn't look up.

"The pretty necklace you made for me." Her cotton nightgown swished as she squirmed within it. I smelled Ivory soap, peppermint, and tree bark.

Twolly went into the cedar chest at the end of her bed and pulled out a wooden box I remembered well. Inside were her jewelry-making tools and supplies. She returned to her bed and tilted the bedside lamp's shade to cast more light near her. The chain of Sunny's necklace was snapped into three pieces. The topaz stones below a delicate silver pendant had not been damaged.

"I'm glad you didn't go to New York. I would have no one to fix it," Sunny said.

Weeks before our graduation, Twolly had been invited to study at a prestigious art school, an honor almost as rare as a woman getting into Harvard. She had apparently turned down the offer.

"There are jewelers in this town, Sunny," Twolly said.

"None as good as you. What's under those clothes?"

Twolly looked. "Something I haven't opened yet."

"Who's it from, and can I open it?"

"None of your business, and no."

Under a layer of laundry, there was a package addressed to Twolly, the handwriting my own. The package I had intended to mail her the day I died. For whatever reason, she could not look inside.

"What happened to your necklace?" Twolly poked inside her box.

"I caught it on a branch."

"How on earth did you do that?"

"I went to hang upside down, and it swung away from me."

"When was this?"

"A few minutes ago."

"It's pitch-dark out, and time for bed."

"I know." Sunny flopped stomach first on Twolly's bed. "I was wondering what it felt like to be a bat."

"You are such a peculiar little thing." She stopped her search for a moment. "That's why Razi liked you."

I had not been in a room—in a house—near a block—in almost three months where I could hear someone who loved me speak my name. Not since the séance that Grams had demanded and I had attended. Not since Andrew left for Yale. My edges began to shake.

"I liked her, too," Sunny said into a pillow. "Do you miss her?"

The box shut with a *thup.* "Yes. Very much."

"Does her old beau?"

Doors, drawers, and lids slammed closed at once. The night was not particularly cold, but they watched the first exhales after the shock condense before their eyes. The sisters looked at each other.

"That's a doozy of a draft," Twolly said as lightheartedly as she could.

"I'll say." Sunny studied the room for another explanation.

"I'll need to use my little soldering tool to fix your chain. It'll have to wait until tomorrow." Twolly went to put the box back in its place. A slip of paper pushed out of the chest as she shifted possessions around inside.

"All right, then. Good night." The little girl kissed Twolly on the cheek before she left. She opened the door, pausing at the threshold. "Bury deep in the blankets tonight. There might be spooks about, Twolly." She ran down the hall, laughing loud enough to silence fright.

My dear friend turned off the light and tucked herself inside a cave of layered cotton. I sensed that she was awake and concentrating, in prayer. Twolly believed in such things. When her breathing slowed and shallowed, I picked up what had fallen to the floor.

I read as well in starlight as in sunshine. The postcard was stamped September 15, 1929. There was a picture of Boston Harbor on the front. On the back:

> *Twolly,*
>
> *Sightseeing now. Visiting cousins. I am well. I will let you know my new address soon. Not settled yet.*
>
> *Regards, APO*

Andrew. My Andrew. I wondered what he was doing that night, months after his visit to Boston. Was it snowing outside his dormitory? Was he reading in a cold room or smoking a cigarette with a crack in the window? Or was he in the company of friends? In the company of a nice young woman? Possibly, was he thinking of me?

Twolly's room became frigid again, and she buried herself deep in her blankets in response. I tried to ice away the memory of the burn of his touch, the warmth of my affection for him, the heat of my heart that no longer beat.

I had no such success that evening.

I DECIDED to spend the night with Twolly. Amy went to her parents' house. She was clearly exhausted and fragile when she hugged her great-aunt good-bye and promised to cook her a lovely breakfast in the morning.

Twolly's night sitter helped her upstairs and into the bathroom. When I heard the shower running, I went into the dining room to glance through the boxes again. Perhaps there was a postcard or letter from Andrew somewhere among Twolly's collection. I poured out everything from her boxes and flicked the photographs back inside. She had a sentimental streak, and she was a pack rat. If there was a hint about Andrew, I would find it. And then, wedged under the inside flap of one old brown box, a telegram.

V893 12=LAFAYETTE LOU 763 R 1940 JAN 19 AM 8 43
MRS LEONARD LAMBERT=
10001 MYRTLE PLACE BLVD LAFAYETTE LOU=
TWOLLY EMMALINE DIED. I AM GOING TO PAY MY RESPECTS. MAY I VISIT YOU NEXT WEEK. I PLAN TO TAKE THE TRAIN INTO LAFAYETTE. PLEASE SEND REPLY TO WESTERN UNION OFFICE ABOVE. SORRY I HAVE BEEN OUT OF TOUCH=
REGARDS=
APO.

The return address was in Philadelphia. What a coincidence, I thought. In the year that telegram was sent, 1940, the Andrew O'Connell I had mistaken for my own was living in that city. That man had been named a partner in his firm that year, too—Fitzhugh, Kohl, and O'Connell—and he had married a young woman from a prominent Pennsylvania family on Christmas Eve.

That winter, why was my Andrew in the city? Perhaps he went to visit Warren and Anna Tripp, his oldest friends. Or perhaps he went to see distant relatives who had emigrated from Boston and settled there decades before. Could he have been only passing through, a stop on his trip to Emmaline's funeral? Maybe he decided, on the spur of the moment, to visit Twolly, who would be only a two-hour train ride away from New Orleans.

Or did he live in or near Philadelphia at the time? Perhaps he was an attorney in a nearby town, or a banker, or a photographer. Moving through their separate lives, did the two Andrews—mine and the stranger—ever cross paths, bump into one another while buying a newspaper, ask the other for the time? Had my Andrew become an anonymous man among many?

Anonymous. Only a few letters I had sent under my pen name, Barrett Burrat, had yielded replies. I heard from Jenna

O'Connell, a remote cousin, and Tulane University, which had no record of his whereabouts after he received his bachelor's degree in June 1929. To cover other possibilities, I had written every other Ivy League law school besides Yale. I was surprised to receive rather prompt responses from each, but was disappointed to learn he had attended none of them.

Although I had little to go on, I knew he had not vanished. The telegram was proof he was still alive a decade after he left New Orleans.

When I returned the full box to the place Amy had left it, Twolly passed through the dining room and went into the kitchen. The family had cleaned up everything from their meals and snacks. There was a warm patch of air by the dishwasher. Twolly filled a teakettle and found a bag of ginger snaps in her cabinet.

She stood there oblivious to me, nibbling a cookie in that mousy way she considered savoring. The letter I had sent her weeks before, on faked Tulane stationery, was near the phone, opened but unanswered. I was curious to know why she wouldn't reply to the phantom alumni representative who wanted stories of her college days. When Twolly glanced at the clock, I pushed the letter to the middle of the counter. Perhaps the letter had become a familiar object, something she now ignored.

I wanted to talk to her so badly. I wanted to know if her life had been as happy as it seemed to be. Did she enjoy being a mother? What kind of man had her husband been, and did he deserve her? What did she do to fill blank hours? Did she ever think about what she gave up by not going to study in New York?

I heard the kettle's whistle long before it became audible to her. I flinched as it screeched into her range. Twolly moved slowly under a lavender silk nightgown and well-loved yellow plissé robe. Her ankles were chicken thin above the white ballet-style slippers as the treads squeaked against the tile floor. Spicy orange tea warmed the room as she filled her cup. Twolly stacked four ginger snaps on a bone china saucer and put it gently on a tray along with her tea.

Nearly every light was still on downstairs when she settled in her den and turned on the television. She thumbed through a *Reader's Digest* until the ten o'clock news started. By the time the sports segment came on, she had finished her snack and was beginning to drowse in her overstuffed chair.

I hovered on the ottoman next to her small, straight shins, which gleamed in the lamplight. "Twolly, I can't believe your old bag of bones is still around." Although only another like myself could have heard my voice, I wanted to speak aloud, in case, in some way, Twolly could understand. "You remember how much fun we had? I hope so. We were such a pair."

Her eyelids slipped closed with the grace of butterfly wings. I lifted her cheaters with the help of the air and placed them on the end table. She pursed her lips, then relaxed them, as if she'd given someone an affectionate kiss. I told myself it was meant for me.

"Look at you. You're still healthy. You're looked after and content. You're not lonesome, thank goodness. It's lonely being dead, Twolly. Jeepers creepers, you wouldn't believe it. Everyone is always going beyond, once this all becomes too much—or not enough.

"I've had fun, or couldn't you guess? You wouldn't believe how many books I've read and how much I've seen. I could diagnose any disease or teach the history of almost any period. I know Italian and German and French now, so I could be a translator. For a long time, I helped the ones like me. I taught them what they needed to survive. I mean, you don't have to eat or drink or remember to breathe or anything like that. But you have to learn how to get around without tearing things apart. How to deal with having so much time. How to stay entertained. Once you learn that you shouldn't cause others pain."

I remembered Andrew's eyes, their depth and brightness drained, in the weeks before he left New Orleans for destinations unknown. The night I saw the light disappear.

"Did he send you a letter now and then? Did you ever see him again, and speak of me when you did? Tell me it didn't hurt so bad. Tell me you laughed. Please tell me he knew how much I loved him. Truly, I loved no one more than my Andrew."

I'd spoken his name aloud, not in a thought. My form rippled into vaporized gooseflesh as I heard my memory answer in his voice, *Razi,* that whisper of content, as if he were breathing me in and out in equal measure.

My hand was suspended above her knee. I couldn't touch her. "Where is he, Twolly?"

Twolly snuffled and woke herself up. She blinked rapidly and raised her right hand to her face. "My glasses." Her left hand passed slowly over the end table and found her cheaters where I'd placed them. During a wide, feline yawn, she clicked off the television and the lamp.

She walked into the kitchen and began to turn off lights on her way to bed. Kitchen, dining room, foyer, overhead den light. She walked into her sitting room and stood in front of her table of photographs. "God bless my family and friends and may they always know I love them. May you all rest in peace. Amen." She blew a kiss to the room before she turned off the light. Then she inched toward her bedroom, humming a tune from our college days, and gently closed her door.

NEL HAD BEEN between for eight months when he decided to learn the languages in which his favorite operas were written. He figured if Ralph Waldo Emerson could learn a handful of languages without the benefit of recordings, he could do it with them.

In the silence of night in the public library, Lionel sat with headphones floating around what would have been his head, repeating phrases. We slipped into high schools and used their listening labs. Lionel studied textbooks to learn to read and write the language as well. He practiced constantly. His accent was flawless, unmistakably Italian.

He made me go with him to see Federico Fellini movies so he could test his new tongue. Only the surreal ones amused me. So he wouldn't cheat and read the subtitles, Nel suspended popcorn boxes in front of his face to block the bottom of the screen. For months, he didn't listen to a single Italian opera—although it tortured him—in preparation for his virgin experience.

"It'll be like figuring out the words to 'Louie, Louie.' You can mimic every sound, but you don't have a clue what he's singing," Nel said. "Now imagine that a switch flips in your brain. The words become clear. You're not just mouthing sound anymore. Wouldn't that be spectacular?"

"Copacetic," I said.

It was February when he decided he was ready for his first listen. We filtered through the front door of the library with the best CD collection. He found his favorite opera and nervously fiddled with buttons and knobs to get a disc player to start. In the meantime, I settled with a book in front of a window that no one had covered with a curtain. As I read, the sounds of the piece were thin, filtered by his headphones. Within minutes, I heard him crying.

The sound, the timbre, was not of the ones between. It was within the range of human hearing.

"Nel, what's wrong?"

"I understand every word. It's beautiful."

Bathed by the glow of the streetlights outside, Nel lay flat on the floor, spread-eagled, sobbing like a jilted lover. The CD jacket was next to his hip. His chest heaved as he bellowed his own rendition of an aria in *La Traviata*. His singing was awful, but so heartfelt that I dared not make a joke.

I sat next to him on the taupe-carpeted floor, inches away from a twisted staple and nail clipping. He wiped away tears that weren't there. He sniffled although nothing clogged his nose. Now and then, he flicked his rakish hands into the air to accentuate a series of rousing notes. Each line of lyrics was sung off-key, but no one could have suspected he wasn't a native speaker.

Nel writhed along the fine line between agony and ecstasy. I could hear it in his voice. I could see it in the way he smiled as his big hazel eyes squinted against phantom tears. He was in pain. What he was feeling required—needed—a body to complete it, to make it whole.

I hated opera, but as I sat there with him, I realized that I, too, could understand every word. Within earshot of Nel's lessons for so long, I never noticed I was learning. The language had seeped into me.

"Alfredo, Alfredo, di questo core non puoi comprendere tutto l'amore," Violetta sang to the lover she'd left. *Alfred, Alfred, little canst thou fathom the love within my heart for thee.*

I noticed the decorations near the children's section. Hearts arched over a display of books featuring holiday projects and young teen romances. Even in that light, I could see the pink bulletin board paper, rosy doilies behind smooching cartoon people, and blushing cupids. I didn't turn away fast enough—a background of blooms—the taste of icing on my lips—the sound of his voice telling me for the first time—

A rush turned me cold under my gossamer edge. A loneliness that I dodged with distraction during the day hummed in time with the music's vibration.

"I miss it, Razi." Nel settled down. His eyelids appeared puffy. The opera continued.

"What?" The particles at my throat were tight.

"Before. The way the music would make my skin prickle and my heart race. How some part of me had to move when I heard it—my foot, or my fingers, or my head. I felt it, you know? Not just in here," he said, tapping a loose fist against his chest. "And then there are the memories connected to music. The songs that played during an evening with a good bottle of wine and a good lover. Walking home through the humid streets of this city after I've left him warm in his bed, hearing whatever came out of the cars driving by. The crickets." He stared up at the ceiling covered in ugly acoustical tiles. The space between us filled with red wine, musky cologne, a blast of exhaust, and mint—the smells of a wonderful night he could recount in excruciating detail if he wanted to. "That's what I wanted. I wanted to feel this music all the time. I shouldn't have been a human resources director. I did the wrong thing. I did what I thought I should do, not what I wanted. And I can't take it back."

I burst into arid tears. My edges shook, but without breath, without a body, the release was hollow, incomplete. I hadn't allowed myself to feel that way since Andrew left for New Haven. Or when I thought, at the time, he had left for New Haven. Seventy-one years, five months, nevertheless. Nel sat up and reached his arms out to me. His gesture was so automatic that he didn't think to stop himself.

I missed Andrew so badly in that moment that I forgot to raise my hand to keep Nel away. The instant our vaporous forms met, there was a second of solace—an embrace meant to soothe. The sensation was only a memory of what comfort felt like. We pulled away simultaneously, our forms agitated, disturbed. We had mingled what should have never had contact.

We glanced at each other. He was crying again.

"I miss him," I said.

"I know you do, honey. Wouldn't you feel better if you talked? After all this time? You can trust me." Nel knew Andrew as a footnote to my life, but I knew Nel understood that he filled chapters.

"There is something I want to tell you. Last week, I received an obituary from someone who has sent me correspondence about Andrew over the years. The man in the obituary—he was born in Illinois. He isn't my Andrew."

Lionel gave me a puzzled stare.

"My Andrew was born in New Orleans. I'm certain. This man I've followed, he has Andrew's name, he lived Andrew's life, but he isn't mine. He isn't the man I loved. I've been mistaken."

"Not once in all these years did you bother to see him? In person?" Nel said. "What harm could one visit have done?"

"You have no idea, Lionel." My voice was weak but ominous. On any other night, he might have pushed me to explain myself, but he was clearly exhausted with his own pain. No matter how curious he was, he didn't have strength to interrogate me. I met my friend's full hazel eyes. "I do wonder what happened to my Andrew."

"Without you." He reached his hand along the floor between us. I reached toward him. We didn't touch. We couldn't. It was pointless.

❧

THE MORNING AFTER Amy's family met to sort pictures, Amy made a wonderful breakfast of French toast, fresh blueberry and peach salad, and strong coffee for her great-aunt.

Twolly left the table, quite full, and went straight to her bedroom, where she began to paw through the drawers in her lingerie chest. She tossed at least four decades' worth of old dainties to the floor. Even when we were young, she was notorious for hiding things from herself. She muttered tame curses under her breath as she searched for items she was convinced were there.

Amy stared into a wide closet packed with boxes. The clothes bar dipped under the weight of Twolly's wardrobe. Every shoe was lined up on the floor, but not a single pair matched. Amy sighed as if exhausted. *Just start,* she muttered to herself. She began to remove boxes, unlabeled, and stack them on the floor.

"Oh, honey," Twolly said, "please make sure you remember how they were put in there. I'll never find anything out of order."

"Yes, ma'am." Amy almost smiled. "Any luck, Aunt Twolly?"

"I'm not finished yet. I know those photos were in here a few years ago."

Amy stretched deep into the closet and wrestled a large wooden jewelry chest from the space. I had seen it before, when Twolly was still young, in the bedroom of her parents' home. Amy placed it on a pile of boxes and began to pick through the drawers. It was full of quality costume jewelry, pristine Bakelite bracelets, tiny empty cardboard boxes, receipts, coins, hairpins—

"Aunt Twolly, this is a gold mine."

Twolly turned to her great-niece as a lacy panty twirled off her finger. She squinted through her cheaters. She was still looking when Amy lifted a delicate silver chain interrupted by clear peridot rectangles.

"You did this. I recognize your style." The drawer was full of similar pieces.

Twolly returned to her exploration. "I did enjoy that period of my jewelry making." She slipped a drawer from its place and put it on her bed. "You can take that."

"I couldn't," Amy said.

"Please, honey, take it. The whole box, in fact. You're the only person I know who'd wear anything in there these days."

"But wouldn't your children—"

"Wouldn't appreciate it. I went through that not too long ago anyway, after Sunny died. We had shared jewelry from time to time. Your mother and aunt got what they wanted." Twolly turned back to her sorting.

Amy returned the necklace to its place. "Thank you so much. I'll give back what I don't think I'll wear."

"Keep it."

Before she closed the drawer, Amy gently raked behind the thick row of necklaces and found two small boxes. The first was empty. The second I recognized.

The hinge of the box groaned as Amy lifted the lid. A faint pansy scent escaped the darkness, and Andrew's scent escaped me. There was his ring, circled by the color of his eyes. I refused the desire to touch it, trace the inscription, return to the questions—

Twolly exhaled and watched the air turn gray and thick

under her nose. Amy shivered from top to bottom, quick as a seizure. Condensation on the old, drafty windows turned to ice. The two women looked at each other as they slowly lowered the items in their hands.

"Loretta!" Twolly clutched her bare arms. "Where is she? The sitters always play with that thermostat. Loretta!"

"I'll take care of it." Amy shut the narrow drawer, the ring box hidden.

I warmed my old friend again as I wondered how she had come to possess and keep the ring I left behind. Twolly of all people would have figured out that the wide, masculine band was meant for him.

By the time Amy returned, Twolly had found what she searched for. "Look. Here are some pictures of your great-aunts and grandmother." They sat on the bed, their hips almost touching.

The first several photos were of Twolly and her sisters, their skirts long and hair growing out. Fashion after the Crash. The following ones, stacked underneath, were from a time before. A photo of Newcomb's campus, the tiny oak trees bushlike on the perimeter of the grounds. A group shot from one of her classes, vague but familiar faces staring back. I saw Anna Whitcomb before she became Mrs. Warren Tripp.

Twolly lingered a moment as she touched a photo of her and me. In the snapshot, she kept her end of the seesaw anchored down while I reached for the clouds.

Then, the second to last one, facedown, was turned upright. "What a terrific picture." Amy studied the image.

I was asleep on the divan, but not alone. My body nested into his side. Our heads touched. My blond locks framed his excellent profile. His arms circled me loosely, as if I'd been held tight earlier and his slumber compromised the hold. I remembered: a shutter click had awakened me. Before my eyes focused, the culprit was gone. Drowsy, I patted his chest. He awoke slowly, yawned, hugged me close. *Time to go home, Cinderaziela,* he said.

"Aunt Twolly," Amy said. "Who's this?" She held out the photograph.

Twolly's reach was hesitant, but she accepted it. She skimmed the back, then looked at the picture. "That's Razi. She was one of my most cherished friends. She's been gone so long." Twolly paused. "What a strange coincidence. I dreamed about her last night. We were playing marbles outside, Razi and me. In the dream, it was Good Friday, 1927, the day it rained so bad and everyone was afraid the levees were going to break for sure and drown New Orleans. That was the year of the big flood, you know. Anyway, in the dream, we were in her backyard. She had a circle, and I had one. We kept shooting into each other's space until all of the marbles were mixed up. Then a big gust of wind and rain came, and they all blew away. A clap of thunder made us jump. She looked at me and said, 'Hey, Twolls, what are we doing out here in this weather? I think we've lost our marbles.' And she laughed at her joke. That's so odd. I haven't dreamed of her in a long time." Twolly stroked my sepia chin.

"Who's the young man she's with?"

"She had so many beaux. Boys noticed the adventure in her eyes, and they liked what they saw. And she liked their variety. Goodness, she was bold with them. She'd disappear at a dance and come back with her lipstick rubbed off from kissing." Twolly gave the photo to Amy.

"Look at them, how they're holding each other, how they fit." Amy touched the points where our bodies met. "He must have been special. Don't you remember his name?"

"So many years ago." Twolly paused, then flinched. "It was Andrew." His unmistakable essence escaped her, its rush intense.

"Andrew what?"

"It's been ages. I can't remember everything."

"Do you remember what he was like?"

"He was a decent, well-mannered boy. Respectful. Smart, very smart. He was supposed to be a lawyer." She smiled, but it was guarded and sad. His scent mellowed. Twolly suddenly stood up. "Ooh, that cane syrup I had with breakfast coated my bowels too fast. This old plumbing."

I KISSED forty-seven boys. Twenty-seven—including my first, Jimmy Reynolds—received nothing more than a quick peck. The rest, I'll admit, I necked with in varying degrees. Of those remaining, fourteen were seriously kissed and nothing more (although ten tried to go further), eight explored north, and three reached south. Of the last five, each touched me bare, although only three saw me that way. With two, I almost had to heed Mrs. Sanger's advice. The funny boy who was good with his hands was too eager, and I never got to call him Champagne in person. And the shell-shocked doughboy with the furry chest was easily distracted by noise, especially those indistinguishable between pain and pleasure. That leaves only Andrew, who knew the color of my other cheeks in daylight.

Truth be told, my hands were far more curious than theirs. I sought texture in odd places. A loose cuff invited me to the smooth underside of a wrist. From a tilted neck, the silken cord that begins behind the ear and disappears in the shoulder. Spread wide, my hands traveled the spine—slate flat blades, tumulous ribs, sinew levees, square waist. Hard cube knees under my grip. The collapse as the surface of my hand moved horizontal between hips. A moor on the chest, sometimes full, sometimes sparse, nourished above the thick red knot of vessels underneath.

When one delighted in those soft and secret places, I knew. I felt his breath and blood rise, and I echoed him, embraced his solid urgent rush. I was alive, aware, ignited, unafraid, my flesh a surge of pleasure, and when the crest gave way to the fall, I flowed. With them, my body reveled in its demanding corporal want. The sensations were their own rewards. I expected nothing else.

On occasion, one would remind me of others before. Suddenly a boy's hand I held was that of one who preceded him—the turn of his knuckles, the brush of his shoulders—and for that instant, the memory of a distant beau was as strong as the grip of the new one. At times, the recollection put the old name on my tongue, and I would have to excuse away the mistake. I could not admit that my senses were sometimes tricked, that a present moment could summon so convincingly, seamlessly, the past.

Then there was Andrew. He let me touch him with a patience, an anticipation, that no other would. I was free to run my fingertips, the flats of my hands, my lips, across his skin with maddening slowness. Through instinct as much as his requests, I learned to change pressure, direction, speed, when his breathing altered, his muscles rolled. I could not feel separate from him when his heat blended with my own.

Much to my delight, he turned to me for the same exploration. Every nerve danced to meet his touch until my entire body positively hummed along with the harmony he created. The pleasure would culminate in bursts or in waves, and he discovered my reaction was rarely predictable but always savored.

I craved a closeness with him that I never had with anyone. The rise under my skin wasn't only blood and oxygen. An ascent, weightless as dawn, seized my body when he looked at me, when I thought of him, when we touched, and I called it love. My Andrew, who kissed my life wide open, insisted that our union reached far beyond our bodies, if only I could see.

❧

SCOTT WAS ASLEEP and Amy was going through her family pictures when the phone rang. She dashed into the kitchen to grab it, cursing that she'd forgotten to turn off the ringer. The answering machine picked up. She let it play through Scott's outgoing message.

"Hey, it's me, Chloe. Anyone still up? I know—"

"I'm awake," Amy said once the phone was at her ear. "Is something wrong?"

"Just calling to say hello."

Amy twisted her lips and squinted her eyes. "How's the new job?"

"Great. I'm working a ton of overtime on this database project, but for some reason, I don't mind. I think I finally love what I do. Oh, guess what? They're sending me to a conference in New Orleans in late October. The muckety-mucks get big hard-ons around here about professional development."

"That's more than three months away." Amy sounded disappointed. "Will you have time to visit?"

"Aims—please. Do you think I can sit through three days of burned hotel coffee, salty cookies, and active listening?"

"Then that's a yes."

"They'd have to get all Clockwork Orange on me. Strap me down and put drops in my eyes. What are you up to?"

"Work mainly. I went to my Aunt Twolly's last weekend to collect some family pictures."

"How'd it go?"

"Fine."

"You did okay? I know it must have been hard, what with losing your grandparents so recently. And considering what he did with your grandma's things."

"Well, we just have to get over it, don't we?"

"I think I'd want to hang on to what was left as long as I could, you know?"

"He was a peculiar man. You know that," Amy said.

"He was an eccentric. Guess it goes with the territory."

"Maybe if he'd taught aerospace engineering or psychology, but he didn't. Composition and rhetoric, how ordinary. Anyway, there's no use dwelling on things I can't figure out. It's done. Time to move on."

"Do you still miss your grandma a lot?"

"Yes, Chloe, I do."

"So what's the deal with the family project?" Chloe took the hint from Amy's curt tone. "You're collecting pictures and making copies?"

"Of what's left. Why?"

"Are you doing that scrapbook thing? News articles and stickers and locks of hair and whatnot? They must do it for the rubber cement fumes."

Amy grinned. "Digital photos. I'm using the marvels of modern technology so the whole family can have copies."

"Hell, one day, some moron will figure out how to put chips in everyone's heads so they don't forget a damn thing. Imagine—family history like you've never known it before. We won't need pictures then."

"Collective memory without the mystery," Amy said.

"That's so Carl Jung meets Silicon Valley or something."

"You can write the program to make it happen."

"No, thanks. Sometimes forgetting is a good thing."

Amy stared at her reflection in the microwave door. "Absolutely."

SEVERAL DAYS had passed since Amy's weekend with Twolly and her family. One evening, Scott found her in the dining room with their computer and a scanner on the table. She flipped through one of many envelopes of pictures that she'd taken home with her. Scott had a small envelope in his hand as well.

"The people we bought this house from—was their last name Burrat?"

"No." She didn't look up.

I had not checked the mail that day. Responses to my letters about Andrew had been so sparse. Scott ran his finger along the flap's edge. When I glanced, I saw Benjamin Beeker's name on the return address, handwritten. I still awaited replies from Twolly and Warren Tripp Jr., and hoped that the batch I'd sent to O'Connells in Philadelphia might prove fruitful.

"I don't think we have any neighbors with that name either," Scott said.

"No."

"It's a personal letter, I think. Someone must have the wrong address."

Amy quickly reordered the photos in her hand.

"How's the project coming along?" he asked.

"Kind of slow. I haven't figured out exactly how to organize everything yet." She slipped the photos back into their place. "Are you going to bed?"

"Soon. It's almost eleven. What about you?"

"I might stay up for a while."

"Okay."

She ducked her face near the computer screen and clicked away at an even pace.

"Aims, I'd like to know about your visit. You didn't tell me anything."

"What do you want to know?"

"Well, how are your parents, for starters."

"Dad sprained his knee during a closet cleaning mishap, and Mom is agonizing over color choices for the master bathroom."

"No where-are-the-grandnestlings-for-my-empty-nest jabs?"

"One."

"How's the greatest Great-Aunt Twolly?"

"Moving more slowly in body but not in mind."

"And how was it, going through all those old pictures?"

"Fine. We had a few laughs, and Aunt Twolly got to tell old stories."

"It wasn't upsetting?"

"Why should it have been upsetting?"

"Well, you were there because of what you promised your grandmother. It must have been a little sad."

"Is that what you want to know about the weekend? If I sat around the table wringing my hands and bawling my eyes out?"

"That's not what I meant."

"Then what did you mean?"

"Honey, I know there's something going on in your head. I know what it means when you start keeping the house so neat. Something is bothering you, and it doesn't seem to be getting any better. I want to help."

"There's nothing you can do. But I appreciate your concern."

Scott flushed at the condescension. "How am I supposed to respond to that?"

"By leaving me alone."

"I've given you nothing but space." He leaned over the table closer to her. "I haven't pried into the reason why there isn't a speck of dust or a germ on any surface in the entire house. But I'm tired of it now. I'm tired of worrying about you. I'm tired of forced conversations and attempts to get your attention. I've tried to be understanding, but that hasn't done a bit of good."

"You don't know what I'm dealing with."

"No. I don't. So why won't you tell me? I'm your husband. Who are you going to talk to, if not me?"

"I want to work this out on my own."

"Work what out? What?"

"I don't expect you to understand. A lot of complicated—memories—came up after they died. Things I hadn't thought about in a long time."

"Like what? Were you molested or something?"

"Don't be ridiculous."

"Then what are you talking about?"

"You know how you can hear a song that you haven't heard in a long time, and you suddenly remember being somewhere or with someone when that song played? It's something you haven't thought about in years. But you remember it very, very clearly. You can feel it. For me, it wasn't a song. It was pictures. Pictures I hadn't seen in so long that I nearly forgot their meanings."

"You haven't told me the problem. You've only told me what started it."

"I don't want to talk about this anymore. Why don't you go to bed?"

"Stop shutting me out," he said.

"Don't shout at me."

"Put yourself in my place for ten seconds." He gripped the top edge of a chair. "How would you feel if I did this to you? It's like our lives stopped after your grandparents died. I'm sorry you lost your grandparents in such a short time. I know how much you loved your Grandma Sunny. And I know you loved your grandfather, too, in some way, and that it must be really hard to forgive him for what he did to your grandma's things or for being so overprotective or for whatever grudge you hold against him. But that's not the problem. I know it. You're trying to create order in a life that wasn't chaos to begin with. Why? Whatever it is, it's shut you off from me."

Scott took a quick breath. In the moment he paused, a wisp of Jem's scent hung in the air, brief as a banished thought.

"When was the last time we watched a movie together?" Scott asked. "Or ate a meal at the same time? What about a conversation? I'm not even talking about the big one you've avoided that starts with a *B* and ends with a *Y*. And oh yes, while I'm at it, let me be predictably trite enough to wonder when we last had sex."

Amy sat with her arms folded against her chest. Her blue-green eyes squinted at a corner of the computer screen.

"Fight back."

"I don't want to fight with you."

"Then talk to me."

She finally looked up at him. "I can't."

For a moment, they stared at each other. Losing his temper wasn't a natural reaction for him. The air started to cool almost immediately, despite Amy's curt refusal to tell him what she hid so well. As the room settled, Jem's essence rose powerful as chloroform around her. I recalled the conversation Amy had with Twolly. The questions Amy had asked were about Sunny's first husband and their son.

Scott left the room without another word.

Dear Mr. Burrat—

I haven't written a letter in a long time, so I apologize for how it might sound. And I'm sorry I didn't write sooner. I hope I haven't delayed your work.

Of course you know Simon Beeker was my father. Daddy died in December. He would have been the best person to help. But I'll tell you what I can.

Daddy always told us that Mr. O'Connell was good to our family. Daddy's grandmother was his housekeeper (Emmaline Coteau was her name) for many years. Mr. O'Connell's family was very wealthy. The kind of rich that wasn't hurt much by the Great Depression. Sometime in the late 1930s Patrick O'Connell—Andrew O'Connell's daddy—died and left plenty behind. There was some stock in AT&T and RCA. Those were young companies at the time. Mr. O'Connell (Andrew) signed his shares over to my great-grandmother Emmaline even though she stopped working for his family soon after he left New Orleans. He really took good care of her through the end of her life Daddy said. He made sure she had what she needed for food and doctor bills and keeping up her house.

Now before my great-grandmother died, Mr. O'Connell and my great-grandmother set it up that my daddy Simon got her stock. That's how he paid for his tuition at Howard University. Daddy got to thank Mr. O'Connell for his kindness after my great-grandmother died. As Daddy told it, Mr. O'Connell didn't want to spend a night in the city again (you must know about how his girlfriend died). But he came for that funeral and they had a drink together that evening. (Daddy liked to go on about the joint near the river where they went. It was a place no one was going to look twice at a black man and white man talking together. Good music, good beer Daddy said.) Mr. O'Connell didn't have to do what he did, but he wasn't a typical man of his day. My daddy couldn't say enough good about him for how he took care of my great-grandmother.

It's because of Mr. O'Connell that my two sisters and I got to go to college and my mamma and daddy had a good life in their late years. My daddy kept hold of that stock as long as he could. He cashed shares only when he needed to. To tell you the truth, none of us knew what Daddy had until my sister Sarah was going off to Spelman. Daddy gave her a check to pay for four years of tuition and living expenses the day she graduated high school. We couldn't figure out how he did something like that on a history teacher's pay. But then he told us what Mr. O'Connell had done.

You know how older people get, telling the same stories over and over. Daddy told us the same ones from time to time. To be honest, I forgot a lot of the ones he told when I was a little boy. But I do remember that he always spoke of Mr. O'Connell with lots of respect.

Oh, I guess I have something to say on my own, now that I think about it. They kept in touch—my daddy and Mr. O'Connell. Holiday cards and letters now and then mostly. But when I was about 8, we went to his house. I don't know why exactly. I vaguely remember Daddy bringing a big box with us to drop off. Anyway, we kids already knew that Mr. O'Connell had helped Daddy go to college. We understood this was an important visit. Back then, we had to take a train from New Orleans. I had never been on a long train ride. I thought I'd watch the whole trip. But the movement of the train made me sleep the whole way. Mr. O'Connell picked us up at the train station in a new blue Chevy. I remember how people looked at us. There he was, this white man, picking up a family of black people. In the 50s. You can imagine the stares and whispers. And he didn't look uncomfortable at all even though he shook our hands in a formal sort of way. He had these very interesting eyes, too. You couldn't help but notice them because of the color. Anyway, I remember Daddy rode in the front seat, and I was afraid the police were going to stop us. Mr. O'Connell just drove like it was the most normal thing in the world.

Mr. O'Connell's house was beautiful. It had two stories. I remember I liked the stairs. His wife was very nice to us, but I got the feeling she was a little uncomfortable. Still, she put all the kids in the den—my sisters and me and their kids. We had cookies and milk and some of the molasses bread my mamma baked. There was a record player. We didn't have one at the time, so this was a treat for us. We kids never saw each other again, but I never forgot how Mr. O'Connell made us feel welcome in his house.

My sister Sarah could probably help you the most. She said she got a letter from you, too, but I think she's been busy with work and handling Daddy's estate. I'll remind her to write you. Also, you didn't give me your phone number, and my son couldn't find it when we checked the phone book on the Internet. My card is in the envelope, so you feel free to call if you have more questions. That might help me think of more to tell.

Good luck.

Benjamin Beeker

Without warning, I remembered watching Simon in Andrew's room the day after he left for places unknown. Simon ran his thin fingers against the bookcase that had become his, along with dozens of volumes stacked inside. He walked to his new desk and noticed paper in the small garbage can nearby. Simon picked up the can to empty it. He stopped in the doorway, pulled my last letter to Andrew from the trash, and studied the dark brown stain that had seeped from one side of the envelope to the other. He sniffed for a clue to its source. Then Simon slipped the letter into his pocket and patted his hip as if to promise his protection.

I looked at the business card Benjamin had sent. He was a plant manager at a chemical company. He had written his home phone number in a blank corner. I wished I could telephone and ask him to search his thoughts for the childhood stories he assumed were gone for good. I wondered if he knew what his father had done with my last words to Andrew.

I AM NINE. A few weeks ago, I found out how a woman gets a baby. No storks dropping them down chimneys, no cabbage patches full of an infant crop. An act of love and nature. There is logic in what Mother told me. A man, a woman, pollen and seed, bud to blossom, blossom to fruit. Cause and effect, my father would say.

I know how the baby grows inside. I've seen the drawings. There are things I still don't understand, though.

Mrs. Delacourt's middle daughter comes to visit after a suffragette luncheon. I know, because I eavesdropped, that she is in her fifth month. Margaret remembers me and asks about my schoolwork while her mother prepares a plate. I tell her about the new microscope my daddy bought me and the slides I made of plants and dead bugs. She claims to have a weak stomach and admires my curiosity. Margaret jumps suddenly. Her hands clasp the sides of her belly.

"What's wrong?"

"Nothing. The baby kicked."

"Kicked?"

"Do you want to feel it?"

I press my palms gently against the soft cotton drape, the tight skin underneath. A quick thrust bends my fingertips. Several sharp nudges follow, then stillness. I think of the drawings, the concentric ovals around a curled little body, the layers protecting it.

"It doesn't breathe, does it? There is a cord that gives it oxygen."

"Yes." Margaret looks startled. "Later, though, it will practice with the water."

"With the water? Oh, in the amnion."

"How did you know?"

"I read."

"Does your mother know you know that?"

"She gets me the books."

"What do you think about what you learn?"

"It's fun. It's like solving a mystery all the time."

"That doesn't disappoint you?"

Suddenly, I remember Grams's Christmas party last year. I had pulled off Santa Claus's hat and beard before he escaped through the kitchen door. Uncle Roger swiped the hat from my hand, grinned, and said, *You're in on the conspiracy now, Razi. Disappointed?* I paused, smiled back. *Now I have something good to tell.*

I beam at Margaret. "The finding out is much better."

❧

I AM TEN. After several rounds of blindman's buff, we decide we want treats and beg for pennies.

My mother quickly finds a few dollars, but no change. As Mother digs in her bag, Mrs. Villere whispers, "Oh, there's Frances Bonaventure," as she hands her son a dime for him and his sisters.

A woman pushing a carriage walks ahead of a stairstep of four children. From the drape of her dress, it's obvious she's carrying again. She comes closer, and Mother waves.

"Is she expecting—again?" Mrs. Villere asks.

"Poor dear." Mrs. Delacourt clucks her tongue.

I take Mother's bag and slowly poke the contents. My playmates call me to hurry. "Aw, I'm coming," I say. Mrs. Bonaventure comes straight to the bench. Mother and her friends greet the woman.

"My, how your children have grown," Mother says. "How old are they now?"

"The baby will be a year next month." She points to the row of children, two boys and two girls, who obediently hold hands. "Seven, five, four, and two and a half."

"They're darling," Mrs. Delacourt says. "Aren't you all?"

"And the Lord will bless us again in the New Year."

"Congratulations," Mother says. "I hope Mr. Bonaventure is doing well."

"Oh, quite. Busy, busy, but then, which of our husbands is not?"

"So true," Mother replies.

"Well, we must continue on our walk. I promised them ice cream if they behaved. Come now, children. Have a lovely afternoon, ladies." The children follow behind like ducklings.

I tuck a nickel between my fingers and keep digging. I wonder why her flesh, almost ashen, doesn't stretch quite right on her face, why her bosom hangs low. I feel a sympathy for her I don't understand.

"Poor dear." Mrs. Delacourt *tsks* again.

"He's a beast," Mrs. Villere says. "There would have been a six and a three, but I'm sure you heard what happened."

"I should have Snitchy send a box of oranges this winter," Mrs. Delacourt says. "Two boxes. They all need their vitamins."

"Raziela, have you found your pennies?" Mother says calmly.

I hold up my nickel. "Will this do?"

She nods, then looks at me in a way that makes me think she wishes I hadn't seen what I did.

I WATCHED Nel and Eugenia stroll around her lovely old home. Late fall was a lonesome time for Eugenia. The people who lived in her house planted few flowers during that season, and she didn't have much to tend. Her pace was a little faster, her attention to cuffs and collars more frequent. We all had our tricks to ease us through the quiet, vacant moments. With Nel that cool early morning, she seemed comforted.

During the few months that Nel had been between, the two had developed an affinity that made me think they each saw someone they missed in the other. He felt soothed by the orbit over the grounds, and Eugenia enjoyed the garrulous company. They shared a common interest in classical music and would often hum together in enthusiastic, if slightly off-key, duets.

When I turned to watch the first pink streaks of the sunrise, I saw Noble pivot the corner and come toward me. I waved, and he returned the gesture.

"Eugenia will be beside herself—so many visitors to begin the day," I said.

"She is expecting me. We've met on this day for years."

I considered the date. November 2. I remembered my Sunday school lessons. It was All Souls' Day. Almost two centuries had passed since Noble last breathed, and he still held fast to the practice of a faith that he truly believed had betrayed him. He looked agitated, vulnerable. "I didn't know Eugenia shared this—observation."

"It is especially meaningful for us, Razi." Noble paused, kept a thought to himself. He glanced at Lionel and Eugenia. "How is the new one? Still at your heels?"

"He's fun. You should try it sometime."

Noble smirked but with some degree of humor. "You think me melancholy."

"Deny it."

"I have an appointment with the gentle lady."

As we approached, Eugenia fluttered her hand at her chest and laughed. "Oh, Lionel, you are so comical."

Nel's grin remained wide when he greeted Noble and stopped moving. Eugenia paused as well. I told Nel it was time to go.

"I want to ask them each something first," Nel said.

I wished for a sleeve—a well-stitched, thick cotton weave—to pull him away. I sensed that he was about to ask about matters that came out in their own time, if at all. His inquisitiveness bordered on nosy of late.

"Eugenia, when was the last time you left this yard?"

"Oh, my, well, I went shopping the morning before the bees came."

"Why not since?"

"I have no material needs any longer, Lionel. Whatever is the point?"

"Isn't there anything you want to see? Don't you wonder about how the city has changed? How the world has changed?"

Eugenia batted her eyes. "There is nothing I can do about that, precious. Besides, this is where I always wanted to be. My garden. The Yankees tried to destroy it all, my home, my garden, but I was a fine shot, yes I was, and I saved enough to start again. I was nearly finished, and then—I've told you that story."

"Yes. The bees," Nel said. "But the ones you kill, Eugenia, it's not their fault."

"I certainly wouldn't want such a thing to happen to another." Her voice was thinly sweet. "It is an awful way to die, Lionel. You cannot imagine the swelling inside and out."

"Nel, let's go. Noble came to see her privately," I said.

His face was calm, but his eyes were troubled. "In a minute. Noble, may I ask you a question?"

"One."

"What do you have left to do?"

"Explain."

"There has been plenty of time for you to see or explore whatever you wanted to. You're still here. I'm curious to know why."

Noble straightened, inching himself only slightly taller than I, nowhere close to Lionel's height. "This is my home."

"Anywhere can be your home."

"You stay as well," Noble said.

"I haven't decided where to go next."

"And I have, monsieur. I belong here. I belong close to what remains." Noble's glance toward me was a warning. I knew what, in part, kept him in New Orleans. I would admit to no one that I understood Noble in a way I didn't want to.

Nel pitched back on his heels. "What does that mean?"

"I agreed to one question."

"Close to *what* remains? Your people are all long gone. The city isn't anything like it was when you first got here. So I can only think there must be something you want to accomplish, see, do, understand—something—which is why you stay."

"You will make yourself mad, Lionel Mulberry, going on like this. But I will indulge you. What do you have left to do?"

"I'm trying to figure that out," Nel said. "Am I the only one?"

The three of us—Eugenia, Noble, and me—glanced at each other. Eugenia had never led someone to join a last breath for his own good, but Noble and I had. There were some who simply would never be able to cope with our experience, the feeble-minded, the insane, the children—like Donna, the first one I ever helped with a release. Then there were the ones who had become too preoccupied with questioning what had been, and there was little they could do to change circumstances once they were gone. When they were taken to sit with the dying, they were grateful. They were ready for the wondering to stop. I feared that Nel was on his way to this end.

"Lionel, precious, what I have observed about you modern men is that you keep yourselves far too busy." Eugenia began to drift again. Stillness made her anxious. "But you are a Southern man, too. It was in your blood. Your capacity to enjoy a promenade with a charming, pretty lady must take precedence."

"Walk with me, Nel," I said.

"It is a lovely morning," Noble said. "A beautiful morning to behold."

Nel politely said his good-byes, but he was clearly hurt. The dew evaporated under him as we swept across Eugenia's lawn. The stir of the air awakened a brilliant bed of pansies. I pushed the scent aside, refused to admire the abundant petals Eugenia protected from insects and ice.

"I know what you just did," Nel said. "You denied yourself the smell of those flowers."

"Yes. Today isn't the day you'll learn why."

❧

CHLOE SAT on the back porch steps with a large piece of luggage at her knees. Her head pivoted in quick shifts to look around the quiet backyard. Hot as August was, she didn't seem uncomfortable in her sharp black linen suit. She looked like a woman of purpose, a force to reckon with.

Amy drove up ten minutes later. She didn't notice her friend until she had slammed the car door shut. For a moment, she looked perplexed. "You're not a mirage, are you?"

"Nope. It's me in the flesh." Chloe walked down the steps and opened her arms. The two hugged tightly.

"What are you doing here?" Amy asked.

"Surprise."

"But you said you weren't coming until late October." Amy opened the back door.

"I still am. This is a sneak preview." Chloe rolled her luggage into the kitchen with precision.

"You just showed up out of the blue? Without notice? What if we'd been gone?"

"Aims, I haven't seen you since you two bought this house. Show me around."

The suitcase was abandoned in the guest room for a tour through the home. Chloe stopped to admire the bookcase, pressed her hands into the luxurious fabric of the living room sofa, and rubbed her fingertips along a textured wall. As Chloe commented on Amy's knack for interior decorating, she looked for signs of disorder and found none. They finished the tour in the kitchen. Chloe went to the bathroom, and Amy got two glasses of water.

Chloe entered the living room. "Fine little trapping of domesticity you got here." She dropped into Scott's chair and grabbed her drink. From the shallow bowl on the coffee table, she took a few marbles and rolled them in her hand like dice.

"We like it. Quiet neighborhood, lots of trees, good property values. We've been so sucked in that we make sure we're in town whenever there's a tax vote."

"The creep of Republicanism?"

"Blatant self-interest, perhaps."

"Same thing, yes?"

"Depending on your definition." Amy sat still in a way that she hadn't in weeks.

"Hey, that's a cool necklace. Where'd you get that vintage beauty?"

"My great-aunt Twolly. That jewelry chest you saw in the bedroom is full of beautiful pieces like this. You'd like digging through it."

"Will do. So, where's Scott? I miss hugging men whose pants will stay loose at the crotch."

She laughed. "He won't be home until about ten." Amy paused. "So you really came without telling anyone?"

"Okay, Captain Jigsaw is responsible. He thought you'd be happy."

Amy's eyes softened, and her mouth bowed up. "No kidding." Then she looked at Chloe without a blink. The smile ebbed back.

"He said he's still enjoying the pharmacy biz."

"He's talked about going for an MBA to work in the pharmaceutical industry."

"The big money. The time is now. Baby boomers are getting older, and they're going to want drugs, drugs, drugs to cure it all, especially aging itself. Somebody will make a killing."

"My mom had one hot flash and dashed off for hormone replacement therapy."

"Pill or patch?" Chloe asked.

"Pill."

"Mine's patch. I tried to get her to think about soy, herbs even, but she's so conventional—what are you smiling at?"

"Same old admonition of the woman who bore you after twenty-five hours of labor," Amy said.

"And the always maternal Nora Richmond, from which you sprung, has become a paragon of a new wave?"

"Hardly. She's clamoring for grandchildren. But that's a topic for another day." She began to twist her wedding ring in a way that made Chloe anxious.

"Well, you know what? I'm hungry. What about you?" Chloe asked.

"I could eat."

"Take me somewhere nostalgic. I'm in the mood. I actually drove around LSU for half an hour before I got to your place. Strange sameness and strange changes in this city. The student ghetto is pathetic as ever, but the new apartment buildings south of campus are amazing. Who's got money to live there?"

"It's called credit—or Daddy."

Chloe jerked up, dropped the marbles into the bowl, and smoothed her pants. "Shit, everyone should suffer the way we did. Builds character. Makes you appreciate what you get once you've worked for it."

"How very Republican."

"Shut up."

Amy washed each glass, dried them, and placed them in the cabinet before they left for dinner.

SCOTT CAME HOME to a quiet house. He knew Chloe had arrived because her rental car was parked in the front and a tightly packed suitcase was on the guest bed. He showered and dressed for visitors, choosing shorts that zipped and a T-shirt instead of clean underpants alone. With a half-read book and a glass of orange juice, he sat in his chair, a nervousness drumming at his fingertips. He read paragraphs three and four times over and glanced at the time. Around eleven o'clock, he paced between the kitchen and dining room, peeking out of the windows.

Chloe and Amy walked in the back door, laughing. His face relaxed when he greeted them.

"Catch me." Chloe ran into his arms, and he lifted her off the ground. When he placed her down, she kissed his cheek with an exaggerated smooch.

"Look at you. Man, you're in shape. But otherwise, you haven't changed a goddamn bit." Chloe whapped him in the belly with the back of her fingers.

"Goddammit, neither have you."

Chloe laughed. Amy busied herself with putting her purse away.

"Had a good time, girls?"

"My guts are gummy with cheese fries from Louie's, and I got to embarrass a row of underage kids at the movies. Banner evening," Chloe said.

Scott made eye contact with Amy, who removed her watch and necklace. Chloe thwarted the silence by announcing she was going to the bathroom.

"I found her on the doorstep," Amy said.

"Did you brush her and offer a saucer of milk?" Scott asked. "Can we keep her?"

Amy grinned slightly and shook her head. "Just for the weekend." She moved as if she were about to reach for him but turned around toward the cabinets instead. "Thank you, Scott. I'm glad to see her." She stretched for a glass.

"You're welcome." He ran his fingers along the back of her head and gently squeezed her neck. She poured water from the tap. "You guys had fun?"

"You know Chloe. It's hard not to have fun with her."

"She seems like she's doing well. She looks great."

"I think she's hit a stride. It suits her." Amy faced him, took a sip, and placed her drink on the counter.

She looked fragile. Her clothes were too well pressed, her hair was too well coiffed, and her face was too appropriately painted. Amy stood with her arms down and wrists tilted like a doll about to toddle across the room. Her fingers splayed out to stretch away the residual tension of working at a computer that day. Before she could grab her glass again, Scott trapped her against the sink, hugging her.

"Scott."

"I'm glad you had a good time."

Amy patted his back. "Let me go. I have to bathe."

He stepped away as she walked past.

"Bath time," Amy said on her way to the front of the house.

Chloe walked in a second later. "We have—what?—twenty minutes alone now?" She was barefoot. She wore a thin cotton robe over men's pajamas, and her hair was held back with a thick headband. Her face was shiny clean.

"Want something to drink? A snack?"

"No, thanks."

"How much did you guys talk?"

"I did most of it. Catching up, that sort of thing. I figure I need to ease into the territory, you know? We haven't seen each other in almost a year. It didn't seem appropriate to bust out with, 'So what's with the obsessive-compulsive thing again?'"

"It's no better than when I talked to you—and now she lives in front of the computer."

"She doesn't know you called about—whatever this is?"

"No."

"Didn't think so."

"I'm really worried. I've tried to think if I did something to start this or exacerbate it, but I don't think I have. Something happened after her grandparents died. Something she won't tell me."

"Did you try to talk to her at all?"

"She was evasive. She said she's having to work out some things in her head, and there's nothing I can do about it."

Chloe pitched herself up to sit near the sink. "That's it?"

"She gave me some explanation about seeing some pictures that made her remember things she'd forgotten."

"What pictures?"

"She didn't say."

"Photographs or something else?"

"She just said pictures."

"Oh."

He stared at her until she met his eyes. "What?"

"She didn't mention a video?"

"Spill it."

Chloe sat bent forward, her hands curled around the counter's edge. "I didn't think it was a big deal, so I didn't tell you about it when we talked. I sent her this video I found in storage."

"When was this?"

"Three months ago. Some tape we made about our nefarious political days. Our impressions. I thought it was kind of nostalgic. There's a part where she talks about her grandparents. She couldn't believe old Sunny was a pro-lifer and that her grandfather was pro-choice. She thought he was really conservative—he had a yard sign for every Republican presidential candidate since she could remember—so that was, well, out of character."

"That seems harmless enough," Scott said.

"I have to be honest, though. I didn't watch the whole thing. I stopped at some point when we were waxing philosophical. Our intensity got excruciating. And then I dropped the tape off at a friend's who dubbed a DVD for me."

"Maybe that had nothing to do with what's going on."

"The timing is suspicious. Sounds like she started to wig out around the time she got it. Might have been a bad judgment call on my part. I thought she might get a kick out of seeing it. I guess I was wrong."

"Your intentions were good."

"They led right to hell." Chloe lightly kicked her heels against the cabinets. Her lips parted, but what came from her was a tinge of Jem. *Hmm,* she murmured, too low for anyone to hear. "I'll do what I can, but don't expect me to blab if she opens up.

If she swears me to silence, she's got it. All I can promise to do is convince her to tell you."

"That's more than I had when I woke up this morning."

"No guy's ever gotten teary-eyed over me. Not like this anyway." Her comment made him tuck his chin near his chest. "If I have any influence on the big scheme, I'm not letting you guys fuck this up. Nobody is going to chicken out of dealing with whatever's going on. Not you. Especially not Amy." She pitched her head against the cabinet and stared at the ceiling. "When you lose your nerve to face things, you lose more than what you didn't get."

"So what did you lose?"

"Aside from my self-respect now and then and a couple of jobs? Might have been a man named Ephraim. But the timing was all wrong. Somebody ought to figure out how to synchronize that shit."

WHILE SCOTT AND AMY got ready for bed, Chloe wandered into the front room. She parted the bookcase doors wide. Her fingers dipped into the separations among the spines as she read them carefully, novels, biographies, essay collections, a dictionary, and reference books. Of those that interested her, she glanced at the covers, back and front. She chose a well-worn favorite of Scott's and placed it on the little table near the rocker. Chloe then sat in front of the drawers, running her fingers along the deep, straight carvings on each one. When she opened the right drawer, she traced the arcs of the dovetailing and tapped her finger on each peg that held the wood together. A century-old breath, the one all could detect, blew out. Chloe smiled at the odd scent, an aroma like good tobacco and spices. The only items inside were candles of all sizes and a matchbox. With both hands, she pushed the drawer closed and leaned to open the other.

It stuck a little as she pulled. She didn't know the trick that Amy had discovered, one that Andrew always used—an even tug up at the handle and a smooth slide out. Chloe moved the drawer until it was nearly out of the bookcase. She held the bottom with her left hand and ran her fingers along its sides. Her touch was slow, exploratory, sensuous. I backed into a corner, vibrating, chilling the room against my will. Never had Amy or Scott left the drawers open so long, and the smell was unusually powerful, overwhelming me. I could see Andrew's bloodstains within the interior—cold, brown, lifeless.

Chloe's left hand slipped. The drawer knocked flat to the floor. As she lifted it up to replace it, she tilted the back in first and tried to close it all the way. It wouldn't fit. She pulled it out again and inspected the rear side. A thin panel of wood jutted from the bottom. *Oh, shit,* she muttered, looking inside to see what was damaged. She held the drawer on her lap and jiggled the panel, which began to slide out. A paper rectangle fell between her legs. Chloe pulled out the false bottom slowly, and photographs dropped to her thighs like petals. Drawer aside, Chloe held a fan of photographs before her.

Each one was of me.

"Aren't you freezing in here?" Amy walked in and glanced up to notice that the fan wasn't on. Then she looked at Chloe. "What happened?"

"These fell from under the drawer."

Amy sat next to Chloe and took the photos one by one.

"I was admiring how well this bookcase is built, and I accidentally dropped the drawer. A panel came out—along with all of this."

There I was, bare. Shadow and light, my body curled into itself, curved along the roll of the earth, blurred by wildflowers, silhouetted against the sky. I remembered Andrew's fingertips nudging the arch of my back, pushing the edge of my heel, meeting the cup of my palm. At times, he blended me into the landscape as if I'd sprouted from the very spot on which I lay. Other times, I was as exotic as a bird of paradise among weeds.

When he looked at me, I felt a radiant nakedness deeper than my skin.

"She's beautiful." Chloe stared at each picture, turning them over to find no writing or marks.

"Who's beautiful?" Scott appeared in the doorway.

Amy extended her arm and handed him a small stack. Scott didn't blink for several moments. His smile was ever so coy and serious. How strange it was to see a man look at me that way again.

Chloe passed another picture to her. "How old do you think these are?"

"Twenties, probably," Amy said.

"Look at this one. You can tell her hair is bobbed," Scott said.

For a long while, Amy studied me. I lay on the ground, my breasts and pelvis covered with flowers. My face was in profile, softened by late-afternoon light and the hangover of a nap. I remembered that day, what happened after he took the photo, his heat below me, the breeze above.

"It's so naughty. Some cute little flapper posing for someone," Chloe said.

"I wish I knew who she was." Amy studied four others. "She almost looks familiar."

"There's not even a studio mark," Scott said.

"Last one, my porno pals." Chloe passed the photo to Amy.

I came close enough to see it was one of the last photos he ever took of me. I am naked, a length of beads between my breasts, one hand curled at my left hip, my eyes closed, the corners of my mouth soft with content. I trusted him when he said that no one else would see me so completely.

❧

SATURDAY BEFORE Valentine's Day, 1928. Twolly says I look moony-eyed. I can't deny it. Everything is bathed in spectacular brilliance. Everyday aromas have transformed into magnificent perfumes, and the simplest meals are delectable. Ordinary noises are symphonic. My flesh is as sensitive and responsive as the silk of a spider's web. I won't say it—can't say it—but I know exactly from what I suffer.

The surprise Andrew has promised for Tuesday thrills more than frightens me, and Twolly knows it. She's almost as anxious to find out what it is.

"Dinner at Commander's." Twolly lies flat on her back on my bed.

"Too public."

"Flowers."

"Expected, don't you think?"

"Candy. Really big box."

"Too predictable. I'm telling you, you can't judge this book by its cover." Andrew, underneath his reticent smile and tailored suits, is a work of unexpected whimsy. Two weeks after the first amazing kiss, he sent me a crossword puzzle that he'd made himself. Several boxes had thicker lines than the rest that indicated a secret message would be revealed. Once I solved it, the staggered boxes spelled out, left top to right bottom, U R C A T S M E O W. For Christmas, he gave me a cricket box that housed a real cricket. The Chinese believe it represents a fighting spirit, he said. In January, he mailed a tiny package containing an origami crane. Its tail had a narrow note attached to the end that read, "Flatten me." I hated to ruin the delicate folds, but I followed the instructions. The enclosed message was, *I'm breaking a cardinal rule to be this earnest, but itswanderful to beak around such a good egg. That's no tail—feather you believe me or not. Affectionately, Andrew.*

Twolly rolls to her stomach and kicks her heels in the air. "Jewelry."

"Too soon."

"Razi, you're positively goofy over each other."

"I don't wear enough baubles to give him a clue that I'd even like that."

"Would you?"

"Wouldn't mind."

"Dinner on a riverboat, dance afterward, dark corners for necking."

"Tempting. But he's going to pick me up at three o'clock. Too early."

"Didn't he give you any hints?"

"No, and I begged him. He can be so secretive. It's awful charming."

"You never tolerated such games from other boys."

"Other boys weren't so clever."

"So what do you have for him?"

I jump to my feet and scamper to my dressing table. "It's a bit of a treasure hunt without the map. He's forced me to compete with his creative flair." I find the red thread in the same place I'd left it. I twist the thread around my headboard and loop it around my room. "I'm going to run this throughout the house. He'll start in the front parlor and make his way in and out of rooms until he finds his gift."

Twolly stares at me from behind the intersecting lines. "Oh, that's ducky."

ANDREW ARRIVES EARLY that day to pick me up. Before we leave, I make him follow the trail. I give him an old spinning wheel spool upon which there is a scrolled note: *Follow this thread; there's nothing to dread; your Valentine surprise is straight ahead.*

His blue eyes spark. As he walks, he wraps the stray line on the spool. Poor Grams is trapped on the davenport until the game is finished. I've forgiven her and my father for mercilessly teasing me as I prepared Andrew's surprise because they are holding their tongues now.

The game ends after several trips up and down the stairs, pirouettes around each dining room chair, circles around every item in the parlor, a brief waltz through my father's study, and dips from different spots in the kitchen. His gift is on the back porch wrapped in a huge box that contains a series of other boxes. In the end, after our noses are sufficiently cold, he opens his final package—a pound of penny candy separated in wax paper rows. On top of the licorice sticks, there is a small card. I had spent hours on the words now concealed within the envelope. Even though I mean what it says, I'm afraid of how he will react. I've never written such a thing to a man in my life.

> *What sweetness lies in wait each time I bring your lips to mine, a confection so perfect that its syrup infuses my daydreams and becomes real when I close my eyes.*
>
> *Razi*

Andrew swallows hard. He stares at me. I quietly look back, trying to read his dazed, flushed expression. "My God, Razi," he finally says. "Thank you." He takes my face in his hands and kisses me with stunning, yet delightful, force.

He is still blushing when we go inside to grab our coats and leave. I receive only one wink from Grams as we scamper out.

He has a queer little smile on his face as we drive to the mysterious rendezvous spot. He's as talkative as usual, but he's nervous. He drums his fingers on the steering wheel in a way that isn't bored or playful. His foot taps the floorboard when we stop at signs. That makes me nervous. I have seen him flustered only once, the night we met.

I don't say a word when we end up in a neighborhood I have never visited. There are shotgun houses lined along the streets, with windows and doors closed tight and sealed with strips of cloth. A few houses have dormant trees in the tiny front yards. Little children stop their games and stare at the car as we drive slowly down the dirt road. I wave at them, and they wave back, smiling and pointing.

Andrew parks the roadster in front of a narrow house painted conch shell pink. "We're here," he says. I sit stunned until he opens the side door for me. "Hello, Simon," he tells a boy about eleven years old who is mending the wooden fence in front of the house.

"Good afternoon, Mr. Andrew." Simon has two nails trapped between his lips. He smiles, which creases the corners of his eyes and makes him look grown up. "Ma-Maw's been expecting you." He grabs the nails by his narrow-fingered left hand and nods to me. "Good afternoon, Miss."

"Simon Beeker, Miss Raziela Nolan. Simon is Emmaline's grandson."

"How do you do?" I say.

"Fine, Miss. And you?"

"Well, thank you."

"You better get on over, Mr. Andrew. You know how she is about being prompt." Simon bobs his head, as if in approval.

Andrew glances at his wristwatch. "I'm not late."

"No. But she just—well, she just glad to have you, is all."

"Would you mind letting her know we're here? I have some preparations. Thank you."

"No, sir. Good day, Miss Nolan. You have a musical first name."

"Thank you, Simon."

I watch Simon run up the clean, solid porch steps. Andrew touches my hand. When I look at him, he dangles a scarf in front of my eyes. "You trust me, don't you?"

"Yes."

"At least you didn't hesitate." He blindfolds me and spins me around.

I take his arm and hear the dry, dead grass scrunch under my shoes. I smell a stew cooking slow and long nearby. Someone picks a guitar within earshot. A whispery tinkle reminds me of a table being set. A hinge creaks in the distance. I am led a little farther.

"When I take it off, I want you to look straight ahead until your eyes adjust. Then I'll let you turn around."

I blink and focus on the wide stripes of his tie. "I'm fine now."

"Then turn."

This garden would make an English lady die of envy. In the dead of February, the small backyard is a blush of blooms. A redbud tree weeps its rosy promise of leaves. A row of camellias is heavy with pink flowers. In the right corner is an exotic Japanese magnolia so perfect it looks watercolored. Nearby, a patch of early roses curl open like the hands of sleeping infants. Toward the back of the yard, there is a dormant crape myrtle draped with yards of sheer pink ribbon and decorated with tiny silver bells. Underneath is a table covered with a white cloth, two cushioned chairs, and a setting of china.

"Remarkable," I whisper.

"Let's sit down." He raises his hand to direct me toward the table. He pulls out my chair, seats me, and eases into the chair on the other side. A small wood-burning stove at the base of the tree puffs pecan wood smoke. Across from us are budding azaleas, which line the back of the house.

Emmaline appears in her back door and moves forward with her beautiful smile and a tray. "Good afternoon, Miss Razi, Mr. Andrew. I'm gonna set this out here, and you call if you need. Here's a little bell, just in case. You have a nice visit, now." She lays out three plates and pours coffee. I swear she winks at him.

"Thank you, Emmaline." Andrew grins tightly.

I am struck dumb. I look at what she placed on the table. There is fruit on one plate and tiny sandwiches on the other. Her famous petits fours are stacked in a pyramid in the center. The frosting is narcissus white with miniature flowers of pink petals, yellow centers, and light green leaves.

He raises his eyebrows as if he is waiting for me to speak.

"You amaze me, Andrew O'Connell."

"Likewise."

"Thank you."

"You're welcome." He takes a sip of coffee, black as usual.

I reach for the snacks and build my own little stack of cakes. We nibble in silence for a few moments. "Emmaline makes the best petits fours I've ever had." I wipe my mouth with a pressed linen napkin.

"I know. You mentioned that to me."

"When?"

"The night we met. You finished some before we walked to the park."

"I'd forgotten."

"You called them 'ambrosia.'"

"Did I?"

"Yes. You know what the mythology is about ambrosia, don't you?"

I think for a moment while I swallow another one. "Food of the gods."

"Indeed. Which imparts"—he pauses, watches my eyes—"immortality."

My body rushes with momentum, but I am floating as I fall. "That's what I told you when I was up in the tree. That I wanted to be immortal."

"That's what I remember." He raises his cup. "To that lifetime of trouble you intend to cause. And to the immortality of your delightful soul."

I return the toast. Everything inside my body has turned to marmalade. To distract myself, I leave my snack on the table and walk up to the crape myrtle that is so simply and beautifully decorated. "Did Emmaline plant all of this?"

"Yes. Her family has lived here since she was a girl. Before she worked for my family, she was with another. The lady of the house was clearing out her family home's garden, and she gave the plants to Emmaline. Most of the trees and shrubs have been growing in her garden for close to thirty years."

"How did you know this was here?"

"By accident. She got sick one day, and Mother thought she would be more comfortable at her own home. She was too ill to walk all that way, and I didn't think the streetcars came close enough to shorten the walk adequately. I shouldn't have been driving then—I was maybe fourteen—but Mother didn't drive at all, and Father was away on a trip. And neither would have come to this area." He pours more coffee for us both. "Her mother was still alive, old as Methuselah and so frail. Her daughter—Simon's mother—wouldn't be home for a while. They both lost their husbands to the Spanish flu back in 'eighteen. Well, I got Emmaline comfortable and went outside to get more wood for the fire. It was about this time of year. I couldn't believe what I saw. One wouldn't expect it, wouldn't you agree? She was in no mood to talk that day, but I asked her about it when she came back to work. Ever since, she's told me about the state of her garden as the seasons change. Everything she plants blooms pink or close to it, she said. It's her favorite color."

"She obviously takes a great deal of pride in it."

"Aside from her family, this is all she has."

"Seems to me she has you, too, in a way."

"Emmaline deserves a second time around. She's earned it. She's worked hard since she was old enough to walk. I promised myself that she will never want for anything. She's been good to me all my life. Loyalty works both ways, don't you think?"

"Among honorable men, anyway."

He smiles reflectively and walks over to me. I have calmed myself down. Andrew reaches above his head and unties a loop of ribbon. His hand snuffs a silver glint. "Razi, you're quite a good sport."

"I am, aren't I?" I laugh.

He suppresses his chuckle. I twist an edge of ribbon between my fingers, level with my heart. He puts his hand on my shoulder. The ribbon drops. I place my hands flat on his chest under the clover-leaf lapels and slip my palms to his waist. I suddenly remember the stray freckle on the front of his left hip, an inch below where my right thumb rests.

"I think—I think that I have never enjoyed someone's company so much as yours." Andrew keeps his eyes on mine.

"I would have to say the same of you." I force myself not to look down. His gaze makes me lightheaded.

"And I believe I've never had so much fun."

"And I believe I've never met someone so smart and charming and handsome." I want him to kiss me. I would first if I weren't so curious about what he's going to say. I feel through the tension of his hands that he is absolutely focused on the moment. An intensity emanates from him, as if he wills himself courage he doesn't think he has. I am delirious with the waves under my skin.

"And you're venturesome and bright and lovely."

"You're going to make me blush."

His hands skim down my arms, and he links his fingers at the small of my back. "Razi," he says in a voice that makes me feel as if he has breathed me in and won't let me go, "I love you." He is so matter-of-fact, I almost think he's kidding.

"I love you, too."

Then he kisses me with lips so limber I nearly bend in half over his arms. The first few seconds, he is entirely responsible for keeping me on my feet. I have fallen for him, and I know for certain that he has for me.

"Here." He reaches around my neck. "So you don't forget."

He clasps a delicate locket that hangs an inch above my beating heart. I open the tiny latch. Inside, it simply reads, "For Razi. Love, Andrew."

"Thank you, darling."

"You're welcome."

A ridge of dampness collects along the black line of his hair. I rub it dry with my thumb. "Jeepers creepers, were you anxious. Haven't you done that before?" I laugh.

"I never meant it like this." He gives me an affectionate grin.

"Me neither." I wait for the panic. When I don't feel it, that scares me even more.

HE IS SOMEWHERE with that camera. He says every photograph is practice for the ones he'll take during his travels around the world. Lately, he takes the camera wherever he goes, in case he sees something to capture. Most of the photos don't satisfy him—the light was wrong or the subject left a blur or his focus was poor—but he keeps the ones that he likes in a little box. What possesses him, I have no idea, because he spares nothing the lens. Inside that box, I've seen a hodgepodge of what turned his eye—a sunset on drowsing morning glories, Emmaline's hands around a bone china teacup, men chatting outside the Pickwick Club, a freshly painted Creole cottage. I love them all. Andrew takes the commonplace and recasts it as incredible.

I roll on the grass and snuggle my chin into the blades. One meets the edge of my lip, and I bite. As I chew, I rest my ear on the ground. The grass struggles to straighten itself under my weight. I hear it groan.

"You haven't dressed?"

"Why bother? No one out here but me, you, the birds, and the bees."

Andrew holds the camera at his hip. "Exhibitionist."

"Voyeur." I lie on my side and curl my knees into my belly. Grass fringes every curve. Slowly, he raises the camera up to his face. He steps aside, back, aside again. He's behind me. "Put that down. What if it goes off accidentally?"

"It won't."

"Andrew."

"Let me."

"You've been in the sun too long."

"No one else will see them. You know I develop my own."

I turn only my face to look at him. That glint isn't there, not the same one I know anyway. "Okay, I'll make you a deal. You tell me your middle name, and I'll let you."

"Too easy. I'll give you three guesses. If you miss, I get to take your photograph. If you're right—well, what do you want?"

"You have to trace me with a feather until I beg you to stop, and you don't."

There—there's the libidinous spark I expected. "I accept the terms."

"Now, now. It's so obvious. You were a fool to suggest the game, Mr. O'Connell. Your middle name is your father's. Patrick."

"No. Don't move."

"Percy. A popular name in these parts."

"No. Stay still. The way the light touches your back—"

"Pierce. A name with some history."

His hand strokes along my spine and pushes my rear further into the tuck, a sweet blind path of desire humming through my skin. "Better luck next time. Don't move." The shutter snaps once, twice, three times. Andrew kneels down at my side but doesn't touch me. I lie flat on my back.

"Beautiful," he says distantly.

I place my hand on his chest and feel the center of the maze, the point where his vessels begin and end. What I want—soon, now—we are not prepared for me to ask.

AFTER HE RETURNED from his early morning exercise with his Saturday running group, Scott cooked breakfast—pancakes, eggs, ham slices, fresh fruit salad, and homemade biscuits. Amy and Chloe sat on the back steps drinking coffee in their pajamas while a pair of cardinals, sparrows, and three squirrels nibbled at the feeder. The girls barely spoke, but they were comfortable together. When Scott called them in, Chloe kissed him on the cheek, and Amy gave him a light peck on the lips when he turned to her. He was content in a way he hadn't been in a while. So was Amy. After they finished eating, Scott cleaned up before he left to entertain himself for the day.

While Amy showered and dressed, Chloe amused herself. First, she looked through the jewelry chest's contents. She tried on bracelets and admired necklaces. When she found Andrew's ring, she read the inscription . . . *why, it beats so I can love you* . . . gave a puzzled smile, and slipped it on her thumb. Once the jewelry was put away, Chloe went into the front room. She studied the bookcase, ran her fingers along the walnut carvings, and opened the doors. The rich, dusky smell encouraged her to nudge into the shelves.

I struggled to hold the air still, noiseless, and warm. That focus gave me respite from the unpredictable surge. Only a few feet away, on a small table, my naked body lay exposed, along with the emotions connected to the man responsible for the photographs. His ring was a reminder of the answers I didn't have a chance to give. As much as I wished I could admire the sleek, polished circle again, I refused to bring it into the light through my own volition. And the bookcase, with its one original, wavy-paned door and the other flat, too-perfect replacement—what it represented and what it held was more than I was prepared to acknowledge. Not yet.

Chloe went to the corner of the room, where a few photo boxes were stacked on a narrow set of shelves. She selected one at random, which contained several photographs from their college years. Smiling, Chloe settled on the living room sofa and began to glance through the snapshots.

"Good, you're entertained," Amy said as she walked in. "Want more coffee?"

Chloe nodded. "That jewelry is gorgeous. You said your aunt made some of it?"

"Yeah," Amy shouted from the kitchen. "She specialized in metals and stones."

"Did she make that ring? That silver and blue one?"

"Maybe, but I doubt it. She liked to make necklaces and bracelets."

Chloe flicked through the photo box quickly. With a perplexed frown, she started to look at each one carefully. Moments later, Amy handed her friend a huge mug and sat down with her own little cup in the oversized chair.

"I never did ask what you thought of that DVD I sent," Chloe said.

"Embarrassed and amused."

"I don't know if I've ever cared about anything so much since."

"Too much effort."

"To be honest, I didn't watch the whole thing. Did we talk about the die-in?"

"No. That came later that summer, I think," Amy said.

"Remember we got lost in the French Quarter? Got bad directions. That girl who was driving. Jesus. Those prairie skirts over her Sasquatch legs. And she ran almost every stop sign. Nearly hit a couple of drunk guys."

"I don't remember."

"She had the best outfit for the event, though. A black veil and a dress covered in metal coat hanger chain mail. Hard core."

"You flung yourself on the ground wailing, 'Patriarchy has murdered me.'"

Chloe laughed. "No, no. 'Patriarchy is murder!' And then you chalked my outline after my death throes stopped."

"A dozen chalk figures stomped out by pigeons and tourists right in front of St. Louis Cathedral."

"We should have used spray paint."

"We would have been arrested."

"For the cause, Aims, for the cause."

"What was the point of it all? Nothing changed."

"If we don't follow our passions, we die, if only at heart."

"Quotable Chloe."

"I should have my own column." Chloe sat up, akimbo, looking purposeful. The box of pictures remained open between her knees.

Amy picked up a remote control and turned on the radio. She scanned the channels until one played music instead of commercials. That station's weekend programming always included early jazz. With a pop of air to a button on the receiver, the radio switched to contemporary popular music. Amy mashed the remote, but the channel wouldn't change. Chloe watched her thrust the control adamantly.

"Didn't know you were such an old jazz fan," Chloe said.

"I'm not. It was something to listen to. You know, I can only catch this station during the week. It's strange. All of our electronic equipment is possessed."

"Can I ask you something? Where's Jem?"

Amy held the cup to her lips and swallowed hard. "Rhetorically?"

"He's not in these pictures. A good number of them are from our college days. He was here then."

"They're in another box."

"Why?"

"That's the way I separated them."

"Why?"

"It made sense to me."

"He was a good guy, that Jem."

The man smell emanated from Amy as if he had run through the room.

"Say something," Chloe said.

"Scott is going to cook that chili you wanted tonight. He went out to find some decent avocados. You like those in your chili, right?"

"Yeah, that's right. Speaking of Scott. He's worried about you."

"You've been having secret conversations about me?" Amy paused, scowled. "That's why you're here, isn't it?"

"How many men would do this? Give him a break and some credit. And FYI, there are no secrets. Not between us. But he knows you're keeping something from him." Amy was silent. Chloe leaned toward her friend, intense and serious. "I swear I won't tell him, but tell me—what's the problem?"

Amy looked outside the window as she folded herself into the chair. Her little body shuddered with tension, ready to run. "Scott doesn't know about the baby."

"You never told him?"

"He would be crushed."

"You really underestimate him. I mean, he married you knowing you lost Jem."

"The competition was finally over. He won."

"That's not fair. He doesn't see it that way."

"He does, deep down. And if he knew that I was pregnant before . . ."

"He'd leave you?"

"No. It's just that—Chloe, he really wants a baby. And I can't. Not now. I'm still too ambivalent about what happened, even after all this time. I go through months and not think about it, and then sometimes it flares up. Sometimes I want that baby I lost, and sometimes I'm relieved I lost him."

"If Scott's ready for a baby, and you know why you don't want one—at least not now—you should tell him the truth."

"What do I say?"

"You just tell him. It's better than what you're putting him through now."

"It's been so long," Amy said with a sadness that made the room feel dark.

I AM HIDING something from Andrew. I cannot feel the pessary snuggled and sealed against the neck of my womb, but I know it is there. For several weeks, I have practiced its fit. The strangest secret I've ever kept. Before, with others, the desire was only biology and curiosity—my body compelled by instinct, my mind by inquisition. I could have—they were willing—but there was always a moment to pause and turn back. I did not pursue the chance again.

Until now.

Andrew holds the rail of the walking bridge in the park. A beautiful spring sunset bathes the creek below. Small fish pierce the light to kiss the air. He looks at me without anticipation—it is a simple gesture, an acknowledgment that I'm near. He says nothing, but his eyes invite me closer.

"I have to ask you something." I wrap my arms around his

waist, press my face into his back. He rests one hand over mine.

"What is that?"

"We never said we wouldn't, and I'm not saying we should, but if you want to, I want to. So . . . ?"

Andrew remains silent and doesn't move. Then he stands tall. "Are you—?"

"I'm ready. I'm sure."

He turns around, breaking my hold. "Now?"

I exhale a nervous laugh. "No, not this minute."

He stares at me. "What if something happens?"

"Remember, I know about these things." My hands flatten against his warm chest.

"Are you absolutely certain? This is serious. More serious than anything that has happened between us before. As serious as marriage."

My reach descends to the front pocket of his trousers. As I expect, his body gives me the answer that he will not reveal with words. "Andrew, say yes."

Not here, I tell him, *the magnolia scent is too strong.* We continue to walk farther on the property than we've ever been, where grass grows to our thighs and the green stirs with startled mice. He holds my hand and lets me lead. A chirping red flutter darts past, followed by its tawny reply. This will be no different, I think, except for the way what I've held will touch me. I look behind. Andrew doesn't smile, but his face changes, especially his eyes, moon nimbus blue, calm and luminous. Over his shoulder, he carries a bundle of blankets corded together, cushioning a thermos and a little box of cookies.

What about there? I ask, and he agrees. The ground is mossy under the oak, whose tannin will not let grass compete with its roots. As he finds a flat, shady spot to lay the blankets, every nerve hums unfamiliar. I am no stranger to his body, or mine to his, and although what is about to happen is no casual affair, no moment of free abandon, I should not feel so anxious, so innocent. An early summer gust catches the back of my neck, and I shiver.

Andrew tucks his socks in his Oxfords near the tree. He walks up with his arms open and holds me gently. His chest is damp from the shadeless trek. I smell a marsh breeze—it's him, hot green salt—and the kiss I plant at his throat comes away more wet than it was given.

We lie on the palette on the ground, so cool there, and we work our way through zippers, buttons, and buckles. Once naked, we twine our hands only, facing each other. I want to tell him that I love him, but I don't have the air to say it. Instead, I kiss him on the mouth, his lips warm and lissome, slow, cautious, they part, his tongue at the edge of mine, we join through the element of life itself, I gasp as he draws in and out, anticipating a coming rhythm.

I push him down. He watches as I run my hands over him, alternate pressure feather light and muscle deep. When I move where he enjoys it most, his eyes close, he sighs and groans, bending into the touch, wanting. My lips join the travel, moist trails blown cool by the wind, and then taste that virgin part of him again, the last time it will be, his soft fold curled under the firm cleft above. He urges me away, not now, wait, it's too soon. He grips my arms to pull me down, but I refuse. I'm not done yet. *Let me touch you.* The quiet springs that rush underneath, they rumble when I find them.

Andrew grabs my wrists and pins me to the ground. That light in his eyes, promethean, melts me to the spot. He kisses me, roughly, but his power has no harm, only desire. His mouth accepts my breasts in turn, tremors of his tongue stir my flesh to peaks, I call without words, don't stop, and I release at my core, a ripple of heat arching me into him. Slowly, so slowly I ache, he carves wet paths down my belly and legs, his hands slip from my ankles to my thighs. With a nudge, he lowers to the center where my legs meet, his firm tender incendiary kiss turning my breath to smoke, my body rolling under him.

He leaves his hand below my navel as he reaches for the box on the blanket. Andrew looks at me. I bend my knees and check that the pessary is in place. *We're safe with this alone,* I say. *Feel, so you'll know.* Gently, he reaches into me, pauses, withdraws. I open my arms to him. Andrew holds me tight, kisses my face, and whispers that he loves me. *I know.*

When he moves into me and I surround him, the fullness where we meet consumes my body. Each movement urges me deeper into him—an impossibility by design—we are only flesh—but that desire will not go away—I want to reach a place under his skin, under mine, I know it's there—now he kisses me, our voices muffle—I smolder, but I am not quite ready—then he thrusts, back tense, a wondrous noise in his throat.

Andrew pulls away. *Oh, that couldn't have been right,* he says with an apologetic glance. I laugh. *Sweetheart, you just need practice,* I say. *You're not upset?* he asks.

No. Have a cookie before we try again.

Andrew lies on my belly and eats five cookies. I stroke the wavy black strands away from his brow. At his dark thatch below, there are gold filaments that I have left on him. I curl to pull one free. What holds me to him now is no more and no less tenuous than this thread that coupled us.

❧

ON CHLOE'S LAST NIGHT with them, Scott made the chili he had promised.

"Can I have a clone of you, Captain Jigsaw?" Chloe dropped into her chair. "I want a man who can cook."

"We're a malleable half of the species. We can be trained as long as it involves precise measurements," he said.

"You were never trained. You've always cooked."

"Survival. My mom didn't. She hated it. Dad used to say that was why they split up. He starved for fifteen years and got tired of it."

"New line for wedding vows: in feast or famine." Chloe reached for the bowls filled with salsa, cheddar cheese, red onions, avocado, black olives, and sour cream. On a heavy trivet, there was sweet cornbread kept warm in its iron skillet.

Scott drank the last mouthful of his fourth beer and rubbed his glassy eyes. "Want another brew?"

Chloe nodded, her mouth full of chili.

He returned with three open bottles and placed them on the table. Amy sat next to Chloe, and Scott settled across from them. They loaded their bowls with toppings and silently downed the first spoonfuls.

"Raise up. To old friends and what ties them," Chloe said. They clinked bottles.

"We haven't done this in years," Scott said. "How long has it been since I cooked and we got drunk?"

Chloe crumbled a wedge of cornbread into her bowl. "No one's drunk, but we're on our way. But to answer your question, it was the summer after we finished college. The clinic protests were over, you were about to move to Ruston, I was about to move to Virginia, Aims had her new job, Jem was packing for Tennessee."

"Just us? No, I remember lots of people there," Scott said.

"Turned out that way. Somebody showed up unannounced, and then in a matter of a couple of hours, your apartment was packed. Is that right, Aims?"

"You're right," Amy said.

"Hey, I saw your puzzle under the guest bed. What kind of masochism is that?"

"It's a challenge. I have to focus on the junctures instead of the big picture."

"Remember when Jem used to hide pieces?" Chloe asked. "You'd tear up the apartment looking for them. And then, like magic, the missing bits would appear in place when you weren't looking."

"At least it didn't happen as often when he moved out. The bastard."

"You got him back good, though. Remember that time you put a roofie in his beer? He was so sensitive to stuff like that. Passed right out. You spent about an hour giving him this Bo Derek meets Bob Marley look."

Scott laughed. "He blamed you. What guy braids another guy's hair as a gag?"

"That was so goddamn funny. You remember that, Amy?"

"No."

"No?" Chloe scraped a gummy crust of cheese from her spoon. "Oh, that was before I introduced you to them. First year of college. I was living across the hall from you boys with that redheaded cheerleader. She had such a crush on you. She only dated nerds because she believed they made better husbands. Smart, never cheat, good providers. You so could have had her."

"I'm not—I wasn't a nerd."

"You're a nerd. And you know, Amy looks like her, the same complexion and nice, balanced features and petite build—sort of like that girl in the pictures we found last night, too. But my roommate—what was her name?—anyway, she had green eyes and big fakey knockers and no control with the eyeliner. Maybe that's why you didn't like her. She wasn't natural, like our girl here."

"Amy was natural from the first time I met her," Scott said. "You two were handing out condoms in front of the student union. You introduced us. We were having that get-to-know-you, what's-your-major, you-know-such-and-such conversation. Then a guy who was screaming about twenty feet away stopped preaching to people walking by and started yelling at her. The Jezebel rant. Remember what you did, Aims?"

"I walked up to him and said. 'That's no way to talk to a virgin.'"

Chloe choked on her beer. "You did that? I don't remember that at all. And I'm sure he believed you, with that little innocent face."

"He started waving his Bible at the crowd again," Scott said.

He looked at Amy until she returned the attention. He smiled softly.

"Scott dropped his book sack and had his arms raised to fight," Amy said.

"You didn't need my help, though," he replied.

"Hell, by then, we knew how to push their buttons on and off," Chloe said.

"You both should be ashamed of yourselves," Scott said without conviction. "Torturing those pious people like that."

"No way. You know how misogynistic and holier-than-thou they were. Now speaking of shame—" Chloe flicked her spoon in the air. "Someone didn't have a gram of it when that book in the living room was purchased."

"What book?" Scott asked.

"You know. That hold the orgasm, hours of bliss, tantric sex book."

"Oh, yeah," he said.

"Any book that refers to a man's *wand of light*—Scott, come on."

"There's nothing light about my wand. And I'm not allowed to do that."

Chloe and Scott nearly asphyxiated. Amy shook her head but grinned a little behind her almost full bottle.

"That's not entirely true," Scott said as soon as he could speak. "That last part. It happens, but it's supposed to be different. No fluids involved, if you get my drift."

"So how's it working for you?" Chloe asked. "Aims, give it up. Has your *sacred temple* lit up and new heights of passion been achieved?"

"He's just reading, Chloe," Amy replied.

"Well, the cover is still clean," Chloe said.

"Oh, for crying out loud," Amy said. Scott began to laugh again.

"Sorry," Chloe said. "Anyway, I looked at the pictures mostly."

Scott took a full draft. "Figures. Really, I read about it in some other books and thought I'd see what it's about. It's not a religion, but some people do it as a religious practice. I think it's interesting. The idea that two people can achieve such a level of connection through something so primal. A transcendence, I guess. And it's sort of scientific and psychological, too. The couple shares their energy, but it builds as they keep going. Lots of emphasis on breathing and eye contact. They lose sense of time and place, sometimes go into other states of consciousness. Like a runner's high maybe. That's how I make sense of it. Anyway, it's pretty deep."

"That's the kind of sex I have when I'm stoned," Chloe said.

"This doesn't require drugs," Scott said.

"Quick way to the same end."

"It's not the same," Amy said. "It's spiritual, Chloe."

"How do you know that?" Chloe traced the top of her beer.

"Yeah, how do you know? Have you been reading the book, too?" Scott's pupils were dilated so much that his irises were simply outlines. A rush of heat escaped his skin and flashed across the table. Amy flushed and returned his gaze for an instant, without the reciprocity of intent he certainly wanted.

"I'm more aware than you think," Amy answered. She bent her head toward her bowl. Scott looked at each of the women in turn. When Chloe met his eyes, her expression showed that she had no idea what had prompted such a reply.

"Anyone for seconds?" Scott asked as he left the table.

ONE AFTERNOON, when the two of us were supposed to study, Andrew spent almost two hours listening to Grams proselytize. He wasn't being polite. He was interested. Because he didn't express outward disdain, like me, or kind tolerance, like my parents, Grams felt she had her first captive audience in years.

While I concentrated on organic chemistry, she told him about mediums and spirits and the manifestations of evidence she had seen. She tried to goad me into joining them when she said spiritualism was a scientific religion—those who practiced collected proof that the veil between our worlds was very thin indeed.

Grams has a terrible crush on him now. When Andrew comes to my house to study, I kiss him hello, take his jacket, and settle in the dining room alone. On those days, Grams mysteriously has no visits with friends or one of her four remaining children. She drifts into the parlor, coiffed and coutured, as if she's surprised to see him. Their voices drone in the background for half an hour or so, until he graciously excuses himself from the conversation. I tease her later. *He's too young for you, Grams. What would the neighbors think?* She brushes the air, but with a coquettish twitch.

This Saturday afternoon is no different. We have exams soon, but Andrew doesn't miss court with my grandmother. I eavesdrop as they enjoy each other's attention.

"May I see it?" Grams says. "*Narrative of the Life of Frederick Douglass, an American Slave.* For which course are you reading this?"

"None," Andrew says. "The other day, I noticed that my copy of this work was out of place in my library. Simon—our housekeeper's grandson—doesn't know that I know he reads my books. I found this in a box of donations I had to pick up for my mother. Her charity is starting a library at an orphanage."

"Stealing from orphans? I'm surprised at you."

"I doubt the children would appreciate this particular text."

"The boy's people—are they educated?"

"No, ma'am. Simon is the first in his family to be schooled past fifth grade."

"How old is he?"

"Twelve."

"Should he be encouraged this way? A Negro boy—he is a Negro, isn't he?"

"Yes, ma'am."

"What chance does he stand to use his knowledge, as a person of that race?"

"If one follows such logic, why should Razi pursue her studies, as a person of the female sex?"

"A woman should have interests of her own."

"Of course. You told me once of your confinement. You said being forbidden from intellectual pursuits didn't help. The neurasthenia only worsened."

"Yes. One's mind must remain active." She pauses. "Certainly, the Creator meant for us all to be thinking beings in some way."

"I agree. Then if I may conclude, Simon is as entitled to seek knowledge as you or I. He's a smart boy. Wouldn't it be wrong to discourage him or take away his books, no matter how he gets them? Why deny him what he enjoys?"

"At least he's not getting into trouble. But he shouldn't raise his hopes. There is a certain place where each person belongs."

Andrew does not reply. At first, I wonder if he's considering a retort, but he is always so quick with an answer. From my father's chair at the dining room table, I focus my attention in the other room. The follicles on the back of my neck tingle. I hear a murmur, the sound of Grams whispering.

"I wouldn't ask such a thing," Andrew says suddenly.

Again, no sound.

"There are exceptions," he says.

"I suppose there are," Grams replies.

"She would say rules are made to be broken."

Grams clears her throat. "Then one must be prepared for the consequences."

Before he can respond, I walk into the room. "Mr. O'Connell, aren't you late for another appointment?"

"We were having a nice conversation," Grams says.

Andrew stands up and squares the row of buttons down his torso. "Agreed. Until next time, Mrs. Burrat?"

Grams gives the Douglass book back to him, eases from her seat, and approaches the stairs. "Good afternoon." I swear, she winks at him as she turns on the landing.

"She's an old lady, darling," I say, "set in her ways about the world."

"Your Grams is not just any old lady. Opinionated, sharp. The nut didn't fall far from the tree." Andrew throws his arm around me and leads us to the dining room.

"You said nut, not fruit."

"Right."

I sit back in my father's chair at the table, Andrew to my left. I tap a pencil against my physics notes. "What was she whispering about?"

"She's afraid your expectations are greater than your chances."

"For what?"

"To get what you want," he replies.

"And what does she think that is?"

He opens a textbook. "It's all right in front of you."

❧

THANKSGIVING BREAK my senior year, 1928. Andrew thinks I'm studying ahead for a tough exam, but I'm not.

On my bed are application packets to Harvard and Yale, their medical schools. I have told no one—not Mother or Daddy or Grams or Twolly, especially not Andrew. If I get in, well, then I'll figure out what to do. If I don't, the disappointment, or relief, will be mine alone.

Packets to five other medical schools were mailed weeks ago. There is no doubt in my mind that I will be accepted to Northwestern. My grades are excellent, the courses I've taken appropriate, my letters of recommendation glowing. I have no such confidence about the Ivy League schools, well aware that brains aren't enough. I'm too proud to use influence that isn't my own—which has been tacitly offered—or to rely on anything other than my own wits, as I always have.

I want the adventure that Chicago promises, an anonymous place where I am nothing but myself, early mornings with wind like blades, evenings when I can abandon my books and find the places where jazz has been born again. Apart from the soil of my birth, I want to see how I grow. When I promised Daddy that I would go to Tulane, it was with the understanding that he would let me go when it was time, that my concession was insurance for future freedom. By all indications, Daddy, as well as Mother and Grams, is keeping his part of the bargain.

But there is Andrew. The unexpected variable. As much as I want to believe that our love affair is one I indulge with blasé sophistication—I am a modern woman, after all—and expect to fizzle on its own, I know it isn't. Not the tiniest bit. No other boy, any I once claimed to love and indeed had in some mimicry of the emotion, has ever tempted me to change what I thought the course of my life should be. I enjoyed their attentions. Even those I loved the most, I never missed them much when they were gone.

Here, I write my name on top of the Yale application, and what am I thinking about? That the haze of his shaving cream evaporated from my fingertips before I woke up this morning, that I didn't see him at all today, that I will ring him if he doesn't ring me first, simply to say good night and I love you.

I've gone mad. I've always been so rational, so methodical about my pursuits. Single-minded. Steadfast. When I overhear whispers that wits like mine are wasted on a girl, the slights only make me more determined. I am proud of every A, the marks of my future. I ignore ladies, who barely know me, who occasionally say to my face—to my mother—that overeducated girls become barren women. I know what I am. I know what I want to be. I have known since I was child, when I discovered that the human body is a machine so great that it repairs itself and makes more of its own kind.

When will I return to my senses?

❧

AMY PLACED a mug of coffee on the nightstand for Chloe, who had finished packing her suitcase. Chloe tossed the bag to the ground and rolled it into a corner. She reached under the bed to pull out Scott's puzzle. Outside, the lawn mower whirred past the side of the house. Amy stepped near the window and brushed her fingers along the gathered curtains.

"Something dawned on me last night." Chloe traced her thumb along the junctures of Scott's puzzle. "It's not only the miscarriage that's bothering you. It's Jem."

"It's been eleven years."

"Almost to the date. The anniversary is this month. But by now, it shouldn't tear you up to hear his name."

"If it happens to you, then we'll talk."

"Oh, stop. Just stop. Why push me away when you know it only makes me more persistent?"

"It's none of your business."

"Yes, it is. We were friends before we met Jem or Scott. I give a shit whether you're happy or miserable. I give a shit whether you're freaking out. I give a shit whether you're about to sabotage your life."

"That's true. You did your part to talk me out of marrying Jem."

"That's not fair."

"You did. 'You have a great job, Aims, right out of college. You're so lucky. Why leave it? He'll wait.' And 'It's the twentieth century. No woman has to chase anything but her own dreams.'"

Chloe didn't respond right away. A look of remorse settled in her eyes. When I glanced at her, I thought of Twolly, whose well-intended guidance I had quickly dismissed. I remembered the ring box, closed, left on my vanity the morning I died.

"You didn't have to marry him," Chloe said. "You could have moved with him, but you didn't. You decided not to, remember?"

Amy stroked the folds of the curtain. "You didn't help, Chloe. All the reasons not to were political, rhetorical. Not reality. I loved him enough to marry him."

"I didn't think you were that serious about it. About Jem, sure, no doubt. But I didn't get the impression you wanted to actually do it. A wedding, all that."

"We thought about eloping."

"Didn't you want some time to yourself? You two had been together for three years. Didn't you look forward to living alone, just to try it?"

"It was an idea. It might not have been terrible."

"Does this all still hurt that much?"

Amy gnawed the corner of her lip. A dozen scents released from her—patchouli, cinnamon gum, grilled chicken, roses, sweat, rain—overwhelming out of context. "I still have nightmares. The car crashes, and no one finds us. I wake up from my coma, and he's being eaten by maggots. Or my grandfather's telling me Jem's dead, and he's crying so hard he can't breathe. Or I miscarry, and the fetus is dangling out of my body, drowning in Jem's blood that's pooled up in the floorboards."

"Jesus." Chloe held her coffee mug and stared at her friend for several seconds. "I think about him. Sometimes, I'll hear a song or catch a rerun or smell something that triggers him. I feel like we've had a chance to catch up. I let him in."

"I can't do that."

"Then what you're telling me is that you never really got over him."

"Of course I did. I moved on, didn't I? I married Scott."

"Different issue. What happened to make you so upset? Scott thinks it's because you lost your grandparents."

"He's right. That's still bothering me."

"That's only part of it. Best I've figured out, you snapped after I sent the video."

Amy didn't turn around. Her entire body tensed. The layers of muscle on her arms and calves drew into cords. Each breath was shallow, measured. She wanted to keep it hidden, buried, almost forgotten. "I wasn't prepared to see him."

"Honestly, I didn't know what was on the whole thing. And I certainly didn't know it would make you so upset."

"On the tape, he gave me the look."

"What look?"

"He had this funny wink, very fast. He'd squint right before until I'd look him in the eye, and then . . . But there was the little smile, too, with it, no one else could have noticed."

"I don't remember that."

"You wouldn't. It was just for me." Amy rubbed her eyes hard. "I'd forgotten what it felt like when he looked at me that way. It all came back. Every bone in my body turned hot. Then I couldn't make it stop. All those memories. Whatever kept them stored away broke. There was a rush of sensation all through me, then nothing. And for days afterward, sometimes I'd get overwhelmed with a sound or the way my shirt rubbed against my arm or a smell. Like my body remembered and reminded the rest of me."

Chloe sat cross-legged on the bed and watched Amy's back. Amy controlled her breathing as if to pace what she might say next.

"I don't feel the same with Scott," Amy said.

"What?"

"That passion." Amy lowered to the ground, clasped her shins between her arms, and propped her chin on her knees. "Have you ever had sex with someone, and it felt like you'd slipped away from this world, that you never trusted or loved someone so much in your life?"

"It's been a long time."

"I love Scott. He's a good man—kind, responsible, sensitive, intelligent. He's a wonderful husband. But it's not the same as it was with Jem. Making love with him was transcendent. There was nothing like it. The feeling was incredible, inside and outside of my body. I can't explain it. With Jem, the connection was almost unbearable. With Scott, it's comfortable."

"Did you ever give yourself the chance so that it isn't?"

"What does that mean?"

"You love Scott—I know this—but not like you loved Jem. You'll never love someone like you loved him. It will never be the same. But I think it could be as strong. You have to be willing to give it your all. As long as I've known you, you've never done anything halfway."

Amy shook her head. "I should have married him. I should have done it. No matter what you or anyone else said. If I would have married him, we wouldn't have been on the road that day, at that time. It never would have happened—"

"You don't know that." Chloe moved to the ground and clutched Amy's arm. "Goddammit, it wasn't your fault. It wasn't Jem's. That trucker fell asleep at the wheel."

"Had we just left the hotel later, like he wanted. I pushed for leaving at dawn."

Chloe jolted Amy gently. "Stop torturing yourself."

"Our baby would be ten."

Chloe pressed her forehead against her friend's. "Amy, listen. You have to get over this. Whatever it takes. See a counselor, grieve for your baby, grieve for him. And let Scott help. Never mind the history."

"It's too much," Amy said.

"You didn't survive to live this way."

AFTER CHLOE LEFT, Amy stopped her frenetic upkeep of the house. Dishes remained dirty in the washer, dust collected on tabletops, and an occasional crumb remained on the kitchen floor. The laundry was separated in baskets and placed in their closets. No longer did Amy iron all of their work clothes at once. She pressed hers before bed, and Scott returned to his haphazard attempt to remove wrinkles from his shirts in the morning. Magazines lay open on the sofa, junk mail mingled with bills on the counter, and lint gathered into small tumbleweeds under the furniture.

Instead of doing housework, every evening Amy sat in front of the computer scanning photographs and retouching them. For each, she changed subtle contrasts and sharpness. She seemed to want them all to be flawless.

A week after their friend visited, Scott stood in the kitchen doorway and watched her click dots of color across an image. "I can't take this anymore. You have to talk to me."

Immediately, Amy stopped her work and began to shut down the computer. "It has nothing to do with you. Is that what you're worried about?" she said.

"This has gone on too long—whatever it is."

Amy went to the bedroom, and Scott followed. She turned off the lamp on her nightstand. He held the doorframe with both arms. Amy twisted under the covers, her face toward the wall. He climbed on top of the blanket and laid a hand on her hip.

"Good night," Amy said.

"Give me a kiss."

She rolled slightly and acquiesced with an arid peck. He kissed her cheek, earlobe, neck. Amy gave him no response. Slowly, he pulled his arm away.

"Are you cheating on me?"

"That's ridiculous."

"You won't come near me."

"I'm not having an affair."

He sat against the headboard, looking down at her. "I've tried to be patient. I've waited for you to come to me. But all that's happened is, the house has been immaculate and we're falling apart." Amy did not reply. "You can't use your grandparents as an excuse anymore. It's been months since they died. None of this makes sense."

"I'm dealing with a lot. Everything will work out."

"When? Our life together has stopped. Dead in its tracks. No moving forward. Don't you want a family? Didn't we always agree we wanted a baby?"

"Scott, let me go to sleep."

"Is that it? This all started right after Twolly's birthday. Did something happen that you didn't tell me? Did someone upset you? Your mom? Crazy cousin Julie?"

"No."

Scott clutched a pillow against his chest as if it breathed. He stared at her back, which hardly moved beneath the covers. "Tell me. If you're having an affair, just tell me. I want to know." His voice was hollow. "How could you do this to me?"

Amy sat up, cross-legged, not touching him. "I'm not. I would never do that."

"What else am I supposed to think?"

"It's complicated. After—before—God, how do I tell you?" Silence. He was waiting. "I was pregnant—"

"What?"

"It wasn't yours."

"Then . . ."

"After the accident—"

"Oh."

"I miscarried. The doctor told me when I woke up from the coma."

"Why didn't you tell me?"

"No one else knows but Chloe."

Scott reached for her hand. She didn't pull away. Jem's scent infiltrated the room, the smell coming from both of them. "I'm sorry, honey."

"I am, too."

"I'm glad you told me. I swear." He exhaled, almost a laugh. "I was afraid you really were cheating. This we can handle."

"Sure." Clearly, she felt no better having admitted part of the truth.

"There's something else. I want to know."

"Chloe sent me a DVD a while back. Part of it was when we were at the clinic. Some of it was interviews, well, mainly just she and I talking. And she had some footage at the end. I didn't remember her taping it." Amy wiped her nightshirt under her nose. "It showed him."

"Who?"

"Jem."

"Okay."

"A lot came back to me. Memories. Feelings."

"And?"

"I realized how much I miss him."

Scott moved back toward his side of the bed. "You miss him? Okay—you know what—I know that shouldn't bother me. He's dead. It's not like you could run back to him. But it rubs me raw because it's affecting us now. He's been gone for years, and this is my life—our life—and somehow, he's appeared right in the middle of it. What am I supposed to say?"

"I don't know. I don't know why I feel like this."

"I sure as hell don't either."

"I loved him."

"I know."

"You don't understand. My life was taken away from me then," she said. "The shock was so awful. I thought I was dreaming. My grandfather was standing next to the bed, rattling the change in his pockets. I asked where Jem was, and he said, 'We thought we'd lost you, too.' Then Mom pushed him away and said she was glad I was awake, she tried to distract me, but I made her tell me the truth. Then I knew I was awake—my face and pelvis and leg were killing me. They had to sedate me. Mom was there when I came to again, and she told me that I'd been out for six days, and Jem was already buried." She paused. "You can't understand what it's like. Losing someone like that."

"Of course I do. He was my best friend."

"He was more than that to me."

"Even after all this time, you've never gotten over him?"

"I was—I am."

"Do you love me?"

"Yes."

"As much as you loved him?"

"I can't answer that."

Scott twisted his shins over the bedside. He stood tall and wide-legged, his fists pressed into the joints of his hips. "He's still got you, and he's dead."

"I wasn't your first love. You weren't mine. That doesn't mean I don't love you."

"In the event the winner cannot fulfill his obligations, the first runner-up will—"

"That's not how it is."

"Then how is it? I'm your husband—you made a commitment to me—and all this time, I've been nothing but a consolation prize."

"That's not true. I married you because I love you."

"Or the closest thing you could get to Jem?"

"You."

"Bullshit."

"Scott—"

"I don't want to hear it. I can empathize with the way it must feel to lose a baby. That you didn't even know you were pregnant, well, that must have been awful. And as for Jem, I'm no idiot, I know you loved him. He was your fiancé. Yeah, you bothered to tell me that before we got married. Who knew that wasn't the biggest secret?" He shoved his pillow under his arm. "But now. What about now? Old feelings can't replace your life, Amy, and they for goddamn sure shouldn't replace me."

"I'm sorry."

"Right." He grabbed a pillow and clutched it to his chest as he turned to leave. When he swept through the bathroom, he flicked off the light. A moment later, the door to the guest room slammed shut.

Amy curled into a tight ball on the mattress.

PART THREE

THREE WEEKS after Amy revealed her secrets, Scott was still living in the guest room. On the nightstand, the Big Ben never lost time. Each morning, it awoke him with its tinny ring. His weekday routine had not changed. He put on his exercise clothes, ate a small breakfast, stretched, and jogged for nearly an hour. After he showered, Scott found pressed slacks and shirts in the closet, the one across from the perfectly made bed where he hadn't slept. He always looked surprised when he found the clothes, perplexed because he had not ironed them himself, but made no comment about who had done the work. On his way out, he had stopped reaching for the soapstone box on the dresser. The route was different then. His watch and wedding band, both of which he still wore, had a new place next to the alarm clock.

Sometimes, when Scott came home, the house was silent. The answering machine held a message, *I'm still at work. Don't worry. Don't wait up.* He unbuttoned and unzipped as he went to the bathroom, where he bathed quickly. He had dinner in front of the television and watched reruns of programs from his childhood. Once he got bored, he went into the room to read or work on his puzzle, only after he left lights on in the other rooms. At bedtime, if he fell asleep before she came home, his rest was never deep. The smallest sounds roused his bleary eyes open.

And other nights, if she hadn't stayed late, he found her at the dining room table, which was now a studio of forgotten photographs. They would say hello at least, acknowledge each other, but they would not make eye contact. On those nights, Scott had dinner standing up at the kitchen counter. After he ate, he went straight into the spare room and quietly entertained himself. Now and then, he would look up and listen to the distant buzz of the scanner. He slept better those nights, but not much.

On Saturdays, he left early to meet his running group. The anticipatory grin on his face, the attention to hair combing, and the trouble he took to match T-shirts and shorts was worrisome. When he returned home, a few minutes later each week, he stocked the refrigerator with food he liked after a long run—pineapple juice, soy sausages, preservative-free bread. As he went to shower, he passed through rooms tinged with dusting spray and tile cleanser—and everything was in order. If he stayed home, he cooked lunch that they didn't eat together and stored the leftovers before they spoiled. If he left, Scott put a note on the kitchen counter. He was gone for hours and only came back once with a purchase, a new book.

Every Sunday, by nine thirty in the morning, because the heat grew flowers well into September, he mowed and edged the entire yard. If he noticed a drooping bed of plants, he set the hose on it while he drank a glass of water. He took a long, cool shower, then washed his soaked work clothes in a small load. For a few hours, he flicked through movies and news programs. He cooked supper, and they ate in shifts, each cleaning up after themselves. There had been a time when they went to bed early on Sunday nights, together, without discussion, routine as much as ritual.

AMY NEVER NEEDED the alarm, although it was set just in case. She lay on her back for several minutes before rising from the center of the bed. As soon as she got up, she pulled the covers straight and arranged the pillows, creating symmetry despite the missing one. Her pressed clothes hung on the closet doorknob, as they had every weekday morning for the last two months. She used the smaller bathroom to bathe and fix her hair. In the bathroom that joined the master and guest rooms, Amy applied her light makeup. She dressed slowly, perhaps selected a necklace or earrings from Twolly's chest. Two rings never came off her fingers, her wedding ring and a narrow silver band inset with red coral. She often had a big breakfast that didn't involve cooking—cereal, granola bars, fruit. Occasionally, she packed a lunch.

The house was always quiet when she returned from work. If she didn't stay late, Amy bathed, dressed for bed, made a simple meal enough for two, and ate as she watched the news. She cleaned and straightened the house. Later, with a determined expression, Amy went to the computer that was set on the dining table. Her office chair from the guest room replaced one straight-backed wooden seat. She pressed tiny cushioned nodes into her ears, turned music on low, and focused on the bins of paper in front of her. One by one, she scanned photographs and studied them on her monitor. The cursor moved, the mouse clicked, the images flickered until each one was as crisp and brilliant as the technology allowed. When he came home, she greeted him tersely. At bedtime, she brushed her teeth in the dark, in the bathroom they did not share.

Those nights she worked late at the office, Amy received at least one call that disconnected soon after she said hello. Sometimes there were voices behind her, mutterings about pixels or code, and sometimes there was only music. She came home to a trail of lit lamps, which she turned off one by one. Amy didn't bother with the house on those nights. There was nothing to tidy anyway. She took a long, hot soak in the little bathroom and read a few pages before she went to sleep.

On Saturdays, she woke up early as usual. As soon as Scott left the house, Amy went grocery shopping and put away everything when she returned. She set about cleaning every room.

Occasionally she would leave for the day, a note scrawled on a pad, but she never brought anything home. If she stayed, Amy monitored laundry while she watched a movie or read or touched up photographs on the computer.

The lawn mower woke her up on Sundays. She had breakfast in front of the television. By the time he was in the shower, she was in the bedroom with the ironing board and baskets of laundry. She ironed her outfit for Monday morning, but didn't iron his clothes. She had only done so during the worst of her cleaning fit. Amy folded her laundry—and his, as she had before, according to habit. When she placed his basket in the closet, she was surprised to see the row of pressed khakis and Oxfords. She touched the sharp, starched lines every time.

❧

I HAVE THE POWER to stop him.

As Andrew opens the drawers to his desk and bookcase, tossing my letters into a crate, I could make loud noises or start a fire or turn the temperature in his room to an unbearable extreme. Distract him. Give him the chance to reconsider. He doesn't know what he's doing. I know that he is not going to sit and read my words to him, because the sound of my voice in his head will mangle his heart all over again.

I could wrap around his shoulders, whisper into his ear, *Andrew, darling, don't.* He cannot hear me, but I have seen what happens when I touch him. He must believe it's a dream when he wakes with his hands gripping the air near his pillow. I am under those hands, his memory of my chin, shoulders, hips, too real, now distant. I am under those hands, my memory of his thumb against my lips, his fingers woven into mine, his palm flat below my navel. He knows something is wrong. The air should not feel as alive as the woman whose flesh he knew better than his own. Sometimes—I know my Andrew—sometimes he wonders if he's going mad.

I have the power to stop him, but I don't. I should not interfere. They are his to destroy.

He takes the crate under his arm, walks quietly downstairs, and closes the door to his father's study. The midnight blue drapes shut out all light so that the gold piping has no sheen, no color. From a far corner, he pulls a chair close to the hearth. He drops the box to the floor. Andrew takes a letter and tears it into little pieces, throwing them into the fireplace. One scrap has a drawing of a girl turning a cartwheel. The night I wrote that letter, we had spent the afternoon in the park reading under a tree and watching children scamper across the grass. He stacks kindling on top, spreads it out to catch fire.

A match turns to a cinder under the paper, but the wood doesn't light. He throws in several matches, and bits of wood start to burn, giving off smoke. He takes another letter and throws it near a weak flame. Gray puffs surround his fingers. Andrew's body gives more heat than the hearth itself.

The door slams against the wall as the light comes on above us.

"I knowed I smelled smoke." Emmaline walks into the room.

Simon appears behind her with a bucket of water and a quilt twisted around his long neck. His eyes relax when he doesn't see a fire. "You got the best nose, Ma-Maw."

With a pivot of his head, Andrew glances across the study.

Emmaline approaches him slowly. "Mr. Andrew, what you lighting a fire for in the dead of August?"

"I'm getting rid of some papers."

"Some papers?" She glances at the crate. "Simon, put those things away. And close the door when you go out."

Emmaline rolls Mr. O'Connell's big leather chair next to Andrew. "Those ain't school papers."

"No." He stares into the fireplace.

"They Miss Razi's letters?"

"Yes."

"Why you want to do that?"

Andrew tucks his elbows on his knees and wraps his palms around his forehead.

"I know you miss her. Your heart broke and don't feel like it ever going to mend. I know how you feel. When my Huey got the Spanish flu and die, well, it felted like the sun went cold and God wouldn't do nothing to keep me warm again. But you know what, baby, that's how you know you love someone with all your heart, when the world get so cold without them."

He reaches for the matches and begins to light them, one by one, pitching the flames, blue as his eyes, into the darkness.

"I seen how she lookted at you, how she talk in that sweet voice when you was around. Miss Razi, she love you. You think she would want you burning her letters like this? Trying to forget her? You not going to forget her. Ever. She going to live inside your soul till you die. You a young man, and you gonna love someone again, and Miss Razi would want it that way. But she would want you to remember all the good times and feelings you had for her. That what going to teach you how to love next time."

The fire suddenly takes with a violent rush of yellow and orange. It illuminates a silver trail along his cheek, breaking jagged through his unshaved whiskers. Andrew scrapes his face against his arm as he leans to grab the box. He takes a fistful and moves to throw them into the flames.

"Andrew, honey, don't." Emmaline places a hand on his forearm.

"I can't bear to have them," he says, his voice in fissures. He holds the crate on his lap with both hands. The tears run like quicksilver.

"Let Emmaline keep them safe. For when you ready."

"They're private. They're mine."

"I won't read them. Trust me, honey." Emmaline places her strong hand on his shoulder.

He gathers each fallen letter from the ground, places them into the box, and gives them to her. For a long while, Andrew quietly cries, Emmaline pressing circles around his spine, humming a song both solemn and joyful. I want to kiss her cheek. I blow a little breeze, and the stray coarse hair by her ear tickles her face.

"Thank you, baby," she whispers. The way she says it, I don't know if she means Andrew or me.

❧

TWOLLY DOZED in her recliner late in the afternoon. An arts and crafts program played on the television, turned up loud enough to conceal an occasional snuffle. She hugged a large red damask pillow to her narrow chest. She wore a loose cotton top with matching pants. On her feet were slipper boots.

Oblivious to the noise, Amy sat on the den floor, quickly sorting through a turquoise suitcase. There were three clear plastic bins in front of her: photographs, postcards, and various papers. She read nothing, took no second glances, flicked each item in the appropriate hollow. Images and words slipped past faster than I could take them in. A postcard landed address side up. At the bottom of the message were Andrew's initials.

"Miss Twolly," Loretta said. "Time for your four o'clock pills."

Twolly cracked open one eye. "You remembered my applesauce?"

"Yes, ma'am. It's all on your table." Her daisy petal nails glanced against the wood. "Don't you drift off again. You been doing that lately."

With a smirk, Twolly sat up tall. "Catnaps. Beauty rest."

"You pretty enough. Amy, you mind seeing to her pills? I got a pork roast need basting for y'alls supper."

"Only if you made that pecan glaze," Amy said.

"Scott coming? I got those molasses sweet potatoes he likes, too."

"No, I came alone this weekend."

Loretta scratched the side of her close-cropped head. Her

russet eyes focused on Amy. "You tell that boy we miss him, you hear? We haven't seen him in a long while. Miss Twolly, I don't see them pills going down." She left the room.

Twolly pinched one of half a dozen pills and grabbed her glass of water. "I don't know why she cooks for me so much. I barely eat anymore."

"She gets to test her recipes. She's working hard on that cookbook."

"She is quite a chef. I like a girl with aspirations. Here go the jelly beans."

Amy clasped the last handful of miscellany and tossed the smaller pieces in the bins. In her hand was a letter still in its envelope. "You're sure you don't mind my reading through all your things? Pictures are one thing, but cards and letters—"

She took a bite of applesauce. "What's to hide at my age?"

"If you're sure." Amy looked at the addresses on the envelope, typed with a clean ribbon. The postmark was still legible, April 19, 1929. It was sent to Miss Etoile Luna Knight from the New York School of Fine and Applied Arts. With a cautious lift of the flap, Amy took out the letter. Twolly had been admitted to the prestigious school, and nearly everyone who had learned the good news was far more excited than she had been.

"Your art school acceptance letter. Why didn't you go?"

She pushed the red pillow behind her back and stretched her willow limbs. "It would have been such a bohemian thing to do. Little old me, all the way in that big city."

"But you were so talented. Everyone thought so."

"I never gave it up entirely. I still made jewelry now and then until my hands couldn't do the fine work anymore. All ladies had a respectable hobby once upon a time—embroidery or flower gardening or cake decorating."

"This was more than a hobby. It was a gift." Amy placed the letter in one pile.

"Thank you, sweetheart. I know you can't imagine what it was like then. Girls just didn't run off to art schools. It was practically a scandal that I went to college at all. Experts then said education made women better mothers and wives, but that didn't make people less suspicious of those who went. It wasn't natural. What did they need it for anyway? You know, Leonard fought me when our daughter wanted to go to college. I insisted. He thought it would be a waste of money. She would just be there to meet a husband. I reminded him that we were *both* college graduates, and that we'd met three years after I had my parchment in hand. I told him his engineering degree kept us fed, and mine helped me avoid being a bore at his important office parties."

"Did you ever regret not going?"

She pruned her lips and squinted her eyes. "Regret is a strong word."

"If you could make the decision again, what would you choose? Honestly."

Twolly stared at her great-niece. She settled back and cupped her hands on her lap. "I would go."

"What changed?"

"I never found out if I was a special talent. I never found out if I was brave. The only girl I ever knew who didn't seem afraid of anything was Razi. The world be damned. How well she did in her studies, how confident she was, the things she believed in and fought for, like birth control, such a scandal it could have become. It must seem so strange to you, Amy. Your generation has such freedom." Twolly glanced into the distance, in my direction. "You know, I never told anyone this."

"What?"

"I never actually declined the acceptance. All of my friends encouraged me to go, Razi especially. I couldn't make up my mind. And then, just when I thought I'd worked up the nerve to tell my parents I was going, Razi died. Going to New York alone was one thing. Going to New York alone without knowing she was a phone call or telegram away, I couldn't."

"She was your good luck charm."

"No, she was my talisman."

Amy's silence mirrored my own.

"A shame, when you think about it. Neither of us got what we really wanted." Twolly seemed to detach from her thoughts, but the mist in the room suggested otherwise. She was thinking of Andrew and didn't want to. His essence was strangely distilled, but powerful.

"It's so sad what happened to her," Amy said.

"The Lord shouldn't take people so young." Twolly stood up and glanced at the bins on the floor. "I'm going to the potty. Listen that I don't fall in."

Loretta entered the room with a spoon coated in thick orange batter. "I thought you might like the scrapings. You okay, honey? Your eyes are all watery."

"Allergies. Too much old dust." Amy left the room to blow her nose.

Loretta didn't notice the breeze that stirred the bin of postcards.

October 18, 1969

Twolly—

Warren kept the silver necklace you made for Anna years ago and gave it to his granddaughter. It was Anna's favorite. He wanted you to know.

APO

July 9, 1955

Twolly—

Conference is a petty bore. However, the weather is perpetually sunny and pleasant, unlike what we're used to. The Golden Gate Bridge is magnificent (see back).

APO

I DOUBLE-BOUNCE the diving board and splash into the pool. After I surface, I drop my face in the water, fill my cheeks with a mouthful, and float aimlessly for a few moments. Two glasses shatter on the concrete nearby. Waves rush against my slack body. My head pulls above water as his arm crosses my chest and his hand grabs the pit of my arm.

Andrew lifts me over his shoulder and shakes. "Don't you die. Don't you die, Razi. I swear to God, don't you dare die on me."

I spout the water down his back. "My hero." He lets me down.

"What is wrong with you?" His face is red, and there are two clear puddles lining his bottom eyelids. He breathes as if he's been swimming sprints.

"I was only kidding." I touch his chest firmly. I sense the currents rushing below his skin and bones.

He pulls away. "You scared me half to death. That wasn't funny."

"It will be later. Rather convincing, don't you think?"

"Too convincing." He frowns. His whole body trembles.

I expect him to crack a smile, but he doesn't. "I'm sorry. It was a joke."

Andrew looks me straight in the eye, defies me to glance away. "Don't ever do that to me again. I swear my heart stopped."

"Andrew, please. Melodrama doesn't suit you."

He walks toward the garden chair where he placed his towel. "I'm serious, Raziela." He rubs his head and face, pulls the towel around his neck. "What if you'd slipped off the board and really hurt yourself? Be careful."

"Don't worry."

"I worry about you all the time." He stares at me until I stare back.

"I know, and you shouldn't. I'm careful as I can be. So is Gertrude."

"Your luck will run out at some point."

"I will not stop the Boyless Parties, and I won't stop leaving the pamphlets."

"Would you if I insisted?"

"What do you think?" I glare at him, unsure whether he's joking.

"I'm waiting for a late-night telephone call from your mother telling me that you're in custody. There's a sock full of bond money in my dresser drawer."

"Oh, that's so sweet." I smile, relieved. "You shouldn't worry, really."

"Perhaps I shouldn't, but I do." He runs his fingers through his damp hair until it's sleek as a black seal. "What would I do without you? You're my match."

"You sound like Grams."

"Your grandmother isn't as crazy as you think."

"I love you, Andrew. Isn't that enough?"

"For now, perhaps. But I'm your match, like it or not."

"I'd say it's a matter of timing, if finding a true love happens at all."

"What a generous statement from one so pragmatic. Your grandmother would disagree that it's timing at all. It's part of a plan. Every soul ever made has a perfect partner, she believes."

"She also believes in ghosts, darling."

He rushes the distance between us to catch me in his arms. "Bella Rah-zee-aye-lah, how you maykah me crazy." He kisses me on both cheeks. "You are such an irresistible troublemaker."

ANDREW HOLDS the door open for me to pass, and I link into the angle of his arm when he catches up with me. He carries a box from his favorite haberdashery under his left arm, a new dove gray shirt and violet tie with narrow magenta stripes. This is not the first time we have picked up a purchase downtown, or lunched at D. H. Holmes, or stood waiting while the other has admired a watch or a hat. This cold November Saturday afternoon on Canal Street, through the bustle and hum, I feel as if our steps answer each other's in a way they haven't before. I am simultaneously bewildered by and drawn to the sensation.

"I'd like a chocolate egg cream," Andrew says. "What sounds good to you?"

"Two straws."

He clinches his bicep, which pulls me into him a little tighter. "Which fountain?"

"What block are we on?"

Before he can answer, Gertrude suddenly strides into our path from a niche outside a shoe store, pulling the lapels of her winter coat around her shoulders.

"Why, Andrew, how nice to see you." She does not look at me, not directly. Then in a whisper, "Razi, dear."

"Mrs. Delacourt, good afternoon. And how are you?" he says warmly.

"Fine, fine. Oh, do you have a moment? I want your opinion about something my husband has his eye on." Her look tells us to follow. She walks ahead as if we're strangers.

"Gertrude, were you lying in wait?" I ask with as much humor as I can muster. I have not seen her in a couple of weeks. The next Boyless Party isn't for another month. Something is wrong.

She doesn't turn to face me. "I saw you two walking this way. A lucky chance. I need to speak with you."

We follow her into a department store and into an inconspicuous corner. She actually crouches next to a support column. Andrew releases my arm, and I sense the heat of his hand near mine.

"Should I come back in a moment?" Andrew asks.

"Can he be trusted?" Gertrude asks.

I glance at them both. "Yes."

"Face each other. Don't look at me. Listen. Snitchy has been raided. That isn't the problem, entirely. He's been able to keep it out of the papers by giving away what came in. But the shipment had the usual items, his wholesale purchases, you understand, and what he allows in as well."

"They checked the fruit crates."

"He usually has his different goods shipped separately, or mixed, but this time they came all at once. A larger shipment than usual, and for some reason, that tipped off someone at the port. Someone who turned out to be more appalled about finding certain paraphernalia than bottles."

"What's happened?" My body is a furnace. I want to take off my coat.

"Nothing yet. He's claiming there was a mistake with the shipment. That some of it didn't belong to him. That may not take him far. His wife does have a reputation." She smiles briefly. "He has a couple of favors to call in. He's not happy to use them in this way, I tell you." Gertrude meets my eyes. Her almond shapes narrow to slivers. "We can't be seen together, dear. The next party has to be canceled. It's temporary. I need to find out how much word has spread."

"What can I do?" I ask.

"The impossible. Keep quiet. Don't implicate yourself. You have too much to lose." She looks at Andrew, then at me again. "I promise, this is temporary. When it's safe to begin again, we can if you wish. We'll have to take a different tack. If desperate women come to you, you're absolutely safe still. You don't know what I know to help them. As for the rest—"

"This can be maneuvered," I say. "There are other ways."

Gertrude smoothes the front of her coat. "You're too brave for your own good. Be careful, dear. You will do so much more from a physician's office than a prison cell." She grins with mischief, finally. She's worried about me, about us, but Gertrude is a woman of adventure. We understand each other.

"Yes, ma'am," I say.

"Andrew," Gertrude says, "Razi tells me that you're a young man of rare character. Prove her right."

She peers around the column, then strides out of the store with her shoulders wide, pushing the air out of the way.

I need a still moment to decide what I will do now. I think of the grateful women who have left Gertrude's house with a sense of control that had been denied them before. That freeing force is not so easily stalled. In an instant, I think of what my mother said when she learned women had won the vote: *Our daughters have a say from now on. Oh, the fear of what you'll tell them.* Her laugh was merry, proud—and conspiratorial. She hugged me close for a long time.

Andrew remains quiet. He watches me. His expression reveals conflict.

"What I've been doing is my purpose. It's something I hold true. I'm not afraid."

"I know you're not," Andrew says. "Fear would at least dissuade you."

"You're angry."

"Yes, but I'm not sure why. Come on. Let's have that egg cream. I'm suddenly ravenous."

He allows me to pass first. I take his hand. He returns the pressure. When we step into the street, he releases my palm and offers an arm to keep me close.

❧

ONE WEEK before our senior year first-term exams, January 1929, Andrew and I study in the library. Without glancing up from his book, he asks, "When will you hear from Northwestern?"

"Early spring I think. What about Yale?"

"Same time, I'd expect. Do they have a nursing school, too?"

"Probably. I don't know. Why?" I stare at him until he looks up.

"Have you ever thought of that instead?"

"Instead of becoming a doctor? Never."

"It's still medicine."

"What's your point?"

"Women doctors aren't particularly well received."

"That's hardly a reason to become a nurse. As if that notion would even discourage me. I'm perfectly capable of doing what it takes to be a physician."

"Without a doubt."

"Ever since I was little, that's what I wanted to do. All during high school and now, well, I could have taken domestic science courses, but that's hardly science. It's a consolation prize for all those girls who want something more but someone tells them they can't have it. No matter what job a woman gets these days, there's always someone who says she shouldn't have it anyway."

"Some situations can be worse than others."

"If you haven't noticed, men don't intimidate me. I can handle myself."

"There are different kinds of men. You're being idealistic."

My chest becomes a vacuum. He means naive. "I know I'm going to have to be twice as smart to get half as far. I don't care."

"Don't get angry."

"Too late. Why did you even broach the issue?"

"I was merely curious." Then he fidgets. A roll through his shoulders, not so subtle that I can't read it.

"Tell me."

Andrew eases himself into his chair and tries to look as comfortable as possible. "What if we married?"

"What?"

"Hasn't it crossed your mind?"

"Not especially."

"It hasn't?"

"Not in a way that made me consider giving this up."

"I wouldn't ask you to do that."

"Aren't you now? Become a nurse. How could you? Would I question why you don't choose to be a court reporter instead? Never. No one will ever interrogate you about your aspiration to become a lawyer. You get to pick what you want to be, and people think it's grand. Don't you think I notice that dismissive look in people's eyes when they find out I'm truly working to get a degree, not a husband?"

"You're exaggerating."

"Then ask your mother what she really thinks of me."

"Honestly."

"Would it shame you if a wife of yours worked?"

"Why should it?"

"The truth."

"It doesn't matter what other people think."

"You didn't answer the question."

"No."

I collect my books into a pyramid and draw them against my chest. "I don't know whether you're lying to me or yourself."

"Neither. Razi, you have my full faith. I would be proud of you, regardless of what you chose to do."

"Until someone asks you who wears the skirt."

Without a good-bye, I walk briskly from the library. I am too furious to cry. A sharpness streaks through the core of my body. What do I feel, what is this edge? Is this the edge of his love for me, where it ends, beyond reconciliation? Sooner or later, it was going to happen, wasn't it? Andrew was bound to buckle under the strain of a practical world and consider what part he was expected to play to strap us in our proper places. I'm angry at myself. I should have anticipated this, prepared for its implications. I am many things, but I am not naive.

I FOLLOWED the rule for the most part. I didn't interfere with the lives of my family. Rarely, I did cheat, and then only on their birthdays, only on my best behavior. Mother, Grams, and Daddy didn't acknowledge that they sensed me—no wistful glances around the room, no sniffs, no tears. The physical changes in them were abrupt, without seamless days and nights gently letting me know they aged.

When they died, I was not there. I would have been a distraction. I might have caused them afterthoughts in the awareness of their deaths. Had any of them stayed, I would have gladly taught them what they needed to know. If there was something beyond, I hoped there was explanation for them about what happened to me. If not, it was just as well they didn't know about the alternative.

After they were all gone, now and then, I went to the graves and polished the stones. The Burrat tomb was almost full—great-grandparents, infant great-uncle, Grandfather, Grams, some symbolic part of Uncle Roger—a beatific, feather-winged angel keeping watch on them, over my Grams, who hated such fairy-tale simplifications of the unknown. How Grams gained entrance into that Catholic cemetery, I have no clue. Her baptismal and confirmation certificates aside, she hadn't attended mass in decades. I wondered if she had chosen to return to my grandfather, a devoted wife in death as well. In another part of the city, in a small Episcopalian cemetery, the Nolan tomb held my bones, then Daddy's, then Mother's, the order in which we left each other.

The bones, where cold and intuition eat at the marrow.

How simple, how obvious, the reason we were not to visit our own graves. Being so close to my remains, what was left of my body, reminded me of its absence. My flesh was dust, but even that could be sifted, felt, an outline sketched into a rotted silk lining. I wanted the pallid, calciferous scaffolding back, the anchor for muscles, the core of every movement. I wanted pain and pleasure in its physical form again.

I was not alone.

Once, Noble appeared as I was burning away weeds from the edge of the Burrat tomb. He watched the plants wither, disintegrate, and join the earth again. "I never thought to do such a thing," he said. "I take them out at the roots and blow them away."

"Why are you here?" I asked. "Changed your route?"

"I come here rather often." He almost touched the scapular around his neck. He began to drift away, toward the old tombs.

"Noble—"

"Good day, Razi."

I trailed behind him, curious. His wife and children were buried in a mass grave somewhere in the city. Not in this place. He stopped in front of a dilapidated tomb that was clean and well tended. The weather had worn the inscriptions, but they were still legible.

"Leave me alone." He blew dust away from his name. Noble began to mutter the Act of Contrition.

I had seen him in such moods before, the memories as sharp as the events. His emotion had been stirred by an anniversary or a birthday, perhaps the midsummer hum of mosquitoes, the descendants of ones whose poisoned saliva made his family bleed to death under their skin. This time, he hovered at the foot of his grave, in prayer, apologizing for his mortal sins.

Noble turned to spot me hidden among the stones. He knew I was still there. I moved toward him.

"You will not understand," he said. "Such pain, worse because it is not of the flesh. The body is simple, no matter your science. Agony reaches far deeper. All those days and nights I burned the candles I made with my own hands. Filling our rooms with His light, our prayers. People at my storefront shouting, 'Open the door and sell us your candles,' while my wife and children vomited blood in my hands."

"Noble, there was nothing you could do then. No one knew that mosquitoes carried the yellow fever virus, much less how to stop the spread."

"I was bitten as well. My arms and neck were covered in bumps."

"No one understood why one person got sick and another didn't."

"But why was I spared to watch them suffer? Such devotion I had shown to Him and the Virgin Mother. Such faith. And I was not the only one. My children, my wife, they prayed. They had trust in the Lord." Noble glanced at me. "I lost them all, one each night, my wife, my four babies. As if God had chosen to prolong my agony as He ended theirs."

"I'm very sorry."

He reached toward the sealed tomb entrance but didn't touch it. "I was rarely sick. I was never injured. I died in my sleep. At peace, to some. I was never at peace. Such a burden—the desire to have faith as strong as the desire to abandon it. I prayed for the burden to lift, but it did not." Noble faced me. "When I was called to go, I refused to pass the gates. I disobeyed. Why honor a father who won't ease his child's pain? And in the instant I refused, I realized the fallibility, that all I had been told was not gospel." His smile was bitter.

"Why do you come to your remains, Noble?"

"The ache for my body eases the ache of my soul."

"So why pray when you don't have hope for an answer?"

"You are lucky that you have never believed. I wish I still did not."

MORE THAN TEN YEARS had passed since I checked on Simon Beeker. The fifties were history. It was 1962.

He walked down the banquette with his head immobile above his long neck. That stretch of vertebrae, as if he had one or two extra, is what I recognized first. Then I scrutinized the proud, intelligent face that still bore his grandmother's nose and his father's Caribbean eyes.

He nodded cordially to neighbors along the way. The briefcase in his right hand looked heavy, but he did not stoop to equalize the weight. Simon's left arm swayed with military precision. With each upswing, his wedding band glinted in the autumn morning sunlight. Coils of gray spiraled throughout his close-cut hair. His suit was navy, well fit, and he wore a white shirt and orange block print tie. He was forty-six, but he could have been mistaken for being a decade younger.

The high school grounds were quiet, too early for students to arrive. Simon walked into the red brick building and whistled down the bright hall. He took a drink from a fountain, inspected his image in a half-glassed door, and checked his watch.

In a classroom, he placed the briefcase on the desk and withdrew a stack of papers. Exams, graded. On the board, he began to write a list of names from the Civil War. Along the walls were posters of family trees, some that went no further back than two generations, some that included only first names on earlier branches, many with empty or question-marked dates. Simon had done his own, too. He included his parents, grandparents, aunts, uncles, cousins, half-siblings, his wife, and their three children.

The back wall had a large, neatly painted wooden sign screwed into the masonry: *Those who cannot remember the past are condemned to repeat it. George Santayana, 1863–1952.*

Simon dusted his hands away from his body. He reached into his briefcase and took out a battered textbook. The print on the cover was outdated, a typeface familiar in the Depression years, when modernity was embodied by bold sleekness. The second book was much older, well loved. He opened the cover and turned the first few pages slowly, copyright, title page, inscription. A first edition, *Narrative of the Life of Frederick Douglass.* To Mr. Simon Beeker. Regards, Andrew O'Connell. Simon's smile was resolute.

Moments after the bell rang, young people began to enter his classroom.

"Morning, Mr. Beeker," they said as they placed homework assignments on the edge of his desk.

"Good morning," he replied. Simon watched them file into their seats. He looked as if he had something important to say.

SEVEN WEEKS had passed since either spoke a complete sentence to the other. Neither attempted to find the humility, or courage, to make amends. The silence, more than their physical separation, grew in its power to keep them apart for good.

On Saturday, Scott returned close to noon to an empty house. He grinned as he went to shower. His musty salt odor barely masked a ginger essence that wasn't his. The smell had followed him home before. Someone from his running group had his attention. The intensity, however, had changed. Its presence wasn't a passing thought. In its strength, there was danger. He had not crossed the line yet.

As he removed his running clothes, he whistled a Sousa march, something he had not done in many weeks. Another tune began once the water hit his back. Droplets flew vigorously over the curtain as he washed. After the soaping was complete, he stood quietly under the spray. An open bottle of shampoo tipped over the tub's edge. *Shit,* he muttered as he turned off the water and tried to collect what hadn't run down the drain. Scott paused, sniffed the bottle. He recognized the familiar almond aroma around him, but it was not the shampoo he had used. The scent belonged to Amy, but her toiletries were in the other bathroom that she had been using. While he dried off and dressed, he was silent and skittish. He looked around as if he realized something was missing.

Scott spent most of the day in his favorite chair, watching television and reading. Late in the day, he got up and went into the front room. He opened the bookcase to find a volume in its usual spot, but it was not in the place where his fingers landed. Scott skimmed every title on the front rows, then shifted books around to look in the back.

Amy suddenly entered the room. She grabbed my revealing photographs from the place she'd left them among her own. Scott looked at her harshly.

"Where's the dictionary?" he asked.

"In there. As usual." She turned to leave.

"Everything is out of order. It's not here."

Amy stood next to him. "You probably left it somewhere."

"No, I didn't. You must have moved it."

"I haven't moved anything." She stared at the rows, befuddled.

"Then what happened in here?"

"I didn't do this."

"Maybe you don't remember doing it."

"I didn't." Amy glanced at him suspiciously. "Maybe you don't remember moving anything."

"I haven't been in here for weeks."

Amy began to walk out of the room. "Log on to the Internet. Look it up there."

He followed her. "I still want the dictionary."

"It's somewhere. It couldn't have disappeared."

She entered the bedroom and opened the closet. As she kicked her shoes to the floor, Scott blocked the doorway and scanned the tops of the furniture. Amy walked past him to the chest of drawers where she kept her nightclothes. He dropped to his hands and knees and crawled to the foot of the bed. Scott peeked underneath, then moved to the right side, his side, and stretched his arm.

Amy stood nearby as he pulled out the dictionary. Several marbles rolled from under the bed, bouncing against each other. A thin layer of dust covered the dark blue hard cover. Scott sat down and whipped his finger against gray haze. As he grabbed the thick spine, he noticed a narrow rectangle poking from the top of the pages. Scott slipped it free. He stared at the old photograph of them at a pool, before they had married, before they were pushed into the deep by a devilish, bearded friend.

Scott didn't move. Amy peeked over his shoulder.

"Chloe," Amy said. She could only assume it had been her friend's doing.

"Why?"

She sat next to him. "To make a point. To remind me."

He did not pull away when she took his arm and laid her forehead on his shoulder.

IN THE DARK, across from each other on the sofa, they tried to begin again.

Amy had not told Scott because the way she felt changed from year to year. In those first few weeks after Jem died, she mourned for the baby she had not known her body held. She confided in Chloe alone, the one person left whom she trusted completely, the one person she could not disappoint. Her grief was complicated. She wouldn't have welcomed the pregnancy under different circumstances. She had been using the birth control pill and had not missed a dose. The failure was a shock, a betrayal of her responsibility. She remembered having a light cycle that month, unusual but not unheard of, and days of light nausea. She blamed the stress of Jem's leaving for her body's malfunction.

Almost certainly, all things considered, had Jem not died, she would have had an abortion. But it was only speculation, she realized, because the moment she learned what had happened, she wished the loss undone.

During the long weeks that she healed, back in her old room at her parents' house, her first job on hold, she caught herself turned sideways in mirrors, imagining the steady convex swell. Her parents would have been aghast if she had been pregnant, more so because she could not marry and make things right. But Amy knew her mother would have slowly recognized that there was a grandchild on the way, and the tragedy of Jem's death would bring more sympathy than shame. There were times she was tempted to tell her mother about the pregnancy. As a mother, she could imagine her daughter's pain. By then, however, Amy felt confused—relieved that she had no decision to make on her own, no child to raise by herself, angry that she had lost Jem in another way she didn't expect, that the accident had decided the fates of them all, ashamed that she would not have wanted the child, surprised that sometimes she did more than anything.

Then, after she left the nest again, she rented a new apartment and returned to a job that had been temporarily filled by someone else. Through those long work days, Amy realized that she could not have cared for a baby alone. Secretly, with guilt, she was glad that the choice had been made for her. That is, until the quiet of her apartment became too much and she wanted something, someone, there to hold. Someone to need her again.

The baby would have been born in May. During the first week of that month, she imagined the event of a birth that never came. Amy remembered calling Chloe and crying so hard she couldn't stop. Her friend was living in Virginia. Chloe was ready to board the first available plane. It took a three-and-a-half-hour discussion to calm her. Amy would have named the baby Jeremy if a boy, Michaela if a girl. It had Jem's dark hair and her blue-green eyes, his long fingers, and her tiny seashell ears. Amy wondered if the burst of emotion and imagination was normal. Chloe assured her that it would have been more disturbing if she'd had no reaction at all.

Then each year, the child she envisioned grew. He was a boy. Little Jeremy's presence was rare, but Amy felt him completely when he appeared. She dreamed of him. Sometimes he ducked around supermarket shelves and doorways. She once confided in Chloe about her specter child. Chloe did not poke fun, did not tell her to get over it. Jeremy was a part of her, even if no one had ever seen him.

She wasn't sure why she had not told Scott about the miscarriage. When their friendship rekindled, she wanted to focus on their happier moments. By the time she had fallen in love with him, she noticed that she thought of the child less often. Amy knew Scott wanted children of his own, and to her knowledge, there was no reason to worry about whether she could conceive again. However, Amy still wished, at times, that the baby had been born. That he was Jem's child complicated her admission; there was too much history among the three of them. Amy believed Scott would understand, but she feared what she would unleash by talking about it.

Then, almost a year before, when Scott initiated the first tender proddings, inquiring whether she was ready for a baby of their own, the specter child came more frequently. He no longer resembled her, but he would not let her forget he was hers.

When Amy finished, Scott took her hand. "I'm sorry. I wish I could have helped you somehow."

"I'm sorry I didn't tell you."

"You just did."

That night, they lay in separate beds, but neither slept well. They both knew there was more between them than the child who could have been.

❧

"YOU WERE like that as a child, weren't you?" Andrew says.

I look up from my book toward him. He points to a girl several yards away. She is seven, maybe eight years old. Her strawberry blond bob tumbles into a shag each time her hands touch the ground and falls with two delightful curves along her cheeks as she stands. She moves so quickly and the space between her knees is so wide that her dress doesn't fall to her dainties. With a toe pivot, her cartwheels turn into walkovers, her back and thighs curve with hidden strength to pull her up again. A little boy no older than four attempts his own cartwheels but looks like an arthritic frog instead.

"What do you mean 'were'?" I stand up, tuck the hem of my skirt into my garter bands, and toss my cloche on his lap.

Before Andrew can grab me, I run toward the children, brace myself against the momentum, and spin ten perfect cartwheels. The little girl's jaw suspends from her high bunny cheeks, but the boy claps. I bow toward them, which only makes the boy cheer and the girl join him. They line up on each side of me, and we three acrobats spin across the ground, cartwheels and somersaults, the grass springing back to life when we release it. We collapse to the ground, dizzy, and I lie facing the sky, my abdomen screaming with laughter. The children giggle nearby. As I calm down, a woman's voice stage-whispers behind me, *Susan, Herbert, come here right now.* I pitch my head back. A woman not much older than myself glares at the mess of us, meets my eyes. I can only smile. *What have I told you about these shenanigans, little girl?* she says. *Ladies don't behave so shamelessly.* That last sentence was meant for me. Susan obeys, but before she walks away, behind her mother's back, she blows me a kiss. I pretend to catch it on the tip of my nose. Clumsy Herbert steps on my hand but gives me a most precocious grin as he steadies his gait.

When I stand to brush the blades away, I see Andrew sitting with his spine flush against the tree, deciding whether to be amused, embarrassed, or appalled.

"You shouldn't have done that," he says with a paternal tone that betrays the glint in his eyes.

"Why not?" I fluff and primp myself back into respectability.

"It's indecent."

"Depends on what you were looking at."

Andrew can't hold the scowl any longer and laughs. "Their mother looked angry."

"Livid."

"What kind of mother would you be?"

"That assumes I want to be one."

"Humor me."

I tuck my hair under my hat and thumb to the page I had been reading. Andrew lays his book flat on his thighs. "Honest. I wouldn't hide anything, like pretend I'm happy when I'm not or fail to give the facts of life. I'd be indulgent. I don't mean I'd let my child have lollipops for supper, but I would want her to become an individual, not force her to be something she doesn't want to be. And affectionate. Children like to be held and kissed and petted. Respectful, too. A child should be allowed her own opinions about things."

"You would raise a child the way you were raised."

"I suppose you're right. So what kind of father would you be?"

"A good provider, of course. My children should have every necessity. Good educations, too, and what extras I can afford to encourage their interests. I also want my children to be safe and secure. That's important to me. Even though I expect to be very busy with my work, I want to be attentive to them. Suppose my child wants to talk to me, about his day or any such thing. I should listen, not put him off." He pauses, looks at me. "I agree with you—children need affection. Sometimes that can be as important as kind words, don't you think. And I want the child to know I love him and for him to love me, not only because I'm his father."

"Like you were raised." I knew in my gut that Andrew spoke of aspirations, not of models.

"At the foundation, yes, of course."

"You would make an awfully cute daddy. Cream of wheat on your shirt, a damp patch on your trousers."

"Do you think I'd be a good father?"

"Haven't you always been good at what you put your mind to?"

"Yes."

"No different in this case. It's all in what you want."

"I think you'd be a good mother."

"Do you? Why?"

"The child would never question how much he—"

"Or she."

"—or she—is loved."

My throat opens to reply, but I haven't a clue what to say. Such a strange little reason, as if that were reason enough. Absolutely sincere, almost as if he'd thought about it before. Finally, I pat his knee. "Thank you, darling."

Andrew gives me an affectionate smile and turns back to his novel. As I look at him, I picture his face as an old man, the wrinkles unable to obscure the handsome geometry there, and I'm scared half to death by the sight.

I AWAKE FROM A NAP, wet, and Mother tries to dress me in dry clothes. I am barely two years old. Naked, I scamper across the room to look out of the window. The summer storm taps a fast rhythm against the roof, which I try to mimic with my little feet. A thunder roll echoes in my belly. I pull the ribbon from my fine blond hair and circle it around me.

"Raziela, come here." Mother holds a dress on her lap.

"No, no, no, no, no," I sing.

"Then I shall get you and tickle you silly." She rises from her knees and begins to inch toward me.

I squawk, run through the door, wobble down the stairs faster than I've ever gone—Mother exclaiming, "Oh, slow down!"—and whip through the living room. My father looks up from his magazine as my blur and trailing red ribbon approach him. A moment later, he lets out a trumpet blast of a laugh.

As I struggle with the back door's knob, Daddy says to Mother, "Our daughter is indecently exposed. Shame on you."

"She takes after you, darling," Mother says.

I slam the door closed as their footsteps approach. By the time they are outside, I am in the middle of the backyard with my face to the sky, giggling as the drops create rivers down my body. A metallic trail of water parts my lips. A thunderclap startles me. I scream with more delight than fear. Slowly at first, I spin, my ribbon above my head. I close my eyes and spin faster. The grass peeks between my round toes and licks my ankles. My breath is shallow with joy—I have only enough air to bellow my giggles.

Then I hear my parents. I stop in mid-twirl and watch them hug under the narrow jut of the back porch, their cheeks wet with tears. They are laughing so much that they have to hold each other up. They look funny. I point at them and say, "Don't cry," which only makes them laugh harder.

Daddy releases my mother and kicks his shoes down the steps. He pulls off his socks and walks toward me, unbuttoning his shirt, which is on the ground by the time he takes my hand. "The water's fine, Claire." He starts to sing "Beautiful Dreamer." I hold his finger and twirl under him.

Mother's slender feet join ours. Her voice harmonizes with

his. I let go of my father and turn several clumsy pirouettes away. Their bodies move into a close waltz. Mother clutches Daddy's wet undershirt against his chest, and Daddy nudges a drippy curl of hair behind her ear.

I clap as the song ends. "Again, again!"

Daddy opens his arms. The water splashes my sleek legs. He gathers me up, his whiskers stippling my wet face, pulls my mother into us, and begins to sing as the rain falls in time to the music.

AMY CONTINUED to visit Twolly almost every other weekend. Invigorated by the attention and the photo project, and perhaps the cool October weather, Twolly had begun to clear rooms she hadn't touched in years. Full closets were purged of clothes that had miraculously come back into style, a boon for Amy's wardrobe. Old business records filled several garbage bags. She set aside all snapshots and miscellany for her great-niece.

While Twolly and Amy were distracted by their organizing, I scoured the boxes for signs of him. I had yet to find a single letter that Andrew had sent. My memory kept a tally of the postcards he'd mailed—dates, locations, business or pleasure, and, I realized, no mention of a family. Within several weekends, I discovered a pattern of correspondence from Pennsylvania, which often conveyed Warren and Anna Tripp's regards for Twolly.

Months earlier, as Barrett Burrat, I had sent a concise letter to the only Warren Tripp Jr. I could find through a computer search. I had received no response, and I especially wanted one after I found a reference to Andrew's work, a direct acknowledgment I'd never seen before. In November 1953, Andrew wrote, *Classical education dead. Moot court worst ever. I fear for their clients.* The postmark—Philadelphia, Pennsylvania.

Twolly, too, had not replied to the letter asking for her memories of friends and fun at Tulane and Newcomb. The letter was still on her kitchen counter, a layer of dust on the torn edge of the envelope. I knew that her days were not so full to cause such a delay. Although I didn't want to, I had begun to resent her silence.

One afternoon, over cake and coffee, Twolly placed a bright yellow hatbox on the kitchen table. The interior was half full. Amy pushed the layers around. There was nothing but dust, photographs, and paper.

"These are from my girlhood," Twolly said. "Look at my hair, how long it was. My sister Fleur would braid it so tight that I always looked surprised. Maybe that's why I don't look my age. She firmed me for life." She lifted an Easter postcard. "I hope I have a picture of me with that bonnet. You know what? There's another one of these boxes somewhere. My daughter's old room, maybe. Or the attic."

"One room at a time, Aunt Twolly. Don't wear yourself out." Amy gently closed the box.

Twolly watched Amy trace the daisies on the placemat. "This all isn't taking up too much of your time, is it?"

"I want to do this. Honestly. I don't mean to sound morbid, but you're the only one left." Amy reached across the table. The photographs she had already scanned were organized in a new, acid-free box labeled "Knight Family" on all sides. "Where do you want me to put these?"

"The closet we're cleaning now. At least you'll know where they are, too." Twolly finished her coffee and wiped a creamy mustache from her lip. "Ready to start?"

Amy grabbed a large envelope on the edge of the table. "Wait. I want to show you these." One by one, she laid out the photographs Chloe had discovered under the drawer.

Twolly looked at three and giggled. "Oh, my. Oh, my. Where did you find them?"

"They were hidden in our bookcase."

"Bookcase?"

"We bought it in New Orleans a few months ago. My friend Chloe—you met a long time ago—she found them under a drawer. I kept forgetting to bring them to show you. I thought you could help me figure out how old they are."

My friend peered closely at another, then another. Suddenly, the perfume I once wore released from her. "Oh, my God. It can't be. It's simply not possible. How in the world—"

"You're not offended, are you? I thought you'd find them interesting."

"I'm not offended. That naughty girl. After all this time, still shocking people." She waved my naked body in the air with one hand while the other pulled more images toward her. "This is Razi. She had quite a lovely figure, didn't she?"

Amy's eyes glimmered. "Are you sure?"

"Without a doubt. There, see this one? That impish little smile. That's Razi."

"I didn't recognize her. So who took the photos? They're not like any nudes I've seen before from those times. These are more artistic."

Twolly didn't look up. In a blast, his scent filled the space between them. "A beau. It must have been."

"Was one of her boyfriends a photographer?"

"Most people had little Kodaks in those days."

"The quality is more professional. Even the paper feels different. Thicker." Amy paused and ran her thumb along the white edge of an especially revealing shot. "Could it have been the same boy in the picture I found a few weeks ago? Andrew."

"Andrew. Of course."

"Quick—before you think too hard—what was his last name?"

Twolly caressed my face, shaking. "Oh, honey, I can't remember everything. It's been so long."

"Why are you blushing?"

"I—a girl shouldn't see her dear old friend naked like this."

Amy smiled mischievously. "Is there something you want to tell me?"

"No."

"You're trembling. And you're flustered. Did you have a

crush on him? Aunt Twolly, did you have a little romance with this Andrew?" Amy pinched Twolly's arm, barely touching her skin. "Or maybe one that wasn't so little? It was the 1920s, after all."

"As if—no indeed," Twolly said, indignant, as she gathered the stills into a pile. Her movement stirred the smell of him in billows. "I'm freezing. Aren't you cold? Did Loretta touch the thermostat again?" She left the room hugging her shoulders.

Amy rubbed her arms hard, then stored my photographs in the envelope. When she left, the air above the table remained icy. I could detect nothing except Andrew's scent, his scent alone.

I was unsure what to make of the strength of his presence.

CHLOE HAD NOT abandoned them. Although she didn't call their home, certainly aware that neither would reveal much if the other were present, she kept in touch. Sometimes when Amy checked e-mail, there was an inquiry or reply from her friend. The communication was so brief in writing that they must have talked at some point to fill in the gaps.

Scott received messages, too. Chloe sent an occasional joke or link to an item of interest, sometimes with a little note that stated she hoped he was okay. Days after Amy told him of the miscarriage, Chloe wrote to him: *You know about the pregnancy now. I thought she'd told you a long time ago. I couldn't have told anyway—it wasn't my place. I'll bet you're pissed and hurt, but be kind to her, Scott.* He had written back, *I'm trying but the miscarriage isn't the issue. No doubt you know what I mean.*

The evening after he replied to her e-mail, Chloe called. Amy was still at work, and Chloe knew this because they had spoken minutes before.

"Sit down," Chloe said, "because you're not going to like what I'm about to say."

He leaned against the kitchen counter. "What?"

"You're going to have to face how you feel about Jem, too."

"Don't make this my problem. I'm not the one still carrying a torch."

"You're still carrying a grudge. It's ridiculous at this point, and it's not fair. He had no idea how deeply you felt about her—"

"I'm sure he sensed it."

"Who didn't think she was the cutest little demure thing they'd ever seen? You know you weren't the only guy who had a crush on her. Jem got one hell of a rise out of that. Amy never noticed because she's dense that way. You know it firsthand."

"What's your point?"

"You never believed they belonged together, but you based that on what Jem was like before they met. When we first got to know each other, he wasn't the most upstanding guy. I did worry a little when they started dating."

"Chloe, you tried to set her up with me a couple of times. You were more than worried. You were playing matchmaker, and not for him."

"She was such an innocent. I wanted to watch out for her," she said.

"So did I."

"And we were both wrong about the whole thing. Whether or not it makes sense to you, they worked. Their devotion was real. Their love was real. What do you think would have happened if Jem hadn't died?" Scott was silent. Chloe waited another moment. "Would they still be together?"

"Who knows?"

"You're hedging. You know they were one of those couples who actually could have made it. That bugs you. Even now. Even though he's dead. Even though you got the girl. But the truth is, you still see this as a pissing match."

"She still loves him."

"Of course she does. If you were the one she loved first and you were dead, would you want her to stop loving you?"

"I would want her to move on."

"That's not the question."

"I suppose I wouldn't want that to happen."

"This is what I've been thinking. You cared about Jem. I'm sure you loved him in that distant way men do. There were a lot of good times, and except for Amy, there was nothing else between you. He would be glad that you and Amy are together. He would want this to work out, for both of your sakes."

"Nice try, but the fact is, she's not over him."

"She told you that?"

"She told me about the DVD. Whatever you caught there did something to her. Get this straight. I can deal with the miscarriage. I was actually relieved when I thought that's all she was hiding. Then she told me how much she still misses him. If it were just that, I could handle it. I'm not an asshole. I'll admit it—I miss him, too, sometimes. But when she started cleaning the house like a maniac and became celibate overnight—that's not normal."

"No, it's not."

Scott rubbed the back of his neck and sighed. The room began to smell of freshly mowed grass and a dry-cleaned suit.

"What?" Chloe asked.

"I just thought of his burial. There was an empty chair next to his mom. She made sure no one took the seat. I knew it was meant for Amy. I remember thinking how glad I was that I didn't have to see her sit there. I felt like she was spared a part of the unbearable." He was silent. "But she wasn't spared. That's it. She took a shortcut."

"Hmm. That simple?"

"It's a place to start."

Dear Mr. Burrat,

My wife has been reminding me to write you for weeks. I finally made myself sit down to reply when I got your second letter. I hope this hasn't stalled your work, not that what I have to say will necessarily help your research that much.

It's really too bad that my parents are dead because they would have written volumes for you, but my mother died in 1969, and my father died in 1975. Mr. O and Dad got along well, it seemed. They shared an interest in current events, so that's what they would talk about most of the time. Now, my father could argue about anything until he was blue in the face—get downright obnoxious sometimes. But Mr. O would listen respectfully, give his side on the issue, and change the topic. My father would try to egg him on, but nothing riled up Mr. O. I admired his composure, even when I was a kid. I'm sure you've heard this from other people you've interviewed.

You referenced a note that you obtained, dated November 1953, and asked for confirmation regarding Mr. O's residence at the time. I was in my last year of high school then, and I recall that he came to dinner every few weeks. He was at Penn Law for two semesters and lived somewhere in the city, an apartment I would assume. Before and after that, however, he would come to visit my folks and his relatives in the area about every other year. He came alone often; rarely did his wife join him. Mrs. O was a great lady from what I recall. She was a small blond woman with a nice laugh. Mom got along well with Mrs. O. They seemed to have a lot in common.

I always got the feeling that Mrs. O didn't quite measure up for my parents, though. Occasionally, they would talk about Mr. O's sweetheart who passed away. They would get unusually nostalgic—and sad, very sad. They had liked that young woman, Rahzee. They would shake their heads and say "Poor Andrew" whenever they'd bring up her name, and never in Mr. O's presence. I got the impression that it was a taboo subject.

I rather miss seeing old Mr. O. He was a quiet, generous man. He gave me good advice when I was trying to pick a law school and wrote a recommendation to Boston University on my behalf. That alumni edge got me in more so than my grades, I'm sure. In the early days of my career, I would occasionally call him up for advice. He had a knack for bulletproof arguments.

He truly cared about my parents, too. He kept ties with them no matter how far apart they lived. I guess that's how it goes with old friends. I know that's true for me. Mr. O was devoted to them, even in the end. He was on the first plane out when they each died. I was devastated by the loss of my parents, but the toll seemed especially hard on him. You could see in his eyes that he was a deeply sensitive man.

You didn't mention whether Mr. O is still living. Is he? If so, would you mind sending me his number and address? I'd like to check on him. My parents would appreciate it if I did. I shouldn't have let him get so far out of touch. You know how to reach me if I can be of any further assistance.

Very Truly Yours,
Warren Tripp, Jr., Esquire

At least I had new leads to follow, more connections to draw me to Andrew again. I simply had not anticipated that he would take a quieter, less prestigious route toward the same goal. I fully expected him to attend Yale, what he always planned, and puzzled over why he chose not to go. Although the letter from Warren's son was affectionate and helpful, it told—as others had—of an Andrew I hardly recognized. To think that the interactions between him and Warren had lost a former zeal. And still, what truly became of him remained out of my reach.

ANDREW AND I talk on the veranda, and a girl I don't know approaches confidently. He greets her with a warm handshake and introduces us.

Corrine is a girl he once loved. He has told me that they were steadies in the fall of their second year in college, but the romance was over by the following spring. Andrew enjoyed her company until he realized they shared few interests. At about the same time, she hoglawed out of school—a scholar she wasn't—and spent her days shopping and lunching. He ended it, and was grateful that the parting had no drama. He sensed she had only been trying to figure out how to get out of it, too.

I notice that Corrine is a traditional beauty with bright, wide blue eyes, amber hair, and a full mouth and bosom. Her smile reveals even ivory teeth, all the same size. We learn that she is doing charity work and is engaged to a young man who graduated from Loyola. Then Warren suddenly appears, gives her a brusque hello, clamps Andrew's shoulder, and pulls him away. Andrew calls out his apologies.

"He's a dear," Corrine says. "The most mannerly boy I ever dated."

"I'd say the same."

"Does he still have those long discussions about politics?"

"He hasn't figured out that cynicism is chic."

"Well, at least he has a passion about something."

"He certainly does."

"I'm sure we've never met before, but your name seems familiar. Isn't there a Mr. Nolan on the Cotton Exchange?"

"My father owns an advertising business."

"Really? Then how did you meet Andrew?"

"His birthday party year before last. Lots of people from school were there."

"What are you studying?

"Science. I'm going to medical school in the fall."

"Really? How does Andrew feel about that?"

"He's going to miss me."

"Oh, look, there's my fiancé. It was a delight to meet you. Give my best to Andrew, would you? Have a lovely evening."

"Thank you, Corrine. You have the same." She disappears through a group of girls. I follow behind, and she lands on the arm of a man in his late twenties. For a moment, I scan the dance floor. A couple of stags notice that my arms are free.

"Good evening, Miss Nolan," says a voice to my right.

"Jimmy Reynolds. I haven't seen you in ages. How's every little thing?"

"Dandy. How's the old girl?"

Before I can answer, he rushes me to the edge of the dance floor, away from the stag line. This violation of etiquette amuses me. I look up at his face. He hasn't changed that much since he was twelve. Freckles along his nose, cowlick at his temple, crescent scar on his chin. He has finesse now; he understands where his hands go.

Whether it's from the heat outside or Jimmy's hand, the last of the bath powder at the small of my back melts toward my coccyx.

"There goes the dainty dusting I gave myself, right down the spine." I say.

"Excuse me?"

"The icing has melted down the cake."

Jimmy cuts his eyes at me, then laughs.

"Where've you been hiding yourself?" I ask.

"Alabama. Mobile. I'm managing my father's new hardware store."

"Enjoying it?" I notice two boys stamping the ground, waiting to step in.

"Sure. He's paying me a decent salary. College life seems to suit you. Someone told me you're blowing this joint."

"Medical school in Chicago."

"Really?" Jimmy leads me into another corner. "Stag narrowly avoided." He stares over my shoulder. "In a minute, sport."

"What did you mean by 'really'?"

"Well, you're smart enough. But nobody figured you would actually go through with such a pipe dream once you found a man to settle on. It's just not done, old girl."

"Watch me," I reply with a little more venom than I intended to spit.

"In any case, this may be the last dance I get with you."

"Why's that?"

"I'm engaged."

"Congratulations. Who's the girl?"

"She's from Mobile. Peggy. Very sweet, good family. I'm nuts about her."

"You're blushing. You're such a peach."

The song ends. Jimmy releases my hand but lightly presses his fingers into the middle of my back. On the periphery, the two boys who were making a dash try to move in casually, but the band puts their instruments to the side. Break time. I wink at them, tap my watchless wrist, nod toward the bandstand, and beckon with my finger. They smile, then flinch at each other.

"No special guy for you?"

"And spoil all of this attention? Never."

He laughs and puts his hands in his pockets. "I've heard otherwise."

"I've had a steady for more than a year. Andrew O'Connell."

"There's talk of a betting pool on when you'll get engaged. Quite a coup, snagging a fellow like that."

"No coup. I'm irresistible. So is he."

"Let me know where you land, will you?"

"Pos-a-lutely. It was so good to see you, Jimmy, honest to Zeus. Your Peggy is a lucky girl." My hands latch on his shoulders, and I give him a soft peck on the cheek. Because I can't resist, I lightly pinch the scar on his chin. "Slide into second."

"What a memory. Thanks for the dance. Good night, Razi."

Our hands meet and brush apart. I cannot find Andrew, but I see Anna near the punch bowl. As I approach, she waves.

"We're being neglected again." Anna rolls her eyes.

"As if they don't see enough of each other." I take a dainty cup of pineapple punch and look in the boys' direction. Warren flicks ashes off the porch while Andrew points his clasped fingers at Tom and Alan.

"I shouldn't complain. This is all over for Warren soon enough. We're moving after the wedding. I found out yesterday. Philadelphia. One of Andrew's cousins got him a job there."

"You don't seem excited."

"This is the only home I've ever had. I don't want to leave everyone. I'm not brave in that way. Not like you. You'll be leaving soon enough for your own adventure, but it's one you want. I always thought I'd live and die here."

"You don't have to be there forever, Anna."

"I know. Look at them. Warren loves to get Andrew stirred up, and he falls for it every time."

"He couldn't survive without a good debate."

"He adores you, you know."

"I had a feeling."

"I saw you talking to Corrine earlier. Nice girl, but those two never made sense together. There were other girls, too, of course, dates now and then. For a long time, I thought Andrew was too picky. No one seemed good enough for him. Their families weren't respectable enough. That wasn't it. He wanted a girl he could talk to, one who wouldn't just agree with him about everything. Remember the dinner party last December?"

"Of course I do."

"Well, I confess. I thought it was strange that you left us girls after dinner. I'd heard you were a bit of a baby vamp, so I wondered which of the boys you were really after. Then Warren told me what happened. He said you two didn't agree at all about whatever the argument was over, but he respected that you stood your ground. As for Andrew, well, he's known Andrew since they were little, and he said he's never seen that old boy more taken with a girl in his life."

"That's kind of you to mention."

"It's the truth. I'm very fond of Andrew. We like seeing him so happy."

The band comes back, and a fast number starts up.

"I don't know about you, but I came to this party to dance. Shall we?" I hold out my hand, and she guffaws loudly.

"You're a kook."

We shimmy across the dance floor. Couples part to let us by. Several stop in mid-step and begin to clap. Tom notices us first. He gestures a time-out among the boys. Warren stares at me and grins like the devil. He knows who's responsible for this scene. With no warning, Warren hooks his arm at Andrew's waist and grabs his wrist. The crowd sways with laughter. The drummer misses a few beats, and both the trumpet player and the clarinetist squeak a whole bar. I expect Andrew to brush off his friend, but instead he takes the lead—Andrew is slightly taller and stronger—moving them in our direction. Anna and I barely keep time as we laugh at our beaux, who suddenly take every step seriously. The song ends with a clamor of hurrahs and applause. We all bow to the audience.

The band transitions into a slow, easy tune. Andrew whisks me into him. He sweeps his chin lightly down my cheek. "This is better," he says.

AMY WAS READING in bed when he knocked on the door. She pulled the covers over her hips and bare legs before she called him in. Scott entered the room like a stranger. They made eye contact again, finally, but there was no hint of the easiness that was once between them. He sat on the edge of the mattress. From the calm look in his eyes and the drop of his shoulders, it was clear he had no intention of fighting.

"I need to tell you something," he said.

She closed the book on her finger and faced him.

"We both know I was jealous of Jem because he had you. I won't apologize for the way I felt. I cared about you then. I knew Jem in a way you never did. I didn't think he deserved you. I never admitted how I felt because, one, it wouldn't have changed anything and, two, deep down, I wanted to see you happy. You were happy with him.

"By the time we ran into each other after I moved back here, I had managed to grow up. I'd had a few girlfriends, you know all that. When we started hanging out, I really didn't have any expectations. It was just nice to catch up. It was strange not to have Chloe or Jem around, and I realized that—before—our friendship had depended on their presence. Our connection wasn't with each other. It was through them."

Amy remained silent.

"Remember that night you invited me to your boss's Christmas party? We got bored and went for ice cream? It was freezing, and you took my arm as we walked back to the car. You didn't mean anything by it, nothing romantic anyway, but that's when I had no doubt you were absolutely comfortable around me. I knew we were good friends."

"I remember," she said.

"When things started to change between us, I realized I'd only been infatuated before. I liked the idea of you. I was surprised when I felt somewhat guilty for falling in love with you. We didn't talk about Jem, but he always seemed to be around. I did wonder what he'd think. And then I felt guilty because I felt that I'd won. As if I'd been vindicated somehow, like this was the way things were supposed to turn out. That's awful, I know."

She didn't reply and began to smooth the flat sheet against the mattress.

"Maybe we should have talked more about Jem. It had been so long, though. He had been dead six, almost seven years by the time we started to date. But I underestimated him—when he was alive and after he was gone. And you underestimated how much he still means, too."

"I didn't lie to you."

"No, but you did hide. We never talked about his death. Sometimes, we mentioned something we'd all done together or a movie he liked, but nothing else. I have no idea what you went through after he died. And then, for me to find out that you were pregnant. What good did it do to keep quiet?"

Amy wouldn't look at him. "It was my private issue. No one had to know."

"I'm not some stranger on a plane. I'm your husband."

"That doesn't give you a right to my every thought."

"But it's like you don't trust me."

"I trust you. There are some things too hard to talk about."

Scott placed his hand on her covered shin. "Listen. I'm still angry. I can't breathe sometimes, this feels so bad. But I love you.

I want to work this out. I think we can. You'll have to want it, too. Deep inside, you probably believe that you and Jem would still be together if he hadn't died. I agree. But that's not how things turned out.

"You have to make a choice. We can salvage this relationship, if you truly love me, if you truly want to, or we can go our separate ways. In either case, you're going to have to confront Jem's memory. If you don't, well, I can't imagine how very sad your life could turn out to be."

"He's dead. What else is there to confront?"

"How did you feel about missing his funeral?"

She curled her bare knees inches from her chin. "It didn't matter. He was gone."

"Do you know what the funeral was like?"

"Chloe told me later."

"Did you talk to his parents after the accident?"

"A couple of times."

"Did you know his mom had an empty chair next to her at the grave site for you?"

Amy almost looked up but jerked her muscles in check. "No."

"She did. You got along well with his family. Jem said that a couple of times." He paused. "Did you ever go to see them later?"

"No."

"So you've never been to his grave."

"No," she said, her voice constricted. She tucked her head onto her bent knees.

"This is as bad as it gets. The truth is out. Part of you still loves him, but the other part loves me. I know it. Right now, you get to choose who wins out. I love you, but I'm not willing to linger much longer. For your sake, make peace. Knock if you need me."

He stood up, smoothed the hair away from her forehead, and kissed the crescent of skin he revealed. As he walked away, Scott looked tranquil and resolute.

DURING THE NEXT few days, their paths crossed more often, but they still retired to separate rooms. She brought work home instead of staying at the office. His schedule changed again so that he didn't have late evenings at the pharmacy. Although the dining room table was still a genealogical disaster area, a corner had been cleared so that two people could eat at the same time. One Saturday night, they watched a movie together. Amy made popcorn.

Before she went to bed, earlier than Scott, as always, Amy peeked into the guest room to tell him good night. Each evening, they chatted a little longer—how far had he gotten on his puzzle, what she was reading now, what tomorrow's schedule would be—and whether she noticed, she had stopped tying her red plaid robe and clutching it as tightly at her chest.

When the lights went off, Amy did not slip under the covers alone. Jem was beside her. He misted across her open eyes. She stared straight at the ceiling, thought projecting into the space. There were times her face revealed her feelings, a cheek-blossom smile, soft lids with a softer lip, narrow brow wrinkles and tight jaw. When she cried, she wrapped into her pillows as sound roared under her sternum and suffocated at her throat. There were times that his hands moved within her own, over her, remembering. Little by little each night, as Jem's essence dissipated before she fell asleep, the sheets began to hold hints of the man who once shared her bed.

Then one morning, she went through her usual routine, left for work, and returned twenty minutes later to an empty house. Amy carefully hung her outfit and changed into a T-shirt and shorts. She dragged a sturdy chair under the attic entry, gripped the cord with both hands, and yanked with all her strength. The hinges stretched and groaned. The ladder fell out halfway.

Amy brought eight boxes of various sizes from the attic into the front room. She emptied the contents of each one across the floor, spreading the treasures into a single layer. School notebooks, photographs, men's clothing—several shirts for different seasons, a green windbreaker, brown belt, two pairs of jeans, a paisley tie, one holey pair of boxer shorts—brochures, news clippings, yin-yang button, brush, toothbrush, bottle of cologne, postcards, incense, scraps of paper, cards, letters, a small diamond ring.

She stripped to her dainties and selected a pair of faded blue jeans and a wash-worn flannel shirt. Her petite body shrank into the drape of the fabrics as she sat among the items. Amy placed her hands on opposite shoulders and swept her fingers slowly downward. Her fingertips brushed the white thread patch at her right shin. With a hesitant stretch, Amy reached for the incense and cologne. She inhaled the arid, exotic spiciness of a russet-colored stick. Then, the top off the cologne, she brought the scent to her nose. A sharp, soft whimper lifted in her throat, and her eyes turned glossy. She pressed two fingertips to the bottle's opening, angled the vessel until the amber liquid touched her, and anointed herself at the hollow of her neck.

She wiped her cheek with a flanneled arm. Her wedding band caught at the first knuckle and came away with a jolt. She let it roll inches away, it could not go far, and then reached for the ring Jem had intended for her. It fit still and looked delicate on her fine hand.

For hours, Amy cleared spaces among the mementos and held each one, studied each treasure in turn. She took breaks but never for a second longer than necessary. She wasted no more time.

After four that day, she called Scott at work to say she was home. She asked him to give her time alone, well into the evening.

"Why? You're okay?" he asked. "You haven't, you aren't . . ."

"Please, Scott. There's something I have to finish."

"I'm leaving now. Don't do anything. Stay there."

"I'm okay. You don't understand. I can't face him with you here."

"What?"

"Jem. He's out. I brought him out."

"You're scaring me. I'm coming home."

"Don't. You don't need to see this. Please. Go to the movies, get something to eat, come home later, well after dark."

"You're not going to do something to yourself?"

"Nothing you should worry about. I promise."

When she hung up, Amy went back into the room and grabbed a stack of cassette tapes. The fall light paled as she listened to dozens of songs, some over again. All the while, she fondled the shirt that swallowed her whole.

Night inked into every room. Only the dim streetlights guided Amy's steps to the bookcase. She found the disc she had stored there and placed it in the DVD player. With the pictures moving, she fast-forwarded to the end. The frames slowed to real time when Jem's sandaled feet appeared. The volume rose at the sound of his voice, a strong baritone.

When the party shots began to roll, Amy cried. She had not seen any of the footage from this point on. The camera panned a dining room connected to a small kitchen entry. There, near the doorway, Jem's shoulders—covered in the shirt Amy was wearing as she watched his image—arched out and down. Two arms moved across his lower back. Jem suddenly turned his face to the lens and shook his head, clearly communicating *not now.* As the camera moved back, Amy could be seen pressed against him, her face near the political buttons he wore, her nose touching the yin-yang symbol on his chest. The microphone hummed with music and chatter. Jem told her, *It'll be okay. We'll have the whole drive up. Sex in at least one strange bed . . .* He nudged her, and she smiled. *Thanksgiving will be here before you know it. This is only temporary.*

A blood-iron gust escaped her lips as the wail rushed from her core. She did not stop it, did not try. Her body, overwhelmed, rocked with the intensity. So much at once.

I wanted to take her to me, the instinct to comfort. I wanted to brush the wet streaks from her face and stroke the length of her back. My touch could not be trusted to soothe. Instead, a cool, sweet breeze began to spiral around her. Amy's tears evaporated before they dropped to her chin. She breathed more steadily. She looked up and noticed that the ceiling fan was not on. She wiped her dry cheeks with mild surprise.

When Scott returned close to eleven, Amy was in the front room in the rocking chair, still surrounded by Jem's possessions. In her lap were his clothes that she'd worn that day. Scott called to her, frightened. She answered him.

He stood at the doorway but did not turn on the light. He stared at the floor.

"I won't be home next weekend," she said.

"Where are you going?"

"New Jersey."

I could not follow Amy on the trip. I knew all too well that shared grief is a misery too raw to witness.

DADDY ONCE TALKED to Andrew as easily as he did to me. Now they stand across from each other near the stairs, avoiding each other's eyes, silent. Grams spaces dining room chairs around the circular table she had my father take from the attic and centers one large candle. Mother draws Daddy's wingback further into a shadow, out of the way.

My grandmother begins to pace near the front door. She pulls the curtains away from the window and peers through the wavy glass. Her appearance is no different, but she trembles almost imperceptibly. Mother sits on the edge of the davenport. With a gentle caress, she sweeps a lock of amber strands smooth against her temple. Her cheeks are pale and taut; she looks too thin. Daddy is completely gray, and his eyebrows appear frozen at the skin. Andrew blinks as if he has just awakened from a restless sleep.

At the knock, Grams rushes to the door and opens it with force.

"Good evening, Mrs. Burrat." The woman's eyes are black, so black her pupils don't exist, and her hair is a burnished pewter. Long, spatulate!fingers reach for Grams, and the two women clasp hands briefly. She looks at the others in the room, inspects them, and nods. The brilliant violet scarf around her neck falls to her flat bosom. When she drapes it back into place, her silver bracelets rattle, and one ring of five snags on the fabric, pulling a filament loose as spider silk. Her dress bodice is fit close, but her skirt falls in an antiquated cascade of layers.

Oh, the costume is perfect.

My grandmother introduces Madame Boliva to Andrew and my parents. She takes each person's hand and searches their eyes. I will Andrew to cross his left one, the strange trick that always made me laugh, but he doesn't. He shows her no disrespect. His eyes are brighter tonight than they have been in weeks, but the shine is feverish and the color is subdued. My parents bow their heads after the greeting. Mother slips her arm around Daddy's waist, and he rests his hand at the small of her back. When he kisses her forehead lightly, Andrew looks away.

Their complacency is maddening. This time, they've humored my grandmother too much.

Madame Boliva asks that the candles be lit and all other illumination extinguished. Andrew offers a packet of matches from his pocket, and Daddy turns off every lamp, even the porch light. The table's center glows while the rest of the room fades into vague shapes. She invites them to sit. Madame Boliva, then Grams, Andrew, Mother, Daddy.

"I have been called here tonight to reach the spirit of Raziela, beloved daughter, granddaughter, sweetheart," Madame Boliva says. "She has recently left our world but is not far away, I assure you. In the next few moments, I will ask that we join hands to connect our energy. Please do not be alarmed when I slip into my trance. I may vocalize strange sounds and move about. This is not unusual and simply a manifestation of my powers." The woman pauses to look at each person's face.

Yes, your powers.

"Are there any questions before we begin?" she asks.

"Will she appear?" I am surprised at Andrew. What is he thinking?

"Materializations are rare, but it is possible. There are many other signs the departed can use to show that she is with us. She may appear through ectoplasm, a mysterious whitish substance, or she may manipulate objects. Does anyone else have a question? No. Very good. Then we shall begin. Please, everyone, join hands. Hold tight. Close your eyes. Breathe deeply, for breath is the essence of life. In your minds, picture your Raziela. Keep her image fixed before you."

Madame Boliva begins to sway, first from side to side, then clockwise, her forearms pressed into the table as she links hands with Grams and Daddy. "Oh, spirits, open your portal. Allow one of your own to join us now. We ask for Raziela, dear Raziela. Join us, loved one, join your family."

I peek under the table. Madame Boliva has removed her right shoe. A toe reaches toward her left ankle and scratches. I wait. There's something under that skirt, I know it.

"Spirits, find Raziela among you. I beseech you to invite her to return for a moment. Bring peace to this grieving family."

No one speaks. Daddy opens one eye, scans the table all around, and closes it again. I want to hug him.

"Wait. I feel a presence," Madame Boliva says. She squints her eyes to look around, then locks her spine and sits with her bosom pitched forward. She blows lightly on the candles and makes each flame twist. "It is a bright energy. Oh, how it nearly blinds me." Although everyone's eyes are supposed to be closed, she still whips her face over her left shoulder and winces. "Listen. There is a growing wind." From her throat flows a strange noise, a waver more than a wail, but it sounds as if it comes from the opposite corner of the room.

Grams immediately straightens her back. Andrew opens his eyes and looks around the room. Mother and Daddy tighten the clasp between them.

"Mother. Call to your child," Madame Boliva says.

The woman who told me to be silent in Sunday school but did not expect me to believe says nothing. She is crying, mercury streams at her cheeks.

"You cannot speak. I understand. Father, is it in your power?"

"Raziela. Rah—zee," he says, as if this is a macabre game of hide-and-seek.

"Oh, it grows stronger."

"Raziela, come to us," Grams whispers.

Madame Boliva starts to shimmy at the hips. Tiny bell-like sounds rise around her. Above the table, there is no vibration in her hands. "She laughs. She is not sad."

Oh, for the love of Zeus.

Suddenly, the bottom of the front door turns blurry. A naked child emerges through the oak. She had been no more than three years old. One so young I would not have expected to wander. As Madame Boliva implores me to come to them, I approach the little girl.

Her form is opaque. She has been between at least as long as I have, six weeks, perhaps longer. I can tell that she once had olive skin, wide brown eyes, and brown hair. She realizes that I'm coming toward her, that I see her, and she doesn't move. Her hands dangle at her chest like a squirrel's. *Yes, I see you. I'm Razi. What's your name?*

Donna.

Don't be scared. Are you lost?

She nods.

Why did you come in here?

The bells. They're pretty.

Stay with me, Donna. Don't leave. I'll help you.

I am furious, that this sham is being performed in front of my family, that this child roams naked and no one has helped her, that I did indeed join them tonight, only to witness their ridiculous complacency. With a gust, I suffocate the candles. Madame Boliva demands that everyone remain in place—my spirit is there.

Donna leaves my side and takes a book from Grams's end

table. She holds it in her hands, then releases it with a little push. In this darkness, they can barely see it float right-side up toward the door. When it hits the leaded glass, the book falls with barely a thump. The noise makes the vision real.

Donna shoves a vase toward the ground. It doesn't break. She giggles. She grabs as many magazines as her arms can hold, and a paper geyser suddenly erupts to the ceiling. Donna claps, and the lights flicker with every meeting of her tiny palms.

Come here, little girl. Don't touch.

I try to immobilize her with an electromagnetic cyclone, but the energy pulls out of my control. The framed photos near the stairs rattle against the wall. The glass shatters. Needle-sharp splinters fall to the wood floor, the sound of a thousand miniature bells. Each photo—of Grandfather, me, our doughboy Roger—drops to the ground. My uncle Roger's face drifts toward my feet. Glass shards spike through his head, neck, shoulders. How strange. He had died in a rain of shrapnel and bullets.

Madame Boliva watches the torn pages flutter. "We acknowledge you, Raziela. What message do you have for your loved ones?"

My family searches the room with anxious eyes.

The child walks around the table and taps each set of clasped hands, which pulls away at the contact—Mother and Andrew, Andrew and Grams, Grams and Madame, Madame and Daddy. My father drapes his arm toward the empty space. Donna immediately crawls into his lap and wraps her arms around his neck. When he appears to press her small dense form into him—an embrace of instinct—she curls against his body and places her right hand on his chest.

"Claire," he says, frightened—his torso jolts forward in a tremor—the chair rocks under him.

"Leave him alone!" I yell at the child, who sits up straight, turns to me, and jumps down. I realize in an instant that Donna has no idea what she has done.

"She reached you, Father," Madame Boliva says.

I rush toward her—I want to hurt her, burn her skin, melt away the costume. This woman has no clue what she called forth. She feels the heat, protects her face with her arms, and screams.

The circle breaks. My family shouts in reply, tearing away from the table. I am furious, and the walls knock—I cannot control myself—the more I try, the louder they get, until Daddy staggers to the light switch and exposes the tableau.

Everyone is standing. Mother's hands are pressed to her mouth. Grams stares at the ground by Madame Boliva's feet. The medium points her toe near her loose shoe and the fallen bells. Andrew hangs his head, his fists in knots. In a corner, the mysterious child holds herself, her eyes wide and brimming.

"She reached you," Madame Boliva says, her voice authoritative. "What a dramatic display. Even I have never felt something so strong. She is powerful."

"Madam," Andrew says, "you have absolutely no idea."

"That was not my daughter," Daddy says. His right hand guards his heart.

"You cannot question what you witnessed. And you, Mr. Nolan, she made contact with you." Madame is firm, sincere.

"That was not my daughter." Daddy storms toward her and kicks the bells across the room. "I don't know what trickery—what strange mesmerism—you brought into my house, madam. It was a cruel thing to do to a family at a time like this."

"Barrett, please," Mother whispers.

"Leave. Now." Daddy is enraged enough to strike the woman.

Madame Boliva lowers her face, steps into her shoe, and walks to the door. She lets herself out. A metallic breeze flows past her, warning of a violent storm on its way. The knob mechanism clicks softly as the door closes.

Daddy swallows hard. "Lily, don't you ask me to do this again. Ever."

"Darling," Mother says.

"Claire, don't—I need a drink." Daddy rubs the sweat from his brow and heads toward his study.

"Oh, what happened?" Grams says. "Never have I seen such a thing. Never have I felt such a presence."

My mother peers at Grams, then Andrew. She can't deny what she has seen, but it is not her nature to discuss what she hasn't settled in her own mind. Andrew, who is usually so quick with appropriate words, remains silent. Instead of sharing his thoughts, he takes my grandmother's hand, then Mother cradles her left arm. Andrew's entire body becomes tense and rigid when Grams and Mother begin to cry.

Within moments, Mother steels herself. "Let's get you settled upstairs," she says finally to Grams. "Andrew, you're welcome to stay. I haven't seen you in a while."

"Thank you, but I should be going."

Grams kisses him on the cheek, then Mother clasps her hands on either side of his tense jaw. "Oh, Andrew," her voice breaks, strained and weak, "don't become a stranger." She kisses him, too.

"Yes, ma'am. I'll say good night to Mr. Nolan and see myself out."

AS ANDREW walks down the hall toward my father's study, I turn to Donna, who is still in the corner. *Come with me, baby. We can't leave yet.* I urge her to walk ahead. She moves slowly, looking in every direction. I am tempted to hold her hand but know I should not. I'm unsure of what might happen.

Andrew stops at the study's threshold, squares his shoulders, and summons the will to walk into the space. Daddy stands in front of his desk, staring at his wall of books.

"Mr. Nolan, I'm leaving. I wanted to wish you good night," Andrew says.

"You know what she did once?" Daddy's back is to the door. "She took every book on the shelf and rearranged them in the opposite order. Aristotle to Yeats, top left to right and down, became Yeats to Aristotle. It took me a month to realize what had happened. She never let on about what she did. She waited for me to find her out." He tilts his head back briefly. I hear him swallow. "Everything is out of order, Andrew. She should not have gone first."

"Yes, sir."

Daddy turns around. His glass is coated with a brown glaze. He attempts not to blink. When he does, a tear hangs at his lashes. "How has it been for you?"

"Difficult."

"With feelings. I know you have them."

Andrew stares at him. He holds his breath and tells the truth. "Agony."

"I think she's here sometimes. I sense her. Smell her. It's my mind playing tricks, I know. I know. My baby—" Daddy's voice cracks. "My baby would find that funny, appropriate. The imagination at work. Does that happen to you?"

"Yes, sir."

"It's as if, for that instant, she's not gone. What's strange is that I live for those moments. If I didn't have them, I don't think I could bear this grief. What happened tonight—" He fills his glass again. "Want some?"

"Yes, sir."

Daddy takes a second glass from his desk drawer and pours a double shot for Andrew. They drink in silence within yards of each other. I raise my ethereal hand toward my father's face and wave a breeze to dry his tears. When he appears to look at me, I startle and the room echoes with a succession of firecracker pops.

"Did you hear that?" Andrew asks.

"Automobile backfired."

"No. I hear those all the time."

"Your own unique shellshock, perhaps."

"Mr. Nolan, I—" Andrew swallows a mouthful and squints against the burn. "I want you to know—that I loved—love—her."

"Andrew, don't you think I could see that?"

"Yes, sir, I suppose you could."

"I have something. I wasn't sure when I should give it to you. For some reason, I thought there would be a right time. A best time." He takes a small metal box from a side drawer. Andrew reaches across the desk to take it from him, then pauses.

The letter I'd forgotten on my way to his house that day. It had not been thrown out with my belongings.

"I thought Claire was cleaning out her room too soon. I was afraid something important would be thrown away. I found a package addressed to Twolly on her vanity. I put a few items I thought she'd like to have in there, too, some jewelry, and mailed it to her. She sent me a note to say she was glad to receive it. And that letter, it was already addressed to you. It was sealed then. I never opened it, I swear."

Andrew places his empty glass on the desk, takes the envelope, and touches the seal. My scent, the one only he has ever known, rises between him and my father. "Thank you."

"Well, yes, you're welcome." Daddy wipes his face and finishes his drink. "When do you leave for Yale?"

"Three weeks."

"I'm glad you're going. She would want that as well." He pauses. "I will miss our discussions."

"I will, too. You are a formidable debater."

"And you are a true champion." Daddy extends his hand.

Andrew shakes my father's hand with respectful seriousness. Daddy, however, doesn't let go when the gesture should end. He looks at the man he has grown to love as a son, although he has never admitted so. I wince as Daddy bursts into tears, covers his face with his free hand, then reaches that arm toward Andrew, drawing him in. My daddy clings to Andrew.

When they step apart, they mash their arms into their faces and clear their throats.

"Good luck, Andrew. You're a bully fellow."

Andrew tucks my letter into the front pocket of his trousers. "Likewise. Good night, Mr. Nolan." He leaves with his expression composed and uncompromised.

I want to go with Andrew this instant but know I cannot. Not yet. There is the naked three-year-old child near my hand, alone and lost, who demands my attention. For a long moment, I stare at my father as he stores away the whiskey and straightens his clothes. *Daddy, I love you.*

Donna stands next to me. She nudges my edge. *I want my daddy, too.*

❧

ALTHOUGH THE LATE OCTOBER NIGHT was cool, Chloe and Amy didn't have their drinks in the warm and ornate lounge at The Columns on St. Charles Avenue. They seemed to like the privacy that the chill allowed them in the small alley on the side of the old mansion. Chloe snuggled into the shoulders of her pea coat. She pulled a lapel to the side, ripped a sticky conference name tag from her shirt, and rolled the paper into a cylinder. Amy zipped her jacket to her sternum. At a round table under half-bare tree limbs, Chloe entertained her friend with stories of three recent bad dates and one promising fellow she'd met at work and lunched with, alone, on several occasions.

"He's the first guy I've met in a long time who makes me lightheaded when he smiles." Chloe gnawed the end of a plastic olive skewer. "My hormones must need balancing. It's ridiculous at my age."

"Oh, enjoy it. It's good for your circulation."

"So are you going to tell me about your trip to Jersey? I've been very well behaved by not asking. But you know I'm dying to find out."

Amy sipped her merlot. "I took a late-night flight to Newark on that Friday, so I rented a car and stayed in a hotel near the airport. The next morning I drove out to his parents' house. They were very kind, very welcoming."

"Had you told them why you were going?"

"I talked to Brenda—you remember his mom—before I left

town. I wasn't sure they'd want to see me. As it turned out, they were apologetic that they hadn't kept in touch after the accident. His mom said the family had such a hard time with Jem's death that they couldn't think of much else. Then she said, later, she didn't want to interfere with how I had moved on."

"Ironic. That might have made a difference." Chloe reached for the other olive in her martini.

"Brenda said she'd dug out some of Jem's old toys and pictures and other things if I wanted to see them. It was up to me. Whatever I needed. Then she and Doug offered to leave the house to give me privacy. That really surprised me, and I never would have asked, but that's what I wanted. So she brought me upstairs to his old room. It's a guest room now, but it had the same furniture, same double bed. I almost started to laugh because the couple of times I went to visit his folks with him, I slept in his older brother's room, but I'd sneak over in the middle of the night to Jem. You know."

"Aims, I had no idea you would dare such a thing." Chloe laughed.

"He couldn't believe it, either, but he didn't send me out."

"Of course not."

"I did ask his mom to stay with me for a little while. There wasn't much I could tell her about the accident, because I've never remembered much. I remember seeing the truck in the distance and telling Jem it seemed to be going too fast, and then the next thing I saw was my grandfather's face when I woke up from the coma. Brenda told me about his funeral and how much they missed him, even still. Then they left me alone. I wandered the house and matched pictures of him in different rooms. That was strange for some reason. Sometimes the angle and perspective were just right, and I could hold the photo, line up a window or doorway or picture, and there he was."

"Weird," Chloe said.

"Then I had a late lunch. His dad had cooked and left a smorgasbord for me to pick through. A couple of amazing pasta salads."

"Jem used to make that exotic one with sun-dried tomatoes. Remember?"

"His dad's recipe. Doug had made some, but I couldn't eat much of it. Jem's tasted exactly the same. I couldn't swallow. I didn't expect food to make me cry."

"I'm not surprised."

"For the rest of the day, I watched a stack of videotapes his mom had left in his room. Some were old Super 8s that had been transferred. No sound." Amy paused, a hesitation more than a break. "You know what's creepy?"

"What?"

"The . . . our . . . baby, as I've imagined him growing up . . . It's Jem."

"Well, of course. You'd seen baby pictures of him before, right?"

"Never film. Jem moved fast when he was little. Turned corners with military pivots. He didn't do that as an adult."

"So?"

"It's just strange," Amy said.

"And the rest of your visit?"

"I had planned to go back to the hotel to eat that evening, but they asked me to stay for dinner. I accepted to be polite—I thought it might get to be too much, I didn't want to lose it in front of them—but everything worked out all right. We shared stories about Jem and talked about ourselves while his dad cooked a fabulous meal. We laughed, more than I expected. No one broke down until later. Doug had started to stack the dishes, and he looked at me and started crying and said he hoped Jem had known how much I loved him."

"Amy . . ."

"We all were a mess for a while after that," she said, her voice small. "They invited me to stay there for the night, but I didn't. They had been so gracious and open and understanding, but I needed to go. The next morning, I went to his grave site. That little Episcopalian church, it's so peaceful there. The landscape reminded me of the part of Tennessee where he would have gone to graduate school, all those trees and hills and green. I realized he'd chosen a place that was much like his home. I sat on the ground next to his plot for a good two hours, just talking. Aloud. I felt like a freak, but it seemed right. It made the experience real. Once I was done, I couldn't believe how different I felt. Relieved. Truthful. And I didn't know if I could do it—would do it—but I brought the engagement ring with me."

"You of all people wouldn't get rid of such a thing."

Amy leaned back and took a small sip. She looked up into the sky faintly dotted with stars. "There's a lot I never got rid of. When I healed enough to move around after the accident, I went through everything, but all I did was box it up again. I had the ring stored in the attic for a long time. I decided that it wasn't necessary to keep it any longer. His gravestone is flat, with one of those flower holders on top, so I dropped it inside. I felt better knowing he had it back. I didn't want some stranger to have it. Its history is too sad."

"You're wrong. Only the ending breaks your heart."

"You know, sometimes you know just what to say."

"I'm goddamn brilliant. I'm really proud of you, Aims. Sincerely. Jem would be proud, too. But he always knew you were more of a scrapper than you looked," Chloe said. "How are things between you guys?"

Amy sighed. "We're still in separate rooms, but we're trying. I'm trying. I've been thinking about my grandma a lot. How she must have been with her first husband. I mean, you can see clearly in pictures that something was special between them. It wasn't because of the war." She finished her wine. "I know she was devoted to Poppa, but her love seemed practical. I saw it and didn't think about it. And that's how I've been with Scott. I didn't realize it. And you know, I don't think Jem would want it that way, for my sake—and Scott's. Through all of this, I figured out that I love Scott and he deserves more than I've given him. He's given me no reason and no excuse to hold out."

"As bad as he's hurt, he still loves you. He's a rare specimen, and he loves you as if he has no other choice. He made a promise before you, me, everybody, and God. For better or worse. It will get better. Much better."

"I never thought of you as a romantic."

"Shh, don't tell."

"The truth is out now. That must be what motivated you to put that picture of me and Scott in the dictionary," Amy said.

"What are you talking about?"

"When you came this summer. When we were at critical mass. You went through our picture boxes, right? Didn't you take one out and move it?" Amy looked like she needed another drink. "It's what made me tell him. Finding it was the turning point."

Chloe sucked the pimento core out of her last olive. "Why would I do something like that? It's not my style. Subtle, I am not. I'm sure there's a logical explanation."

ON AMY'S last night in New Orleans, as she and her dearest friend slept in double beds in the same downtown hotel room, I rushed through the city where I was born. With the speed of a runner, I traveled across the chaotic commercial nightmare that was now Canal Street, through the restored splendor of the French Quarter, into the still-standing places where speakeasies once lured the intemperate, along the river tamed against its desire to change course, and among the streets of Uptown, where I had grown.

I stopped in front of my family's home. The key-shaped porch, square across the entrance and round on the opposite side, had been stripped and painted recently. As I moved up each step, the beautiful and terrible flood of memory returned, the one that churned me as I sped through the city I loved. Through each room—front parlor, Daddy's study, my room—I experienced every moment again, my life in layers of time, a baby, a child, a woman. To pause and linger would have intensified the onslaught, torn me apart.

The rush didn't stop as I moved out and away, south, toward Audubon Park, where I had climbed a tree and wished for something I thought I wanted and received much more in return, where I slipped Andrew kisses, where the seesaw that balanced Twolly and me had long since disappeared—

East toward Tulane University, where my sex was never an obstacle because I refused to let it be, where I was an A student and at the top of my class and the one who was sure to make it, by golly, where I kissed Andrew behind the largest oak on campus—

Farther east, to a Victorian house painted in its original glory, the way it was before a banker and his wife bought it, where they bore an only son, where he grew into a man who was brilliant and gentle and handsome, where I died moments before he could hear what I came to tell him—

Then finally, southeast, toward the Lower Garden District, where a Confederate lady strode in a ceaseless orbit around the home she had saved from Yankees and protected from invaders—

"Eugenia."

"Raziela, so good to see you. It's been seven months, hasn't it?"

"Yes."

"Not so long a time, to us anyway." Eugenia stopped to kiss the air near my cheek and continued her walk. "How do you like your new home?"

I struggled to answer. My thoughts were caught in the memory of the afternoon I told Eugenia I wanted to touch him and how she had merely sniffed at the ramifications of such desire. "Oh, it's very quiet there. A nice little neighborhood. The couple is darling."

"Are you training there?"

"No."

"Why are you here, Raziela?" Her tone lacked curiosity and hinted at insight.

"Amy—that's the young woman's name—came to New Orleans to meet a friend. I followed."

"Why?"

I could have drifted the miles to visit her at any time during the months I'd been away. I could have skipped this wee-hour conversation, and she would have never known I was in the city. Why had I come? I glanced at her old home. Its owners had hung a paper skeleton on the door. Halloween . . . Andrew's birthday.

Eugenia cut her eyes to me. "You look different." She flounced the skirt of her dress away from the ground. A dead bee rose airborne for a moment, then fell back into the grass. "You're glowing."

"I am? I am." I remembered Nel's peculiar luminance the weeks before he left—and realized what was happening.

"What has occurred since I last saw you?"

"I can't stop thinking of Andrew."

"Oh, sugarplum," she said with the sweet empathy of a good mother.

MRS. O'CONNELL sips her water and cranes ever so slightly to glance left. Her pewter bun holds every strand of thick hair away from her high forehead and cheeks. The crystal glass and her diamond ring absorb the glow from the chandelier. After she wipes her mouth with the linen napkin, she pivots right. The narrow cross on her sternum doesn't move. Her chin bobs in genteel recognition. Mr. O'Connell nods, but he smiles in greeting. Black wavy fringe circles his head like a low-set crown. His coal eyes consume his pupils, reflective light fractures on each edge.

"Andrew," his mother says, "the Hemphills are here, but Corrine isn't with them. Such a lovely girl. When did you last see her?"

He turns to his left, raises his hand. "Months ago. She might be married by now."

"Oh, certainly not. We would know."

"Razi, congratulations," Mr. O'Connell says. "Andrew said you were accepted at Northwestern."

"Yes, sir."

"It's not too late to change your mind about another school," he says.

There have been conversations about me between Andrew and his father that I wish had never occurred. Ones I did not sanction. "I appreciate Northwestern's history of admitting women. Such tradition is important."

"How were your grades at the time you applied to schools?"

"I competed well."

"She'll graduate magna cum laude," Andrew says. "A chance at valedictorian?"

"I'd never have any fun if I studied that hard."

Mr. O'Connell laughs. "Yes, enjoy your youth. When you look back on the years, you'll want to remember the frolic, not the drudgery. When I was at Yale, some of us fellows staged races with those high-wheel bicycles to impress the young ladies." He leans into the table and exposes his wattle. "Look at this scar. I nearly decapitated myself from a fall. The blood was terrible. Ghastly. A lady and two of my friends fainted."

"So they lost their heads," I say.

"Ha! Yes, very good." Mr. O'Connell raises his glass to me and drinks half.

"Mrs. O'Connell," I say, "Andrew mentioned that you are leading an effort to raise money for your charity. What a rewarding endeavor."

"Why, yes. The orphanage is in such a state. The ceiling leaks, half of the windows don't open—can you imagine the diseases trapped inside?—and I won't begin to mention how many children sleep in each room. Abominable. The poor sisters do what they can, but without an appeal to the parish, well, circumstances would only worsen."

"Are there plans to renovate the building or relocate?"

"Renovate. We've almost secured a temporary home. An unrelated but pressing issue is their food, however. They all look malnourished. When a group of us visited the home, we saw hundreds of cans of food. I never fed Andrew such things. Children need their fresh fruit and vegetables."

"One of our family friends might be interested to help. Mr. Richard Delacourt."

"Delacourt. Why do I know that name?" Mrs. O'Connell drinks her water.

Andrew nudges me under the table. I slice my eyes toward him. His lips turn under until they disappear like a monkey's. He knows what has happened to Gertrude of late—and how precarious the situation is for me. Gertrude's pamphlets have been intercepted a second time. The rumors have already started to spread. I was questioned once, briefly, and based on Andrew's advice, answered as literally as possible. I volunteered nothing and told the truth: yes, I knew that there were certain materials in Newcomb's library; yes, I had told other girls, and no, I had no idea how long they had been there—could have been a few months, maybe more.

"Oh, yes, Delacourt. He has an import business." Mr. O'Connell flicks his nail against the rim of his empty glass.

"Yes, sir. Oranges and bananas, primarily," I say.

"No, there is another reason," Mrs. O'Connell says.

"What could he do for the children, Razi?" Andrew asks.

"Delacourt. She was involved with suffrage. Yes, I believe that's right."

"Mother, what does it matter if it's for your cause?" Andrew says.

"Do you know, Raziela, if Mrs. Delacourt was so affiliated?"

"Yes, ma'am. She was."

"Indeed. I myself was opposed to the whole idea. I did go to one meeting. There was a moving picture of a man who drank and beat his wife and children. Some of the ladies cried. Then a woman dressed in some costume came onstage and said that all such things would end once women got their freedom. Ridiculous. Some men are worse than others, but all men are as they are. No vote will change that."

"Good men serve as good examples," I say.

"Yes, yes. This Mrs. Delacourt, I'm not finished with her. Wasn't her name in the papers recently?"

"No, ma'am."

"Something about a raid. Lewd paraphernalia."

"Perhaps you've fallen prey to gossip, Mother." Andrew's gaze is fixed on me. I can read his mind: Keep quiet.

"No, ma'am, there was no such thing in the papers." I am telling the truth. No printed article has appeared, although one could at any time. There's something more insidious and interesting about boxes of feminine sanitary supplies filled with birth control devices and pamphlets than that liquid that titillates this city's prurient appetite.

"I was certain I had read an account," Mrs. O'Connell replies.

"About the orphans," I say. "Mr. Delacourt is a generous man. He would do this favor."

For a long moment, Mrs. O'Connell studies my neutral expression. The only thing we have in common is that we both love Andrew, and she tolerates the fact only because she expects to soon be rid of me, even though she disapproves of the reason why I'll be leaving. "Then thank you, Raziela. Could you arrange an introduction?"

"Yes, ma'am. I believe it's each person's duty to help someone in need, even if the gesture is small."

"How true. Oh, look, the first course has arrived. Raziela, have you dined at Antoine's before? The food here is simply a delight." She leans toward her husband. "Mr. O'Connell." She does not call him Patrick, in public, if ever. "Dear, please put your napkin on your lap."

"PEPIN."

"No. Turn your face a little to the right. Pull your shoulders down. Hold." Click.

"I know parts of you your own mother hasn't seen for fifteen years, but you still won't tell me. Why do you use it in your initials, then?"

"I have no objection to the consonant itself."

"This isn't as fun as it used to be." I pause. "Percival."

"No."

"Pericles."

"That's all for today." He places his camera in its case. I look at him through a verdant cascade of willow branches. "Take a nap with me."

Andrew removes his shirt and stretches flat on the ground. He knows how much I like to sleep against his bare skin. I press the side of my face into his sternum and smooth the hair on his chest. His fingertips curl into my left upper arm. I am about to drowse. . . .

HE DIDN'T KNOW she was watching him from the dark bathroom.

Scott sat cross-legged on the bed with the puzzle. There were fewer than fifteen pieces left to place. He caught one between his thumb and middle finger, held it above the image, and moved it in a languid zigzag, looking for its home. He twitched his left eye as the part snapped into its notch. Quietly, he mimicked the roar of a crowd. Amy palmed her mouth to stop a giggle. Neither noticed the strange little shadows moving across the floor.

The next few clicked into place with ease. Without looking, he swept his hand against the coverlet to grasp the last three. He found no more. *Dammit,* he muttered, and slid off the bed. He searched the top of the duvet, under the puzzle board, and beneath the pillows, then crawled across the wood floor like a greyhound.

Amy stood in the doorway. "Lost something?"

"The last three pieces. They're here. I counted all the pieces before I started, like I always do."

She dropped to the ground and helped him. After they had both covered the entire floor, he checked the box itself. Amy suggested that the pieces might have been caught under the blanket. They took everything off the bed except the bottom sheet and shook it out. Scott frowned and crossed his arms.

"They'll turn up. They always do," Amy said.

He glanced at her, then scanned the floor again. "I was so close to being done."

A muted plop made him turn his head. There, near Amy's left ankle, was one of the missing pieces. "Open your hands."

She held her palms wide in front of him as she looked down.

As he reached toward her, another fell. Scott sat on his heels, inspected Amy's hip, and shook the hem of her robe. Three marbles dropped and rolled across the floor. The last puzzle piece landed in his hand.

"Scott, really, I haven't—" She touched the pocket. Her finger disappeared into a hole, then wrapped around a loose thread. She pulled, and the pocket hinged open. Amy parted her lips to speak, but the words had vanished.

He rattled the pieces like dice. "Well, well, perhaps a little mouse is responsible." Scott kneeled at the board to finish his work. "It's not nice to tease people."

"I didn't. I haven't been coming in the room when you're not here."

"Denial will only worsen the penalty."

"I swear I didn't take them." She took a breath. "I think we have a poltergeist."

"A poltergeist?"

"Explain all the things that get rearranged around here. The misplaced objects."

"We don't have a poltergeist." He crouched back on his heels.

"But in the movies—"

He laughed. "People are their own poltergeists. It's their energy that builds and builds until weird things start to happen. There are no ghosts."

"How do you know?"

"How else? I read it." Scott crawled within arm's reach of her. "You're just a bundle of kinetic energy, aren't you? Now tell me the truth. You took the pieces."

"I didn't."

"Then you shall suffer the wrath of the whalebite." He suddenly clamped his hand around her leg an inch above the knee.

Amy yelped with surprise and jumped back. Scott attacked the other leg in the same way. She darted through the bathroom and into their bedroom. She was about to whip around the doorjamb when he caught her at the waist. Amy bent into him, an unpredictable maneuver, and spun free. He stood at the crosswind of both doors.

"What shall it be now?"

She sat on the bed, catching her breath. Amy clenched her teeth to stop a playful grin. Scott tucked his fists at his last ribs, angled his elbows back, and drew air into the top of his bare chest. "I know how to torture you," he said. He approached slowly in a Herculean pose. "Nondairy creamer. Beverage-dispensing hats. Irregardless."

"Plain yellow mustard. Daytime talk shows. Misuse of *aggravate.*"

"Gilligan's Island." He dropped his arms. "Leaky faucets. Wool clothing."

"Open cabinets. Drivers who don't signal. Missing puzzle pieces."

"No prelude kiss."

"No scratch at the nape later." She took his hand and guided him to sit. For several moments, she traced figure eights on his loose fist. "Come back to sleep in here."

"Are you sure?"

"Are you willing?"

"Are you ready?" he asked.

"That's your question to answer now."

Scott leaned close, and when she didn't move away but toward him, he kissed her softly, as if he'd suddenly remembered how. "I'll get my pillow."

The light was off when he came into the room. The electric alarm read nine seventeen, earlier than their usual bedtime. Scott tousled the sheets and moved underneath. Amy was on her back. He nudged her to roll on her side and pulled her into the arc of his body.

He left his alarm clock in the guest room.

❧

After Nel learned the languages used in his favorite operas, he spent hours in music libraries listening to everything from medieval polyphony to twentieth-century minimalism. His passion was intense. No longer was his love unrequited. He was happy when he researched. Now and then, when he looked up from a book, Nel told me he could study forever.

Eighteen months into his time between, he decided he wanted to play the cello.

"How in the world are you going to learn the cello? You'd have to study somewhere. I don't know, perhaps you can teach yourself to sight-read music. Regardless, cellos make noise."

"I can practice at night," he said. "We don't sleep."

We left our stake at a university's music school when Nel found a private cello teacher. We became the quiet tenants of an unsuspecting landlord who tried to show children the beauty of instruments that weren't attached to amplifiers. Nel would watch the sessions carefully. In the evenings, he would make me join him in a music store near the French Quarter to listen to him.

In the beginning, Nel didn't touch the cello. He had mastered using the air to animate objects long before. It was a simple trick to maneuver two things at once. He blamed his screeching bow on rusty skills. I assured him that he sounded awful because he was supposed to. He had never played an instrument io his life.

I agreed that Nel needed to be alone to practice. To fill the hours, I returned to my strolls near hospitals and nursing homes to collect both the determined and bewildered who lingered nearby. As Nel had said, they needed me. However, for the first time in a long while, I drifted through the halls and watched people die. I wondered how they could release themselves so thoroughly into the atmosphere. What pulled them had pulled me, but I had remained. I had stayed. Wanted to stay. Why didn't they as well? How could they be at peace, knowing what they left behind?

For a moment, no more, I wondered whether my Andrew was dead and whether he had paused before the air absorbed him completely.

Early one evening, after I had been away for more than two weeks, I returned to the music store to see Nel. I was knocked for a row. As I entered the room, I thought I heard a recording, but there was no hum of a machine. "Wow, Nel, that's really—"

He was touching the instrument. His shins framed the cello's feminine curves. His fingers gracefully pressed the strings on the neck. Level with his belly, the bow rocked. Nel watched his hands. He did not close his eyes or gaze at the ceiling. He wasn't only feeling the music.

"Nel, what are you doing?" My outburst shook the storefront windows.

The bow dropped. He looked at me, startled. "I thought I'd gotten better."

"I didn't think it was you until I saw you. That's against the rules."

"Holding an instrument?"

"Touching. Touching anything. Touching anything is against the rules."

"Rules were made to be broken." Nel squeezed his knees together against the cello's sides. "I couldn't play well when I held it at a distance."

What stunned me as much as the cello in his hands was the way he looked. Nel was hidden in a strange glow, a luminescence I had never witnessed between.

"Nel, what's happening to you?"

The strings whined from contact with some part of him. "Look, you don't understand. I always wanted to learn how to play—"

"That's not what I'm talking—"

"Let me explain. When I was a little kid, we didn't have the money for me to take lessons. My dad would let me go into a music store now and then to look around. The man who owned the shop was always nice to me. I didn't touch anything or bother him. Then one afternoon—"

"You don't understand—"

"Listen. Please listen."

"All right." I had to avert my gaze. The sight of him was unnerving.

"When I was twelve, for no reason at all, the shop owner let me play some of the instruments. Everything was either too complicated or loud. But the cello, it was so lovely. I was tall when I was young, so I didn't feel like it was too big for me. The old man pushed my fingertips until the strings made channels in my skin. He told me to pass the bow smoothly. There was almost a human sound. I felt the deepest parts of me answer with that same hum. As if I had strings of my own inside.

"My dad walked in as I was drawing one note into perfection. He stared at me and said, 'Lionel, get that sissy piece of crap out from between your legs. There's only one thing shaped like that I'd care to see near your crotch.' I passed the cello to the old man and thanked him for his kindness. I never went back."

"Your father wouldn't even let you go in the store?" I asked.

"I wouldn't let myself go in. There was no use torturing myself."

"Lionel—"

"It's okay. I know what I'm doing."

"Listen, you play beautifully. You're a natural. Honest. But—"

"I wanted to do that my entire life," he said. "Now's my chance, and I'm dead. All I can do is repeat the memory of that one note because that's the only one I ever felt whole. That's when I knew good and goddamn well that I wasn't all thumbs the way my father said I was. I would have been good with my hands, but not the way he would have liked. So I forced myself to be content with merely listening. I was a dandy of a listener, too. Expressive, you know, my body always moved with music. I couldn't help it. That's what I was meant to do. You know, if I'd been born to a different family, or if my father had believed in giving us more than just the necessities, if he'd—"

"Stop it, Lionel." I throbbed as if I still had veins.

"Why don't you ever want to talk about anything important?"

"It's the past. We can't change it."

"But you know what moments you could have changed. The ones that could have made a difference between then and now. I've seen all of mine, like exits on a map. I realize now that I was wrong to blame my father. I wasn't powerless. I was just scared."

"You were a child."

"And what were you?"

"What's that supposed to mean?"

"What if you'd been accepted to Yale? Or Harvard? What if you hadn't left the ring behind? What if you had gone back to get it? Tell me, Razi, if one thing had been different, would you be dead now? What would you be?"

"You have a hateful little streak in you, Lionel Mulberry, I swear. I never should have told you any of that."

"Why not? Because I know your secrets? You know all of mine by now."

"An air of mystery becomes a man," I replied.

"If that's your criterion, your Andrew is as attractive as they come."

I ignored him.

Nel popped the air near my shoulder so I'd look at him. "I don't know why I'm being allowed this time to—"

"No one's granting you permission."

"Okay, I'm *taking* the time to make up what I lost before. What I never did. Something's changing," Nel said. "Each time I achieve what I meant to do before, I feel a sense of resolution."

"What are you telling me?" I prepared myself for the real answer he wouldn't give me that night. That would come soon enough.

"I'm going to enjoy playing that cello. It's going to feel cold and hard, but that will not change the way the notes sound. Music is food for the soul, and mine has been starving for a very . . . long . . . time." He looked at his hands around the neck of the cello. "You were right, though."

"About what?"

"I ache for my body so badly. What I wouldn't give for a sneeze, a stretch, a yawn, a cry, an orgasm. The more I play, the more it hurts. The more I touch, the more I remember, the more my form changes. It's like when I got migraines—the pain built up so much until I passed out. But when I awoke, I was on the other side of the pain in a peace so immediate I didn't want to leave. I'm beginning to feel that peace all the time."

"But you shouldn't look different. It doesn't make sense."

"Touch me. I'm solid. It's strange."

"No, Lionel. I won't."

"Just once can't hurt you."

"I'm not worried about me."

"All right, honey." He plucked each string in turn. "Are you leaving again?"

"I will if you want me to." I looked at him fully. He was unbearably beautiful.

"Stay and listen, won't you? Don't leave me alone now. I'm afraid, to be honest. And I miss you."

"Didn't Bach compose for cello? I like Bach."

Nel smiled. "You must have heard that somewhere. Challenging work."

"Tonight, for your pleasure, a solo performance by Mr. Lionel Mulberry."

"I always wanted to hear that," he said.

❧

AMY ENTERED the sitting room with a flashlight and approached the bookcase. She was swaddled under layers of long shirts, thermal underwear, and corduroy pants. It was November. The electricity had gone out in their house again, and it was the only one on the block with the problem. Within the last few days, the power had fluctuated so much that they were afraid of fire. I had tried to calm myself, tried not to frighten them, but I no longer had control over the flares of thought that extended beyond my form and interfered with their routine and comfort.

"Don't forget, the electrician is coming tomorrow morning." Scott walked into the room after her. He wore the thickest sweatshirt he owned, a bright yellow stocking cap, flannel-lined blue jeans, and two pairs of wool socks. "You know, with a house this old, the wiring was bound to go out at some point."

"It was built in the early forties. How bad could it be?"

"Knob and tube. Antiquated," Scott said.

"Maybe your mice with the marble fetish have chewed the lines in the attic."

"You know, I didn't think of that. I have traps up there, too."

"There'd be a rodent morgue if that were the case."

Scott moved to sit in the rocking chair, and I slipped into a corner. "I was looking forward to seeing the finished product tonight."

I hadn't watched Amy's last months of progress because every time I neared their electrical equipment, it ceased to function. During the past week, when the lights worked at all, Amy had put in the final hours on her photography project. Every snapshot she selected had been scanned, every pixel of each one touched up. Her patience was magnificent. Her attention to the minutiae was rewarded by a collection of images so clear, so bright, that the people almost seemed to move. Amy had arranged to spend a long weekend with Twolly to document all the names she could remember and collect any stories her great-aunt might share.

"I'm really pleased with it." She rested her fingertips on the edge of the second bookcase shelf. "I just wish Grandma Sunny could have seen it."

"I know, Aims. She would have been really proud of you."

"What have you read lately that you'd recommend? I want a break from fiction." Her flashlight tracked the titles.

"That book you got me on Hinduism a while back was interesting."

She turned the light on him and watched his features. "Really?"

"Yes. And don't look at me like that. I didn't even think of the tangential reading material. Intriguing as it was."

"Where is it?"

"Third shelf, left side."

Amy located the volume, closed the bookcase door, and stood reading the back cover with the flashlight. "I'll give it a shot."

"Even if the book bores you, you'll like the illustrations. The colors are so vibrant. I can see you figuring out how to use such color palettes. If you end up moving into interior design like you've considered, I think you'd do some pretty daring rooms."

She glanced up. "Daring?"

He rocked back and forth on the tips of his toes. In the haze from the streetlight, Scott looked like a bootless little boy ready to build snowmen. "You'll try something just to see how it works. The way you dress, combining all those vintage pieces in a way that's unexpected."

"Is that why I'm asked if I'm European? I dress *daringly*?"

"Probably. And why you won the award for that magazine spread last year. It was so bold. And years ago, the way you'd make Chloe go to antiabortion meetings to figure out where they were coming from."

"It wasn't only to understand them. It was part of the strategy to figure out their tactics to come up with ours."

"But it took—what does Chloe say—clit?"

Amy laughed.

"Your grandfather liked that about you."

She dropped her arms to her sides, flashlight in one hand, book in the other. "What?"

"Your daring."

"How would you know?"

Scott rubbed his hands together, building heat. "I just remembered one afternoon we were visiting your grandparents, not long after we got married. You and your grandmother went upstairs for some reason, and I was alone with him. And out of nowhere, he said—yeah, I remember this because the words he used were so unusual—he said, 'Your Amy, she's venturesome. That's a rare beautiful trait in a girl.'"

"And what did you say?"

"I said I agreed, and then he changed the subject."

I watched Amy as she thought about her grandfather's words. From the space around the bookcase, a clean salty smell began to spread into the room. I felt a tremor of memory begin to tear from me, out of control again, forcing Andrew to emerge with excruciating clarity. But the bookcase wasn't the only source of the scent, and neither was I.

"He said that?" Amy asked, her voice tight and high.

"Yeah. I don't know why I didn't tell you before. I guess I thought you knew he felt that way."

Amy raised her right hand, the flashlight within her fist, and wiped the side of her cheek. "I had no idea Poppa Fin thought that."

Poppa Fin.

Light and motion and sound exploded in the house. As Scott rushed to protect Amy from what had erupted—their expressions stunned and frightened—the room grew colder than it had ever been, suspending that pure brine in space until I could take it in, take her in, take in the fact that he had been so close—

PHINEAS

That word is on the top of the box. The name of a shop I don't recognize. From my fingertips, Chinese red paper and silver satin ribbon drop to the ground. Valentine's Day is two weeks away, so what is this? When I rattle the gift, there's a dull *thump, thump.* A delicate pansy scent reaches my nose before I see the brilliant blossoms inside. A fine white feather blows free. My fingers stir the petals until I touch something hard. My heart rises, and my gut sinks. Then I realize—

I SLAM THE DOOR and pull her on the bed. "I know his middle name now."

"Finally. That was one joke played out too long. What is it?"

"Phineas, but—"

"Andrew Phineas O'Connell. That's not so bad. Why'd he—"

"Etoile, listen. I know his middle name." She stares at me. "He proposed. Had his grandmother's ring and everything."

"Oh, my God." I clamp her mouth until she extricates herself. "What did he say? What did you say? Where is it?" She grabs my hands and finds nothing shiny but the one little ring I always wear. "You didn't."

"I didn't do anything. We agreed to a postponement."

"Have you gone cuckoo? Postpone what?"

"The decision. Until we hear back about our applications. March, probably."

"What does that have to do with the price of beans? He

wants to marry you. And if you'd stop being so ridiculous and bullheaded and—and modern—well, you'd realize you want to marry him, too."

"I don't know that."

"You love him. Isn't that enough?"

"It's complicated."

"No, it's not. You're two sides of the same coin. You're what poets can't put into words. You're a perfect match."

"Spare me, Twolls."

"Don't miss your chance. Marry him, Razi." She takes my hands in a sisterly embrace. "Who gets to love someone as much as you love him twice in a lifetime?"

EMMALINE places a cup of coffee and a saucer of ginger snaps on the end table near Twolly. My dear friend thanks her, and the look they share is an entire conversation. With quick steps, Emmaline crosses the study and closes the heavy door. Andrew does not mutter a word.

"I couldn't come into town without seeing you," Twolly says, "even though it's a short trip, for my friend David's—I'm leaving the morning after their reception."

"You didn't have to."

"I know. I wanted to." She reaches for a cookie, nibbles an eighth of it. "Did Emmaline make these? They're wonderful. She's such a terrific cook. Our housekeeper always puts too much baking soda in whatever she makes. Cookies like crackers. My little sister Soleil throws them to the grackles. Those birds will eat anything."

Andrew pulls a cigarette case from his left pocket. He leans over the couch for a match from his father's humidor. His right hand is bandaged, protecting the deep clean slice under his little finger. He lights the cigarette, closes his eyes. The first drag is long, like a kiss.

"I've only seen you smoke at parties."

"New habit."

"What happened to your hand?"

"I cut it. An accident." His tone warns her not to ask for details.

She sips her coffee and finishes her cookie in two bites. "So when are you leaving for school? It must start soon."

"Two weeks."

"I heard New England will be simply beautiful in the next month or so. All the leaves turning colors. Not like here. We're lucky to see that for a week."

"New York is out, then."

"I'm not going. I thought about it. What's the point, really? I never wanted to be a world-known artist or anything. Anyway, I don't want to be away from my family right now. Not now. Considering. I hardly know my sisters anymore. I missed out during these past four years."

"They were good ones."

"Yes, they were." Twolly holds the cup in her thin, long fingers on her lap. She stares down. A moment later, the dark pool ripples once, twice. She clenches her jaw and discreetly wipes her lashes. "Andrew—"

He peers through the tobacco fog. The cigarette is half burned.

"Can I do anything for you?" she asks.

"No."

Twolly clutches her handbag and moves to sit next to him. Andrew continues to smoke, hard gusts held tight. In her purse, she finds paper and a pencil. She scrawls a few lines against her knee. "Here." Twolly stuffs the paper into his left palm and holds his fingers closed around it. "That is my address and telephone number. No matter where you are, ever, ever, I want you to let me know. That's all. I don't expect long letters. A simple note will suffice."

"Why?"

"I care what happens to you."

He doesn't respond. He doesn't pull away. Twolly doesn't let him go. Andrew suffocates the cigarette nib with three blunt taps. He needs to cry, with her, again. That happened only once that I witnessed, two weeks after I was buried. The tenderness between them was familial. At least, I had thought, they aren't so alone in their sorrow.

"Do you promise to write me?" she asks finally.

"One condition." Andrew doesn't turn. "This is never spoken of again. You know too much." His face pivots like an owl's, controlled and cautious.

Twolly stares at his eyes. She leans back. She must notice the absence of light there, the fissures in the blue that have begun to change the color completely. "If that's what you want. I expect I'll be in my parents' home for a while. Eligible men aren't exactly lining up at the front steps."

"In time."

The door folds open. "Hey, old sport. How about a—" Warren halts before he gets into the room. "Sorry. The Negro boy didn't tell me you had company."

"How are you, Warren?" Twolly releases Andrew's hand.

"Hey, good to see you. I'd heard you went back home to Shreveport."

"I'm in town for a visit. I thought you and Anna had moved to Pennsylvania."

"We are," Warren says. "It took a little longer to get ready to move after graduation and the wedding. We leave on Monday. My job starts the following week. Come on, best man, let's go to the movies. I'm bored. Twolly, do you want to join us?"

"I don't want to go," Andrew says.

Warren strides over to the window and tucks the sheers behind midnight drapes. "You're pasty. What about a round of tennis? A little cruise? I have Father's roadster."

"No."

"I'll leave you boys to your fun." Twolly kisses Andrew on the cheek and squeezes his forearm. "You promised."

"You promised." Andrew stands and puts Twolly's address in

his pocket. His hand lingers within the space, then visibly, forcefully, clenches into a fist. "Thank you both for stopping by." He rushes past them but stops with his back in the doorway. "And Warren, you know the boy's name is Simon. Use it."

Twolly and Warren stare into the hall, then at each other.

"He's not doing well," Twolly says.

"No. Breaks my heart," Warren replies. "He's not himself at all."

WHEN SHE opened the door, Sarah Beeker Washington reached her arms across the threshold. She hugged the older woman tightly and kissed her cheek as if they were old friends. Once they separated, Nora O'Connell Richmond introduced her daughter and son-in-law.

"I know them already," Sarah said. "They bought Daddy's—Mr. O'Connell's bookcase. If I had realized who she was then, I would've given it to her." She embraced Amy warmly. "I owe you a refund. I can't keep what doesn't belong to me."

The living room was furnished with a beautiful camelback sofa, two wingback chairs, and an antique opium table. Sarah had eclectic but elegant taste. Over coffee, they visited without the stilted small talk of virtual strangers. There were no awkward moments. The bond between their fathers had extended to them.

As they talked, none of them could figure out why Sarah had received another letter from Barrett Burrat. In that last note, she had been instructed to search her father's house again, closely, to look for items that may have been in Simon Beeker's possession and forgotten for decades. Her brother, Benjamin, had referenced a box in his letter, which may or may not have existed. She was given the names and phone numbers of Andrew O'Connell's heirs, who would have to grant permission for a review of any documents left behind. When Sarah called Nora, more than forty years after they had first met, Andrew's firstborn daughter cried when she learned of the treasure Simon had taken great care to preserve.

Amy searched the room the entire time, faking a stretch or straightening some part of Scott's clothing. I knew what she looked for. I'd found it in the office in the back of the house. A footlocker, stenciled "S. Beeker," was tucked against a wall.

"Mrs. Washington, would you mind if we got a peek at what you found while you two catch up?" Amy asked.

"Of course not. Down the hall, last door on the right."

Amy nearly sprinted out of the room, with Scott trailing behind. The footlocker's hinged top was open before he walked through the door. She glanced to her left and noticed a large, clear plastic box with her and her mother's names taped to the top. The envelopes inside were addressed in Andrew's handwriting, his letters to Simon Beeker and Emmaline Coteau. Amy chose to begin with the footlocker.

A film projector was the first item out, followed by six canisters that Amy judged as full when she held them. Thick twine batched three sets of letters. Under the letters were boxes filled with film negatives, photographs, his old camera, and unused developing paper. There was a catalog from a photographic supply company. A moving-picture camera was wrapped in an old flour sack on top of his college yearbooks.

Amy looked at the first letter in a bundle. "Mr. Andrew O'Connell, St. Charles Avenue, New Orleans, Louisiana. We've been up and down that street a hundred times. But there's no return address." Her fingers tugged at the tight, knotted string. Scott handed her a small pocketknife to cut it apart. She didn't move.

"What?" he asked.

"I'm actually nervous. I'm about to meet my grandfather." Her hands trembled as she slipped the yellowed stationery from the envelope. *"Barely Thursday, November 1, 1928. My Darling Andrew, Where your tongue lingered tonight, there is a sweet solferino bruise made darker because my hand cannot leave it alone. I am abandoned to an ache deeper than the skin. Yours, truly—Razi, your little succubus."*

"Oh, my God," Scott said.

"Oh, my God," she echoed. "Do you think he wrote back?"

"The question is, what did he do back?"

"Scott, really." Amy shook her head in feigned disgust. "I can't imagine they're all like this. And that he kept them. And that he ever let them out of his sight."

"Read another one."

"Wednesday, December 7, 1927. Dear Andrew, How delighted I was to receive the little monkey figurine. He's on the dresser looking at me now. Twolly was here when I got it, and she pestered me until I told her what it was for. She thinks you're a peach of a fellow to listen to me on my soapbox. I swore you got a word in edgewise, but I don't think she believed me. I do get passionate sometimes. Everyone gets used to it. Sincerely, Razi."

Amy flicked through the stack, glancing at postmarks. There was one without a stamp. It was the last letter I had written to him, the one my father had saved, the one Simon had salvaged. The bloodstain on the envelope had not faded.

"Why didn't Aunt Twolly tell me that she knew Poppa Fin long before he married my grandma? She didn't tell any of us. And what about that 'our fathers knew each other from business' explanation about how Poppa and Grandma met? Aunt Twolly knew him first, and I'll bet knew him well."

"But why didn't your Grandma Sunny tell the whole story?"

"What if she never knew?" Amy asked.

"Knew what?" Nora said as she and Sarah entered the room.

"Did you know that Poppa knew Aunt Twolly from college?"

"No, that's not right. She went to Tulane—Newcomb College. He went to Oxford. Their families knew each other."

"Are you sure?" Amy asked.

"Mr. Fin went to Tulane first," Sarah said, "then to Oxford to study philosophy, and then Boston for law school. Daddy said my great-grandmother Emmaline got letters from England and Boston now and then."

"What? Law school?" Nora said. "He never practiced law."

"No, but he had the degree. He taught the subject. Didn't you know?" Sarah was clearly surprised.

"Poppa was a rhetoric professor. He retired from the university in Lafayette." She paused. "Rhetoric. My God, it figures." Nora looked hurt. She pointed at the bundles near Amy's lap. "What are those?"

"Proof."

THE STORIES Sarah Washington remembered most were her father's accounts of his reunions with Andrew—Fin—O'Connell.

During Emmaline's funeral service, Simon had turned to scan the pews. He knew that Andrew had received the telegram about his grandmother's passing, and Andrew himself had confirmed that he would attend the funeral. Seated alone in the back was a solitary white man, his black hair carefully combed. They nodded at each other when the family made its slow walk down the center aisle and out of the church.

Simon greeted Andrew after the burial. As he reached out his hand, Simon noticed that the man's eyes had changed. Simon had remembered them as the darkest blue he'd ever seen, what he imagined was the color of the middle of the sea, but that reunion day, the irises were a strange blue-green. Against his fair skin and black hair, Andrew's eyes looked—as Simon said—haunted.

When Simon spoke his name, *Thank you for coming, Mr. Andrew,* the young college man was corrected. *Fin,* he said. *Simply Fin. A classmate exposed my middle name, and I was on the Oxford rowing team at the time. The nickname stuck, I prefer it now. I don't go by Andrew any longer.*

He didn't need an explanation. Simon—twenty-three, a freshman at Howard University, the new beau of a lovely girl named Liza-Beth—realized that what he had witnessed the summer of 1929 had shattered that gentle man at his core.

That night, after they met for a drink in a club known for its swing, Simon asked if he could keep in touch. Fin said he would find Simon first. Fin had graduated from Boston University with his juris doctorate the previous June and was traveling until he decided what he wanted to do. At the end of the evening, Simon asked why he had not attended Yale as he had planned. Fin replied that going would have invited too many memories. Nothing more. They shook hands. Simon never thought he'd hear from the man again.

Occasional postcards and letters passed between them for several years. Then, when Simon moved his family to their second home, he rediscovered a collection of boxes his grandmother had left for him after she died. Her instructions had been clear: See that he gets them one day. Simon asked to visit Fin one summer in 1958 and was surprised to receive a positive reply. Although the Beeker family was welcomed, the largest piece of luggage Simon had taken with them, a footlocker, was left at the station. Fin O'Connell refused to even know its contents. On the ride to the O'Connells' home, throughout a pleasant conversation, Simon remembered that Fin kept his hand in his right pocket, twirling change with a steady rhythm.

The speed of a prayer, Sarah said. *Daddy said he rolled that change at the speed of a prayer. My father had a strange way with words. I think he read too much.*

❧

AMY BREATHED sharp when the razor ripped an inch-long strip of epidermis from her ankle. The bath water turned pink at the site where her foot submerged. She finished shaving and rinsed the almond-scented conditioner from her hair.

Scott poked his face through the door. "Want to watch the DVD tonight?"

"Sure. It won't take too long," she said. "Only three of the six canisters were any good. The others didn't develop. They couldn't be transferred."

"I was reading those letters again, and—"

"You know, there's something inappropriate about your fixation. She's my dead grandfather's dead girlfriend." Amy laughed.

"We both have good taste in women. Listen, I found that ring slipped in with one of the letters. Do you want me to put it back with the jewelry?"

"No, I'm going to put it in a bookcase drawer. I think it belongs there, with the pictures of Razi." Amy stepped on the white mat, and watery blood ran toward the floor.

"What happened?"

"Just a slice." She wrapped the towel around her body.

"You're bleeding everywhere." He handed her some tissue. "I didn't realize Razi's last letter and that ring were connected."

"Neither did I." Amy pressed the cut with the wad of paper. She said nothing more. She didn't tell him she had found Andrew's ring, out of its box, balanced on its side, on top of her jewelry chest one morning and carefully read the inscription again. When she ate her breakfast, the letter was out of its envelope, spread flat, at her place at the table. Amy had searched the room with her eyes, held her breath, and tilted her ears from side to side. Then she nodded, as if she understood directions given.

"I'm going to load the DVD player," Scott said.

Amy hobbled to the sink, found bandages and antiseptic, and propped her foot on the tub to inspect the injury. The flow was still steady. She kept pressure against the broken skin for several moments with one hand, rubbing a towel against her hair with the other. Amy breathed deeply, then sighed. I cooled the air to ease the flow at her foot. She shivered.

I smelled her blood—and Andrew subtle, diluted, within it.

The day she found the bookcase, perhaps Amy had sensed him, too, his bloodstains like tannin within the drawer where he hid images of my body. A recognition deeper than the flesh, beyond the conscious, ordinary awareness of the senses. Almost instinct, the way an animal knows the members of its pack, a baby knows her mother, two people flood with a mysterious urge to embrace as lovers.

Amy covered and taped the wound. She walked into her bedroom and stood before the full-length mirror in the closet.

There she was. Naked. I saw Andrew again, altered. The shape of her eyes, the cut of her nose, a familiar freckle—how could I have missed that surprising dark spot on that fair skin?—on her left hip. Her auburn hair, proof of the recessive strand that had run like hemoglobin through each of his black follicles, dormant, waiting. Amy slipped her palms over her breasts and down the arcs of her hips. In that motion, I saw myself. The small pink-tipped peaks, smooth flat abdomen, slight curves below the waist.

As she grew up, had he ever looked at his venturesome granddaughter from across a room, in his quiet way, and saw something, someone, he missed?

From a hanger, she pulled the big white robe Scott never used. Amy slipped into it as she stepped toward her nightstand. Slowly, she opened the drawer and reached for her diaphragm. I watched her rub the edge with spermicide. Amy placed her foot on the bed, crouched, ready to slip the contraceptive into her body. Then, after a pause, she placed it back in its case. When she turned to leave, she seemed relaxed, prepared.

Amy walked into the dark living room. A forgotten Louis Armstrong CD played in the background. "What's going on?"

"Sit down," Scott said from the shadow on the couch. "I thought we should make this an event. A premiere." She accepted a glass of merlot and curled on the cushion next to him. Scott turned on the machines and pressed play.

The first reel, mostly landscape. The picture jumps, but not because the film is bad. Andrew, behind the camera, stands up above the windshield and captures the verdant flood cut by the gravel road. An egret lopes across the shot. Suddenly, I'm the focus. I wave briefly. The steering wheel is difficult to control, I'm a terrible driver, really, scared to death that I'll wreck Mr.

O'Connell's automobile. The picture returns to the land, the flat wild tangle of June, each tree an oasis of shade.

Second reel. Graduation day, Wednesday, June 12, 1929, after the ceremony. Three sets of parents greet each other on the lawn: the Knights, the Nolans, and the O'Connells. Obviously called, they wave to the camera.

"My great-grandparents," Amy said. "I recognize the Knights, but—oh, the older people, those are Poppa's parents. My great-grandmother, she's so stiff, but he looks friendly enough. The other two must be Razi's parents. I wonder who that woman is, with the white hair, holding Mrs. Nolan's arm. A grandmother maybe? Her father—he's gorgeous."

The picture goes black for a moment, then returns to the families. Mr. O'Connell and Mr. Knight chat seriously. Nearby, the mothers nod and look for their children. My father struts across the field of vision. When he disappears, Mr. Knight and Mr. O'Connell exchange small white cards and shake hands. The lens drops to the ground. Up again, the three friends stand with their arms linked. Twolly and I kiss Andrew on his cheeks. His blush turns the color of soot. I begin to sing and shimmy. Twolly joins in. I grab my mother and Grams, Twolly grabs her mother, and Andrew walks away laughing.

"Take it back," Amy said. The film rewinds to the start of my dance. "That's him. That's Poppa Fin. Look. He's laughing. Really laughing. My God, look at him so happy."

The final reel. I float into view. My eyes are closed, my hair spread like moss in the water. I look absolutely peaceful. I open one eye and smile. My body pivots, and I reach for the diving board, pulling myself up, my mouth in a pucker. The lens turns right to catch Simon standing with a rag and bucket. His expression shows he is watching us kiss with interest. The image goes black. Moments later, the picture shows the rim of a white iron table on which the camera is balanced. In the distance, Andrew cradles me at the edge of the water. I cling to him, laughing. He moves as if he's going to throw me in, but I grip tight, refuse to let go. Suddenly, we fly forward, our force against the water making a splash so big droplets hit the lens. When we come up, we swim into each other's arms.

"Want to see it again?" Scott asked.

"Yes."

They watched without speaking. Louis's trumpet bleated in ragtime.

"Why didn't he tell anyone? About her. About before," Scott said.

"He left everything behind when he left New Orleans. He wanted to forget."

"That makes no sense. They obviously loved each other."

"It makes sense. He didn't want to remember. He didn't want to share her. She broke his heart. It's painful to love that much and lose it." Amy ran the last five minutes again. When it was over, she turned off the machines and looked at her husband in the dark. "I'm just like him."

"No, you're not."

"Then your love is truly blind."

"You're not like him. The truth didn't kill you."

Amy set her empty glass on the coffee table. She took his glass, finished the last sip, and placed it next to hers. Near the glasses, in the small shallow bowl that had always been there, every loose marble in the house had come together. She did not notice. With her hand, she nudged him against the arm of the sofa. "That's why I married you, Scott Duncan. You're sincere in your delusions about me."

"It's not delusion. You just don't see what I do."

She kissed him with affection. He didn't move. She kissed him again, tugging the tie at her waist. Amy linked her hands behind his neck. "I've been unfair to you, terribly, mercilessly unfair. I'm sorry. Do you forgive me?"

"Yes."

"If we had a boy, I think Andrew is a nice name."

"I'm partial to Mordecai. Or Spike."

"Maybe as a middle name." Amy kissed his throat.

"Are you sure? Where's the diaphragm?"

"Let's risk it," she said, looking into his eyes. "Now where's that book?"

BECAUSE OF THE PROPOSAL I can't accept or refuse, because of the future we can't see, Andrew and I carry on, locked in a stalemate. Neither of us will budge. Neither of us will let go. If anything, the uncertainty makes us cling tighter, as if the love one has for the other is strong enough to break the other's will. Even though I have accepted Northwestern, and Andrew has accepted Yale, we pretend there isn't a moment we will actually have to part.

I cannot give in. It isn't the idea of marriage, no, not entirely. Perhaps becoming someone's wife years before I expect to be is a concession I can make. But why bother, if there will be such a distance between us? Married or not, faithfulness depends on trust. I trust him, as he can trust me. If I marry him and postpone my medical studies—how can I? why should I? but if I do—what I fear is that the drive will fade with each year, those three years of law school, being a wife to him, my energy redirected to hearth and home. Will there be an unexpected child, even with the best precautions, unexpectedly wanted, one I might secretly resent years later? Will I resent Andrew for being that important?

I cannot forgive him for not giving in to me. What makes his desires more important than mine? What traditions hold him so tightly that they are more powerful than his love for me? Because if he truly loves me—right—if he truly loves me, he will see that my future is no whim or wish, not a mere dream but a purpose. And if he believes that I am meant to love him, he must also believe that I am meant to help and heal. Of course, I know what people would say—what kind of man stalls his own plans, allows his wife to wear such pants? And I know, in every moment—past, present, future—when there is only the two of us in those quiet, intimate spaces, the world feels miles away but is only a veil apart.

Why not have everything at once? What is three, four years compared to a lifetime? Without the distraction of the other, perhaps one of us will finish in record time. And if our love is true, it will tolerate the distance, no matter how far. Absence, they say, makes the heart grow fonder. But can my taut little muscle endure such fullness? Would missing him erode my will, his will? I don't expect him to deny himself his aspirations, either. What will our letters say between the lines? And could I, my flesh not so weak as it is want, bear the separation from his touch?

Why him? Why now? Why not?

THE SATURDAY after graduation. The elder O'Connells are on the Atlantic Ocean, going to Europe: destination, Switzerland. The trip was intended for Andrew, a bachelor's adventure, but he refused to go. He believes persistence will break our indecision, that one of us—that I?—will give in.

"What are we going to do?" he asks.

"We'll decide when the time comes. Don't spoil it."

"I can't wait any longer. I need to know."

"What's wrong with what we have now?"

"Razi, we can't linger like this for three or four years."

I peer into his face. He is so serious, and his irises shine. "Who's lingering? I love you just as much as I ever did."

"But you won't marry me."

"Why? We'll be apart. What would it matter? Isn't it enough that I love you?"

"Then are you turning me down?"

"No, darling, I'm not, but it's not so simple. We both have big plans for ourselves. I don't want you to give up on yours."

"And I don't want you to give up on yours."

"But you want me to wait."

Andrew perches at the edge of the settee. "It only makes sense. I come into my trust when I turn twenty-five. I'll have my degree by then, and I'll be able to provide for us and pay for your schooling."

"Why don't you wait? I'll have what I need for tuition and living expenses. Daddy has taken care of that. You could support us while I'm in school. You would have no trouble finding a job. Then, once you get your trust, you could go."

"But once I'm at school, then what? Where will you be?"

"Then I'd get an internship somewhere near you. New York, maybe."

"Why didn't you just let my father get you in?" he asks.

I can't believe he said it. "I told you. That wouldn't be right."

"Because your acceptance would be through his influence, not your own merits. That doesn't matter. You're smart enough to succeed there. You know it."

"I do know it." I take a deep breath, long enough to decide whether I'll tell him. "The school rejected me." Andrew blinks, confused. "I applied to Yale. Harvard, too. I didn't get in."

He bolts up from his seat. "Why didn't you tell me? I could have had Father put in a word for you. In the right ears—"

"That's not the point. I didn't get in. I don't want his influence, covert or otherwise. What kind of a trade would he have had to make? What would his motivation have been to do such a thing?"

"He admires your spirit, despite what he thinks of women and their place. It's a compliment. My father is not so easily swayed."

"Neither is his son."

"What have I ever asked of you? When Mrs. Delacourt was caught again—and you distributed what was left and let women know where it was—"

"Only if they knew what to ask for."

"Word spreads. You were an innocent girl before, when all

they thought was that you'd been led astray by youthful curiosity about such things. You and she had been smart enough to have those parties for women with no influence. Women who would never volunteer to tell police what they knew once the rumors filtered to those circles. But you threatened to make yourself a real suspect, someone in cahoots with her, to continue in any way. And did I once insist you stop? No. Did I want you to? Yes, desperately. For your protection. For your own good, your future—and ours."

"They don't want me, Andrew. They want Gertrude."

"No, they want Mr. Delacourt. You know what he does to earn his living. There are people in this city who are willing to take his place any way they can. They'll simply use this scandal as a way to draw attention away from what they truly want. You and Mrs. Delacourt would be nothing but a diversion."

I could not argue. My silence urged him to continue.

"And as much as I think people will treat you badly and call you an unnatural woman, even in your very presence, have I ever asked you to give up on becoming a doctor? Have I put my foot down? Have I discouraged you? Have I given you any reason to believe I would interfere?"

"You've danced around the issue. Nursing school, I recall."

"An option. That is all. I meant nothing more."

"I don't compromise."

"There is a difference between compromise and compromising. One allows for negotiation. The other undermines who you are." He pauses. "I'm only trying to be sensible."

"Then if sense is the crux of the matter, if we are both to get what we want at the same time, why don't we wait and reapply somewhere with a school for each of us?"

"Would you do that?"

I freeze. "Would you?"

"Is that what you want?"

"No. That's not what I want. It's not what I planned."

"I'm willing, goddammit, if it means I don't lose you."

"You won't lose me."

"What if Yale had accepted you, too? What would you have done?"

"I can't think about 'what if.' It doesn't change the present."

Andrew starts to cry in a fast hot tense silence. I am suddenly afraid like I've never been in my life. "Yes, it does. It's changing us now, right now. That matters. Don't I matter, too, Razi?"

Without warning, I spring into tears. "You have no idea."

"I love you," he says.

"I love you."

We don't speak for several moments. Instead of calming ourselves, within our own thoughts, we both cry harder. He is vulnerable in a way that makes me ache. I go to him, take his face in my hands, wipe the tears with my fingertips. Andrew clasps my wrists to his chest—his hard, forceful breath at my pulse—and kisses me with a pressure desperate and angry. I return the kiss with a different passion, one that lets him feel the truth he doubts—I do love him, so much that I cannot be rational.

Our lips part open. His palm caresses the cradle of my skull. Near his loins, my hips lie flat. We remain embraced, and we look at each other. I know that glint. My own mirrors in his eyes.

The quiet house rumbles with the steady patter of footsteps along the solid, creakless stairs. Inside his room, where a humid breeze rushes through the open windows, there is only enough light to discern the placement of things: his bed, his desk chair, the bookcase. Neither of us reaches for a lamp. I undress as he opens a bookcase drawer, finds a little metal box, and locates the pessary. When he comes to me, I am lying on the sheets, his quilt a knoll near the footboard. *I don't think there's enough jelly,* he says. *As long as it stays in place,* I reply. *Don't worry.* He draws my legs over his shoulders and gives me a hurried, intense kiss. An ecstatic shiver urges him away. With a smooth, gentle curl of his fingers—he is practiced now—the membrane cups the seal of my womb.

I watch him take off his clothes. He is shadow, shade, line, the dark parts of him only darker now, his penis an angle of light against his groin. I wet my hands and guide him into me. My limbs twine across his back.

The rhythm is his, steady, forceful, his body hovers above mine, he arches deep, skims my nipples, he does not rush, he does not hurry, motion in the measure of time. I lift into his throat, kiss him in the hollow, feel his groan as much as I hear it. He stops. His arms slip under my shoulder blades, he draws us in, breast to breast, breath to breath, his mouth barely touching mine, I reach my tongue but receive no reply, the air between us heavy as rain, the depth of me full. Where no one can see, I hold him close, release, hold him again. *Don't move,* he whispers, his lips a glaze on my mouth. He tips my chin with his to direct my eyes upward and open.

We belong together, he says. *To each other.*

When I try to turn my head, he pushes his arms upward, his fingertips at the base of my skull. His weight lifts slightly away from my chest, and I feel him breathing, the rhythm in perfect concert with mine, in, out, I feel spread wide and full. I cannot look away now, I don't want to, he is within every draw I take into my body until I cannot tell the difference between our breaths. A ripple begins under my navel, the waves move toward the surface of my skin, break through, take Andrew into the crests and troughs—I am pulled into his swell—our waves extend beyond us both, merge and emerge, return again and again, the intensity unyielding, beyond flesh, bone, blood, muscle, nerve, thought, desire, memory . . .

He releases me gently and rolls me on my stomach. Andrew holds my legs closed with his knees on either side, kisses my neck, softly at first, then takes my flesh in his mouth, teeth in the skin, tongue soft over the folds. I call to him in the language beyond words, I feel his cleft at my coccyx, now at my lower spine, he can curve no further, my nape in his firm jaws. With the whole of his hands, he takes my hips up and back. He moves ahead, inward. I press toward him as his touch crosses over my belly, down, where my being collapses to that one spot and expands from the same place, once, again, again. I push his hand away, the rhythm between us even, my back wet with drops from his brow, his chest, the pace quickens, the pitch of his breath rises.

I lean forward, away, turn—he is so close—push him to his back. Easily, I slip around him. Slowly, I rock, the sway gentle as spring boughs, I bend into him, his hands trace the sides of my body. My mouth dampens at his forehead, temples, cheeks, drenches at his lips, the kiss like drowning, my life inside of it, he can fill me no more than he does now. I succumb to his flesh, the strain and softness—

How could I have known when I first brought you to me
that your body is a veil,
that I would want it to fall away
and feel the pure element underneath
embrace me in return?

Under me, he moves, he is so strong, my hips lift with his. We mark the rhythm, his fingertips at the base of my spine, my body arches, one hand at his mound, one hand between his legs. The coming surge draws him inward. He grabs my arms, grounds my palms on his soaked chest, thrusting, the call, *Razi.* I bear witness to our little deaths and resurrections, his before me, mine in reflection—our bodies in tremor, our eyes locked through will on the other. Light springs where none should begin.

I transcend, transfixed.

I collapse onto him. He wraps me gently. An undertow swells straight from my gut. I cry out, startled, amazed, and cling tight. My sobs muffle in his throat. He holds me without question, without fear. He has shown me what I have not believed. He has shown me many times, I know, but this time, I cannot doubt that part of me I have never called by name.

❧

My little succubus, he says, roused into the penumbra of sleep.

The room is aphotic, moonlight consumed by miles of low,

fast-moving nimbostrati. Andrew reaches into the dark and along familiar contours. He finds the shape of my sacral curve with his fingertips, urges it forward. Not yet. The grip on him is warm, rhythmic, practiced. His arms sweep out. Pajama bottoms hit the floor with a gasp. He demands that the movement stop and pulls a kiss toward his mouth. The sky illuminates. He groans as the firmament rumbles.

I feel nothing. He is resistance and pressure. My pleasure is memory alone. Somehow, I have learned to create an elementary solid form, aware that my density is a knit of energy, not matter, not as I had known it.

For him, the sensation is real. Whatever I am, I am here, invisible.

Andrew clutches me—vibration and energy—as he is guided into place. His muscles urge the pace to quicken, but he is overwhelmed, overpowered. Sudden rain batters the roof. Wind blows each curtain horizontal. The thunder is felt as much as it is heard. *Razi,* he says, his voice suffocated.

Hands pinned near his shoulders, spine rolling against rumpled sheets, Andrew opens his eyes. He searches for a return of his gaze, but the darkness prevents such focus. The tension against his thighs relaxes, and he welcomes the freedom. He tilts into the urgency, lifts into its demand, pulls into its release. He closes his eyes again. When the final exhale escapes his body, Andrew sinks into the mattress.

He smiles as his lashes part.

The room incandesces for a second.

He touches his groin, finds moisture without temperature.

Andrew swings his legs to the floor and curls his torso toward his knees. He looks around the room. A choking cry works from the depths of his lungs. He throws a pillow at his desk opposite the bed. *Release me,* he says, his voice plaintive, pleading. *Let me go. Please.*

The storm stalls above us. The thunder is furious, but it can roar no louder than the fierce visceral desire denied me—the part that made me whole—the piece I wanted to reclaim through the fusion of his body with what remains of mine. I know how fragile I am now, nothing but a whisper, a breath away from oblivion like the little girls whose release I beheld tonight.

Andrew gets up and creeps through the room. He grabs a cigarette from its case and fumbles for a match. He pauses at the mirror above his gentleman's chest, unable to make out his own features. I hear him breathe in short, stunted bursts. He walks toward the bookcase where he keeps extra matches in the left drawer.

The cigarette dangles at the edge of his lip. He has not stopped crying. Andrew opens the drawer and finds a matchbox. He stands, strikes the flame, and brings it near his mouth. A bolt strikes within yards of the room. Light crosses itself hundreds of times in reflection, in an instant, back and forth between the mirror and the bookcase doors.

Andrew lets the cigarette fall. The match snuffs out on its way to the floor. I follow his gaze to the point where it ends, near the center of the room where I am, where the darkness should reveal nothing but his imagination. I peer down, look through the layers I have constructed, and realize what he sees.

A white mass suspends in the space where my vagina would be—then disappears.

He is within me.

I move toward Andrew as the lightning pulses, dim and almost distant now. After what has happened, he stands before me bewildered, yet his body is unharmed. I am left with a want that cannot be sated, but the look in his eyes is what I can't bear. Instinct draws me to him, my hands toward his chest. Before I touch him, I can hear the hum of his blood and feel its current, lulling me . . . lulling me.

My form meets his bare flesh at the sternum, and a gust presses through his skin. His heart misses a beat—another—his blue eyes close—he falls against the bookcase with a jolt—glass shatters to the floor—and the night comes back to me—the séance—Donna—her palm on my father's heart—she almost stopped it, didn't she?—the orphan—Donna's hand—a final breath?—the thin silver horizon. Do not touch, this is why, don't you see, this is why the heart beats—

My hands hover above his chest. There are flutters, dim waves of movement, deep within his atria and ventricles. His pulse is silent. One more touch—that is all—he would feel no pain, he would see the black blink and feel the light lift, he would surrender—one more touch—with him, in him, through him, we would release into a vapor pure as our love—

In an instant, my hands resist the deed. I nudge the air with the curves of my fingertips, and a rush of energy spreads from the edges. An electric snap sends a tremor through his body. *Pump,* I say. *Let the current flow again. Breathe, Andrew, breathe.*

He gasps. His eyes open. For weeks, the flawless blue has been draining away. Now, in each iris, a slice of blue is entirely missing. A crescent of white takes its place. When I shift from left to right, the color does not return. After many deep breaths, he sits up and lifts his right arm. Blood trickles down his skin and into the open drawer at his elbow. He crawls toward his desk lamp and squints against the glare when he turns it on.

Without a flinch, he tugs a glass triangle from the meat of his palm under his little finger. The blood rushes forward from the straight, clean cut. Somehow, he pulls himself up and leans against the desk. A red puddle seeps into the envelope left on the blotter, into the last letter I will ever write him, the one he accepted from my father's hand earlier tonight. Andrew takes the shirt he'd worn that day and twists it around his fist. Blood spreads into the fine tight white fabric. As I reach to hold the part that bleeds—I can't bear to see him hurt—I realize the truth.

I am powerless to stanch the damage I've done, so afraid that a part of Andrew cannot be repaired.

IN MY ROOM, in my bed, I reach to my side as if I expect to find more than the empty morning heat of mid-June. I am alone.

Hours before, I had fallen asleep on top of him, his left arm cradling my side, his right hand stroking my cheek and neck. My rest was deep then, so much that I didn't dream and I didn't notice that he'd left me. Andrew nudged me conscious close to two in the morning and drove me home. He walked me to the door. When I kissed him, I knew in my gut and bones what I had to do, what assurance I could give him.

That day, I meet with one of Twolly's former classmates and place an order. Most of the money Daddy gave me for new school outfits is gone—well spent, an investment.

Three weeks later, I pick up the ring. The beautiful silver band is inlaid with a thick stripe of lapis lazuli, exactly what I asked for. Inside, the inscription is flawless. I wait for the panic, and when I don't feel it, I am relieved. The gesture was not made on impulse.

Each day we have seen each other has been a tense increment of good-bye. We talk about Christmas, timing our arrivals and departures five and a half months away. We float in the pool like aimless starfish, toes and fingers changing the trajectory of the other's drift. Alone as much as possible, in unbearable heat, we embrace for no other reason than to hold on. He hasn't asked me to marry him again. He doesn't offer to withdraw his acceptance to Yale and join me in Chicago, nor does he do it outright. He doesn't ask me why I won't reconsider my decision and follow him to New Haven.

Tucked into the mirror of my vanity is a tiny calendar. Underneath, my acceptance letter from Northwestern. On the bottom of the paper, handwritten, is the time and date of my train departure. I leave in eight weeks.

I look at the clutter in front of me and begin to pack Twolly's surprise package. She moved back to Shreveport after graduation. I miss her like crazy and want her to know. Inside, I place a crossword puzzle book, a pretty scarf, some pictures Andrew had taken at graduation, fifteen sticks of Roman candy, a tabloid with my comments in the margins, and a yo-yo. I realize that I've forgotten to buy some Barq's Root Beer, her favorite, and don't seal the box.

I stare at myself in the mirror for a long time. Against my sternum, I hold the locket Andrew gave me our first Valentine's Day. I open it to read the words inside. When I glance right, he watches me from a photograph. Twolly took it, but I stood behind her and winked. In the instant between the moment I called his name and the shutter closed, Andrew unearthed a subtle grin, squinted against flares in his irises, and drew me along the rhumb line connecting our distance. We had not touched, but my body, below and beyond, felt encircled by his pull.

I love him.

The blank stationery lies flat between Twolly's parcel and Andrew's ring. With my best fountain pen, I write,

Wednesday, July 10, 1929

Andrew, my darling,

My love for you is a force of nature.

I know, such words from a woman who holds faith in nothing but what her senses reveal. But I have proof, you see. I cannot doubt the rush under my skin when you turn those unfathomable blue eyes my way, the velocity of my blood when I am naked against your body, and the ebb and flow of my breath when you whisper my name.

You asked me a question, and I have your answer now. Just for a moment, close those eyes I adore, Andrew, then hold out your hand for me.

Always, always,
your Razi

When I seal the envelope, I kiss it. There is no imprint, I haven't put on lipstick, so I draw a tiny rosebud mouth at the flap's corner. On the front, I write his name in my best script. For the hundredth time, I take the ring from its box and turn it in the light. The inscription is his answer, but I know, so that he will believe me, I will have to speak it aloud.

Mother calls me from the landing. Breakfast. I close the little jewelry box, shove it against Twolly's package, and stand Andrew's note against the mirror. I kiss Grams, Mother, and Daddy good morning. My father remarks that I am in a cheery mood, a change from the last few weeks, in which I've been unusually quiet. Why shouldn't I be happy on such a gorgeous summer day? I answer. I eat quickly and tell them I'm going to walk to Andrew's. Mother tells me to invite him to dinner. With his parents gone, she says, he must be lonesome in the house.

I walk the tree-shaded blocks in my favorite green sleeveless dress. The heat makes me dewy. I hope my extra swimsuit is at his house because I terribly want a dip. If not, perhaps I should go bare. The O'Connells are in the Swiss Alps avoiding mosquitoes and tropical heat, and Emmaline will be away shopping until it's time to cook lunch.

My pace quickens. Along St. Charles Avenue, I grin at a college boy who offers a ride in his coupe. His F. Scott hair weeps into his neck from the humidity. He looks familiar, someone who's cut in on me at a dance or two.

"Thanks," I reply, "but I'm limbering up for a swim."

"Mind if I join you?" he says.

"Not today, sport."

As he drives away, I stop in my tracks. Andrew's surprise. The items are still on my dressing table. A sliver of grapefruit curls at the tip of my tongue. Go back home, brush my teeth—forgot to do that, too—sneak it out in a little bag. No one will notice, no one will know.

I can't do this. He's going to want to before we leave. I know him, that decisiveness. A small ceremony, sure, no time for a big event—he knows I wouldn't want that. If we do, it will play on us every day we're apart. That bond on paper and all it implies, stronger than steel. I can't. My plans have been made. Made for years. I can hold the ring until later, keep it safe. It's not time, not yet.

No.

But I'm not saying I'll do it now. I express intent, a promise. He's a reasonable man. He'll understand. And he hasn't mentioned it since that night. He would be surprised, a little amused perhaps. If I give it as a symbol, yes, a symbolic gesture—he would appreciate that. I'm meeting him halfway. I can do this.

Maybe.

Timing. I leave in eight weeks. Between now and then, I can decide. Yes.

It can wait.

ANDREW, my Andrew.

Remember the night you pointed to the North Star and told me that when you were a child, you were afraid the creatures and objects would fall from the sky and crush you? You believed they were there among those constellation points, that if one of those lights went out, like a pin removed from a seam, the weight would tear the rest away and leave them at the mercy of thin air.

You were right. We are.

The day my friend Lionel left, we!went to Jackson Square. Cart mules chewed their oats, fortune-tellers spoke of futures and pasts, tourists marveled at the sights, thieves lay in wait, a brass quartet played, and the locals ignored it all. Nel was happy, content. He had chosen to go beyond alone, the way it had been the first time, almost. No deathbed wait to follow a stranger's last breath. I was unsure whether this would work, if there was a chemistry involved in the release. Nel told me good-bye, as if he were going home after a friendly visit, and drifted into the crowd. I followed his glow. His movement accelerated like a run, and when he shouted, *Falling up!* Nel leapt and disappeared. Completely.

Not so long ago, Lionel found solace in the strangest theory. He said that in the instant two particles collide, an event occurs, a decision is made—what did not happen, in fact, did. The opposite result still exists. The alternative is in motion. We cannot experience the other option in a way that we understand, much less see.

Unless, Nel thought, those moments are woven into our dreams, visits to what could have been, or what is. Or maybe, Nel said, we are allowed only glimpses of ourselves and our lives. What we know is a fraction of vastly scattered possibilities—the position and momentum of every instant in constant flux. We would be overwhelmed by knowing it all at once. Nel decided that if he existed in many different ways, in more dimensions than he could fathom, it didn't matter. He was still Lionel. He was entirely connected in the end somehow, even if it was only memory.

I wonder what would hold the possibilities together, like the bond of water, the tug of gravity, the force of nature. What would we call each whole and the variations created when they are broken, repaired, rearranged?

And how, Andrew—how can I apologize for tearing you apart?

When I didn't turn back to get your ring, to promise a life with you, I had no idea I would miss the chance for good. I stalled that day because I believed in time, plenty to parcel out for the passions I held. You were one, Andrew. I feared that I would give you too much, not enough—my measure in the world based on those proportions I balanced. I sometimes thought, *He is just a man.* I forgot to admit I was just a woman.

That last night I went to you, when the storm clouds stretched a black net wide enough to catch falling bodies, I longed for consummation. I wanted you and what was beyond that want, the experience when we breathed in rhythm and my desires lifted, suspended, drifted away. The moment I saw the fractures in your blue eyes, I knew my love had scarred the man you were meant to be. I admit it now. I should have left you to mourn me alone. I had no right to surround you with my own desperate grief or attempt to take away what your love gave to me—your very life.

There was a word you spoke in the Latin masses of your boyhood—*anima*—and it translated into soul. That same word held new meaning for the scholar you became, its definitions dependent on usage and intent. Anima: soul, spirit, mind, breath, wind. Here, where I am, there is no consensus, no absolute, and no debate about which one, if any, is truly accurate. Like those of us between, like memory, words are images without substance—fluid, malleable, fundamental.

But I can say it now, on my terms, free from connotations—I am a soul. What lifted above the pool that morning did not depend on oxygen for its life. I am a constellation now, too, Andrew—a configuration reduced to its essentials, spread far and wide like the atoms that once gave my body the illusion of density.

I am still Razi, and I still love you. How absolutely possible I always have and always will.

❧

"Aunt Twolly, I have something very important to show you." Amy slipped the DVD into the player. "It's about Poppa."

Twolly sat up straight in her chair and adjusted her cheaters. She watched without a sound as our graduation day replayed before her eyes. "Where did that come from?"

"It's a long story. Do you remember someone named Simon Beeker? Or Emmaline? Think. And tell me the truth."

"I remember Emmaline." Twolly exhaled in a long rasp.

Amy removed the DVD and sat on the ottoman near her great-aunt. "I want to know who that man was. Before he became the grandfather I barely knew at all."

"I made him a promise."

Amy reached into her jacket pocket. She placed two items on Twolly's lap—my last letter to Andrew, and the ring. My dear old friend would not touch them.

"Why didn't you tell me, Aunt Twolly? Who were you protecting—him or you?"

"What do you mean?"

"Was there something between you two? Did something happen?"

Twolly turned a fierce red. Her eye contact did not waver. "Never," she said, her voice strong and strangely youthful. "I loved him like a brother. Always."

"You had the ring that his dead girlfriend—your friend—meant for him. Why?"

"He wouldn't take it." Twolly pressed her lips together.

"What? When?" Amy received no answer. "What happened to him?"

Twolly sighed. With a rush of energy, she described the first time she saw Andrew again, more than ten years after I died. She hardly recognized the man whose eyes had turned an unusual blue-green, who had a law degree he never intended to use and a doctorate in the theories of thought and logic. Twolly believed it was just as well he had adopted the Oxford nickname for good. He was not the man she had known.

After working several years as an adjunct professor, he visited her again. Sunny and her child were living with Twolly at the time. Sunny's first husband had been killed in the war a year prior. Twolly explained that her baby sister knew Andrew and I had been an item once, but that she had been too young to hear the details after I died. By the time Sunny met Andrew, Twolly felt it was his right to tell about his past. She had promised her silence. It was a vow she kept with devotion and ambivalence.

"Your grandfather loved your grandmother," Twolly said. "But even I will admit it was the kind of love you have for someone because you'll die inside if you don't love something. When Razi died, he was broken. The rest of his life revolved around the moment he lost her."

Amy looked down and twisted the wedding ring on her finger. "Poppa never spoke of Razi?"

"No. But she was always just below his surface."

"Why did you have his ring?"

Twolly leaned back in her chair. "Razi's father sent me a package after she died. It sat in my bedroom sealed for months. When I finally opened it, I stored a lot away without looking at what was sent. I was still too close to the grief. Mr. Nolan probably didn't take a second glance at what he boxed up, or I'm sure he would have given it to Fin. That ring box sat in my jewelry chest for years."

"Didn't you try to give it to him?"

"You don't understand, Amy. After he married Sunny, I was his sister-in-law. There were rare moments when we were the friends we had once been. And we never spoke of our past together. It was as if Razi never existed. I hated that, because we had both loved her so much. But I knew if I gave him that ring, it might destroy him. He was so fragile."

Amy picked up the letter from Twolly's lap. "This is the last letter she wrote to him. It relates to that ring. You mean to tell me that he never got the answer she left inside the band?"

"He got it." Twolly looked into the distance. "A few weeks after Sunny passed, I invited your grandfather to come here. I knew I had some clothes and a few pieces of her jewelry that your mother and aunt might want to have. I didn't remember the ring was in the chest until it was too late. He had opened every box he found in the drawers as we looked, and I couldn't very well snatch that one from him. The second he pulled it from the velvet, he put it on his finger. That ring fit perfectly. He made Loretta find a magnifying glass so he could look inside. What does it say again?"

Amy held the circle in her hand. She had memorized the words. *"Why, it beats so I can love you."*

"Yes, that's it," Twolly said. "The funny thing is, he started to laugh at first. A genuine laugh I hadn't heard in so, so long, I wanted to cry. He said he remembered a special afternoon they had together, one of their many intellectual conversations. Andrew had told her that no one knew why the heart beats, and Razi, being Razi, gave a scientific explanation.

"Then he told me about her letter. That one you must have there. He puzzled over what she intended. What had she meant to answer? There was one answer he wanted more than anything but was afraid he would never hear. Then"—Twolly's voice hitched—"he said that he had planned to ask her again, one last time, but he lost his nerve."

"To marry him."

"Yes." Slow tears staggered among the soft lines in Twolly's face. "He said the inscription meant Razi had acknowledged a sacredness between them. In her own way. He wanted her to realize this. It was something he believed very deeply. But he also understood what she was telling him about another question. A ring means the same thing to a man as it does to a woman, after all." Twolly sniffled. "Then, I couldn't believe it. He reached into his pocket and tossed his coins on the bed. He held up a piece of silver. It was misshapen and flat and worn. No one could tell what it was, and if he hadn't told me, I wouldn't have guessed either. It was the locket he had given Razi the day he told her he loved her. He said he'd taken it from her neck himself when he pulled her from the water."

"That annoying habit"—Amy's skin blanched—"how he'd jingle the change in his pocket. It's amazing he never lost it. Did he say why he kept it so long? After so much time?"

"I wish I knew. He couldn't explain when I asked. I guess he just couldn't part with it. My goodness, the poor man." Twolly wiped her cheeks. "So then, your grandfather sat on my bed with that ring on his finger and that smashed locket and cried as if every feeling he ever swallowed was tearing straight from his soul. Cried for the longest time. There's nothing worse in this world than watching someone's heart break."

Amy's eyes pooled. "Unless you have the one that's been broken."

"Yes, you know, don't you?" Twolly patted Amy's hand, then shivered violently. "A nice boy with long hair. What was his name? I've forgotten. I'm sorry."

"Jem. His name was Jem." Amy inhaled and exhaled quickly, her breath frosty. "Why didn't Poppa keep the ring?"

"Fin—oh, goodness—Andrew—it feels good to call him Andrew again—he said it would be safe with me. He got what he needed, he said."

Amy rubbed her hands together. "You kept your promise to him all these years. There must be a reason to talk now."

"It would be so wonderful to talk about those times again, while I still can," Twolly said. "Are you chilly? I swear I can see my breath before my eyes. I don't remember a winter this cold." Twolly pushed herself from her chair and went down the hall.

Finally, I understood why our photos were hidden, why the letter from Tulane remained unanswered, and why our history was never told. Twolly could indeed keep a secret.

The walls knocked, the lights flickered, and the doors slammed shut. Ice crystals spread in fractals on the windowpanes. Amy was not afraid. She breathed a plume from her mouth and glanced around the room. "Quiet. Be still. Rest," she said into the air.

Loretta drops the pills in Twolly's hand one at a time. Twolly chases each with a sip of water and teaspoon of applesauce. After my friend is finished, Loretta leaves the bedside and switches the channel to Twolly's four o'clock program. The volume could wake the dead.

Twolly smoothes the blanket over her chest. Her hands are transparent almost to the bone. Her hair is wispy and white as the edge of an egret's wing. An opaque veil dulls her left eye to beige, while her right remains focused on the television. She coughs heavily and stretches her variegated arm. The box slides under her reach. She tosses the used tissue toward the wastebasket, its trajectory corrected in mid-float.

Near the bed, Loretta has moved Twolly's table and photographs from downstairs. Behind the snapshot of us on the seesaw, there is one of me, alone, my naked back and coy profile lit by the perfect light of dusk. To the left of my figure, Andrew watches me, out of his photo, the true color of his eyes lost in sepia. Although Twolly doesn't often glance at the photographs, she knows they are there. She talks to the images every night before she goes to sleep.

I talk to her, too. I tell her things she doesn't know. I necked once and only once with David Kleinert, a year before her first date with him. Sometimes, just because, I didn't wear my dainties. Her granddaughter Julie has already helped herself to the china stored in the sideboard. Amy doesn't know she's pregnant yet, and she will deliver in October. Once the breath stops, the blackness won't last long. I am afraid, uncertain, but ready now. It doesn't matter whether I converge or vanish.

Twolly drifts into a nap from which she will not awake.

I take her hand in mine.

Her pulse is a burble.

I listen to her inhale, exhale—waiting for the last one—but it is not her respiration I hear. His voice comes to me, breathing my name into him, a whisper, Razi. *I know: it is imagination, memory. My head on his sternum, the rumble of blood and air and words, conversations of the heart, where they come together.*

With the shape of my right hand, I trace the effluvial contours. Such a complicated sweep of sensation and substance I was. I follow the outlines, once, twice, and end at the curve of my face. Where is he in me?

My lips fold along a map of his skin. Thin as want, my flesh remembers the terrain: canyons and hills, peaks and valleys, no part of him uncharted, unexplored. The relief of him, against my own, giving where it will, firm where it cannot, a thrum below the surface, blood as magma, breath as flame. What invisible latitudes join me to him, align our cores, twine rhythms primal, celestial. I open my mouth to say his name, Andrew, *and the map rolls forward. He is here, where he has always been.*

ACKNOWLEDGMENTS

Several sources made all the difference in my research. *New Orleans in the Twenties,* by Mary Lou Widmer, provided details that would have taken weeks to find on my own. Southern women writers of the 1920s, especially Sara Haardt Mencken, provided clues about the period's culture, relationships, and conversations. The Newcomb Archives is an absolute treasure. Gary Zukav's *Dancing Wu Li Masters* made the fragments snap together, an echo that still lingers in my ears.

My thanks to these special people: my family, especially my parents, Ron and Patty, and my siblings, Robbie and Jenny; my teachers, who offered guidance—Dorothy Allen, Jenny Anderson, Charlene Banna, Donald Begnaud, Flo Jakeway Courvelle, Debbie Hargrave, Richard Latiolais, Nancy Mounce, Linda Mouton, and Toni White; and a number of my history keepers—Martin Arceneaux, Jennifer Hull Decker, Laura Souther Delahoussaye, Robert Forbes, Laura Gough, Jody Dreyfus Hampton, Jenny Upchurch Thompson, and Ariana Wall.

For various acts of kindness, support, and encouragement, thank you to Jules and Linda Bourque; Nancy Sullivan Jacobs; Judy Kahn; Jeff Kleinman; Kelly McKinell, M.D., M.P.H.; Lynn Rainach; and Dorothy S. And thanks to Danny Plaisance, proprietor of Cottonwood Books, for the early enthusiasm.

I greatly appreciate several readers who offered helpful comments at different stages—Robin Becker, Matt Beeson, Richard Buchholz, Paulette Guerin, Kent Muhlbauer, and Laura Zuelke.

What would I have done without my brilliant and beautiful friends? Mary McMyne was there from the beginning and gave me excellent editorial input. Benjamin Lanier-Nabors noticed the connections in a way that still stuns me. Nolde Alexius shared her charming intelligence and critical eye. Tameka Cage saw blood and told me so. Jennifer Nuernberg brought a little more Carl to the table. Linda Lee offered a sincere reader's perspective. Victoria Brockmeier gave us both the goosebumps and closed a loop. Katy Powell inspired thoughts on the construction of identity. Joe Scallorns talked me off a few ledges. Alison Aucoin gave me encouragement and a place of respite. Lori Bertman saw me through The Worst Year and always kept the faith. Truly, I'm a lucky girl.

Homage to James Wilcox, the Technical Master, and James Gordon Bennett, the Intuitive Master. They'll simply have to balk at such titles, because that's what they shared with me. Thank you, Jim W., my mentor in so many ways, for your support, your advice, and the critical question, "What does Razi think she is?" Thank you, Jim B., for teaching me the essence of character and for the praise that came when I needed it most.

Intuition and divine intervention worked a strange magic—and there was my agent, Jandy Nelson. Her editorial vision and gut instinct played a part in this miracle. Thank you, Jandy, with the fullness of my heart.

Sarah Branham, my bright and delightful editor, figured out how to make the final bits fall into place. Thank you, Sarah—you made a dream come true. Pos-a-lutely.

To Atria's entire team—how I appreciate your great ideas, hard work, and pure excitement.

Last but not least, my thanks to Todd Bourque, who endured the challenge of living with me in the midst of this. I owe him a thousand bowls of homemade chocolate pudding. How much do I love you?